N. D. Moorjani.
Oct/14th/85.

Search for Happiness

By
DAVID RITZ

SIMON AND SCHUSTER   NEW YORK

Selections from *Santa Teresa de Avila* by Helmut A. Hatzfeld are reprinted with the permission of Twayne Publishers, A Division of G.K. Hall & Co., Boston.

Excerpts from *The Collected Works of St. Teresa of Avila,* translated by Kieran Kavanaugh and Otilio Rodriguez, copyright © 1976 by Washington Province of Discalced Carmelites, Inc., ICS Publications, 2131 Lincoln Road, N.E., Washington, D.C. 20002 are reprinted by permission.

Excerpts from *The Art of Ecstasy: Teresa, Bernini, and Crashaw,* by Robert T. Petersson, © 1970 by Robert T. Petersson, are reprinted with the permission of Atheneum Publishers.

Published by Simon and Schuster
A Division of Gulf & Western Corporation
Simon & Schuster Building
Rockefeller Center
1230 Avenue of the Americas
New York, New York 10020
SIMON AND SCHUSTER
and colophon are trademarks
of Simon & Schuster
Designed by Eve Kirch
Manufactured in the United States of America

1   2   3   4   5   6   7   8   9   10

Library of Congress Cataloging in Publication Data

Ritz, David
  Search for happiness.
  I. Title.
PZ4.R616Se 1980   [PS3568.I828]   813'.5'4   79-24221

ISBN 0-671-25233-X

For their generous help, I thank Roberta Ritz,
Alan Eisenstock, Aaron Priest, Molly Friedrich,
Ellen Flanagan, and especially Ann Patty,
my friend, editor, soul mate and surgeon.

For Alison and Jessica,
the little miracles running around the house

1

I need an idea. I'm looking for a character, a hook, something hot and juicy, something I can really sink my teeth into.

So I'm sitting here frying my brain in this little cubicle. You'd think that the network would give a guy with a hefty six-figure salary a classy office. But not those cheap bastards. They don't give a damn. As long as I come up with something big every couple of months. A different twist. A new angle.

Not that I'm worried. Why should I be worried? I'm in the creative arts, and all us creative artists have dry spells. I've been doing this for so long that I'm used to the blocks. That's what it means to be a professional—not to be thrown by the lean times. I'm doing fine, believe me. I'm on the verge of a major breakthrough. I can feel it coming. All I have to do is move away from the typewriter for a while, let the thing brew. Just back off and be patient.

I've got the NFL schedule laid out before me—it's spread over the top of this cheap metal desk—and if my calculations are accurate (as I know they are), come Monday morning I'll be richer to the tune of five thousand bucks. Gambling is good for the soul. Gambling keeps me sane by keeping my mind off the show.

The show. *Search for Happiness*. How's that for irony? But don't blame me for the name. I inherited it from the sixty-five-year-old bespectacled, emaciated man who was doing this stint before me. Poor son of a bitch. When I met him he had the shakes so bad he couldn't light his own cigarette. But that's what writing soap operas will do to you—if you're not strong. It can work you down to the bone.

Not that weight loss is a particular problem with me. I tend to

7

go the other way. For the last ten years, ever since I started slugging away at these scripts, I've been putting on the pounds. The more I write, the more I eat. (Though it's also true that the more I *don't* write, the more I eat.) Anyway, for a man in his mid-forties I'm still in top-notch mental shape, even though the doc says I should put myself on one of those ridiculous diets that turn people into homicidal nuts. But right now is not the time to think about dieting. Right now I have shows to write, intriguing characters and ingenious plots to invent. Right now I have to go back into myself and see what's there.

There's still plenty left. Sure, I've just gone through a very rough period, so rough, in fact, that it might have thrown a weaker man. You might say it's been something of a professional and a personal nightmare. But it's not going to keep me down. No, sir. I'm coming out swinging again. I'm roaring back.

Ten years—that's right—for ten years I've been churning out this shit, for ten years I've proven myself time and again. So what the hell am I worried about? Everyone knows that I run this show. Everyone recognizes that I'm the guy who makes it all happen. I'm the head writer. I'm the heart and soul, I'm the guts, I'm the source of the story. I *am* the story. Let 'em wait a few more hours, a couple more days. The network boys upstairs aren't concerned. By now they believe in me. They know I deliver. They realize what a tremendous job I do. Who else could turn out fifteen or twenty pages of heart-throbbing script on any given day? My assistants just stand around and stare. They can't believe the way I spin the yarns. Matter of fact, if you ask anyone in the business, they'll tell you that I'm considered something of a natural phenomenon. Al Gonfio, they'll tell you, is thought to be a master of his craft, even if I do say so myself.

You know how most soaps operate? There are organizational charts, there are staffs, whole armies of writers, weekly, daily, sometimes hourly meetings where all these supposedly brilliant brains slurp coffee and try to figure out how to get their characters further into trouble. Personally, I hate the meetings. I avoid them like the plague. I do this shit by myself. I'm not saying that I do all the writing—sometimes I have my assistants actually write the dialogue once I give them the idea—but I always give them the idea. *Always*. I don't need any help. To me, it's

8

nothing to keep a half-dozen hot plots spinning in the air. Right now I have a widow with an abortion problem, a doctor dying to get into his nurse's panties—she's his sister-in-law, by the way—a big bankruptcy and an unfortunate case of child abuse.

It's nothing to come up with something new. I might have a bad day, or even a bad week, but eventually it's going to come to me. It always has. Like lightning. A little spark in the dark. That beautiful creative light that clicks on inside your head and makes everything clear and sensible. That's the moment when you know you're a real writer, the moment you know you're about to make a shitload of money.

I remember when it happened last time. With the nun. With Prudence. With Anna. I was in the same position then as now. I was searching, and all the nifty new ideas were playing hide-and-seek with me. For too long I had fooled around with the character of Baxter MacNiece, a wealthy, silver-haired lawyer who's humping a bunch of hot honeys. I had gotten him enough off-screen pussy to last the average man—which does not include me—a lifetime. I needed to do a whole different number.

I don't know why I thought of a nun. I guess you'd have to say it was a stroke of genius. Because it worked. Dear God, did it ever work! It worked so well that my life may never be the same. That nun, that sweet little nun, did something that no character of mine had ever done before. She came alive. She haunted my nights and my days, she never left my side, she crawled inside my skin—she's still there, she'll always be there —and she whispered and she shouted and she tugged and kissed and kicked at my shins until I got sore and pissed. But there was nothing I could do. Because I had invented her, and she was good, she was so goddamn good I could cry. My Prudence, my Anna, my beautiful and talented Anna.

It started on a Saturday afternoon, about two and a half years ago. I was at the track, which is where I've spent every Saturday afternoon for the past two decades of my life. It was one of those really murderous September days when my money didn't want to have anything to do with me. I had just torn up $250 worth of daily double tickets when who should walk by but Brink Kaufman.

Brink's one of the guys from the old neighborhood. I call it

9

the old neighborhood even though, coming from Orchard Street, ten blocks east of Mulberry, Brink was part of another world. Somehow, though, those two universes—Western Europe and Eastern Europe, Italians and Jews—had a way of spilling over. Deep down, we came from the same place. Their fire escapes looked just like ours.

Brink's all right. He's a decent poker player and, like me, he's got a very heavy nag habit. He calls himself a talent agent. That means he spends a couple of months a year out on the Coast—at Santa Anita—looking up old friends at the studios (guys like me from the old neighborhood) to see what they're writing and producing. He must call me at least once a week to see what's on my mind. If I'm about to write a new character into the script, Brink's the first to know. Then he'll run out that night, catch a couple of Off-Broadway plays and corner an actor who he thinks is going to fit the bill. He takes a quick 15 percent and the next day heads back to the track. Nice work if you can get it.

"I didn't think they let dagos in here, Al." Brink slapped me on the back. Brink was corny. He'd been using the same lines for the last hundred years. Which is why you can't help but love him a little.

"No bullshit today, Brink. You're looking at a defeated man."

"You? Defeated? The hottest soap writer in America? Come on."

"Ass kissing will get you nothing. The mutuel clerks already have it all."

"Then lemme buy you a drink. We'll console ourselves. And if that doesn't work, I know a place down on Rivington where I can get you a gross of crying towels wholesale."

Brink. Brink from the old neighborhood. How could I resist?

We walked over to the big-shot bar. We both had the magic membership cards. Hell, we invented the place. We probably had the first double Scotches the joint ever served.

The place was buzzing. The cigar smoke was as thick as hair on a horse's mane. It was dark and the smell of draft beer hit my nose as soon as we got near the bar. Mike, the bartender, was bullshitting with the boys at the far end of the bar.

10

"Mike!" Brink shouted. "Get that ugly mickey puss over here. We want some drinking-man's whiskey."

I wanted to tell Brink to cool the ethnic crap. But I didn't. How could anyone be mean to Brink?

Mike stood before us, glumly, both hands leaning on the bar. He wore a green-uniformed top and a white apron which stopped at his waist. "What'll it be, gents?" he asked in precisely the same accent shared by Brink and myself.

"Two Chivas's twice," Brink winked. Mike nodded, knowing that meant he should bring us both doubles. Mike knew Brink's language. He should have; he'd been serving Brink booze now for a good quarter-century.

"*Alle tue salute!*" Brink offered as soon as the drinks arrived.

"*L'chayim,*" I gave back, not to be undone.

"*Nu?*" Brink asked, after sipping the cold Scotch.

"*Nu?*" I gave back. I thought I'd play with him a while. I'd give him what he wanted, but I was going to take my time.

"How are the *gonifs* at the networks treating you?"

"Like they always treat me," I told him.

"Underpaid and overworked," he sympathized. Brink was a great one to sympathize. Especially when he wanted something.

"I ain't underpaid, Brink. I don't have to tell you that." I was tempted to reveal my salary. Let him know I was into six figures. And yet, why make him feel bad?

"They couldn't pay you enough, *paisan*. Every web exec on both coasts knows you're the only real storyteller left. You're a diamond in a world of plastic."

His metaphors might be a little mixed, but Brink could butter up with the best of them.

"Enough kibitzing," I said, finishing off my first drink. "I gotta run home and hit the keys. I'm four days behind—with the guy upstairs at the network and the guy downstairs at the bookie joint."

"Listen. Let's talk turkey." Brink turned the conversation back to me.

"I've been waiting," I said, halfway through my second double Chivas.

"What's up?"

"The same crap." I was still playing hard to get.

"Stop beating me off."

"All right. A nun."

"A nun?" he asked in surprise.

"A nun. The Catholic kind. Keep the Jewish girls away. And it'd be better if she were Italian."

Brink smiled. He understood. "Trying to keep it in the family?" he asked.

"Always," I said. "At every opportunity."

"You're not kidding?"

"Why should I kid? I've had two Scotches on your money. You know I'm an honest drinker."

"What are you going to do with this nun?"

"Plenty. But right now I'm not sure. I just know how I can work her into the story."

"How old does she have to be?"

"Mid-twenties."

"Good-looking?"

"Very," I answered.

" 'Nother Chivas?"

"Sure," I said, laying down a fiver before Brink could get to his wallet. "Do it again, Mike." The drinks arrived, beautifully iced over and light, watery, golden brown. Scotch is such good medicine for the soul.

"So a good-looking nun?" Brink recapped, taking a fast slug.

"That's it."

"Tits?"

"Come on, Brink. You're talking about a nun."

"I'm talking to you. You want tits or not. Just answer the question."

Say whatever you want to about Brink, but he's competent. The man was on the case. "Tits never hurt," I told him.

"How long you going to keep her around?"

"Who knows?" I said. "You never know those things. If she's good, hell, maybe she'll last a year. I've had characters last as long as four or five."

"So the money might be good."

"For the right nun, the payoff could be first-class."

"Give me till the middle of the week," Brink said, throwing back the rest of his drink. He had gotten what he wanted.

12

"No rush," I assured him.

"I just want to get back to you before you have a chance to call any of the agencies. You know I hate competition."

"Listen, Brink, you deliver by Wednesday and I won't say a word to anyone. We guys from the old neighborhood owe each other some loyalty, don't we?"

"Bet your sweet ass, *paisan*," Brink whirled off his stool and stalked out of the bar. The agent had his tip; the man was ready to go to work.

Brink delivered. He delivered at precisely 10:35 Wednesday morning. He delivered as he had never delivered before. One look and I knew: My *Search for Happiness* would never be the same.

She stood there, in the doorway of my cubicle, and I thought:

She's an angel. Her beautiful dark black hair was drawn tightly, severely into a bun atop her lovely head. The features of her face were simple and clear and fine. Her eyes were soft, her nose was small, her chin delicate. Her lips were thin, her mouth demure, her coloring olive, deep, Italian. She had to be Italian. She looked innocent. She looked sweet. She looked frail, the way saints are frail, the way nuns are frail. She was quietly but dramatically beautiful.

But even before she spoke her first word to me, I also thought:

She's a devil. She was dressed all wrong. She wore jeans which were faded and too tight, too sexy. She wore big boots over the jeans, and the boots were too clunky, not in the least stylish. She wore a large white fisherman's sweater which was stained and a little ratty. Her clothes were angry and aggressive. Her clothes said—I'm here, but I don't want to be here. She hadn't dressed for an audition.

"Gonfio?" she asked, almost impolitely.

"Yeah," I answered.

"Brink Kaufman sent me," she said.

"I figured that."

"He said you might have a hard time with me."

"Why?" I asked. She spoke with the accent I knew and loved so well—tough and testy hard-core New York City.

13

"No tits," she said.

I laughed. That son of a bitch, Brink. He was really something.

"Don't worry about it," I assured her.

"I'm not."

"You seem pissed," I said, deciding it would be better to level with her right away.

"The idea of a soap isn't real thrilling."

"Then what the hell you doing here?"

"The money. How about you?" I liked her. I liked this chick very much.

"I do it for strictly aesthetic reasons. The literary uplift is really something to see." Now *she* laughed. For the first time, her sour expression turned to a smile, and the smile was small but very, very sweet.

"Brink tell you about the part?"

"No. He just said you'd be worried about no tits, but you'd like the idea that I come from the old neighborhood."

"Where?" I asked immediately.

"Mulberry."

"Mulberry and where?" I wanted to know.

"Hester."

"What number?"

"At 1801."

"I'm 1725, between Hester and Canal."

"Does that mean I get the part?"

"Depends on how much of your catechism you remember."

"What does catechism have to do with the part?"

"It helps to know your catechism if you're a nun."

"*A nun?*"

"Yeah. A young, pretty, innocent nun."

She roared. She threw back her beautiful head and roared. Her laugh was high and squeaky but substantial, and when she was through there were tears in her eyes from the laughter.

"I see I've made your day," I said.

"That's funny," she said, as though she were talking to herself, "the nun thing is very funny."

"You've never worked a soap," I deduced.

"Never."

14

"And you know nothing about *Search for Happiness* or Troy, Ohio?" Troy was the typical Middle American town where this soap opera supposedly took place.

"I know nothing about TV shows," she answered.

"Brink must have found you in a little theater somewhere downtown."

"That's it."

"What's your name?" I asked.

"Anna Calzolari."

"And you think soaps are shit."

"I don't watch them. But I wouldn't think they're my idea of great drama."

"And you want to do nothing but great drama?"

"Listen, I came here on a lark. Your friend Brink—who talks out of the side of his mouth, by the way . . ."

"All agents talk out of the side of their mouths. If they don't, they're not real agents."

"Thanks for the tip," she offered. "He said you might have something extremely interesting. He said the money would be good."

"But you didn't give enough of a shit," I told Anna, "to bother to get dressed."

"I was going to wear my confirmation dress," she quipped back. Anna was quick. And she was also very street. *My* kind of street. I liked her a lot.

"I bet you're not as tough on the inside as you are on the outside," I guessed.

"What is this? Instant analysis time?"

"I'm just trying to figure out why you're here."

"I told you. Brink Kaufman. I was in a play and he saw me. He liked me."

"What was the play?"

"An adaptation of a novel by Kate Chopin. *The Awakening.*"

"Never heard of it."

"It's not well known," she said. "It's from another era."

"What's it about?"

"A woman who's a feminist before her time. Something like Ibsen."

"You're talking over my head, baby. No need to name-drop around me, 'cause I don't give a shit."

15

"I wasn't name-dropping. You asked me a question and I answered it."

"I don't give a good goddamn how feminist and highbrow you are."

"I didn't say I was feminist and I didn't say I was highbrow," she fought back. "I was just telling you about this part I'm playing."

"I got the idea that you're a serious actress. That's what you wanted to tell me, wasn't it?"

"I don't know how serious I am. I couldn't be too serious if I came here."

"This is the first time I've ever been insulted by someone who wants my money."

"Since when do you own this network," she snickered, seeing that I was enjoying the combat.

"How the hell do you know what I own and what I don't own?"

"It's all right to trick," she told me, "as long as you know you're doing it."

"I know, I know," I confessed, unable to resist her honesty. "And that's why you're here, I suppose. You wanna turn a little trick."

"I'm not sure," she said with genuine hesitancy.

"So you want to audition. And you don't want to audition."

"As long as I'm here, I suppose . . ."

"Don't do me any favors, sister."

"You're going to play rough, huh?"

"You've been playing rough since you first stepped in here," I told her. "You're a pretty girl. You've got a pretty face. But if you think it's so hysterically funny to put on a nun's habit, there's no way you're going to be able to play that part. It may be a joke to you, but to me it's real. It's how I keep myself in cigars," I said, lighting one up.

She closed her eyes and tapped her foot. She was studying what I had said. "What the hell," she finally sighed. "I'm here. I came here. I might as well put on a costume. I've done weirder things than dress up like a nun."

I tried to hide my excitement, but I didn't succeed. "Just pretend you're back at the Church of the Most Precious Blood on Baxter Street."

16

"That was our church," she said with some enthusiasm.

"I got my wrists slapped by the same sisters as you," I added. "Only when they were slapping me, they were twenty years younger, and stronger."

Anna smiled her sweet half-smile, looking like a very precious, very delicate child. She baffled me. These Off-Broadway actresses were really something. Most of them were temperamental bitches who thought they were great artists. But this one was different. This one had depth. I knew that she wasn't what she seemed to be. And I found myself fascinated by her strange combination of soft and hard.

"I'll walk you over to wardrobe," I said, "and take you on a little tour of the place. Then we'll round up the director and producer. Don't worry about them, though. They work for me."

"Glad I came to the right guy."

"You should be."

We walked out of my cubicle through the maze of offices and studios that was designated for the soap operas. We were on the third floor of an old building on the West Side of midtown Manhattan, a building, in fact, which used to be a milk plant before the network took it over. It was used for the news division and the soap operas. Everything else was done in L.A.

We passed the sets, the cardboard interiors which were made to look like upper-middle-class drawing rooms, chic restaurants, bedrooms, bars and kitchens.

We arrived at wardrobe and I introduced her to Carmen. "Put her in that nun's habit, honey," I said, "and please, no bad jokes. Then bring her back to my office. When you're dressed, Anna, I'll show you what I want you to read."

I went back to my cubicle and waited. This girl, this woman, had me a little bewildered, a little enchanted. I puffed on my cigar and watched the smoke curl above my head and drift off into the corner. There was something about this chick that was very goddamn strong.

And as much as I thought about her, as much as I found myself obsessed with the smallness and great delicacy of her face, as much as I dwelled on her almost spiritual presence, I was not prepared for what I saw standing in my doorway.

I saw a nun. I saw a goddamn nun. I mean, the woman stand-

17

ing there was a nun. She was standing in the doorway, holding her hands together in the position of prayer, looking toward the heavens. She was sweet and she was real, this nun. And she blinked her eyes at me—her eyelashes were long and dark—and she knelt and crossed herself slowly and with absolute conviction. She was a nun! Anna Calzolari was a nun! The black robes flowed behind her. Her hair was hidden and her face shone with radiance and faith. The crown of white over her high forehead, the modesty with which she walked toward me, the demure way she offered me her tiny, beautiful hand.

"It is good to see you again. I am glad you have returned to our church. We missed you." She was speaking so quietly, so sincerely. "And although it has been a long time since you visited us last, good brother, we always knew you would return. Your soul is too full of God's love to be denied. Oh, but it is comforting to have you back among us."

"This is scary," I said. "This is goddamn scary."

"Why are you frightened?" Anna asked.

She had lost her New York accent. Now she was speaking as though she had been raised in swanky private schools and prestigious convents. She was speaking like aristocracy.

"I'm frightened," I was finally able to say to her, "because you're so goddamn good."

"You must refrain from vulgarity. I implore you," she said softly. "There are so many beautiful words in the English language from which we might choose, so many other wondrous choices. Don't you agree?"

"Fucking A straight, Sister. This might really work. That bastard Brink might have really made himself a little dough."

"Again, you dwell on the vulgar, the material. What matters money in a world where the glory of God is so abundant, so magnificently omnipresent?"

"Holy Jesus!" I swore.

"Holy Jesus indeed. Holy and sacred Jesus," she singsonged to me in the cadence of piety. "Jesus who is Our Father. Jesus who is Our Saviour. Jesus who is our friend."

"This is ridiculous!" I howled. "This is absolutely ridiculous!"

"Nothing that is real is ridiculous, my brother. And nothing

18

that lives need be ridiculed. You understand, don't you?" she asked, gently patting my hand.

"Anna. Enough, baby. Save it for the audition. I don't want you to use it all up now."

"God's love is infinite. God's love is inexhaustible."

"Let's go, sweetheart," I said, grabbing her by the hand. "I want the boys to see you while you're hot." I took my script and led her into the studio where they were building the convent set. This is the scene that had to be taped in a couple of weeks when the young nun—whom I decided to call Prudence; Anna looked so much like a Prudence to me—is designated by the Holy Mother to plead with the man who owns the land on which the convent sits not to raze their building for a shopping strip. Until now, the landlord has been unwilling to budge. He already has signed up such sterling tenants as Baskin-Robbins, Pioneer Chicken and 7 Eleven. The section I had written was a rough draft of Sister Prudence's plea to the mean old landlord.

We walked down the hallway and, I swear before God, people turned around and looked at Anna. One cleaning lady stopped and said, "Good morning, Sister," and without missing a beat, Anna sweetly said, "God bless you, good morning." Now let me tell you something: At the milk plant, no one looks at anyone. We're nothing but a bunch of freaks running around anyway, so for heads to turn . . . well, Anna was really something special.

Dick and Howard were waiting for us at the set. Both these guys are pretty high up as far as soap men go. Like me, they're muddling their way into middle age. Dick's a director who went to an Ivy League school and fashions himself an intellectual lost in the world of crass TV. Which is bullshit. He's a money-grabber like the rest of us, pulling down very decent dough. Howard's the producer, and, in theory, he should be the boss. Except that he's scared of his own shadow and got where he is by sticking his tongue up the asshole of every executive who's ever been over him. A professional bootlick if there ever was one.

Personally, I don't mind either of these guys. They understand that the genius of this show comes from the shadows of my mind, not theirs. They live and die by me, and so do the haughty actors—the guys who think they're all Robert Redford —and the uppity bitches who call themselves actresses. They know they're there because I invented them. If I have an upset stomach tomorrow, maybe I'll kill them off. So they treat me with respect. And most importantly, they know I make more money than any of them.

I introduced Anna to Dick and Howard and she took their hands and gracefully withdrew to the middle of the set where she sat—patiently, silently—as I explained the setup.

"You really got to plead with this landlord. He's about to throw your holy sisters out on their asses," I said. "So read those couple of pages I've written for you, Anna, to yourself. Then take a few minutes and read them to us." I tried to be reassuring, but I saw it wasn't necessary. She was perfectly at ease. She looked at me through the angelic eyes of Sister Prudence. She was already gone, lost in a world of Renaissance churches and black roses, a world of Mary holding Jesus, the remorse, the agony of the oldest of all Catholic sufferings straight from the streets of Naples. Because there could be no doubt that Anna and Prudence were as Neapolitan as the mount called Vesuvius.

She read from my script: "I feel so honored that you came here, Mr. Adams," she said to an imaginary, thin-mustached and sleazy anti-Catholic landlord. "I know how terribly busy your schedule is and how important your time must be to you. Therefore I will speak directly to the point, sir, if you don't mind."

She was brilliant! Right off the bat she was brilliant, and Dick and Howard couldn't believe it! I looked at them out of the corner of my eye. They already knew that I had scored again. This chick was perfect for the part.

"Now I understand, Mr. Adams," Sister Prudence continued, "that you have a wonderful business opportunity, but that, unfortunately, that opportunity is in direct conflict with our sacred duties here at the convent. It is not so much the sisters themselves that I worry about, Mr. Adams. We are certainly capable of taking care of ourselves. But rather, sir, it is the needs—the very special needs—of the children whom we teach. They have been entrusted to us, and if we were to abandon the

20

little ones now, it would be like . . . well, Mr. Adams, it would be something like your sucking my nipples right here on the couch.''

At that point, Anna got up and ripped open the top of her habit, tearing the black cloth to shreds, exposing her lovely small breasts and her hard dark nipples. Her eyes were on fire under the white crown. She was New York street again. Everyone around the set, who had stopped to gaze in wonder as soon as she had begun her small speech, was now flabbergasted. I was flabbergasted. Dick and Howard stood there with open mouths.

"You can take this fucked-up part," she spat in the style of the old neighborhood, speaking to no one and to everyone, "and cram it up your ass.''

Then she stalked off, changed clothes and disappeared before I had a chance to recover.

2

When Anna left the milk plant she went straight for the subway. The streets were crowded and the New York September afternoon was hot and unreasonably steamy. There were tears in her eyes and she felt her heart beating fast. Auditioning for the part had scared the shit out of her—she told me all this later. It had touched home in a funny, frightening way, and she wanted no part of it. She just wanted to get back to her home, to the place she shared with her boyfriend, the unemployed actor, John Palermo.

She stood on the subway, cursing the fact that she hadn't been able to avoid rush hour. She was squashed on every side and her head ached. She was going to be late making John dinner, and that would get John extremely pissed. She worried about that because John had a hell of a temper. John's temper was different. His temperament was artistic. He was an actor, a very great actor, and he was entitled to his eccentricities. In her mind, John was different than all the boys from the old neighborhood who spent their lives bragging and strutting around like peacocks. John had soul and depth. But John—she also knew as she got off the train downtown and climbed the stairs to reach the streets—John was also the same.

She walked the streets like a native, with neither fear nor trepidation. She stopped at a fruit stand and bought a half-dozen tomatoes, just as her mother always had, testing and squeezing them with the wisdom of five centuries of Neapolitan savvy. She took her bundle and hurried down Spring until she reached the corner of West Broadway. There she walked into the huge furniture-depository-turned-apartment-house and got into the freight elevator. She held the button as the elevator slowly, slowly rose to the seventh floor. It was a ridiculous way to travel, but it was a lot better than climbing stairs. Among their SoHo friends, a freight elevator was a sign of great luxury. It beat having a doorman.

She opened the door to the expansive loft that she and John had been sharing for three years, ever since he had quit City College. She had quickly followed by quitting herself. She had gone there because it was his choice, so it was only logical that if he were disenchanted with the place, she would be too.

The loft was long and drafty, dark, damp and ugly. There was a large mattress in the middle where the two of them slept. There were posters hung on the wall advertising plays that John had acted in. Anna had put them there to cheer up the place. She had placed plants in strategic points, and recovered a couch in yellow and an easy chair in bright blue. She had added a number of decorative touches to create a semblance of green optimism and life. But none of her efforts had worked. The place was simply too large, too dreary, too stark. To redecorate, to create something of an atmosphere would have required new walls, a skylight and thousands of dollars. Anna and John were broke, and they had no choice but to accept the loft more or less the way they found it—empty and cold.

22

She turned on the lights which consisted of a few naked bulbs hanging on wires, dangling from the ceiling. The sink was full of dishes from last night. John hadn't touched them. He had promised to clean up, especially in view of Anna's audition to which he had encouraged her—even ordered her—to go.

"What about the soap?" he asked directly, remembering that he wanted to score a couple of grams of coke by the weekend. He was lying in bed, barely awake from his long afternoon nap.

"We'll talk about it later," she said.

"We'll talk about it now!" he demanded, sensing that something had gone wrong. She turned to look at him. His shining brown eyes were beautiful. She loved the way his nose was broad and flat, strong and aggressive. His hair was wild with waves, extravagantly full over his ears and neck.

"Nothing really happened," she mumbled.

"I want to know *exactly* what happened," he insisted.

Anna had to think quickly. This was not the time. She knew that this was not the time. And yet she had little choice. She'd just have to try and be cool about it.

"It was bullshit," she said to John in calm tones. "Total bullshit. You would have laughed."

"They didn't like you, then," he assumed.

His assumption angered her. "Yes, they liked me. I was good. I was very good. But I didn't like them. And besides, I like the play. I'm into that part and I don't want to leave it. Not right now."

"You crazy bitch!" he shouted, now roaring out of bed, naked and angry. "Are you telling me that they offered you the part and you turned it down?"

"I said that I don't want to leave *The Awakening*."

"*The Awakening* is shit. S.H.I.T. It's another meaningless, jerk-off Off-Off Broadway production. And the play pays shit."

"Listen, John," she retorted, "can you imagine me playing a nun?"

"Fuck, yes! Fuck, yes! All little Catholic girls want to be nuns, and you're no different."

"Well," she answered, still trying to be cool, "it made me feel silly and grotesque. I couldn't do it. I simply couldn't do it."

"But you read for the part, didn't you?"

"Yes, I read."

"And you were good, weren't you?"

"I was all right."

"I bet you were dynamite," he said. "I bet you got into that nun's head and I bet you knocked them out."

"I think they liked me, yes."

"And then you told them to shove it, didn't you?"

"The word I used was *cram*, not shove."

John shook his head in wonder. "I can't believe it. I really can't believe it."

"I exploded," she said. "The script was ridiculous. I couldn't read it. I couldn't get through it. I tried. Believe me, I tried. But it was a joke."

"*You blew it!*" he screamed. "*You idiot, you blew it!*"

"Listen, John. I've heard enough about this stupid part. I just don't want to do it, and there's nothing more to say."

"You have any idea what scale is?" he asked, now steaming. "Do you know what kind of bread you threw away?"

"We have some money. The play's running and that teaching job I applied for last month just might . . ."

"The play! The teaching job! Listen, Anna, the play is shit. Hear me: The play is shit, and you're not much better than the play. Actresses like you are a dime a dozen in down-and-out theaters. What you need is a break, and now that you got one, you threw it away. You actually threw it away."

"How about you?" she finally found herself saying.

"What about me?"

"What are you doing all day—smoking grass and snorting coke?"

"I'm out there, baby. I've been out there."

"When?"

"Yesterday. The day before."

"Bullshit." Anna faced him. There were only inches separating their faces.

"I knew this was only a question of time," he said. "I told you that a long time ago, that it would never work, living on your money like this. But you assured me. You said . . ."

"I don't want this thing to get any uglier, John. All I mean is

24

that the part was humiliating, and I want you to leave me alone. I just don't want to play some half-ass nun on a soap opera that turns on empty-headed women. That's not me."

"Then who the hell do you think you are? You're a fucking broad from Little Italy who's trying to get out like all the others."

"I'm out, John. We're out."

"Don't fool yourself. We're still in the same dumpy neighborhood. These buildings are falling apart just like the ones we lived in when we were kids. Don't you see? What we need is *money*. We need money right now!"

"And what are you doing about it?" she asked in rage, feeling tougher, feeling stronger.

He backed off a bit and said, "Do I have to give you a list of the producers I call every day? Do I have to recount the directors I've been chasing? What the hell do you want? Are you interested in punishing me more by having me go over my bloody failures? Is that what you're looking for? A little blood?"

"Stop!" she protested. "I'm an artist, I'm an actress. I don't want to do schlock. I'm not interested in schlock, John, and neither are you."

"Meanwhile, we're starving, and meanwhile you could turn a little trick."

"I'm not interested in tricking."

"This soap would make you act your ass off. You'd have to really . . ."

"Rationalize," she shot back. "You're just rationalizing. It's no good, and you know it."

"I know that I'm about through with this whole thing."

That single sentence did it. She felt herself weaken. Chills raced through her arms. Now he was frightening her.

"You're carrying this too far," she pleaded. "You don't have to take it that far."

"I haven't done a goddamn thing. It's you who've blown it. It's you who are out to destroy our relationship."

She knew that he had her. She had feared that it would come to this.

"Stop talking that way," she begged.

"Mitch Simms gave me a hundred-forty-five-page play that

ne said he wrote with me in mind. He wants me to read for his moneyman next month, and I was hoping that we could get away for a weekend in the country together, just you and me, where we could concentrate . . .''

"We can, we can," she urged.

"Not now," he said cruelly. "Now it's too late."

"Why didn't you mention that before?"

"I don't mention a lot of things, baby," he answered sadistically as he began getting dressed, as he put on briefs and his pants, as he pulled a blue sweater over his head. "I'm tired of these ridiculous scenes. I've had it." Then he put a scarlet scarf around his neck.

"Don't go out," she begged. "Please, John. Not tonight. Stay around. I'm going to make us dinner and . . .''

"Jesus, Anna, you sound like my mother. For Christ's sake, lay off." He put on his shoes, combed his hair. Anna was crying. She knew if he left like this he might not come back tonight. He often did that. Rather than fight with her, he'd teach her a lesson by staying out all night.

"Don't, John. Stay." She grabbed at his sweater. He ignored her, walking to the door, dragging her along.

"I'm getting out," he said. He looked at her with contempt, and yet he looked beautiful to her—fiercely, darkly beautiful— and she worried that he would go to one of those poet or painter women who lived alone and had jars of grass and cocaine and seduced gorgeous actors like John Palermo. She worried that he would leave and never come back. So she pulled on him, trying to keep him from walking out the door.

"Get your goddamn hands off of me," he warned.

But she wouldn't let go, and he spun around and slapped her across the face, knocking her to the floor. The slap stung, but she caught her breath before she screamed, and she watched him slam the door, and she sat there for five or ten minutes before she decided to call me.

3

I was reading the *Daily Racing Form,* sitting around the apartment in my undershirt, sipping on a beer. The ball game was on the tube and I was trying to cool off. Anna had been on my mind all day, and I had just managed to get the picture of her face out of my mind when she called.

"Where'd you get my number?" is the first thing I asked her.

"Kaufman."

"And what do you want?" I asked coldly. "Don't you think you've caused me enough aggravation for one day?" I tried to sound pissed off, but I wasn't. I knew she could tell that I was glad to hear from her.

"It's been a lousy day for me, too. I'm sorry." She did sound remorseful. But I was wary. Sure, the chick could act, but I had the feeling that she was about to do a number on me.

"So you're just calling to say that you're sorry. Is that it?" I asked her.

"Not exactly."

"Now you want the part," I guessed. "You got home and saw that the cupboard was bare."

"I want to talk to you," she said softly, sweetly.

"Well, you're talking to me."

"I'm not good on the telephone."

"You want to get together?" I asked, my heart beating a little faster than I liked. A man of my age has to be concerned about his heart beating too fast. What did she want? I wasn't about to be strung along. Women can be a pain in the ass. Which is why I've never been married. And which is also why I prefer to buy my pleasure. My idea of love is three beautiful air-conditioned days at Caesars Palace in Vegas. The wheel, the blackjack table, maybe a little afternoon sun by the pool and then one of those well-behaved, blonder-than-blond $250 numbers for the rest of the night. And to tell you the truth, I don't give a shit whether she's silicone or not. It all feels real to me.

"I'd just like to talk to you," she said, sounding alarmingly sincere. "You don't bullshit. You sound like the kind of person I can talk to."

"What do you want to talk about? You've already blown the part."

"I know that. You don't have to tell me that. I'd just like to see you, that's all."

"When?" I asked.

"I'm not doing anything tonight."

Holy shit, I thought to myself. What's with this chick? Could she really be interested? I looked at the tire around my waist. Sure, I was a little chunky, but I could see where I could still be attractive to a girl like this. After all, in my own field, I was something of a star.

"I'm busy," I answered, deciding to play hard to get.

"Oh," she answered, letting me dangle on my own rope for a while. There was a terrible silence, and finally I had to fill it.

"I suppose we could meet somewhere, if it's really important," I offered.

"That would be nice," she said, with what I took to be genuine joy in her voice.

"Where?" I asked. I was not accustomed to setting up dates with girls in their twenties. Who knew where chicks that age liked to hang out these days?

"Where do you live?" she asked.

"Midtown. Where do you live?"

"Not far from the old neighborhood," she said.

"Mulberry?" I asked her.

"SoHo."

"I could come down there. I was thinking about that anyway," I lied.

"How come?"

"The festival," I reminded her. "Don't tell me that you've forgotten the date. September nineteenth."

"San Gennaro," she sighed. "It's San Gennaro's night."

"I'll pick you up at the corner of Houston and Mulberry," I

told her. "We can walk through the festival and then grab something to eat. How does that sound?"

"Perfect. I'll be there in an hour."

"See you, kid."

I hung up the phone and wondered: What the hell was I getting into?

I went to my closet and, for the first time in years, regretted the fact that my wardrobe sucked. I've never been big on clothes. I've never cared. Women are entirely too fussy when it comes to things like fabrics and fashions. Which is why I prefer hookers who don't even look at what I wear. They're happy as soon as they see a little green.

But this was different. Anna was something else. And I would have liked to have been able to slip on something classy. Something a little more expensive than the blue blazer with gold-colored buttons that I bought three years ago at Ohrbach's. Oh, well. At least the gray slacks had just come back from the cleaners. They had a nice crease. And the yellow shirt was made of polyester or silk or something shiny. I got it in Miami last summer and it still looked new. I was definitely presentable.

So why was I nervous? Why did I take ten minutes to shine my pair of Nunn Bush shoes which hadn't been shined in a year? I suddenly realized I had a date. A woman had called me and asked me out. Yes, that's what was happening. I cursed myself for being out of hair cream. I could have used a little. Yet looking at myself in the mirror, I was not entirely displeased. Sure, I was a little jowly, a little pudgy. But I still had all my hair, and even though there were strong streaks of gray, the hair was thick. I figured it was probably this mature look that had turned her on. She wanted an older man, a worldly guy who had been around.

The cab ride downtown was swift, the night was cool, one of those the-summer-is-ending-and-fall-is-arriving New York nights. I had splashed on some English Leather and, I must confess, I was sort of enjoying smelling myself. This lady was a real mystery to me, and I was more than a little anxious to see her. To see how this evening was going to progress.

The cabby couldn't get near the corner of Mulberry and Houston. The area was mobbed. Everyone came to Little Italy for the Festival of San Gennaro. Yeah, this was the night that we really showed off. Especially we Neapolitans. Because San Gennaro is *our* saint, the patron saint of Naples who saved our relatives in the old country from plagues and famines and fires and even the smoldering lava of Mount Vesuvius. How could any of us ever forget our grandmothers telling us in their marvelously fluid Neapolitan dialect how, in the Church of Santa Chiara in Naples, a phial containing the blood of San Gennaro would turn from solid to liquid? Every September 19. A recurring miracle, to save us all, all us poor Neapolitans, from the plight of our poverty. *San Gennaro! San Gennaro!* The old ladies dressed in black screaming at the wooden statue of the saint, in the ghetto of Naples and the ghetto of New York City. *Save us, San Gennaro! Give us health, give us wealth, keep us strong, tell us you're there, tell us you care! Let us see your blood flow! Keep us in Thy grace!*

It felt good to be back. The streets were teeming with people, all rushing to get a look at something real. I couldn't help but feel the pride come rushing back. This was my home, and as I approached Mulberry, I could see that those beautiful white lights had been strung across the street. Traffic had been closed off and it was just the people and the smells, all warm and spicy, familiar and enticing.

And when the saint himself was carried by on a wooden platform, I saw that dozens of dollar bills had already been scotch-taped to his arms by those seeking favors or miracles or grace. He was illuminated by small, flame-shaped electric light bulbs. He was a little chipped, a little dented, and he looked, as he always looked, like a very sweet and very inexpensive baby doll. No matter. He was *our* San Gennaro, and I was glad that the people in charge saw fit to keep him year after year. I'm not sure I could stand to see a new, spiffy San Gennaro. The old one, like the old neighborhood, was good enough for me.

Mulberry was sparkling, dancing, dazzling with pushcarts and stands of sausages and peppers, melons and clams and thick-crusted pizzas, cheeses, and raw prosciutto, garlicky mushrooms, anchovies and luscious pastries oozing with cream and booze. The crumbling tenements seemed to vanish behind the festivities.

30

I stopped for a couple of quick *bigné* at the makeshift *pasticerria* set up by my lawyer's aunt, Mrs. Umberto. She wouldn't let me pay, so I gave her a couple of extra kisses on the cheek and fought my way back up to the corner of Mulberry and Houston, trying to find Anna among the crowd which seemed to be growing larger every minute. I kept looking around, standing on tiptoes, going from one side of the street to another. No Anna. For a small second, I began to worry. I wondered whether I was being stood up. But that made no sense. She had called *me*. She had asked *me* out. And then a few minutes later I felt a tap on my shoulder and heard a small voice say, "You seem like you're right at home here."

I turned around and looked into her eyes. Her eyes were smiling, but they were also extremely red. I knew that she had been crying. I stepped back and looked her over. I knew I hadn't been very subtle because she asked, "Do I pass inspection?"

"In one day," I said to her, defending myself, "I've seen you look like a Greenwich Village actress, a nun and now . . ."

"And now?" she egged me on.

"I have no idea. I have no earthly idea."

What *did* she look like? She defied category. She was beautiful, yes. She was soft and she was demure. But she was also improbably, impossibly mysterious and distant and chic. And hurt. I felt her suffering, and I don't know why. To this day I don't know why. But standing in the middle of Mulberry Street, in the midst of the crazy festival, I felt her pain, even though on the outside she was all satin and silk.

She was wearing a peasant-styled tunic, hip-length with full-billowing sleeves and a high collar. It was a dusty rose color, muted and romantic, and when she offered me her arm, and when I took it, I felt the fabric. Heavy satin. The kind of stuff, I thought to myself, that Jean Harlow's slinky nightgowns were made of. Best for showing off nipples. She wore tapered black silk slacks and small black suede boots. The chick was dressed as though she just stepped off the plane from Paris. And on top of that, she wore absolutely no makeup. Which gave her a look of deep depression.

"I think you look like a kid from Little Italy," I finally said.

"Thanks," she answered glumly.

"Who grew up to become a famous actress and decided, on the spur of the moment, to grace the old neighborhood with a visit."

She considered my flattery and decided to return the favor. "You look very nice yourself. I like your blazer. And I also like English Leather."

This was obviously a woman who understood men. Or at least who understood me. We started walking down Mulberry and I loved the feeling of her hand against my arm. I was proud to be her escort, even though I was a little uncomfortable. After all, I was twice her age. And yet it didn't seem to make the slightest difference to her.

"You let your hair down," I said to her. It was thin and black and wispy and barely fell to the top of her slender shoulders.

She turned and smiled at me and said, "Thank you for noticing."

Thank you for noticing! I thought to myself. What else could I do but stare at this woman who had more class and poise than all the girls from this old neighborhood put together.

"Ever want to be the *principessina* of the festival?" I asked her.

"Never," she answered as we passed by a three-hundred-pound *paisan* hawking huge strings of sausages from his stand. The overhead lights twinkled in Anna's eyes and I couldn't see a drop of happiness. Not a drop.

"You weren't the princess type, huh?" I probed.

"I was the kind who might have tripped the princess."

"Rebellious," I figured.

"Rebellious and restless," she answered.

"A lot of brothers and sisters," I guessed.

"Seven. And you?"

"Eight."

We strolled past another row of pushcarts loaded with ziti lobsters, piled high with platters of spaghettini, linguini, olives, finocchi, giant zucchini and squirming calamari. My mouth watered.

"So it was rough," I said to Anna, trying to sympathize.

"It was rough for all of us, don't you think?"

32

"I'm not sure," I answered honestly. "It's not so bad looking back. We got out, didn't we?"

"I don't know. We're still here." She pointed to the tenement at the corner of Mulberry and Broome.

"This is just a visit," I said, nodding at a guy I recognized from high school. "We're just passing through."

"If you say so," Anna replied in a voice that was barely audible.

"You really sound down," I finally told her. "If you'd rather not be here . . ."

"Maybe we could walk over to the Village," she suggested. "I guess I'm just a little nervous about running into relatives. . . ."

"And being seen with an older man."

"Bullshit," she assured me. "That has nothing to do with it. I just don't want to be pinched on the cheek and asked a million dumb questions."

"Enough said. I thought we might drop in on the Church of the Most Precious Blood. But I guess we'll save that for another time."

She laughed a very small laugh.

"One favor, though," I continued.

"What's that?"

"If we go over to the Village I've got to have some Italian food. The smells have really gotten to me."

"I wouldn't dream of depriving you," Anna conceded.

The half-hour walk was strangely silent. The noise from the festival faded. She had let go of my arm and I could tell that she neither wanted to talk nor be talked to. I felt as though she had left me. I worried, but my instincts told me to leave her alone. Out of the corner of my eye I looked at her looking at the beautiful old ruins of the Lower East Side. And as we approached Washington Square, I saw relief pass over her face. The old neighborhood obviously held little charm for her. She just wanted to get out.

Among the hipper atmosphere of the Village she felt freer, more relaxed. By the time we arrived at a place over on West Fourth Street called the Napolitana Kitchen, my tongue was practically hanging out from hunger.

"I love this joint," I said to her, pointing out the long sign in front of the restaurant which had been there as long as I could remember: LASAGNA, RIPITENA, GNOCCHI, PERCIATELLI ALLA SICILIANA, FRITTO MISTO. It was nearly 11:00 P.M., but inside the place was buzzing. The smells from the kitchen nearly knocked me down, and I immediately felt good. This, too, was home. It had been a long time since I was down here, and I had forgotten how much I hated those pretentious, swanky French restaurants where the network boys were always dragging me. I never knew what to order and, besides, I detested goopy cream sauces. Just give me a plain restaurant like the Napolitana Kitchen—sawdust on the floor, beat-up chairs, starched white tablecloths, gigantic baskets of fresh bread on the table.

"This is better," I said to Anna, "much better."

She had been thinking about something else, but my words brought her back. "I'd like a little wine, if I might."

"Just say the word," I urged.

"Lambrusco."

"A particular favorite of mine."

We sat in silence. For a long time she closed her eyes and pressed her fingertips against her eyelids. Then she opened her eyes and sighed and tried to smile. But it didn't work. I wondered: Am I just a lousy date? Am I boring her? Is she tired? Or is she afraid?

"Anna," I said, "you look like you don't want to be here."

"No," she tried to snap back, "not at all. I, I . . . I'm just a little distracted, a little . . ."

The wine arrived and saved her from finishing the sentence. I wanted to take her hand but I guess *I* was a little afraid. I didn't do it. I was too busy trying to figure out what this evening— what this whole, crazy, goddamn day—had been about. All I knew was that right now there was no communication. Just a bottle of Lambrusco and a couple of glasses. I put away more than a few pieces of bread and tried to be patient.

I ordered gnocchi al pesto, and Anna said she wasn't hungry.

"You got to eat something, baby," I urged.

"The wine's doing me good."

"You could stand to put on a couple of pounds," I assured her. "Why don't you have a little pasta?"

"No, really," she begged off. "You go ahead."

"I'll feel guilty. I'm the one who should be laying off. You know I'm really at least thirty pounds . . ."

And then the tears came. They came suddenly and they came in torrents. They came with sobs, and the sobs were loud and everyone started turning around and looking and I realy didn't give a shit about the stares. I went ahead and took her hand and patted it and kissed it. And her hand felt so weak, so wet, so slight. And I said, "Now, now, Anna. Come on, sweetheart. Everything's gonna be all right. You just need to talk about it."

And by then the waiter brought my gnocchi, but I couldn't touch them. Which is an indication of how worried I was. I made her drink a little wine, a little water. I buttered a piece of bread for her and told her to take a bite. I asked her if she wanted me to take her home. By now I knew that I wasn't going to get laid and I didn't care. Or if I did care, I cared more about something else—about Anna herself.

"I shouldn't have called you," she finally said.

"Sure you should have. Hell, you've made my evening. I was with the best-looking girl at the festival." I smiled. I tried to make her smile, but it was no dice. She was still shaking with her sobs, still choking on her tears.

"I thought I'd con you." She continued to weep between words.

"Con the con artist?"

"You're no con artist," she said. "I can tell. You might be tricking a little bit, but you're honest about it."

"We all have to trick," I stated philosophically. "It's just a question of degrees. I learned that long ago."

"I guess that's what I didn't realize today."

"At the audition?"

"Yeah. I blew it. And I thought . . ." She couldn't finish the phrase.

"You thought you'd hustle me for the part tonight."

"Something like that." She stared into her wine glass. She couldn't look me in the eye.

"Mind if I smoke a cigar?" I hated to be crude, but I really needed to smoke. This chick was really shaking me up. She didn't respond. She was too busy trying to settle down, so I lit up. As soon as the tobacco hit my tongue, I was much better off.

"I feel silly," she managed to say.

"You're entitled to a little cry." I tried to help her.

"It's more than that."

"The old neighborhood can be a drag. That was a lousy idea. Sorry."

"No. It was a good idea. It's just that my head was spinning. I wanted to tell you that I felt close to you. I felt like I knew you my whole life. I felt like I grew up with you. Like you were an uncle, a real friend."

I was confused. I no longer knew whether I was being hustled, whether I was being liked, or loved, whether I was being used or whether I was being needed. All I could do was to keep listening and wondering.

"It's not really about me, though," she continued. "It's about John."

"John?" I asked.

"John Palermo. The man I live with."

"Oh." My heart sank. I guess deep down I knew it was coming. It was too good to be true. There had to be a John.

"Tell me about John," I managed to ask out of simple decency, though I really didn't want to hear about him. I decided to eat my gnocchi, cold as they might be. I needed something to console me. And as I ate, she slowly told me the story.

She told me how she understood him, how off and on, she had been his woman for eight years. John Palermo, the sultry, moody beautiful boy from around the corner, had taken her. And the funny part was that now, a lifetime later, it was not much different than it had been when they were children.

She described how he looked when she had first seen him walking down Mulberry Street. His misty wet eyes. His slouch. She had seen him from her window, through the fire escapes, and she had remembered him from school. John was quiet and John was cool. He didn't hang out with the other boys. He carried around poetry by the old beatniks and went to the West Village where he listened to jazz. He talked about art and she listened because he was the first artist she had ever met. And she thought that he was so different and so wonderful. He was

36

different from everyone else in the neighborhood and she wanted to go wherever he went. She, too, decided that she wanted to be an artist. An artist, an actress: That was the way out, out of her parents' apartment, out of the old neighborhood, out of the tenements. John was her way out of one world and into another. John was everything. And even then he wore black turtlenecks and mud-splattered jeans. Even then his body was splendid.

She went on about his enormous talent and his artistic temperament. About how he was going to be the new Pacino and De Niro all rolled into one. About how he needed help—her help. And how he needed money—her money. I was touched by the fact that she was confiding in me. And I was impressed, even moved, by her candor. She was really letting it out and sparing me none of the details—as if, in truth, we *had* known each other all our lives. But when she was done, I found myself asking her the question I had been wanting to ask her the whole night:

"What about you? What about you, Anna?"

"What do you mean?"

"I want to know about you."

"I'm an actress."

"I've seen that. But I still don't know if you want to act on this soap opera. Do you really want to do it? Are you going to be happy doing it or are you going to hate yourself for doing it? Because if you're going to hate yourself, it's not going to be worth it. And it's not going to work."

"I'll make it work. I have to make it work."

"Why?"

"Because now I feel," Anna said, brushing back her hair, searching for the right words, "that I have to show John that I *can* make this thing work. I want him to see that I can act, no matter what the part."

"You sound like you're selling me. Or selling yourself."

"I don't have to sell anyone, Al. You've seen that I can act. It's something that comes without struggling. I close my eyes and I'm there."

"Because you don't want to be here?" I questioned.

"There's no because, there's no explanation I can think of. It's simple magic that . . ."

"Magic isn't that simple," I interrupted her. "What you did today in the audition wasn't simple."

"It was for me. I swear."

"Then why did it make you sick? Why did you cause such a ridiculous scene?"

"Because it was almost too easy."

"You thought it was dirty money."

"Is that what you think?" she asked me.

"No money is dirty to me. But maybe that's because I don't give a shit about art."

"Come on, Al. You're an artist. You sit around all day and create images. You paint pictures, and millions of people love to look at them. If that's not art, I don't know what is."

She was convincing, but I felt she was only fooling herself. Or confusing herself. "So this soap opera thing doesn't bother you anymore," I said. "Is that what you want me to believe?"

"Listen, right now I'm only interested in showing you and John and the ladies out in TV land that I'm a nun. If I can do that, I have the feeling that a lot of my problems will be over."

"You're tired of being broke," I said sympathetically. I began seeing all kinds of good possibilities for the show.

"Besides," Anna continued, "this is like Old Home Week. And that's certainly nothing that frightens me any longer. That's all past me. Wanting to be a nun . . ."

"What!" I almost choked on a gnocchi. "You wanted to be a sister?"

"Who didn't?" she asked rhetorically, thinking of John's earlier accusation. "Sure I wanted to be a nun. I thought of it as a way to get out of those four cramped rooms with everyone on top of each other. I thought nuns had a charmed life. They had their own rooms, and it was always peaceful and quiet. I would dream about it. I'd think of how great it would be to have the Virgin Mary as my mother—instead of my real mother. The Virgin Mary was so beautiful. And she never screamed, she never had a husband who hit her, or drank, or stayed out all night."

"Sounds like my old man," I said, sucking on my cigar.

"For a long time I cried every time Mass was over. That meant I had to go home. And I didn't want to go home."

38

"So you were a good girl, then."

"For a while," she smiled softly, sipping her wine. "You know how it is down there. It's boring as hell. And you have to be a little cracked to get lost in the Church. For me, it was just another dream that came and went. And when I awoke, I realized that being a nun was the pits. I saw that I wasn't all that interested in charity, poverty and obedience."

"What were you interested in?"

"John."

And so for the next ten minutes we polished off the bottle of Lambrusco as she once again went over all the details of John's brilliance, John's talent, John's past and John's future.

"If this character is such a gem," I finally couldn't help but ask, "what the fuck is he doing slamming the door in your face?"

"He's been frustrated. He needs work. He needs work desperately."

"So he puts you to work."

"Listen," she said, now fortified by those bubbly fermented grapes, "I really do need that part."

"I figured as much."

"And I really didn't want to put you through such changes tonight."

"It was nothing. Nothing at all."

"So you're not angry?"

"How could I be angry when you smile at me like that?" I asked her.

"And you don't think you're being conned?"

"I don't think I'm being conned. I *know* I'm being conned."

"And you don't mind?"

"Keep conning me, baby."

"So I can have another audition?"

"You can have the goddamn part. It's yours."

"Just like that?" For the first time tonight, her eyes were alive. Her cheeks were flushed with color.

"Just like that," I assured her.

She got up and came around and kissed me on the cheek. "I love your energy," she said to me, "I really do."

"Listen, honey," I announced, "I'm tired. That energy you

love is slipping away. So I'm going to put you in a cab, and then I'm going to put me in a cab, and you'll call me tomorrow morning—not too early—and I'll let you know where we go from here.''

''But I got that part? You can really cool things with those other two guys?''

''I can cool anything, as long as I can count on you. You gotta realize that I'm talking about a major role. Five days a week, some rehearsals at night. You're going to have to give up your play. There's no way you can do both things at the same time. But I'll make it worth your while. I'll cut the deal with Kaufman and make sure you get at least twenty thousand for the next six months. I'll keep you in the script for at least that long. And then we'll see how things work out.''

''You can really do that?'' she asked excitedly.

''You're talking to the boss, baby.''

''I want to say that I love you.''

This lady was really getting to me. I didn't want to be this excited. ''It's a little early for talk like that,'' I said to her.

I threw a twenty on the table, and we walked outside. It wasn't long before I found her a cab, kissed her on the cheek and told her, ''You're the craziest broad I've met in at least a week.''

''Thanks,'' she said, and she kissed me back. On the lips.

The cab ride home was painful, and so were the two hours it took me to fall asleep. For a while I considered indulging myself in what I've always considered man's greatest solitary pleasure. But I couldn't stop picturing Anna as a nun, and I couldn't stop trying to figure out how to manipulate this plot to utilize her enormous talents.

Anna was something very special. I hadn't scored, and yet I had. We had gotten together after all, and as I thought about how she looked when I put her in the taxi—like a little girl whose father had just promised her the moon—I realized that I was into something very deep. And there was no telling what was going to happen next.

40

4

Anna awoke the following morning and John was not there. She had expected as much, and yet the disappointment was deep. Secretly she had hoped that he had managed to slip in during the night without being heard. She knew, though, that would have been impossible. Any sound would have awoken her from her troubled sleep. And yet she knew what she had to do today. In some sense, she was changing her life, and she realized she needed strength. The depression which threatened to fill her head had to be shaken loose; the day had to be met head-on.

She dressed quickly and tried not to think about the dampness of the loft, the hopelessly dingy feel of the space and air surrounding her. She walked to the window toward the front of the loft. Her eye was greeted with gray; the day was hazy. It was ten o'clock, and she knew if she didn't go to see Gwen Snodes now, she never would.

In some ways, telling Gwen was going to be the most difficult move of the day. Still, it was something that had to be done. Anna locked the loft behind her and went down the freight elevator. She would walk to the theater.

A dog had crapped outside the door of her building. SoHo smelled bad this morning. She stopped at an espresso bar which was bustling with artists and dancers and hangers-on, and she knew a few; she nodded, she was polite, but she sat alone and looked at a *Soho Weekly News* which someone had left. She couldn't concentrate. Couldn't concentrate on anyone but John. The espresso was bitter. The lemon tasted bad. How would she tell Gwen? What would she say? The truth is always the easiest, she thought.

She drank down the coffee, paid and left. Outside she walked through soot. The same soot, she thought, that she had known as a child. Decades of factory dirt, the soot of centuries, New York's Lower East Side, called by a dozen names in a dozen eras—from immigrant tough to arty-farty and back again. Who cared? At this point, Anna wanted out. She just wanted the money to get out. And she would get it, she thought as she continued moving west across Houston, she would get it and she—and John—would get the hell out. For good. She wanted to feel different, to look different. She wanted sleek new pants, she wanted shoes and scarves, Egyptian cotton and Irish linen. She wanted a new direction. She wanted to do a whole new number.

The sign above the theater which said LIVING ROCK in bold graphic type was dirty. The letters were barely visible. She had not noticed this before. She walked inside. The cigarette butts hadn't been cleaned off the floor of the tiny lobby. And beyond, in the small circular theater, the folding chairs—of wood and metal and plastic—were rickety, chipped, dented. The place looked as though it were falling apart. Only the distant voice of Gwen Snodes—speaking from her closet-office to the right of the theater—raised Anna's spirit. In spite of everything, she loved her friend Gwen.

"Listen," Gwen was saying when Anna walked into the room which looked as though it had not survived several serious storms, "you're supposed to be the good guys"—and she put her hand over the phone and whispered to Anna—"this is PBS, I'm pitching PBS." Gwen listened to the party on the other end and then relaunched her attack. "I'm telling you, Bob. This isn't just another Off-Broadway production. This is quality theater. I've had a couple of calls from *Sixty Minutes*. They're doing a piece on Off-Broadway and they want to come down here and shoot, but I won't let them. I hate the networks. But I promise you, Bob, this is a production that could make you a star. Once WNET picks it up, the whole system will follow suit. Edmund Wilson loved the story. You'll love it, you'll absolutely love it, and the woman who plays the lead is standing before me and I swear on a stack of Anaïs Nin diaries that she's the next

Hepburn. She's good enough to make you weep"—Gwen winked at Anna—"and we've spent God knows how much money on costumes, authentic period pieces."

Anna wanted to stop listening, but she couldn't. She sat down in a chair by Gwen's desk and looked at her friend with only a half-smile. She listened to Gwen's enthusiastic presentation of the theater's current work, and she reminded herself how much of Gwen's life was wrapped up in the theater. Once a public-relations executive, four years ago—at age thirty-three—Gwen had given up a $40,000-a-year job to push this theater. Leaving the PR agency had transformed Gwen. In the days when it was fashionable to do so, she had actually once straightened her hair. But now, sitting behind her desk, her face was encircled with light, golden curls which sprouted from her scalp like flowers, light and springy. Anna marveled at the texture of Gwen's hair and the strength of her face. Her cheekbones were sharp and well-defined, adding to the already aggressive slant of her green/blue eyes. She was tall—nearly six feet—especially large-breasted and not at all plump. She was built like an athlete. She was strong and she was intimidating. She ran the theater single-handedly, and she had been the first person in Anna's life who had said that Anna had talent. Her boyfriend had known John—that's how she and Anna met—and it had been Gwen who gave Anna her first chance to act. She sensed that Anna was a natural, and she also knew that it was just old-fashioned womanly fear which kept Anna from stepping out into the spotlight.

In the initial stages, when Palermo felt particularly threatened, it was Gwen who sustained Anna, who practically threw her on the stage and told her to act. At the time, Gwen was at the height of her feminist convictions, and she saw Anna as a soul in need. Not only did Gwen tackle Anna's insecurity, but she tackled John Palermo as well. She conducted a campaign—soliciting everyone connected with the Living Rock Theatre—to browbeat John until he dropped his objections to Anna's acting. Gwen won, and the production of *The Awakening,* which was mounted five months ago, was Anna's first starring role. Gwen had the novel adapted to the theater with Anna in mind.

"We're sick of *Masterpiece Theater,*" Gwen continued to

sell, "everyone's sick of *Masterpiece Theater*. Get yourself in a cab tomorrow night, Bob, and run downtown and I promise you, there will be nothing local about this production. It's absolutely made for television. So Saturday night I'll meet you in the lobby. Bring whomever you like and afterward I want you to meet the cast. Can I count on you?" A few minutes later the conversation was over, and Gwen Snodes stood up, displaying the great bulk of her beady-crocheted-top Indian tent dress, and screamed. As she screamed, she put her hands to her own ears —as if to capture the scream inside her head—and continued the piercing sound for at least thirty seconds.

"Sorry," she finally said to Anna, "but I had to get that out of me."

"I understand," Anna conceded.

"Oh, God." Gwen tilted her head toward the ceiling and closed her eyes. Her curls seemed to spill on the floor. "Will anyone take this poor production and put it on the air or take it uptown before we run out of money?"

"How much is left?"

"I'm not telling. It doesn't matter. Help is on its way. I've got so many irons in the fire that my fingers are burning. Never you worry, cara Calzolari. You are an artist and your head should not be confused with matters of finance. That's my domain, and one way or another you'll be reading about yourself and horny old Kate Chopin and her *Awakening* in *Time* and *Newsweek* before this year is over."

"You really think so?" Anna questioned.

"I know so. I have *The New Yorker* coming next week. Then the drama critic at *New York* magazine. Isn't it exciting?"

"Gwen, I better say right now . . ." Anna was prepared to get the whole bloody business over with.

"Before you say anything," Gwen interrupted, "let's go out and grab a bite."

"I'm not sure I can eat," Anna remarked sullenly.

"Why? What's wrong?"

"Nothing, except that I'm not hungry."

"Well, if you're not eating, I'm not eating. There's nothing to gain from eating except weight."

"We'll walk," Anna said.

"We'll talk," Gwen replied. "We'll solve the world's problems from a bench on Washington Square. It's an old New York tradition."

The walk to the Washington Square Park had Gwen talking about plans for the production of *The Awakening*. Anna couldn't stop her. She tried a couple of times, but it was useless. If Anna had a tendency toward shyness, Gwen brought out that quality in abundance. She talked Anna into silence, and Anna simply let her babble as they walked beneath the Washington Square Arch and found an empty bench toward the center of the park. The layer of clouds covering the city sky had thickened, and in the far distance the rumbling of thunder was barely audible. The day had grown damp and sticky, and the park looked especially sad. The trash cans were overflowing with litter.

"But I've been talking too much about this goddamn production. Tell me what's on your mind, Anna," she finally heard Gwen say, "tell me what's bothering you."

"I think I'm leaving the play." She said it just like that. Plainly, bravely. She knew that was the only way to get it out.

"You think you're leaving the play!" Gwen turned toward her in shock. Anna knew she was going to have to be strong, and she wished, having broken the news, that she could just get up and run away.

"I have to leave, Gwen. And I have to leave soon."

"Tell me why. Tell me why *immediately*."

"There's another part that's been offered and . . ."

"I don't believe this. I can't be hearing right. We've worked our asses off for nearly a year and you're walking away, going to some other theater. Anna, this doesn't make sense."

"It's not another theater."

"Then what in hell is it?"

"Television."

"Television! Unbelievable! This is unbelievable! What are you going to be doing, selling douche spray?"

"It's a soap."

"A soap!" Gwen practically screamed.

"You're not making this easy."

"You shaft me, you shaft the whole theater, and you also

want me to make it easy on you? Well, let me tell you something, honey, you go find yourself some shrink who'll take your
money and tell you that your shit smells sweet. Not me. The
least you could have done was warn me that you were looking
to get out. The least you . . ."

"I wasn't looking. I didn't know. This agent came to me."

"I don't believe it. We were raided. One of those sleazy
Broadway agents came down and raided us. And you're telling
me that you're doing all this in good faith, without the least
regret."

"I didn't say that."

"Then why are you doing it?"

"It's a complicated story, Gwen. It's long and it's painful,
and I'd rather not . . ."

"Did you read for the part?"

"Yes, of course."

"And they liked you. Naturally they liked you. I should
know. I was the one who first understood just how good you
are. Only to have you wind up on daytime TV. Jesus, Anna, I
can't believe you liked it. Don't tell me you actually liked reading for the part."

"No, I didn't like it. I hated it."

"But you're doing it anyway."

"It's . . . well, it's the challenge and the . . ."

"What kind of part do they have you playing? Don't tell me.
You're a young housewife whose lawyer husband has just died
of cancer, and now you're having second thoughts about fucking your best friend's old man."

"No, it's not that, it's . . ."

"Well, what is it? What soap is it?"

"Search for Happiness."

"I love it," Gwen howled, "I just love it. And tell me, who
do they have you playing?"

"A nun."

Gwen got up from the bench and screamed. "You're leaving
The Awakening to search for happiness," Gwen finally managed
to say between howls of protest and rage. "If that's not the
absurdity of the century, I don't know what is."

"You're presuming too much." Anna began to fight back.
She was tired of taking the abuse, tired of Gwen's arrogance.

"I'm presuming that John Palermo's coke stash is getting low. And I'm presuming that you're being sent out to the streets to do a little tricking."

"Goddammit, Gwen, what do you think you're doing for Living Rock? What in God's name were you doing on the phone all morning? All I've heard about for days now is tricking. I'm sick of it. I'm sick of the whole rotten mess."

"Then why are you doing it?"

"Because I want to do it. You don't understand, Gwen, You're too angry to understand. But believe me, I know just what I'm doing. I know what I want and I know how to get it."

"So Anna's turning tough on me, is that it?"

"Anna's always been tough. Anna's had to be tough," Anna said.

"I'm not buying any of this," Gwen replied.

"I'm not selling."

"You've already sold. I'm just wondering how much they bought you for."

"That's none of your business," Anna snapped.

"You're ashamed," Gwen accused.

"I am not in the least ashamed. In fact, I'm proud. Twenty thousand dollars. I'll be getting twenty thousand dollars for the first six months."

"That's sickening. That's criminal."

"I'm not looking to win an award for Purest Soul of the Year. I'm looking to advance my career, to live, to be seen."

"You'll be seen all right. You'll be seen by eighteen zillion idiot housewives every day while their infants are throwing up on their heads."

"You're not giving me a chance. You're condemning this thing before I ever get started."

"First you destroy our production and then you tell me to congratulate you for such a fine destruction job. Go get Palermo to kiss your ass, Anna. He'll do it, but not me. He'll do any goddamn thing as long as you keep his nose stuffed with snow. I know that bastard and so do you, Anna, which is exactly why you're leaving us. He may not be smart, but he has the instincts of a brilliant pimp. He pushes your buttons at just the right time. Just be careful, though, that you don't do too well, because that'll get him good and scared, and then you'll be back where you started from—looking for another way to keep him home.''

"You misunderstand him, Gwen. John is not . . ." Anna began to say.

"John *is!* John *is!* John *is* behind this whole dirty mess! You're a wonderfully talented actress, Anna, wonderfully, wonderfully talented, and it breaks my heart. This whole thing breaks my heart, and it's a shame, though it is your shame more than anyone else's, because for all your talent you lack the one quality which could really put you over.''

Anna did not answer. Her eyes were swollen with hurt and pain.

"You lack balls," Gwen told her.

"I don't want balls!" Anna finally exploded. "I don't need balls! I don't intend to spend my life trying to get something that has nothing to do with me. My whole sense of myself says . . ."

"Your sense of yourself is nonsense." Gwen's voice was lowered, reconciled to the fact that her arguments were having no effect.

"I'm a woman," Anna retorted. "I'm an actress. I want to act, and I want to love, and I want a career that means something. I want to show John and you and everyone else that I'm capable of . . ."

"Doing shit. You'll be doing shit."

"It's just a part. Can't you see, Gwen, that it's nothing more than a part?"

"It's going to be more than a part," Gwen said with a strong degree of compassion. "I know you, Anna. This part—this insane soap opera part—is going to be your whole life."

Gentle drops of rain began to fall. An old man, seated on a nearby bench, put a copy of *Il Progresso* on top of his head and sighed. Anna looked up to say something, but Gwen would listen to nothing else. Gwen was off. She was walking, almost running through the park. Anna wanted to call after her, to stop her, but that would be pointless. There was nothing more to say —at least not now. A tall man in a cream-colored raincoat approached Gwen under the Washington Square Arch. Anna saw him eyeing her friend's expansive bosom. He must have said something lewd, because Gwen turned and shot him the finger. He quickly turned and went in the opposite direction.

48

For a while Anna thought that Gwen might return, might say something else, might soften the blow. But her friend didn't look back. She disappeared into the gray city afternoon, and for a long while afterward Anna just sat there in the soft rain, thinking of Gwen's words and wondering whether John would be coming back tonight.

5

Anna called me that night, full of questions and worry. She wanted to know when she would see a script, when she would actually start performing. I told her that it would all take two or three weeks, and to be cool.

"I'm going to Vegas," I said. "But I'll be back Tuesday. I've already talked with Howard and Dick."

"And?" she asked.

"They were a little skeptical. But when I explained the situation they were satisfied."

"How'd you explain it?"

"Listen," I said to her, "it's bad enough I have to hear my bullshit the first time. Don't make me go through it again."

The meeting with Dick and Howard had been turbulent. They had tried to pull rank. Dick was especially pissed. He said he couldn't forgive any actress who talked that way to him. I told him that I really didn't give two shits who he was willing to forgive. I told him that Anna was just such a strange broad, that she had flipped out for a few seconds and that's all there was to it. I wanted her for the part, because I wrote the part and I knew what I needed. Dick started telling me how it didn't work that way, how the casting director had to be consulted, how there had to be more meetings and discussions. Bullshit, said I. There was only going to be one meeting and this was it and Anna

Calzolari had the part. Dick started using his big words and kept jawing until Howard—who has no guts but certainly a few smarts—told him to pipe down. Howard told him that maybe Anna wasn't a bad idea. But Dick kept protesting and finally I had to play my ace. "Listen, why don't I go to Mark Costein with this. We'll let him decide."

Mark Costein is the thirty-five-year-old kid who runs programming. Mark Costein isn't about to veto anything I want because Mark Costein knows that I'm making the network money. Mark Costein understands that I'm the guy who makes *Search* go. He knows that I'm senior to every other bastard on the show.

"There's no reason to bother Mark with this," Howard started sucking up. "I don't see why we can't use this actress. She was especially good, and if you can keep her in line, Al, why, I'm willing to go along."

"It's not her I'm worried about," I answered, giving them both the back of my hand, "it's you guys."

That was yesterday.

"So I can consider the part mine?" Anna now asked me on the phone.

"I already told you that last night. Don't worry your pretty little head."

"Will you give me your number in Las Vegas?"

"What for?"

"I might need to talk to you."

"Talk now. What's wrong, honey?"

"For openers, my best friend's deserted me and John's still not back."

"Tell me more about your best friend."

In great detail, she explained what happened with Gwen Snodes, and as I listened, I realized how important it was for her to get into this TV role. She was out there stranded, and she was really looking for a connection with something new. I could feel how much she needed someone to trust. She talked to me a long time, and I kept assuring her that I understood, and when she was through I told her to call me in Vegas if she wanted to. "I don't leave Caesars Palace," I said. "Tell 'em to try the pool, the casino or my room. Night or day."

"I'm not going to forget this favor," she told me.

"It's no favor, baby. Believe me. It's my livelihood. It's my life."

"You're a doll."

"You're a seductive little broad. Good-bye."

I put down the phone and sighed. Anna Calzolari: What were you doing to me? How in the world did you have me caring so much about you?

I thought about her while I threw some things in a suitcase—that's what I love about Vegas; no one gives a shit how you dress. I thought about her as the springless cab sped me out of the city, onto the Long Island Expressway, out to Kennedy. For a crazy moment, I considered calling her from the airport, asking her if she wanted to go. But what would be the point? She didn't need that. I didn't need that. I just needed to get the hell out of town for a few days. I needed a quick swig of that Vegas juice.

I hate airports and I'm not all that crazy about the planes themselves. Which is why I always try to get there in time to throw back a couple of Scotches before takeoff. And which is why I always fly first-class. The champagne helps me forget I'm flying.

I had my portable typewriter—I always lug it around just in case—and after dinner on the plane I actually thought about knocking out a few notes. Anna was still on my mind, and I was a little curious about what I was going to do with this nun. But I continued drinking instead—going from Scotch to champagne to a little Tia Maria on the rocks. The ride was smooth and the sky was black and her small face was still before me. She was too thin, I thought. Much too thin. And yet there was something about her being practically emaciated which was haunting, almost ethereal. This Anna, this Anna who might as well have gone on this trip with me, who might as well have been in this first-class cabin with the bright plastic walls and the drippy stewardesses, who might as well have been sitting next to me, because even as I closed my eyes, even as I dreamed, she stayed, she played inside my mind. . . .

I saw her playing the part of my nun and becoming a big star. Getting big money. Wearing beautifully fashionable clothes and

51

forgetting all that old hippie-dippy nonsense. I saw her changing, changing her mind about herself and about Palermo. I imagined that she finally came to her senses; that she was glad that he had skipped out on her, and when he returned, she wouldn't let him back in. She realized that he was nothing more than a two-bit phony living off her good heart. Now she knew better; now she knew me. And everything was going to change—her world and my show—and I couldn't have been any happier as I heard Captain Bozo putting down the wheels of the plane. I was about to hit pay dirt in Vegas.

It didn't work out that way. Friday was a disaster. The dice practically spat in my face. Saturday was worse. The wheel spun me into the ground. Maybe it was because I had been working too hard or maybe it was because I couldn't stop thinking about Anna; I don't know. But somehow I couldn't stop playing and I couldn't stop losing. I didn't even take time out for a swim. I was afraid that any time off would be my lucky time, my lucky hour at the table.

This is my crazy side, I suppose, but Vegas does that to me. I get there and, like everyone else, I flip. I throw myself into the casino and flounder and splash and most often drown. And usually I'm too zonked even to look up from the green felt and the dice and the chips stash. Usually it's just me and my cigar and the trinkle of sweat down my back.

This weekend had been no different. I didn't care about seeing Shecky Greene or Buddy Hackett. I had heard their routines before. I didn't care about eating. I could do that at home. I just wanted to get on a roll, and when it didn't happen, and when it kept on not happening, I fell flat into the old Vegas depression dumps that no one knows better than me. And for which there is only one cure: tail. An old-fashioned lady of the Strip. I was tired of not scoring, and by early Saturday evening, I was ready to spend some money on a number that was guaranteed to come in. I picked up the phone in my room and called Maxie. Maxie's my man in Vegas.

"I didn't even know you were here," Maxie said.

"Well, I am."

"And you're ready."

I love Maxie. He's the oldest bellhop on the Strip. He's been procuring for me for years. He knows my tastes; I never have to specify. I'm easy. Just give me something very blond and very big.

"Yeah, Maxie, I'm ready," I announced.

"Give me your room number and a half hour."

"You got it—1301."

"One thing, though," Maxie added.

"I know," I said, "inflation."

"It's really a killer, isn't it?"

"What are we up to?"

"All night?"

"Naturally all night," I reminded him.

"Five hundred dollars."

"Holy shit," I said, "this one's really gonna have to have a pair of knockers."

"Don't worry. You're dealing with Maxie. Maxie delivers."

"I'll be waiting," I said, and hung up.

I took a shower and tried to get the $8000 I dropped in the past two days out of my mind. I tried to forget about the action, tried to forget about the show, about Dick and Howard and the fucking ratings. But it was tough, because I knew if my losings continued I was going to need more scratch. And to get more scratch, I was going to have to get more viewers. Which meant a hotter story. Which was why I should have been working instead of screwing around with some ridiculously high-priced lulu.

Still, a man needs to relax. A man needs relief. And release. And to be perfectly honest, I've never been that comfortable around broads. At least not the kind you have to date and court and butter up and hit on. I hate the fucking game. Why can't they hit on me? Somehow I always get shy and the words never come out right. So I find it easier to dispense with all hypocrisy and make a clean, honest purchase. Besides, this way my little dream comes true; I get exactly what I want.

I slipped on my silk dressing gown which, by the way, is the only expensive article of clothing I own. I bought it just for these occasions. I saw it in the men's shop at the Century Plaza Hotel in L.A. a few years back and I liked the colors, black and white, and the pattern, wild horses chasing each other up and down hills. I slapped on a little cologne and inspected myself in the mirror: Could be worse. My teeth were straight and my smile, if I say so myself, was sincere. And when I heard the doorbell to my room I felt the excitement, the anticipation of what I had been waiting for so long. To hell with the dice! I was about to sink my teeth into something real; I was about to take a quick trip to the goddamn moon.

I opened the door and I loved her. I fucking loved her. She was in a red woolen dress which hugged her like a long, clinging sweater. Hugged her ass, which was just unbelievably juicy. Hugged her hips, which would get an Eskimo hot. Hugged her tits, which would bring the priests out of their monasteries and the monks out of their cells. Which got me up so goddamn fast I was scared. Her hair was done up in bubbles and curls and if it looked a little cheap, well, so much the better. Her hair was the color of the sun on a scorching day in Miami Beach. Her eyes were a crazy green, surrounded by a heavy dose of blue shadow. Her eyelashes were as long as her fingernails, which was fine by me. I liked the effect. Here was a whore who looked like a whore.

"Nice to see you, baby. Come on in and make yourself comfy," I offered.

"Thanks. Maxie said you were a lot of fun."

"I'm all fun, sugar," I said, remembering how much I liked these women who had the good sense to sell their charms to the top bidders. "How 'bout a bite to eat?"

"Sure thing," she replied in an accent which smacked of the old neighborhood. I didn't dare ask. I'd rather not know. Anyway, when she sashayed across the room and sank into the yellow crushed velvet easy chair and crossed her legs, the sound of nylon and the sight of thighs made me forget about all talk. I just wanted to look and savor what soon would be mine.

I ordered her a big fat steak from room service and a bottle of decent champagne. While we waited for the goodies to arrive, she had the good sense not to draw me into conversation. She flipped on the TV and second-guessed the answers on the *Hollywood Squares*. She didn't do too well. I helped her out and she was generous with her praise of my intellect.

"You must be one of these executives," she said to me.

"A writer."

"Ooh, a writer!" she purred. "That is *so* very terrific." She wiggled a little bit when she talked. I thought of telling her that I wrote soaps, but I didn't want to prolong the bullshit.

The meat and the bubbly arrived, and she went right to it. This doll was all business. When she was through, she got up, told me how good it all was, kissed me on the cheek and slowly brought the red woolen, clinging dress over her head, stopping so I had time to appreciate her transparent, purplish, very tiny bikini panties, her underwired lace bra whose half cups exposed and lifted—oh, so beautifully, oh, so high—her gorgeous, hard, huge nipples. This was a dish that just had to be tasted. Praised be Frederick's of Hollywood.

She fell back on the superduper, round, king-size bed that Mr. Caesar had provided and began to caress her tits. She half opened her mouth and let her tongue slowly wet her lips. She raised her hips and began rotating them, and then she took her finger and wet it on her tongue and brought it to her crotch. And touched herself, and pressed herself, and pushed aside her silly little nothing panties and opened herself. And I was there on the bed next to her, my dressing gown open and my cock inside the fist she formed with her hand, squeezing me, telling me how good I was, how good it felt to have me sucking on her fabulous boobs—first one, then the other, then back and forth, crazily, madly, pushing them together, all mine, this wonderful pair of $500 tits—and her biting on my earlobes and telling me that now, right now, she wanted me to give it to her, that she had to have it, me, big and ripe, to fuck her to the heavens and back with her long nails in my back and her fat tongue in my mouth and . . .

The telephone. The goddamn fucking telephone.

It wouldn't stop. I'd have to answer it. She moaned a little and then rolled over to one side. I picked up the phone and heard that horrible, faraway long-distance echo.

"Yeah?" I grunted.

"It's me."

Jesus Christ. Anna.

"I've been thinking about this part."

"Anna . . ."

"And the way it's bound to affect my career."

"Anna . . ."

"You sound out of breath."

"I'm just trying to relax."

"Sorry." She sounded hurt.

"No," I was quick to say, "not your fault. Not at all. It's just that . . ."

"You said I could call."

I looked over at Maxie's girl and sighed. "Listen, Anna, I'm glad you called. I really am, sugar. But your timing's not real good."

"Well, it's just that I've been thinking more about Gwen, and how much she meant to me. I feel like I've really dumped on her. . . ."

Oh, God, I thought to myself. Anna was turning around. She was finking out. I could hear Dick and Howard howling now. And for the next fifteen minutes, I had to listen, listen closely and patiently, to Anna explain how she was betraying Gwen while my $500 honey was purring and cooing and doing her best to keep my spirits high. She ran her tongue in and out of my belly button and I had to stop her from biting my ear.

"Listen, Anna," I finally said after realizing that I had been worried over nothing—she was only having a mild attack of the guilties—"we'll talk about this when I get back to the city. You were in a tough spot, but you did what you had to do. As long as Gwen ain't paying your rent, she has a right to say only so much. I realize she's a friend, but sometimes friends can be the least friendly people on the face of the earth."

"I feel like you're a friend," she said to me in a voice which melted my heart and had me half ashamed for being flat on my back while Suzy Q. Hooker was massaging my uncooperative cock with her moist mouth.

I got off the phone with Anna and I tried to remember my place. But I couldn't. Because I had Anna on my mind, Anna and that goddamn nun.

"You're losing it, honey," my million-dollar baby said to me.

"You ain't telling me nothing I don't already know."

"I got some getups in my purse. I don't know what you're

56

into, but a lot of guys like to be taken care of by nurses. Some guys even like . . ."

"Don't say it," I pleaded, afraid that my mind was as transparent as her hot little panties.

6

John came back Sunday and Anna was calmer than she had been in a long time. She borrowed a couple of hundred bucks from her parents—telling them about the part, knowing that they would rather see her as a TV nun than practically anything else in the world—and bought a few new plants for the loft. She called Gwen and, though Gwen was cold and short with her, Anna remained composed; she would stay in the play for another week. Gwen told her that wasn't necessary. She had already found another lead. Fine, Anna thought, that will make it easier for everyone.

With some hesitancy, she made contact with John's candyman and bought him a fresh supply of grass and coke. She knew this would please him—and it did. She wasn't thrilled about his habits, but she was convinced that his needs were special; his talent was so extraordinary that equally extraordinary patience and understanding were required. Besides, she wanted to put their last fight behind them and this, she knew, would be the best peace offering she could make.

When he showed up on Sunday morning she asked him no questions—she didn't dare. And at the appropriate time, when he had rested and showered and eaten and relaxed behind the new dope, she made the announcement that the part was hers in spite of everything. And when she got to the best part, she paused dramatically and then, slowly and deliberately, said, "and the initial contract . . . it looks like the initial contract will be for six months."

"Did they talk money?" she let John ask her, prolonging the moment of truth.

"Yes, they mentioned something."

"And what was the something?"

"Let me see," she reflected. "Oh, I remember. Twenty thousand. They said I should be getting twenty thousand."

"You're a smart chick," John said to Anna, smiling, "and I love you for it."

"Telling Gwen was very rough," Anna confessed.

"What did you do that for? Why can't you do both?"

"They want me five days a week. And there may be rehearsals at night."

"Jesus, you've really landed a role, Anna. You've really done it," John said. "I would have loved to have been there," he added with a touch of cruelty. "I would have loved to have seen Gwen's face."

"Thank God you weren't."

John lit another joint and inhaled deeply, passing it to Anna. She took a very small hit. Too much pot made her alarmingly paranoid.

"I feel good about the part. There are certain things that I have to prove to myself—and to you."

"Like what?"

"Like the fact that I'm real."

"I can feel that," he whispered, touching her breasts, kissing her lips.

"But soon you're *really* going to feel it," she said with sudden joy. "I'm going to take this ridiculous part, I'm going to jump into that nun's habit, and I'm really going to act. And the housewives are going to love me, and my scriptwriter Al will love me, and you'll love me. And by then you'll be starring on Broadway and we'll be eating caviar like it's tuna fish."

"You're a beautiful schemer," he said as he caressed the back of her neck. "You're a beautiful dreamer . . . a beautiful woman."

Anna felt her heart swell. She came to him and kissed his eyes, his neck, massaged his back and told him that his break

58

would come, that one day the world would recognize his acting genius, that she would always be there and never leave him, that she cared because he was so good, so deep down good.

He turned and looked at her and his face, the face of a matinee idol, seemed all gentle and soft to her. She wanted to give this man what he wanted. Already her new part had made them happy, nothing else mattered, nothing else mattered at all as he took her, and she felt his teeth, and she squeezed him. Their lovemaking was frantic, their lovemaking was small bites and sudden thrusts. And she gasped at the pleasure, at the pleasure of the surprising pain. They loved as they had argued, first apart, then together, one challenging the other, going for more, getting more. Excited by the tautness of their bodies, excited by their passionate ambitions, swollen and wet, egos flowing with desire. His orgasm was desperate and hers was long in coming, like the pure expectant joy of the long-waiting woman whose man had finally come home.

I called her the Sunday night I got back from Vegas and she sounded calm, sweet as melted butter, an angel of good faith and hope. Right off the bat, she told me that John had returned.

"So you're really glad he's back," I said.

"Very glad."

"And he's going to stick around this time?" I wondered.

"Oh, yes," she answered confidently.

"Don't count on it," I warned.

"You're too cynical. You don't know John."

"And you've been thinking about the nun," I said, changing the subject, knowing that I was never going to feel good about John Palermo.

"I think I've got her down."

"You better let me write something first. Then come to the milk plant on Tuesday. We can talk then."

"Sure you don't want to talk first?"

"Positive, baby. Vegas sort of used me up and I've got to recover. It's better that I'm alone with my typewriter for a couple of days while I'm on the mend."

"You're the boss."

But neither the words nor the plot came to me that night.

Only thoughts of Anna. And for a long time, staring at the ceiling, I wondered what had happened to the fiery rebel who tore off the nun's habit and scandalized the boys only a few days ago. Now her prince had come back, and she would devote the rest of her life to making him happy.

I was in a rotten mood Tuesday morning, and when I finally dragged my ass down to the milk plant I was a couple of hours late. Everyone was waiting around for me, complaining that we were behind schedule. Dick and Howard were screaming and actors and actresses were chasing after me, wanting to know where the scripts were. My assistants were anxious to see what I had done. If there was dialogue to expand, they wanted to get started. "Fuck everyone!" I screamed. "I'm going to my cubbyhole to drink coffee. In an hour I'll be ready to talk."

They cursed and scratched their heads and went away. I was still cranky from the Vegas fiasco, and I had only managed to write about half of what was needed. The bastards could wait. All I wanted now was a little java and a couple of aspirins. But I had to try to plunge ahead and get this day over with.

"You look troubled, good brother," said the nun who was seated in the chair next to my desk.

"Jesus Christ," I mumbled to myself, looking at Anna who had already put on the habit of Sister Prudence. Her hands were folded patiently on her lap and her lips formed the gentlest and sweetest of smiles.

"Profanity again," she chastised. "I thought we had already decided to restrain ourselves."

"Cut the shit, baby. This has been a bitch of a morning."

"I have come to help. I have come to relieve you of your burdens."

I thought about it for a minute. I hadn't worked out her scene with the landlord. I had spent last night pouring over today's trotters lineup and, to tell you the truth, my mind was still calculating odds.

"Let me just think," I said. "There's all kinds of crap I've got to work out."

"As far as I'm concerned," she said, "my position will be quite simple. I will speak only from the heart. How can I do otherwise? We sisters are uncomplicated souls. Our words are few, our vocabulary is basic, our arguments direct.''

"Say that again," I asked her, "only this time, speak even slower.''

She repeated herself practically word for word, and as I listened I typed out everything she said.

"But what's going to happen," I asked her, "if this fucked-up, mean-ass landlord doesn't listen to you and throws your ass out?''

"Such a likelihood is so farfetched that I dare not contemplate it.''

"Well you better, Sister, 'cause that's what I got in store for you.''

"The Lord does not desert those whose faith is not fickle.''

"Maybe He doesn't, but I sure as hell do. The Lord doesn't have to fool with the ratings like I do. I've got to keep the pot boiling.''

"I am capable of dealing with reality. I may choose to reject a world of arbitrary and meaningless fashion, but I understand fact. I understand hard necessity.''

"So you have a tough side. Is that it?" I asked my friend Anna, my character Sister Prudence.

"I prefer to call it my practical side.''

"I see what you mean," I contemplated, lighting my second cigar of the day. "Just sit there while I knock out a few ideas.''

"I don't mind waiting," she said, fondling a small rosary with her fingers, sitting quietly while I wrote.

The ideas came to me quickly. A few times I'd look up at her for inspiration, and, sensing my glances, her eyes met mine. What a crazy lady, I thought to myself, as I returned to my typewriter, happy that at long last the words were flying.

"Let's get out of here, honey," I said some thirty minutes later. "I think I've got what we need.''

We walked down the hall to the secretarial pool where I had the girls make copies of the scene I had just written. While we were waiting, I told Anna a little about Jeff Rosloff, the man who was portraying the heartless landlord, S. J. Adams: "The guy's an old pro who's pushing seventy. He's been mainly playing an old reliable doctor who recommends Crest to his patients, and he's very happy to have this part. In the old days he played villains in horror flicks. So this should be like homecoming week to him. He looks mean, but he's really a pussycat."

When we arrived on the set Dick and Howard were already waiting, naturally nervous because of their last experience with Anna. I could tell that they were still sore.

"All right," Dick said, trying to establish his directorial authority, "let's get started. Let's see what the genius has cooked up," meaning me.

He thought he was really spiffy this morning in his herringbone sport jacket. To me he just looked like an overgrown prep-school kid. Fuck him; I was about to show him how right I had been about Anna.

Jeff Rosloff was there, and I was happy to see that his waxed black mustache gave him an especially demonic air. I introduced him to Anna and Dick had them both move to the set. For the next half hour they would read the script while Dick blocked the scene. Then in a few days we would actually tape. (I should also tell you that all this garbage involving the nun represented only a fifth or sixth of the complete *Search for Happiness* show. Naturally I had a lot of other plots going at the same time. But Sister Prudence's story is the one that counted. It's the one that changed my life, and it's the only one that really needs to be told. The others pale by comparison.)

"Okay, kids," said Dick the director. "Whenever you're ready just go ahead. I'll try to interrupt you as little as possible. I know this is the first time for everyone. Let's not linger, though. We've got another half-dozen scenes to work out today." Dick was in an especially bitchy mood this morning.

Sister Prudence sat herself on the couch in the office of the convent. S. J. Adams knocked on the door. The sister went to open it, greeted him, asked him to come in and sit down.

"I'm so glad you've taken the time to come here this morning," she said tenderly, reading my script.

"Let's get down to business," the foul-tempered landlord answered.

"I know you have a busy schedule, and it must have . . ."

"I said let's talk now. I didn't want to come. I told you on the phone that there was nothing to discuss."

"Let me explain. Our convent is a great deal more than the physical land that we occupy. It is a . . ."

Dick cut her off: "I'd like you to put a little more emotion into it. I'd like you to . . ."

Anna cut *him* off: "We sisters pride ourselves in having an even temperament. It is important that we maintain our composure, that we speak as clearly and . . ."

"I'm not asking you, Sister," Dick persisted, "I'm *telling* you."

I was about to speak up for Anna, to explain to this tight-ass director that he hadn't even given her a chance to read into the script. I wanted to tell him that the emotion comes later. But I decided to say nothing. I saw that Sister Prudence was capable of taking care of herself, and, besides, if I had said something Dick would have jumped on me for being so late with the script; I hadn't given him a chance to read it beforehand.

"The consequences to the children for whom we are responsible," Sister Prudence continued, "are severe. It is not ourselves who are involved, it is the young lives . . ."

"Money is money," Adams barked back. "You can take your problems to the bishop. If he wants to sign the kind of lease that Baskin-Robbins is giving me, fine."

"It is not a question of money," Anna implored. "It is a question of . . ."

Dick stopped her again: "No, Anna, I'm afraid . . ."

Anna got up from the couch. Now she was angry. But she didn't bother to address Dick. She kept on talking to the landlord: "If you don't understand . . ."

"You're the one, Sister, who doesn't understand," Adams scowled.

"Anna," Dick tried to stop her again.

"I don't like to be interrupted," Sister Prudence said to S. J. Adams, "but if you choose to risk a confrontation, then that is your decision to make." Her neck muscles were strained; her eyes were on fire; her voice was still low, but the intensity with which she spoke was alarming. "I myself," she continued, "deplore confrontations of any sort. But let me assure you, Mr. Adams, even though it might sound uncharacteristic of a servant of the Lord, that once I am pushed, I have not the slightest fear of pushing back."

She stopped, smiled a smile of devastating but sweet sarcasm, and then—improbably and completely uncharacteristically—the technicians and members of the staff who were huddled around the set, broke into applause. Sister Prudence bowed her head, staying in character, while I grinned from ear to ear and Dick turned cardinal red.

It was definitely one of the high points of my soap-writing career, and I would have stayed in a good mood for the rest of the day if Howard the producer hadn't whispered in my ear that the network boss wanted to see me and if, an hour later, the network boss hadn't told me that I was fired.

7

I walked over to the network's twenty-four-story skyscraper from the milk plant, just to give my brain a chance to clear. I had been called in by these sort of guys before. I wasn't worried, at least not too worried. He probably just wanted to know what direction the show was taking. Or maybe he just wanted to meet me. I knew he had heard about me, because there wasn't anyone at the network—anyone really important—who didn't know my name.

I took the elevator designated just for the VIP floors, remembering that there had been a party for Costein about five months ago when he was named programming VP. It came on one of my track days, and I decided I wasn't going. So I didn't. There had been too much hype about the kid, and the idea that someone so young had so big a job—especially a job which ultimately controlled my job—was a little depressing. He was the youngest senior veep in the history of the network. They said he had been raised on a diet of computers and calculators.

A star graduate of Harvard Business and Evelyn Wood. An

egghead with an uncanny sense of what America would buy. He had been at the network for only a few years, and in those years he had successfully risen to the head of sales—he had pitched commercial minutes to the ad agencies up and down Madison Avenue—the head of research and finally the head of a department that he had created for himself: Media Marketing Development, the famous MMD. It was here—with his multimillion-dollar computer banks, his socioeconomic analysts, his Ph.D.'ed psychologists and his complex of research test groups—that he developed his first lineup of fall programming. I forgot what the hell it called for—more sitcoms where you can see the chicks' nipples, something brilliant like that—but anyway, out of all this hocus-pocus came three new pilots which went on the air and hit. Hit the fucking jackpot. Made Mr. Nielsen come twice in the same night. Which is quite a trick. The result is that the powers who control the conglomerate which controls the network started listening to Costein, and giving him more bread, and letting him and his MMD boys buy more expensive toys. The next fall, Costein came in with a new bunch of suggestions —a prime-time game show having something to do with sex and real estate, for example—and enough of the ideas clicked to take Costein up to the executive suite, close to the very top of Sixth Avenue power.

Which was where I was headed, riding up in this elevator, thinking about all the Costein stories I had heard. I was curious, but I still wasn't all that curious. I had seen the network golden boys come and go, shine and fade in the sunlight of Sixth. They didn't impress me. They placed their bets—just like you and me. And sometimes they got on a roll. But I also knew that what's lucky today is limp tomorrow, and these characters were no different than Bennie and Tony and Little Joe and Irv and the rest of the guys from the old neighborhood who studied the *Racing Form* and went to the trotters and sometimes won and mostly lost. Yet I had to be curious about what the kid wanted with me. Curious, but not worried, because I knew that no one in the city could do my job any better than me.

The elevator opened into a reception area. There was a thin Asian girl, young and beautiful with long green boots, who sat behind a sleek teakwood desk and said to me, "Yes?"

"Al Gonfio," I answered, "reporting for duty."

She smiled, and I wasn't sure she understood, so I added, "The kid called for me. Tell him Gonfio's here."

"The kid?" she asked.

"Costein."

She coughed politely and began to raise her eyebrows—which were very thin and lovely—but didn't. "Have a seat, Mr. Gonfio," she said in near-perfect English, "and I'll tell Mr. Costein that you're here."

"Thanks, hon."

I looked around. The furnishings, like the Asian girl, were classy. Not too much of anything. Sparse and lean and expensive. Modern and cold-blooded. The magazines on the coffee table were in French, German, Japanese and Italian. They were slick and glossy, with pictures of villas in Switzerland and new factories in Spain. Then there were a bunch of academic journals, with no pictures, and articles with footnotes about foreign affairs and biology and business. I was going to ask the pretty secretary if she had a copy of the *New York Daily News* around, but I decided not to be a wise guy.

"Mr. Costein will see you," the lady announced as she stepped from her desk, opened the door leading to the inner sanctum and waved me on through.

He was on the phone. I could have told you that in advance. Naturally he had to keep me waiting for ten minutes and naturally he had to be doing something else when I walked in. He motioned to a seat in front of his boat-size desk—more gleaming chrome, more steel. I sat down and looked in his face. He remained expressionless as he talked on the phone. He hadn't yet said a word. He was listening to the party on the other end.

He was very thin, and I guessed that he was well over six feet tall. Everything about him was thin, his fingers and the lapels on his rather routine pinstripe suit, his lips, his eyebrows and his tie. He had a horse's face—not an ugly horse, but definitely a horse—and I had an idea that he must look just like his mother. But the most annoying thing about Costein were his eyes, which were hidden. He wore small, round, tortoiseshell glasses, very thin and professorial, but they were tinted a dark brown and it was impossible to see beyond them. They were the kind of glasses that should not have been tinted. There was something really peculiar about the combination of Ivy League frames and the mysterious darkness of the lenses.

"I see," he finally said, and his voice sounded devoid of emotion. He listened for another long spell, and I started looking around the office. There was a long wall of books to let everyone know that he read, and there was only one small Sony TV. I had expected a console of three or four tubes lined up in a row. The office was L-shaped, and in the corner was a conversational area with a sofa and chairs which looked more like instruments of torture than places to sit. On the walls three large canvases were hung, and except for a few small blotches of blue and green and yellow paint, the canvases were empty. Modern art. Go figure it out. All I know is that there were no pictures of trees or flowers or people.

"There is a point to that," he said into the phone just as I noticed, in the other corner of the office, a pinball machine. "There is a point to that, and I certainly want to take your opinions under advisement. Thank you so much for calling me. Good day." The kid had all the enthusiasm and bounce of an undertaker.

He put down the phone delicately and I noticed how his manicure gleamed. He looked up at me and folded his hands together. His tie was blood red. I guessed he was looking at me —I wasn't sure—and he said, "How are you, Mr. Gonfio?"

"Great, just great," I answered. "Mind if I take a look at your pinball machine?"

"Not at all." He seemed surprised.

I walked over to the machine and saw immediately that it was a custom job. The cushioned circles that had to be hit by the little silver ball carried the names of the network's current prime-time lineup. I laughed.

"A gift from a friend," Costein commented. He was still sitting behind his desk.

"Used to be something of a champ at this sport," I told him, remembering my teenage days at DeLorenzo's candy store in the old neighborhood. They say I still hold the record on that machine.

Costein got up from his desk and walked over toward me, just

67

as I released a ball. When he reached the machine the game had begun. I realized he was probably pissed off that I was wasting his time, but to tell the truth, I didn't give a shit. Besides, I wanted to see if I had lost my touch, and being watched certainly didn't hurt my style.

"It's all in the tilt," I explained to my boss. "Once you get the tilt straight, you can keep the bastard going for an hour."

"I would hope that's not the case, Mr. Gonfio."

"Call me Al, Mark. And by the way," I said, as I flipped the sliver ball back to the top, "what's the record on this machine?"

"I wouldn't have the slightest idea."

"You don't play?"

"No, I don't."

"What do you do for fun?"

"Jog."

"That's fun?"

"It's important. I do some of my best thinking while I'm training."

"Training?" I questioned as I gave the ball one hell of a violent flip.

"I'm training for a marathon."

"I'm sorry."

"I'm not. I like it."

"You got to be kidding."

"I'm quite serious."

"That's the problem. You're too serious. Now take pinball. It's a hell of a sport. I love it."

"I can tell."

"I thought you were jerking *The Nurses* off the air," I mentioned as the ball hit the circle marked *The Nurses*.

"That's under consideration."

"If you give it the ax, are you going to take it out of this machine?" I wondered.

"That's one problem that I haven't yet put on my agenda."

"Holy shit!" I exclaimed after I got away with a very bold tilt, "this baby is loose as a goose. The flipper action's very, very slick. You could really go to town on this machine."

"Mr. Gonfio," he said.

"Al," I corrected him.

68

"We had best begin our discussion. My recreation period doesn't start for another forty minutes."

"Be with you in a second," I said, still working on my first ball, "when I break two thousand I'm all yours."

A half minute later the machine displayed 2225, and I let the ball run down the right flipper. I felt good. I still hadn't lost my touch.

"Jesus, I forgot how much I like to hear those bells ring and see that little ball pop!" I rejoiced.

Costein didn't bother to respond as he walked behind his desk. His arms seemed too long for his skinny body. I felt like asking him if he wanted something to eat, but instead I made a different suggestion. "Why don't we sit over there in the corner, Mark? I think we'd be more comfortable."

That might have irritated him a bit, but I didn't care. His desk looked like it was made from a nuclear missile, and I didn't want it between me and him.

We walked over to the conversational area. I took the couch. Black leather, not much give to the pillow. He took an armless easy chair which looked as though it had been designed on the moon.

"Do you think your girl could get us some coffee?" I asked him before he had a chance to open the conversation.

He hesitated, and then said, "Why . . . yes." He got up and went to the door, giving the order to his secretary, and before he closed the door again, I shouted, "Three sugars, honey, and double cream." A few seconds later she reappeared with my java. He drank Perrier and lime. Fucking sanctimonious jogger.

Costein reseated himself. I wished to hell that he would have taken off his glasses. I was tempted to ask him.

He folded his hands on his lap. He didn't seem comfortable with his height. I had the feeling he was continually struggling to keep himself calm.

"Let me come to the point," he finally said.

"Good." I was ready.

He rang the buzzer on the phone sitting on the coffee table. On cue, his secretary reappeared holding a group of charts. She gave them to the boss and left, almost too quickly, as if she were trying to avoid something which was about to happen.

"Are you familiar with the work of Dr. John T. Flamerton?" Costein asked.

"No, he's one who got by me."

"He's a Harvard business economist, a teacher of mine, and a brilliant, brilliant man."

Costein spoke with what I now heard was a covered-up New York accent. He was straining to sound from out of town.

"Where do you come from, Mark?" I interrupted his little rap.

"The city."

"Where in the city?"

I had caught him off guard and he didn't like it. "Actually," he said, "the Bronx."

"Where in the Bronx?"

"A Hundred and Eighty-second Street and the Grand Concourse. Why?"

"Just curious. But go ahead, make your point. You wanted to tell me something about some egghead."

"Yes, Flamerton, the man under whom I first developed the theory of comparative negative gain. I presume you do understand what I mean by that term."

"Sure, when your horse is gaining, but not gaining enough to show."

"Something like that, I suppose."

"And?"

Costein began placing his charts on the coffee table. "I've had the ratings for *Search* analyzed for the last five years. The apparent gain in audience is deceptive, very deceptive. If you will, just look at the graphs."

"I was lousy at geometry," I said.

Costein reached in his pocket and pulled out a sleek, silver penlike object. He pointed it toward me and pressed something on the side of the object. I half expected a switchblade, but instead of a knife a pointer popped out, a kind of miniature version of the pointer that teachers use to point out stuff on blackboards. I couldn't believe it. Mark Costein packed a portable silver pointer.

"Let me give you a quick math lesson," the kid offered. "I suggest you pay attention."

70

I didn't appreciate being talked to this way, but I decided to let him have his say. It was clear that he really got off on this shit. He began speaking rapidly and got himself wrapped up in all sorts of far-out explanations: theories of the ratings progressions and regressions, total number of TV households versus minimal viewer interest, and on and on. So I sat there, letting it all float over my head. Finally, when he was really getting steamed up and I was really flat-assed bored, I had to say, "Mind if I finish my pinball game?"

The kid didn't laugh. "I don't have to take the time to explain this," he said. "I'm doing so because I want you to understand."

"Understand what?"

"Why we are looking at negative numbers for *Search*."

"What do you mean negative numbers?"

"Numbers that aren't positive, Mr. Gonfio."

"Are you telling me that you're losing money on my show?"

"Money is not the point."

"Money is always the point."

"I'm trying to help you understand how management views your show."

"And I'm telling you that soap operas ain't made in test tubes."

"I'm not talking about test tubes. I'm talking about a scientific composite picture which is not very pretty."

"And I'm telling you," I went on, "that you don't know the first thing about how these shows are really put together. Well, I'll tell you. I drink a couple of beers and go to the typewriter and try to figure out what in the world is going to make those ladies out there cry and laugh and worry and wet and weep themselves sick. Hate to disappoint you, Mr. Costein, but there ain't nothing scientific about it. It's all blood and guts. It's fast and it's furious and it's amazing that it ever comes off. And the only reason it does, the only reason *Search* has survived so long is because of me, because I know how to get the most out of the actors and the director and even the bootlicking excuse of a producer you've stuck me with. But the real reason it works is because I'm a genius—yes, I'd use the word genius—I'm a genius at dreaming up the story. And all those computer sheets and graphs and focus group sessions ain't nothing but jerk-off, nothing but a way for you to have another four dozen people working for you and telling you that you're smart. But I'll tell you right now that you're smart, not because you got yourself nuts with this research mumbo jumbo, but because you got enough brains to keep people like me around, people who know what the hell a real story means. That's the whole thing in a nutshell."

"Except for one small thing," he said firmly.

"Yeah?" I challenged, now cranky and impatient, now really irritated that I had to be lectured by a kid fifteen years younger than me.

"I'm letting you go."

The words flew by me. They were like the silver ball in the pinball machine flying down the slot. I couldn't push the flipper. I couldn't react. If it was one thing I had been sure about—sure about for years now—it was my job. I was already a legend in the business. Everyone in town knew that I ran this show—I was the head writer—and everyone knew I could turn out stories like Detroit turns out cars. I sat there with my cigar stuck in my mouth, looking at Costein's horse face, Costein's tiny tinted glasses, Costein's silver pointer.

"What the fuck," I finally said. "This is ridiculous."

"These are the facts. I've been trying to point out the facts to you. They are simple, but they are substantial, and they all point in one direction. The stories are not working. The stories are flat."

"You got to be kidding."

"I don't kid, Gonfio," Costein said. And I believed him.

"There's something wrong."

"Indeed there is. And that something is you. You've been pampered here, and you've been protected. You've had everyone under your spell, and you've had everyone believing your own myth."

"The other networks will pick me up in a second. They'll throw big money at me."

"You'll certainly have an opportunity to test that theory, won't you?"

I was still reeling. My knees felt weak and my stomach started

72

churning. I started thinking about my debts, my bookies, my long-term and short-term financial obligations. I started thinking about pounding the pavement. At middle age. I was middle-aged, and this kid was telling me that I was washed up. This skinny kid who was running marathons and soon would probably be running the whole fucking network with his computers and his charts and his double-talk.

"Well . . ." Costein said, recrossing his legs and expecting me to pick up and leave. He had done it, he had axed me, and there was nothing left to say. Except . . .

Except for something inside me that said fuck it, fuck it because I wasn't going to go, I didn't want to go, not now. I didn't want to hit the pavement and start hustling as I did when I first landed this job. I was too old for that. I had paid my dues, and who the hell was Mark Costein to tell me that he knew more about this business than me? After a few miserable seconds I found my nerve again, and for some crazy reason I thought about the time when I was eleven and a kid jumped me from behind in a playground in the old neighborhood and somehow I got him off my back and managed to cram my fist down his throat.

"You're full of shit, Costein!" I blurted out. "You're wet behind the ears and you're full of shit! I didn't want to tell you that, but I got to."

"Now that you've said it," he said in his smug non-Bronx accent, "you can get out."

"Not before I tell you a little bit more." I leaned forward and let him have it, speaking with my hands, jabbing the air with my cigar. "Do you know what this whole goddamn thing is about?" I asked him. "It's about money. *Search* is making money all right. If it wasn't, I'd be out on my ass long ago. It's just not making *as much* as you want. Next to the other soaps, it could be earning you more. Now that's it. Tell me that ain't it."

"That's it," he snarled. "Now . . ."

"Now nothing. Now you'll listen a little more. Now we're talking turkey. You want to beef up the revenue on *Search* so you can go to your boss and say, 'Look, I've taken daytime from profits of eight million to twelve million,' or whatever the fuck the scale is. You do that and the boss says, 'Here, I'm moving you up from being president to the chairman of the board, so you take my job.' "

"It's not quite that simple," he protested weakly.

"Listen, Costein, you're talking to Al Gonfio, and I know. I honest-to-God know that it's just that simple. You make money for this network and the network gives it back to you, with a little power to boot. And you think the way you're going to do that is by studying your computers and your math formulas. You think you're going to get there by being the wizard of numbers, by listening to the shrinks and the surveyors you got working for you. Well, I'm here to set you straight. I'm here to cut through the bullshit and tell you that these sheets don't mean shit"—and I got up and took the computer sheets that were in his lap and threw them on the floor. The kid was a little nervous because he thought I might be going nuts, and maybe I was, but I kept talking 'cause it felt good—"these sheets," I said, "are no more scientific than Artie Sappone's joint down behind his uncle's butcher shop on Second Avenue. Ever seen Artie's joint, Costein?"

"No, I'm afraid I haven't," he said smugly.

"Well, if you're lucky I'll take you there sometime. There's a little misspelled sign in the window of the butcher shop that says U Pick 'Em Turf Analisis. And you go there and walk past the meat counter and go into the back and there's Artie and he charges you for tips on the nags. And you know something? He's real good. He sits at this little folding table and he charges you a couple of bucks, depending on the day and the race, and he gives you these tips. Yeah, Artie's been behind this little folding table ever since he was a teenager, and now he's nearly seventy, so you figure he's got to be there a good fifty years. And he's making money. Artie Sappone always makes money, because his customers come back. His repeat business is about the best in the city, and, all in all, I'd say he probably makes a big one a year. Now Artie is good in basic math, and he understands the weather and he certainly knows about the history of many nags. But he's never seen the inside of a school or the outside of a computer. Maybe he'll even have a bad year. But Artie's a winner over the long haul, just 'cause he feels something in his gut for the ponies. And that's everything right there.

Because your Harvard and Yale and your business school bean brains ain't no better than the Puerto Rican palm reader over on Ninth Avenue. Your guys just use fancier words and charge more money. But if you're gonna survive in this game, kid, let me tell you something: Believe what's in your gut. If you think a show is hot because it *feels* hot, then go with it. And the reason I've survived here for so long is because I write from the gut. And if what you're saying to me is, 'Your gut's getting soft, Al,' Well, maybe there's something to that. Maybe I do have to get my ass in gear a little to goose those fucking ratings. Maybe. And I'll tell you right now, I'll say that I'm ready to do that, not because I care about you, Mark Costein, and not because I give a shit about this network, but because I understand this show. It's my show, and I'm not about to start another one. Besides, if you're on the move, I'll take a shot and go with you. I'll put my ass on the line and tell you, Costein, straight out that if I don't produce for you in a month, if I don't gain a few of Mr. Nielsen's precious points in four or five weeks—you pick the time—then I'll come back here, bend over backward, stick a cigar up my ass and let you light it."

Costein laughed. The kid actually laughed. It was a loud laugh, a laugh that came from the gut.

"You should be selling Bibles, Gonfio," he said after he stopped laughing.

"I should be writing soap operas, because there's no one who has a feel for this stuff like me. You see, I understand women, I know what makes them . . ."

"Stop! That's enough. I've got to think about . . ."

"There's nothing you got to think about. You can me and the whole writing staff falls apart. They don't know how to take a leak without me. And that means you got to get yourself a new writing team. It'll take three, maybe four senior writers to replace me, and by the time you find them two months will be shot, and the ratings will be so fucking low you'll never bring 'em back up. You'll lose half your audience, and when you finally straighten out the mess it'll cost you a quarter of a million dollars in advertising to buy the viewers you lost, and you'll be lucky to get half of those. So where does all this leave you, Costein? And what are the people in those big offices down the hall going to say? Just listen to me. I understand money, and I'm going to make money for you, kid. Big money. Give me this month and don't sweat it. I didn't want to mention it, but I got an ace up my sleeve. It just happened the other day. A new part, a new actress. Some very strong stuff. So you go back to your phone calling and I'll go back over to the milk plant and I'll forget that you were a little rash. I'll chalk it up to inexperience.''

"I've never been sold like this before," Costein commented, sounding dazzled and confused.

"You've never met me before," I reminded him.

"I'm astounded."

"You're impressed."

"I wanted to fire you."

"You can't now. You can't afford to. It'll cost you money. You know that I know that."

"You say that, Gonfio, but I'm convinced that your sort of writer no longer understands the enormous technological . . ."

"We've been through all this, Costein. I already told you that I don't know your Flamerton friend and I don't want to know him. I already gave you all the facts. Now you make the decision. But just have the guts to make it from the heart, from the heart, kid, and not from the head."

"You're crazy, Gonfio. I really think you're crazy."

"Sure, I'm crazy, but I'm no crazier than you."

"You don't know me, Gonfio. You don't know who I am."

"I can feel it, kid. You're on the make, and now you realize you need me."

Costein stood up and for the first time he took off his tinted glasses. His eyes were blue. Very blue. He wasn't bad looking. He looked like a horse, but a handsome horse. I could hear the computers turning in his brain. "So you want a month," he finally said.

"That's all I need."

"Thirty days from today."

"Make it forty-five."

"You're welching," he accused.

"I need time to get my new character in gear."

"Forty-five days, Gonfio, and that's it."

"Practice your pinball," I said to him as I got up to leave. "You should take that game a little more seriously."

It was only in the elevator, going down the spine of the building, that I thought I was going to pass out.

8

When I hit the streets, I thought I was going to be sick. When I got into the cab, I thought I was going to be sick. And when I finally got home, I *was* sick. My stomach felt like an elephant had sat on it. I threw my guts up, and then I had the runs and the chills and every other goddamn thing you can think of. I spent all day going over that meeting with Costein, not believing I had done what I did, still amazed that the kid had bought my bullshit.

I didn't know whether to be proud of myself or ashamed. I guess I was both. Because I knew I was right, and I knew I had bullied Costein enough into believing me. But now I knew I had to produce, because suddenly I realized that time was running out, I'd have to concentrate more on the show. I was going to have to come up with something big, because I knew goddamn well that once you're canned from one soap—especially at my age—the next stop is the Bowery. Yes, I told myself, it was time to regroup and reform. Time to shape up and thank God that Costein was green enough to buy my bullshit. Or was it bullshit?

I was flopped out in my easy chair when I glanced at the *Racing Form* and spotted—as though it were meant to be— tomorrow's lineup at Aqueduct. A horse named Mark's Faith caught my eye. Too good to be true. That was it. Fate was talking to me. I called my bookie and put down a G. I knew it was crazy, but the whole day had been crazy, and there was nothing else I could do. I spent the rest of the night drinking Pepto-Bismol.

The next day was torture. Mark's Faith ran next to last and my heart sank. It wasn't just the G; it was what it meant. I looked at my tongue in the mirror and saw that it had turned black. I panicked—I was convinced I had the plague—until I remembered that Pepto-Bismol gives you a black tongue. I couldn't even start thinking about the show—not today. I had my assistants knock out the episodes that were due tomorrow. I didn't want to be bothered. I was a complete mess.

But then I began to think of the nun, and it was only that image, the picture of Anna in Sister Prudence's habit, that calmed me. The nun. The nun was going to have to save my life. I'd figure out something. I'd have to. I'd done it before, and I'd do it again. Even if it were something a little far out, a little crazy. Yeah, I was beginning to feel that it would work. This Anna Calzolari was an amazing actress. And she was a nun, a very perfect and a very strange nun. I could tell my brain was starting to cook already. All I needed was a little spice, or a lot of spice, and soon I'd have myself another hot dish. Who knows?—maybe I'd do something really wicked, maybe I'd get that hot little nun laid. Now wouldn't that be something? I could see Mr. Nielsen's dick rising right this very instant. Hell, yes! Soon my worries would be over. I was about to write my way out of this goddamn jam. I was about to come up with another fucking brainstorm!

It was a little past noon, three days later, and all was quiet on the set. We were about to shoot the second episode of the day. The first—the one in which Sister Prudence tells off landlord Adams—was already in the can. It had gone wonderfully well. Now we were ready to go again. Before I left the floor and returned to the control room—I always watch the show from the control room; I supervise the director and I watch the action the way it's going actually to appear on a TV screen—I winked at Anna who was already too caught up in the part to wink back. I lit a cigar and glued my attention to one of the monitors above my head.

* * *

78

The mother superior is seated at her desk. In back of her, hanging on the wall behind her high-back chair, is a large ornate crucifix. She is an old lady whose skin and eyes are as clear as the dawn. She speaks slowly, and with compassion.

"You must tell me of your meeting with Mr. Adams," she beseeches Sister Prudence, who is sitting in an armless wooden chair across from the mother superior's desk.

"He is a most unreasonable man, Mother Superior," the nun states. "I am afraid that my arguments were to no avail."

"Were you firm, my child?"

"I pleaded our case with great conviction. I tried to let the Lord speak through me."

"And he was not moved?"

"I am afraid that he is not a man of God."

"Why, we are all the product of God," she corrects Prudence.

"You are right, of course. It's simply that Mr. Adams is stubborn beyond all reason. Stubborn, and, I believe, exceedingly greedy."

Mother Superior folds her hands on the desk. She sighs. "I am surprised that you have not been able to persuade this man. For the two years since you have been with us, I have noted your restless spirit. I have watched how you argue, how you pursue a point or project. I sometimes worry that you are too volatile, and often I am surprised by your sudden change of moods. But your combative nature is not without compensation, even charm. You set forth goals and you seem to achieve them. You move forward quickly and decisively. I selected you for this task precisely because, of all the sisters who have blessed me with their devotion, you are among the strongest. You have that streak of tenacity—perhaps because you were raised in a large city—which I was certain would work in our favor."

Sister Prudence lowers her head. Mother Superior gets up and walks around her desk. She stands by the nun's side. Affectionately, she puts her hand on Prudence's shoulder. Prudence looks up. Her face is small, her features perfect. Mother Superior continues speaking:

"I am not blaming you, not in the least. It is something which

I should have done myself, and now I see that my thinking—to ask someone young, vivacious and bright—was not at all a proper strategy. There was no excuse for my not going to this man myself."

"The convent will not be sold," Sister Prudence raises her head and flatly announces. "The convent will not have to move."

The older woman is startled. She had not expected such a remark. "What makes you say that, my child?" she asks with aroused curiosity.

"I say that because it is true. You asked me to do God's work and I assure you that God's work will be done." The muscles in Prudence's face tighten; she is absolutely firm.

"But you've already said that the man is impossible. You've described him as a person who cannot be reached. You've indicated that he's beyond reason."

"Yes," Sister Prudence explains with a touch of steel in her voice, "we have already used many of the tools at our disposal, I have pleaded for mercy and understanding, and my arguments have been sincere. But that has not been enough. So now, if I might suggest, we must turn to other means. We must meet force with force."

Mother Superior stands directly in front of the young nun. She regards Sister Prudence with a mixture of wonder and admiration. "What do you have in mind, child?"

"The force of the law."

"But we are not lawyers."

"Yes, but we can employ lawyers."

"That would take quite a long time. I would have to write the bishop for funds and presently he is on his way to the Vatican. He won't be back until the end of the month, and by then, I'm afraid, it will be too late."

"Please, Mother Superior, let's not worry about funds. At least not now."

"You are naive, my child."

"I am determined to do as you have asked, to fulfill my obligation, my sacred obligation, to this order. You spoke of my being raised in a big city. Well, one thing that taught me, Mother Superior, is that when you are pushed, sometimes the best policy is to push back."

"And you intend to push through the law? You think that the law will work on our side?"

"It is not so much the law as it is the lawyers. Lawyers—if they are smart and powerful enough—can work magic. Lawyers can change the world."

"And that is your view of things, my child?"

"That is my view of this problem, yes. If you so authorize me, I will call the most prestigious and powerful law firm in this city, I will explain our predicament and I will ask for help, simply and directly. If I am refused, I will go the second most powerful law firm, and from there to the third until someone responds to our call."

Mother Superior walks to a corner of her office where there is a small altar holding a statue of the Virgin Mary. Above the altar is a delicate stained-glass window. "Come pray with me," she calls to Sister Prudence. Together, they kneel, and as the older woman speaks, light from the window illuminates her face and the exquisite face of Sister Prudence.

The camera zooms in on Mother Superior's face, then back on Prudence's face, as the screen goes black, making way for a dancing cat-food commercial.

When the taping was over, I was so happy I wanted to celebrate. Which meant the track. We could get there on time, I assured Anna, if we hurried. She was game. She was high from her performance, and going to the races seemed nutty to her. She had never been. And besides, she wanted to be with me. Who could blame her?

In the cab she was laughing about the nun, and I was laughing too. She admitted that playing the part had been fun today. She viewed it as a game, she said. The game is called Saving Al's Nuts, I said. I explained to her something of the ferocious competition for daytime audiences and told her how important it was that I start scoring in a big way.

Once we arrived at the track I felt a million times better. Ah, the track. Why is it that I love it so? Why is it that there, and only there, I feel some sense of meditative calm? There my mind can function and there my blood pressure stops boiling. Of course I've known considerable frustration at the track. But usually I'm able to leave the nagging, petty concerns of my life behind me and concentrate on that most metaphysical of questions: how to make a buck on a bet.

I like the way the track looks and the way the track sounds. I like to see everyone milling around, all the characters I have known for so many years—the crazy old ladies talking to themselves and counting their pennies, the cronies scratching all kinds of wild notes on their scratch sheets, the cabdrivers and the bartenders enjoying their day off, the Japanese tourists with their high-priced cameras, the Puerto Rican guys, the black guys, the hotsy-totsy business brains in their tweed sport coats and leather elbow patches with beautiful Saks Fifth Avenue blondes clinging close, the fat faces, the skinny faces, the sickly and the robust.

"How do you like it?" I asked Anna as we milled with the rest of the throng in front of the clubhouse.

"It's just what I needed," she said. "It's impossible to think about anything out here except money."

"That's beautiful," I told her, "that's the whole idea."

"It feels good, it feels very good, Al."

I looked at her and smiled. In her jeans and her shawl, her oversized circle earrings and her turquoise bracelet, she looked like—well, she looked like a Village actress at the track. Out of place, but happy. And me—I was proud to be her escort.

I asked Anna if she wanted to sit, and she said no, she'd rather hang around the area below the stands, just in front of the track. She wanted to be close to the race.

"Actually, I'm not that crazy about watching the race itself," I told her. "I've seen a couple of jockeys get thrown, and it's nothing I want to see again."

"You mean you come here and you don't look."

"I look. But that's the least enjoyable part. I've got friends who've been betting for sixty years and haven't seen a race yet. I'm not sure that they wouldn't confuse a horse with an overgrown dog. Bennie, for instance. Which reminds me. I want you to meet Bennie."

Anna followed me through the crowds toward the mutuel clerk windows. Bennie was working a ten-dollar window today. There were still fifteen minutes to the first race and not much of a line in front of Bennie. The smart betters, like me, wait till the last minute. We read the big tote board to see how the betting was going. Now I already knew which way I was leaning for the daily double but, just for appearance's sake, I'd wait another few minutes to bet.

"That's Bennie over there, the guy whose head looks a little like a sharpened pencil point. He's a wonderful individual. Been here since Revolutionary War days. I want you to say hello to him."

We walked up to the line, waited a few minutes and, at just about the right time, I put down my money on the daily double. Couple of horses called Alan's Speed and Huey 2 which I'd been studying for the past couple of days.

"Bennie, this is my friend Anna. I wanted her to meet you."

"A pleasure, I'm sure," Bennie said hurriedly. "You here to bet, honey, or just look pretty."

"She's an actress," I spoke for Anna. "A very fine actress."

"I'm sure." Bennie tried to smile—I can't remember his ever smiling before—as he pushed the tickets toward me, but he didn't make it.

"You interested in betting?" I asked Anna as we stepped away from the window with my ticket.

"Maybe a little later."

"Good thinking. Once you get used to the rhythm. Once I've had a chance to show you the ropes."

Alan's Speed never sped. That really hacked me off.

We went to the grandstand where I decided to wait out two or three races. I had planned on hitting the daily double today, and losing made me remember how much I'd been losing recently. In the privacy of my mind, I went over my debts. I had

83

bookies stashed around town like other men stashed mistresses. And they were all hungry—$20,000, maybe $30,000 altogether. I didn't want to think about it. The sun broke through the clouds for the first time and Anna put on a pair of tinted glasses which made me think of Costein. Which made me get down to work.

"Look," I said to her, "I'm glad you're having a good time and I'm glad you came out here with me and met Bennie and saw the boys, but I got to level with you. I know you got problems with your old man, but I got problems of my own."

"What problems, Al? Tell me about them."

I told her the whole Costein story. I spared her no details as the third race came and went. The pony I liked won, but I wasn't about to worry about it. If I had bet, the horse probably would have broken a leg.

"That pig," she said. "He sounds like a pretentious creep."

"I would imagine he's pretty smart to have gotten where he is," I protested, not knowing why I was defending him.

"Smart robot," Anna commented. "He's one of those corporate creeps whose life is dedicated to climbing higher and higher up the big network antenna."

"You've got him."

"I don't want him. And I don't want him driving you nuts, Al. You're too good for that."

I wanted to say "I am?" but I didn't. I loved hearing her talk this way. And while I guessed that was primarily because I got her a $20,000 role, I also detected that there was something sincere about Anna. I was convinced she cared.

"All this beating up on Costein," I said, "is good for our souls, but it's not going to get us anywhere. The other execs are all dropping off like flies, dying of heart attacks, but Costein isn't about to have a heart attack. He's jogging ten miles a day so he can live forever. By the time he's forty his heart will be stronger than the vault at the Chase Manhattan Bank and he'll be running the whole fucking network."

"I can't stand the type. He's the kind of jerk who makes me want to have nothing to do with television."

"We've got to go beyond that, Anna. We've got to figure out how to make your segment on the soap so big and juicy and heartbreaking and hot that we take the ratings through the ceiling and make you a star and make me financially solvent."

"I don't mind ripping off the network. I don't mind one little bit," she said with radical anger. "It would be a pleasure. It really would."

"That's one way of looking at it, I suppose. But another way of looking at it is through Sister Prudence's eyes."

"What do you mean?"

"For example, do you think she ever gets horny? Don't nuns get horny like everyone else?"

Anna laughed. She was having a good time at the track. She was having a good time with me. The fourth race ran and I didn't give a shit. Anna watched the nags kicking up the dirt and listened to me at the same time.

"I hope I'm not offending you," I said to her, half in jest.

"No, I think it's funny. I think this is all very funny. Yes, of course, nuns get horny. Maybe hornier than anyone else. They're cooped up and God knows what goes through their minds. But I think what you're fishing for is something different than horniness. You want this nun to fall in love, don't you?"

"Yes, of course. Love. That's it. She must fall in love. All women fall in love."

"And the love has to be romantic and idealized, very sweet and very true. Wouldn't you think?"

"Couldn't have said it better myself," I said.

"So there has to be a man. A man must enter her life."

"That's exactly what I was thinking. Now I want you to tell me what this man would look like. What sort of man would appeal to a nun?"

Anna smiled as the horses slowly made their way to the gate for the fifth race. For a long time she didn't speak. She just sat there with her chin resting in the palm of her hand. Her hair was as dark and beautiful as any hair I had ever seen. I decided that I loved her wild pink socks. She began to speak just as the horses broke from the gate. She stopped herself so she could watch. The crowd below surged toward the finish line, as always, and as the nags came down the stretch everyone stood and cheered. Except Anna and me.

"Do you know what I think?" she finally said after the tension of the last race had dissolved into thin air. The favorite had come in.

"Tell me," I urged.

"I think she'd go for a blond."

"A blond?"

"A blond who looked nothing like any man she had ever been close to. You know what I mean, don't you?"

"Of course," remembering that my hair, except for some flecks of gray, was as dark as Anna's.

"He'd have to be very blond," she said. "Very light, with very little hair on his chest or his arms or his hands. I think he'd have to be on the tall side, but nothing extreme. And I don't think his hair should be curly. She's seen enough men with curly hair to last a lifetime. Naturally he'd have to have blue eyes."

"Naturally."

"And I also think he'd be very educated. You know, one of those guys who went to Princeton, like his father and grandfather before him."

"Old money?"

"Very old and very established. And his voice should be extremely mellow—that's important. He would have to be calm, inwardly calm, and not given to sudden bursts of temper."

"He couldn't be from New York."

"No, no," Anna directed me. "This guy should be from an old Ohio family and he shouldn't care about New York. Actually, he shouldn't care about money. He's always had it, but his sensibilities go far beyond that. He's sensitive to human feelings and human frailties."

"Is he an artist?"

Anna thought for a moment. "No, I don't think so. He's probably a professional, probably a lawyer. Maybe even the lawyer who handles the case for the convent."

The Lawyer! The fucking lawyer! Why hadn't I thought of that? She was right! Beautifully right! The blue-eyed blond boy had to be her lawyer! Now the wheels inside my head were turning like mad.

"He's a lawyer," she continued, her interest building, "but I think he might write some poetry at night. Maybe just before he goes to bed. He doesn't tell anyone, and he keeps his poems locked in the bottom drawer of his bureau. He doesn't even tell his wife."

"I didn't know he was married."

"Anyone this gorgeous couldn't be a bachelor for long."

Anna talked for a long time. The sixth and seventh races flew by us. I was tempted to run down and place a few bets—my spirits had been renewed—but I didn't want to leave Anna, not even for a second. She was talking as though this guy really existed. I could see that she saw him, and I started seeing him, and I started weaving plots and subplots and then—as she continued telling me how he walked and talked—I started getting a little itchy about the eighth race. I liked a horse named Shirley's Wish and I liked the way the betting was going. The odds looked good and I was willing to risk a G. What the hell?

"Let's stretch our legs," I suggested to Anna, and the two of us walked downstairs. I waited till the last possible minute before I put down my money. Then we got as close to the track as we could—"I want to feel them racing. I want to feel their power," she said, and they were off, and Shirley's Wish came out slow—which was okay, I expected that—and then hung back and then made his magnificent move at the stretch. Anna was jumping up and down, but I remained cool, no real gambler jumps up and down, and she was yelling 'cause Shirley's Wish was coming on, Shirley's Wish was closing the gap and the finish was wire to wire, which didn't bother me in the least cause I had $500 on the nag to win, and $500 to place. I knew my afternoon was made in the shade. Anna screeched and kissed me on the cheek and that felt very good. She had very warm lips and a snazzy little body and now she seemed happy as a little girl.

"You've done it," she said, "you've picked a winner."

Just then the INQUIRY sign flashed on the board.

"What does that mean?" she wanted to know.

"Trouble," I said, trying to fight a sinking feeling in my stomach.

JOCKEY INTERFERENCE. I knew what that probably meant, and I was right. Shirley's Wish, the clear winner, was kicked down to third place. And a show did me no good, no fucking good at all.

"Doesn't matter," Anna said to me. "I'll pick the next race."

I tried to smile, but the thought of my bad luck hung heavy

over my head. Why didn't I leave well enough alone? I wanted to kill the asshole jockey for interfering.

"Sure," I told her with some condescension in my voice, "you pick 'em, honey. It's the last race and it's an exacta. That means if you pick the horse that wins and the horse that comes in second, you'll win a lot of money. Let me suggest, though . . ."

"Let's not do it that way, Al. Let me just read the names. I'll be able to tell from that."

"The names? You'll be able to tell from the names?"

She was already engrossed in reading the card. "Gusher will win," she announced. "And Bebop will be close behind."

Gusher wasn't an entirely stupid choice, but Bebop was a ridiculous long shot. Yet what difference did it make?

"All right," I said. "Here's twenty bucks. Baseball it. That means you'll be picking Gusher to win and Bebop in second— and then you'll reverse the order. Make each of those bets twice, and tell Bennie the numbers of the horses, not their names."

She went, and came back with the tickets. We walked through the crowd to watch the race at ground level.

The late afternoon sun was luscious and her horses came in. Her fucking horses came in. Anna Calzolari hit the exacta.

Now I've been hanging out at the track for a couple of hard decades and one thing I've never done is show any real emotion —win, lose or push. Except for that race. I screamed. I fucking screamed as loud as anyone has ever screamed at Belmont Park. I screamed because my friend Anna, the brilliant and beautiful actress, had picked the exacta and won something like $4000.

"You better get the money from Bennie," she finally calmed down enough to say. Tears were streaming from her eyes.

"Are you kidding? I'm too excited. You go. I'll be standing right next to you."

She got the money and handed the cash to me. "You're crazy," I said. "You picked them. You keep it."

"It's yours. It was your twenty dollars."

"No." I was adamant.

"I can't. I won't." She was just as adamant.

"I won't be able to sleep," I told her.

"Then we'll divide it."

"All right." I could see that was the only solution. Two Gs apiece.

"Let's celebrate," she suggested.

"Fucking A straight," I replied.

A half hour later we were at the Turf Club bombed on Dom Perignon. My eyes were dancing out of my head and Anna was smiling. Our waiter was blond but we decided he wasn't *our* blond because his teeth weren't straight enough and he was a little too short.

"I love what these bubbles do to my head," she giggled.

I wanted to say to her, "I love what *you* do to my head," but I wasn't that drunk, not yet, and I ordered another bottle of the stuff because we were still on our way up.

"We've made a lot of money today, haven't we?" she asked rhetorically.

"This is nothing," I answered, "compared to the money that we're going to make. Yes, sir. This is a place and time to remember, and you mark my words—you and I are going to make a lot of money together, a shitload of money."

There was no doubt about it. She had just what I'd been missing.

In the cab back to the city I was giddy, and Anna was talking about the soap. "You see," she said, "he's really not happy in Ohio."

"How come?" I wanted to know.

"He's trapped. He has a wife who's sort of a pain in the ass. Maybe she's a high-school sweetheart who went to finishing schools back East and college at the Sorbonne, but never changed. She remained what she had always been—a high-school cheerleader—while he, our lawyer hero, was deeply moved by the books he read at Princeton, the humanity courses and the novels and the history of the modern and ancient world."

"Then why did he become a lawyer, for Christ's sake?"

"Good point," Anna granted. She thought for a few seconds and then she said, "His father. His father's a lawyer."

"That's right," I interrupted, "one of the most prominent, let's say *the* most prominent lawyer in Troy."

"And he has this law firm which will go to his son. And his son, who really is a very fine and beautiful person, is also a little weak. Or maybe just so devoted to his family or so trapped by the bourgeois thing, that he finds himself back where he started."

"In Troy, Ohio," I chimed in. "In the middle of a soap opera."

"Miserable and bored, but not miserable or bored enough to really change his life. He's looking for someone or something. Do you know what I mean, Al?"

"Of course, of course! He's looking for a cause. And he's looking for a dame. And I got both for him. I got everything this blond bastard needs to spice up his life. I like this, Anna. I like this very much."

"It must take a long time for Sister Prudence to face her feelings. You realize that, don't you?"

"Listen, sugar, all we've got is time. There's nothing that moves slower than the action on a soap. Nothing, except maybe a couple of horses I picked last week."

"Is this what you intended? Is this what you thought would happen to Sister Prudence?"

"No, and I'm not even going to mention my original story idea. This one's ten times better. It just means making up a whole new dramatic segment to the soap."

"Is that bad?" she asked as the cab headed down Fifth Avenue.

"Not bad, just complicated. But I'm thinking, I'm thinking."

"I'll be quiet," Anna volunteered.

"Are you kidding? Keep jawing, kid. It'll all work out. I was going to have Sister Prudence meet Baxter MacNiece but, until today, I didn't know that Baxter had a son. So tell me where you got this idea about this blond."

"I remember the first time I noticed a blond man," she reflected. "I must have been twelve or thirteen."

"Twelve or thirteen? Come on."

"I'm not kidding. You think about it. How many blonds are running around the Lower East Side? It's a world of dark-haired men which, of course, never mattered to me, until I was sitting in the movies one day and saw a blond cowboy jump on a black horse and chase a few Indians across the screen. I can't even

90

remember the actor's name. There was only his hair, which was the color of the sun, and I thought to myself, My God, there are blond men in the world, and they are gorgeous."

"And did you find one?" I wanted to know.

"I found John. That happened very early in my life."

"But you told me that John ain't no blond."

She smiled, and said, "John ain't no blond. But John, is well, John is gorgeous in his own dark way."

I realized that we had gotten on the wrong subject, but it was too late. Already I could see that I was losing her, and I found myself resenting that bastard. Even hating him. He was in my way. In the way of my work. And I knew it wouldn't be wise to bring her mind back to the soap, because now she was elsewhere. And what the hell, I thought, I had enough to remember. So I dropped her off in SoHo and went back uptown to my place to start writing. And I would have been fine, I would have been happy thinking about our day and our winnings and our story scheming, if she hadn't kissed me and hugged me good-bye back there in the cab with the kind of enthusiasm—I'd call it passion —which I was sure went beyond the bounds of friendship.

A week later I was back in the control room, waiting for the action to start. I wasn't worried. Not one bit. The rehearsals had been smooth. The script was slick; it was exactly right. I knew that I was clicking now. I was riding on a roll, and I was loving it.

I looked down in the studio and saw that they were ready. Dick called for action, and I turned my attention to the monitor. I wanted to see how this was going to look on the tube.

Baxter MacNiece is seated in his high-back swivel chair. The top of his desk is clear except for a Steuben-glass owl. Mac-

Niece is handsome. His hair is gray, his skin tan and clear, his mustache full, dashing. His dark brown suit is custom-tailored, his tie quiet and expensive. His office is imposing.

"Naturally I am sympathetic to your case," he says to Sister Prudence who sits across from him, "but I see certain problems."

"There are always problems in the pursuit of justice," she answers slowly but firmly.

"I'm afraid you've caught me in the middle of a terribly complicated case, and the idea of turning my attention from . . ."

"I did not expect that you would personally handle the matter," she politely interrupts. "I was only hoping that you might be good enough to designate someone else in your firm, perhaps a junior partner."

"We do some *pro bono* work, yes, but this is a very busy time for us, and . . ."

"This is work for which not only the sisters at Ursula will be grateful, Mr. MacNiece, but the Highest Judge of all. He will bless you with His gratitude, I am certain."

The lawyer arches his right eyebrow. He knows that he's being rushed.

"I can make no promises today, Sister. I will take the matter under advisement, and I will let you know."

"Then let me thank you in advance for making the right decision," she says assuredly, "for making the only decision that is morally feasible."

"Yes, yes, well, thank you for coming," MacNiece states as he rises from his chair to show Sister Prudence to the door.

"I will take the liberty of calling you tomorrow," says the nun. "I trust by then you will be able to tell me which of your fine counselors will be assigned to our case."

Baxter MacNiece smiles. Sister Prudence smiles back. She shakes his hand firmly and leaves the office.

"I've got a surprise for you," I said to Anna while she was walking to her dressing room.

"You've decided on someone to play Brian MacNiece."

"That's right."

"You're fast."

"Faster than you think. I told him that we'd meet him for a late lunch today. What do you say?"

"Yes, of course. He's my man, isn't he?"

He had one of those gold tie bars, the kind that go under the knot of your tie. And that, as far as I was concerned, really put the icing on the cake.

He was waiting for me and Anna in the reception area of the Droman Club which, by all estimates, is one of New York's most exclusive. Nine-tenths of their members are purebred graduates of Harvard, Princeton or Yale. There are a few fancier clubs in the city, but none of them admit women for lunch. Which is how I zeroed in on Droman. It also helped that Dick our director is a card-carrying member. Which is how I got us in.

I looked at Anna when she first looked at him, and I saw that my past week's work had not been in vain. I saw her blink nervously and I figured I better hurry up and introduce them.

"Anna, this is Hanford Seames. Hanford, Anna Calzolari."

"My pleasure," he said, and he took her hand and kissed it. I couldn't believe it! He actually kissed her hand! Oh, this was too good to be believed.

Looking around the joint—at the red-leather wing-back chairs and deep mahogany paneling, the somber waiters and the overstuffed, filthy-rich clientele—I regretted that I was wearing that baby blue sport coat and yellow tie that I picked up in Miami last year. Compared to Hanford, who was all muted and flanneled in charcoal brown, I felt a little loud. So I tried to keep my voice down.

"We have reservations," I announced to the maître d' who looked at me as though I had just arrived from another planet.

"This way please," he answered, his nose pointing toward the moon. As we walked across the dimly lit dining room I looked at Hanford looking at Anna and saw that he was pleased. She had somehow put together an outfit which, not altogether right for the Droman Club, was wrong in exactly the right way. She had put her hair back up in a bun, like the first time I had met her, and her fine features, her beautiful chin and cheeks, were without a drop of makeup. No lipstick, no rouge, nothing.

93

She wore an oversized scarlet blouse, the kind that had no collar, and her skirt was jet black and very long. Underneath she was wearing boots. She looked fancy—fancy-bohemian or fancy-actress—and, as far as I was concerned, she was the best-looking thing in the place.

Dick must have had a little clout because we were given a table by a wide, high window which looked down on Fifth Avenue, just a few stories below. Hanford waited for Anna to be seated, which caught me by surprise since I was already reading over the menu. It was nearly two o'clock and I was hungry as a bear. The waiter came—still another snot—and we ordered drinks (Hanford requested a Tanqueray martini), and before the sauce arrived Hanford excused himself and said that he had to make a phone call. I stood up and helped him out of his chair and no one thought that was very funny. When he was gone Anna leaned over and said to me, "You really went out and did it."

"You said you wanted a blond," I told her, "so I got you a blond. What do you think?"

"Is he real? Or is he stuffed?"

"He's as real as they come. What's wrong? You don't like him?"

"Give me a chance, will you?"

"What about the looks?" I wanted to know.

"The looks are first-class," she admitted.

"Not too Redfordy?" I wondered.

"You can't get too Redfordy for me," she confessed.

"Good. Great."

"I think he's very, very pretty."

"I don't want pretty. I want handsome."

"He's handsome and pretty both. And the color of his eyes remind me of the first time I went to Coney Island and saw the ocean."

"Blue, blue, blue," I smiled.

"True blue," she smiled back.

"Wait till you hear him talk," I said.

"I've heard him talk."

"Wait till you hear him talk again."

"You're selling too hard, Al. I'm already sold."

94

"Wait till you see him act."

"You told me he was good."

"Great."

"When do we get started?"

"At the end of the week. I'll have the script for you tomorrow."

"Aren't you late?"

"Very late. But I'm always late. That's my style. Besides," I said, not willing to reveal the extent of this latest block, "I've had to tie up some loose ends on the other segments."

"I'm anxious."

"*You're* anxious. You wanna feel my pulse?"

Just then Hanford returned. It looked as though he had been combing his hair. He sat down just as the waiter showed up with the booze.

"I had to call my father," Hanford explained to us. "He's giving a speech tonight and I wanted to wish him well."

"What kind of speech?" I asked.

"He's receiving an award from the American Historical Association in San Francisco."

"He's an historian?" I presumed.

"Actually, he's a medical doctor who last year wrote a history of nineteenth-century medicine."

"I see," I said.

"Do you come from San Francisco?" Anna asked, speaking her first words of the afternoon to him.

"Yes, I do. But I'm much more interested in where you come from."

I thought that line was a little oily—especially in view of the fact that another man—me—was present. But Anna didn't seem to mind.

"I'm from the Lower East Side," she said flatly. I was proud of her.

"I *love* it down there," he told her. "It's so wonderfully ethnic. In fact, I was jogging around there just the other morning."

Oh, Christ, I thought to myself. Just what I needed. Another goddamn jogger. I downed my Scotch and signaled for more. "Bring us some bread and butter," I told the aloof waiter.

"Where did you start your jog from?" Anna asked.

"Park and Sixtieth," Hanford answered, delighted with the question.

"That's a long way," Anna said with apparent admiration.

"Some people like to climb mountains or catch whales. I just like to run. But we're still talking about me, and not about you. Al tells me you're going to be the next big star on daytime television."

Anna sipped her glass of white wine. She waited for a few seconds and she said, "Al is full of shit."

I really liked Anna a lot.

Hanford, at first surprised, now began to see her more for what she was. "Al sounds like your biggest fan," he said.

"Al's prejudiced," she stated.

"And besides," Al said, "Al's getting drunk." I took care of my second Scotch. Getting bombed in the middle of the day was always strange and not totally pleasant, but here I was in between these two kids—both my invention—and I was having some second thoughts about the whole thing.

"You know, Anna," I said, "there were a lot of guys who read for the part of Brian MacNiece. A lot of big names. Big TV names. I let the word out that I had something important up my sleeve and you should have seen them come running. Yeah, the studio was flooded, and Hanford will tell you, they weren't reading to the casting director or the producer. They were reading to *me*, because they understood that Al Gonfio had come up with the part, and that it wasn't peanuts."

"Have you been acting for long?" Hanford asked Anna, as if I hadn't said a word.

"I've always been acting," she answered him.

He smiled and said, "Are you acting now?"

"Of course," she shot back.

"Listen," I broke in, "let's cut the bullshit and order. I got to eat something before I pass out."

"Well, we don't want Al passing out, Anna, do we? We want Al at the typewriter."

I didn't like the way that sounded, but I left it alone. My purpose was to get these two together. I wanted to get them interested in each other—professionally interested—because I knew that the fate of the show, and maybe my whole future, depended upon the chemistry between them. Besides, I had chosen Hanford with Anna and only Anna in mind. He was my present to her. And right now, I could see that there was no taking him back.

We ordered. Quiche for Anna. Ratatouille for Hanford. The T-bone for me. "Don't forget the sour cream with the baked potato," I told the waiter. "And bring me a beer."

It was going to be a heavy lunch.

"You were going to talk about yourself," Hanford said to Anna. "You mentioned that you were a New Yorker. Have you always been interested in the theater?"

"I've always been interested in theatrics," she wise-guyed him.

He laughed and he looked at her, he kept on looking at her, and I looked at the empty Scotch glass in front of me.

"So you don't want to talk about yourself," Hanford said to Anna.

"I'm sure you have a more colorful background than I do," she suggested.

"Something like the color of your suit," I chimed in.

Hanford seemed amused. Nothing really threw him. He was cool.

"Actually," he said, "I am the result of a mixture of old San Francisco money and old Boston money."

"Then what the hell are you doing hustling acting jobs?" I asked, maybe too brutally.

"Ambition doesn't have anything to do with money," he replied.

"I wouldn't know," I said.

"And besides," he added, "I'm really not that much different from everyone else who was in my eating club in Princeton."

Anna kicked me under the table. Hard. "So you went to Princeton," she said.

"That was the place," Hanford assured her. "You can blame all my culture on Princeton."

"I was wondering why you dressed like that," I couldn't help but say.

"Once a tiger, always a tiger," he quipped.

97

"What's a tiger?" Anna asked.

"A Princeton man," my boy answered, "is a tiger."

Our food arrived and I said, "You'll notice that I'm the only one eating meat."

I ate the meat. I've eaten better. The beer glass wasn't chilled and I wasn't thrilled with the service. I wanted more butter and more bread. Meanwhile, Hanford was brushing back his blond mop and eating slowly and questioning Anna about growing up on the Lower East Side. I could have told him a thing or two, but he didn't ask. I could have reminded him again who got him this role, but I didn't bother. Instead I listened to him tell us about his college production and his year as a model—he did a cigarette billboard one year but turned it down the next because his conscience got to him. He told us how he loved O'Neill and Ibsen and Ionesco and that naturally he was mad for Shakespeare but he really preferred doing Sophocles and Aristophanes. I yawned, but Anna seemed interested and she said something about her Kate Chopin play and he really went for that, he started asking her a million questions about her attitude about the *theater,* and I almost reminded them both that they were about to jump headfirst into the old soap opera cesspool and they could take their fancy notions of *theater* and cram them. But I didn't. Instead I waved to the waiter and told him I wanted a telephone brought to the table.

"Calling the office?" Hanford questioned.

"No," I told him, "I'm calling my bookie."

And while they carried on their artsy-fartsy talk, I chewed the fat awhile with Sam Turbenburg, who's been taking my football money for decades. Funny, but I don't believe in mixing bookmakers. I've got one for every major sport. I'm superstitious that way. I listened while Sam ran down the poop on the exhibition games that were coming up. I pulled a little parlay action and committed myself to a grand. Looking at Anna and Hanford chatting away, I was convinced that I was about to make some big money on this show.

When I was through with Sam I got interested in a little banana cream pie. Anna and Hanford ate fresh fruit and cheese which has never seemed like much of a dessert to me. He kept asking her about life in the slums and she kept backing him off while at the same time letting him know that she liked his style. She was a much smoother operator than I had figured. She did very well at the Droman Club.

"I'd like to know something more about the part," pretty boy finally turned and asked me a question.

"I'm still deliberating," I answered. "Great artists don't like to move too quickly. I'm still in the psychoanalytical stage of the character development." I thought I'd show him that for a high-school dropout I knew a few 18-karat words myself. "I'll show you some script this week and by the weekend we'll probably be taping."

"That's awfully quick," he commented, and I saw my opening.

"You better understand, kid," I said, "that this whole business is fast. This ain't no theater and this ain't no poetry recital. This is let's-grind-out-the-shit, gut-level TV. This is what America wants and loves, and this is what I understand better than anyone in this whole country. That's why we're here today, because I can see what's going to make those housewives come all over their ironing boards. So when I say rehearse, it's time to rehearse. And when I say tape, it's time to tape. And I wouldn't suggest challenging or questioning or any other goddamn thing, because you'll soon learn that at *Search for Happiness,* it all begins and ends right here." I pointed to my head and stuck a cigar in my mouth. Let him think about that one.

I grabbed the check when it came and signed Dick's name. I left an especially small tip.

"I'm anxious to get started, Al, I can certainly tell you that." Now Hanford was showing a bit more respect. "And I can't tell you how much I'm looking forward to working with you, Anna."

I thought that was a bit too much, but she was still digging it, still studying his blue eyes as we all walked out together and said good-bye on Fifth Avenue. "I think I'm going to get in a game of squash," he said, "while the day is still young." And with that he left us.

"Come on over to the milk plant with me," I suggested to Anna, and she was smart enough to come along. She knew I needed some postgame analysis.

99

"You happy?" I asked her.

"My happiness is not your responsibility," she said to me as the cabdriver nearly killed a guy wearing an Indian turban walking across Fifty-seventh Street.

"I feel like it is," I said.

"It's hard for me to think much about Hanford." As she spoke, I could see the mood was changing in her eyes. She was moving further away.

"He's kind of a snob," I declared, "but the kid can act his ass off. You should've seen him read, you should have . . ."

But the more I talked, the more I saw she was not listening. Her eyes misted over. She looked aimlessly out the cab's window at Manhattan's midafternoon fury. "Anna, Anna," I said, "I think this guy is going to be very right."

Yet I knew I wasn't getting across. I could practically hear her rehearsing her lines to John tonight as I thought about Costein's pinball machine, Costein's meanly tinted glasses.

11

A couple of nights later I had to take some time off from my writing. It wasn't going as quickly as I would have liked. It's always a little frustrating when those keys aren't really flying. That usually means I need to take a break. And besides, I had a wedding to go to.

I had to go to Queens, and I hate Queens. And I had to see my family, all six hundred members, and I love my family but I just didn't want to deal with them that night. Still, there was nothing I could do. My nephew Johnny was getting married, and he was a good kid and there was no way I could miss his wedding. I used to take him to ball games and when he came down with his first case of VD a couple of years back I sent him to the right skin doctor. (His old man, my brother Eddie, would have killed him if he had known.) Now Johnny had been going with this girl for about a year—I hadn't met her yet—and they were tying the knot and I hoped that he hadn't knocked her up already.

So I dressed myself in a blue suit and a white shirt and a fancy tie with some Frenchman's initials on it, put on my shoes, slapped on some cologne, went downstairs and gave the cabby an address in Forest Hills. I don't like Forest Hills. It bothers me to leave the city and go over the Queensboro Bridge because there's nothing on Queens Boulevard that really interests me.

I was going to this wedding, but I should have been writing. I should have been writing all day, every available second, because I had to keep that story going. And riding through Forest Hills I tried to concentrate on the show, but it was no use. The cab was too noisy, the streets were too noisy, my mind was too noisy, and by the time I fought my way through the noise the cab pulled up to this large catering hall or recreation center—I don't know what the hell to call it—named Fiorello's. I guessed that this was where all the big-moneyed Forest Hills Italians marry off their kids, and even though my brother Eddie lives in Brooklyn, he figured he was good enough to have a Forest Hills wedding.

And when I walked inside and saw all the people, when Eddie came up and hugged me and I saw the pride in his eyes, I could hardly blame him for wanting to throw a bash. He had been driving a miserable pretzel truck for thirty years now and Johnny was his only son and the bride's family was dirt poor and this was Eddie's way of saying, I've done all right, I can give my kid a decent wedding.

"You look terrific, Al," he said to me, and immediately aunts and uncles and cousins came up to me and kissed me and hugged me and asked me questions about all the characters on *Search*. I guess in some sense I'm the only star in the family and naturally everyone watches the show every day, and naturally I love that. Relatives started bringing me drinks and I thought —what the hell, why not, and I began downing Scotch. The bar was open and the booze was flowing and I wondered when and where they were going to get married. Hadn't someone forgotten about a church? Around then I saw Mama and Pop and they both looked very old and very small, and Mama opened her arms to me and we embraced and she asked me whom I had brought. She wanted to meet my date and when I told her I didn't bring anyone she wasn't happy. "What about *your* wedding, big shot?" Pop said for Mama and I laughed it off; I was used to it, and I had another drink. By then a band had started to play and thank God there was an accordion. It wouldn't have been a wedding without an accordion. Then in the middle of this big hall with fancy cheap chandeliers dripping down from the ceiling I spotted my nephew Johnny. He looked burly and a little confused, and he came over to me and said, "I'm not sure this is right, Uncle Al. I don't feel good about it."

"That's what they all say, kid. Means nothing, though."

"Then how come you haven't married?" he wanted to know.

I took a sip of my third drink and, feeling that my ailments were quickly vanishing, I said, "Because I'm unlucky in love and I know it." Then I slipped five crisp hundred-dollar bills into his pants pocket.

He wandered off and I thought to myself that the kid really is crazy for getting married so young. But at that age you're so horny and so stupid that sometimes you think that the first girl you're really fucking good is the one you have to marry. You think that a hot screw equals love. Well, that was Johnny's problem. As for me, I was feeling fine or maybe even a little better than fine when I happened to see Freddy Bosco who happens to be one of my bookies. He's Eddie's bookie, too, which explains his appearance here, but it still unnerved me because I remembered that I owed him three Gs.

"I saw you slipping something to your nephew," Freddy said, "and I thought you might have meant to give it to me." Freddy comes right to the point.

"You don't miss a trick, do you?" I asked the bum, trying to avoid looking at his face which resembled an overripe tomato plant.

"Just ribbing you, Al, just ribbing you. Hell, you're the one guy I don't worry about. You could buy us all out. I keep telling the boys that soon you're going to be buying your own TV station."

"Don't hold your breath."

"What are you doing about the play-offs?" he asked.

"You going around soliciting? Business isn't good enough, you gotta work the weddings, too?"

"Al, this is Freddy. I'm talking like a friend."

Five minutes later I had put three Gs on the Dodgers and two on the Yanks. I liked the odds.

I also liked the food. There was at least a mile of appetizers, scampi and caponata, four kinds of bread and six kinds of olives. I had another drink and I ate some more and felt good about my bet, felt good about everything, and when I saw Silvia Rowe I felt even better.

She was my cousin Regina's friend whom I had banged a couple of times last year. I had completely forgotten about her for the past few months. Not that there was anything wrong with her—she was a neglected and very passionate lady—but she talked an awful lot, especially about her job at City Security Bank in Sheepshead Bay and the interesting people she met all day long. Tonight she was in a bright-red sequined dress and her lipstick made her lips look tasty and her goddamn bust was big, big, big. She came over and planted a big one on my mouth—the broad was already loaded—and shit, I thought, I've already scored, I ain't going home alone tonight. In her high, squeaky voice she started telling me all about how much she adores the show. They have a television in the bank, and she takes her lunch break when the show's on and she tells everyone she meets that I write it, and where have I been? How come I don't call? And did I know that last week was her fortieth birthday and even though a lot of women feel funny about revealing their age she doesn't have the least reservation because, after all, we are what we are and she looks pretty good for a woman of forty and don't I agree? Goddamn right I agree, honey, and nice to see you, Silvia, have a drink and we'll dance later and who are you with and that's great, 'cause I'm alone and don't leave without checking with me first.

I was on my fourth or fifth drink when Old Uncle Tato, Mama's brother, came over and started telling me in the language of the old country how he missed the wedding parties back in the old neighborhood when they were held in people's houses and we all ate a little prosciutto and a little cheese and that was all. Yeah, I said to my uncle whose speech and face were wrinkly and sweet, I liked it back then, those parties were really something, weren't they?—*ci siamo divertiti, ci siamo divertiti.* My Italian was a little strange, but it's always been strange, more *New Yorkese* than *italiano,* but it didn't matter, 'cause we were having a ball, and I kissed Uncle Tato on the forehead and he told me I had been drinking too much. I looked around and saw all the little kids, the beautiful little kids dressed up in party dresses and suits, and they came over and called me Uncle Al and I passed out dollar bills to all of them, just the way Uncle Tato might have done twenty or thirty years ago, but now he was broke and I had the cash, I had the goodwill to spread because I wrote the big soap opera that everyone watched every day. Suddenly the music stopped and the back wall of the hall folded open and there, on the other side of the room, was a chapel, a big chapel, and I thought to myself, Jesus Christ, it's all here, they're going to get married right here in the portable plastic chapel. The crowd started filing toward the pews, and standing at the altar was a priest I had never seen before and next to him was Johnny and my brother Eddie and there were flowers and everyone was stiff and waxlike; everyone was ready to go.

An organ replaced the accordion and I felt like telling Eddie or my sister-in-law Rosa that the booze should follow, not precede, the wedding, but I was too drunk to do that and it was too late, and besides, it was funny. This was a new-fangled wedding. The bridesmaids wore pink and looked as though they just stepped off a wedding cake and the ushers wore tuxes and looked like a Fred Astaire movie. "I bought a package deal," Eddie would tell me later when I asked him about the procedure. "You leave everything up to Fiorello's and you get a beautiful wedding." So I sat in the first row—in the pew taped off for relatives—and I was a little worried that I lost sight of Silvia. But I saw that Mama was already crying and Papa had nodded out and the priest was talking and Eddie was beaming and suddenly the bride came down the aisle. Her hair was dark and her features were fine and small, she was demure and she was dressed in white in a long, trailing, frilly, costume of a wedding gown, and I immediately thought of Anna, Anna who was never married like this, not in the old-fashioned way or in the new, crazy Queens Boulevard way, Anna who had never gone to the altar but instead rebelled against all this shit, and good for her, yeah, good for her except that her boyfriend was no better than a husband, or maybe worse, but it didn't matter —none of it mattered because she was going to save the show! Anna was going to save the show! That's why I had been feeling so good and why I had been able to tell Mr. Marathon with the hidden eyes to pull his head out of his ass. Because I was right, this gal was going to be dynamite, the sweet little Italian girl whom everyone loves, the nun, the understanding, the wholesome, beautiful nun. I should have taken her to the wedding, I should have let her see all this, because she would have laughed herself sick, but it was really okay, Johnny was marrying this little thing who was innocent and at least looked like a virgin, and Mama was still crying and Papa was still sleeping when the wedding was over. The back wall, which had closed, now opened, and we all spilled back into the banquet hall which was being set up with tables and flowers and we headed back to the bar and drank and the accordion played and I found Silvia and gave her tits a little squeeze—Jesus, I had to fuck her tonight, the booze and her boobs, her big luscious boobs—and just when everyone was sitting down, Eddie, my brother Eddie who bought the package deal wedding, stood on top of a folding chair and shouted, "The guy who was going to take movie pictures just got here. He missed the wedding, so we got to do it over again. I hope you don't mind, but I want everyone back in the chapel, so it looks real."

Everyone looked at each other and not that many people laughed because they realized the seriousness of having this thing on film. I had downed another drink and I didn't care, in fact I liked the idea of a repeat performance, a real-life instant replay, except that Papa had passed out and Mama insisted that I carry him back in the chapel, which I was barely able to do. Somehow the ushers and the bridesmaids got back in formation and there was a lot of stumbling and burping, but the great mass of guests found its way back into the plastic chapel, though, this time around, there was a lot less restraint and a few catcalls and obscene remarks, but that had to be expected since we had been

105

drinking now for hours. A few people, including Papa, snored through the ordeal, while the earnest-looking filmmaker in a pea-green safari jacket made his movie.

The second wedding, the fake wedding, was over and we all deserted the chapel and a couple of relatives fell down but most everyone was merry and mobile as we headed back into the big hall to finish off the food. There was soup and fish and three kinds of pasta and chicken and beef. I ate a great deal because I had to offset the drinking. I congratulated the bride, my new niece Patricia, and welcomed her into the family by slipping her a hundred-dollar bill. She thanked me with a kiss and I told her to watch my soap opera. She said that she'd try. Afterward I danced off the food, I danced to the wonderfully lousy accordion band. I danced with the bride, and my younger nieces who were six and seven years old and the best dancers in the joint. I danced with my sister-in-law Rosa and I danced with my mother who was light and lovely as a child. It seemed as though I danced with every woman there and they were all beautiful, especially Patricia who reminded me of Anna, and somehow I wished that Anna was there and Costein was there. Just so they could see. And sometime around three in the morning I grabbed Silvia who was raring to go. And we went. We grabbed a cab and once inside we tore at each other. I had my hand inside her dress and up her panties and we were like a couple of kids. She was big and moist and hot as a pistol and I wanted to bang her right there in the goddamn cab. We kept at it, we kept on smooching and smacking, and in the elevator of my building she fell down twice and I was scared that she was going to pass out before I got to her. Inside my apartment, on my bed, I got rid of her ugly red gown and saw that she had girdled herself like a mummy, but when I finally got all that gear undone she came rolling out to me, her flesh was freed, her tits spilled in my mouth and I sucked on them like candy and she giggled and told me what she wanted me to do with her pussy—she used the word pussy—and brother, it was one gorgeous pussy, and there we were, slamming and fucking our way to the moon. I couldn't have been happier, I've never been happier. It was a wild, juicy screw, and afterward, when she was zonked out and I was just staring at the ceiling, I realized that my fortune was in that

106

goddamn nun. And, even more, I realized that that nun was going to have to get laid.

12

"He's gone," she said.

"Who's gone?" I asked, not quite aware of who the hell I was talking to on the phone. My head hurt.

"John."

"Where'd he go?" I asked, not really caring and not really understanding.

"I don't know, I don't know. He left about three A.M. We had a terrible fight and I feel horrible. I can't talk to Gwen and I really need to talk to you."

"Okay, sugar," I said, now realizing that I was talking to Anna, "just hold on a second." I looked at the clock by the side of my bed: 8:00 A.M. Jesus Christ. When did I stop banging Silvia last night? Only a few hours ago. I looked over and saw her flat on her back. God, she needed to lose weight. Still, she had a beautiful bush and a great pair of tits. She was smiling as she was dreaming, and I covered her naked body with a blanket. Now I could talk to Anna. "Listen, Anna, you've caught me at a bad time again."

"Then I'll call back," she sounded apologetic, even a little hurt.

"No, no," I quickly said, remembering Costein's tinted glasses and the fact that I was on the verge of occupational collapse. "I can talk to you. I want to talk to you. But maybe a little later."

"Can I see you?" she asked me, sounding so much like a little girl that I couldn't resist.

"You can see me whenever you want to."

"Who you talking to, Al?" Silvia, aroused from the dead, suddenly lifted her sweet head from the pillow.

"No one," I whispered, covering the phone with my hand, "just an actress."

"Is she on your show? Is she famous?"

"Shhhh," I demanded.

"Now what were we saying?" I asked Anna.

"I'm sorry I disturbed you," Anna said, sensing the presence of another woman.

"You did *not* disturb me," I insisted. Watching Silvia rise from the bed and walk to the bathroom, I considered screwing her again this morning.

"We'll talk another day," Anna suggested.

"We'll talk today," I offered. "Let me just think a second." My head still hurt. Silvia was taking a piss. I had to start working. I was way behind. If I got together with Anna, maybe that would do the trick. I put the phone back to my mouth and said, "How'd you like to have lunch?"

"Fine."

"Take a cab here. Meet me at my place at noon." Then I gave her my address and quickly closed the conversation.

Silvia came back to bed and promptly fell asleep. It was hell getting rid of her. It was Saturday morning and she didn't have to work. She said that she wanted to sleep till noon. I told her that was impossible. She grunted and groaned and I had to wrestle her awake. "Take a shower with me," she said. I thought about it, but my head was hurting too bad. I needed tomato juice, I needed bread, I needed to concentrate on cleaning myself up and cleaning her out.

"When will I see you again?" she wanted to know.

"Soon, very soon."

"Why are you hurrying me?"

"I'm not hurrying you. It's just that I'm in a hurry."

"I'm not going. I don't want to go."

"Listen, baby, you got no choice." And when I reached to pull her out of bed she somehow got her mouth around my dick and started sucking me something fierce. How was I going to fight this kind of thing? "I just love to do it in the morning," she

108

said, taking a breather. Naturally I gave in. I climbed back in bed, and we fucked around for another hour. She was still hot from last night and I was still pumping, though God knows where my energy was coming from. She scratched and tickled and giggled and tempted, and there was no way she wasn't going to get what she wanted. The lady liked to play hardball.

"You think I can come when you tape the show?" she asked when we were through.

"I think you can come whenever you want."

"Gee, thanks, Al."

We got into the shower and soaped each other down. I sudsed up her boobs and somehow we wound up on the floor with the shower water attacking my ass, and I supposed that was as good a stimulation as any.

"That's all she wrote, honey. That was my last and best shot," I said to her. "I've got to write today. I got to save the rest of my strength."

I wondered how I was going to make it through the next ten hours. I needed to eat, I needed to sleep, I needed to get rid of Silvia. It was 11:30.

"Hurry up," I told her.

"What's your hurry?" she wanted to know.

"Just hurry," I commanded, and practically dressed her. Last night's red and sequined party dress looked ridiculous and I didn't have the right grooming utensils for her to get her black, lacquered-looking hair in shape. It didn't matter, I assured her. She could fix everything when she got home. Then she started telling me about her bank customers, the ones who always came to her window, and how they chatted with her and how one wanted to be a writer—she had written a short story—and would I read it? Of course, of course, I said, debating whether to give her cab fare. I decided I would—that would be a gentlemanly thing to do—and just when I took out a $20 bill—I didn't have anything smaller—the doorbell rang and I answered it and Anna stood there in a white shawl, looking heartachingly depressed and beautiful, saying, "Is that twenty for me?"

"No," I answered, surprised that she was early, "it's for her." And I pointed to Silvia who was applying her rouge in the mirror over my living room couch.

Anna half smiled and said, "I knew I was disturbing you," and I told her that she didn't understand, that she didn't understand at all. Silvia turned and looked at us and marched into the foyer where we were standing and said to me, "I thought you were going to work today."

"I am. This is Anna Calzolari. She's a very fine actress."

"It's a pleasure," Silvia purred sarcastically.

I realized that I was holding the $20 bill. I didn't know what to do with it. I just wanted to get rid of Silvia, so I told Anna to have a seat on the couch and I went to the bedroom and fetched Silvia's little black evening bag and stuffed the money inside. Silvia came looking for me. She was furious, but I didn't give a shit. "You turn them over pretty fast, don't you?" she accused. I didn't answer. What difference did it make?

"I put something in your purse for cab fare," I said to her, hoping that would expedite matters.

"What the hell are you doing! Giving me a tip!" She was shouting loud enough for Anna to hear. The whole thing was getting messy.

"You're taking it wrong," I explained. "I just meant . . ."

But she didn't wait around for explanations. She stormed out of the bedroom, out of the apartment, looking a little silly in her fancy red dress. She didn't even say good-bye and slammed the door so violently that I jumped.

"It's been a crazy morning," I said to Anna who was looking around the living room.

"I can see. I feel bad that I've broken into the middle of . . ."

"First of all, I want you to stop saying that. And second of all, Silvia's not what she seems."

"I never presume anything," Anna said diplomatically.

"She's a bank teller."

"That's nice."

"She was at my nephew's wedding last night. My nephew Johnny. He got married in Forest Hills. Wait till I tell you about it."

"I want to hear," Anna said. "But first I want to look around your place."

"It's nothing more than a two-bedroom motel room," I explained. "I haven't had time to fix it up the way I'd like to."

110

"How long have you lived here?"

"Five years. But I've been busy."

"I've never seen a place quite like this," she said. She walked into the second bedroom which I used as a study. There was nothing in there except a typewriter on a stand, a typing chair, an easy chair and a stack of maybe five hundred editions of the *Racing Form*. I considered it bad luck to throw them out.

"This is where you do your serious work," she commented.

"Which reminds me," I said, "that we better get started. My appetite's returned."

We walked over to Fifth Avenue and started heading down toward the Village. Anna said there was a nice place around Tenth Street where we could get salads. I wanted meat, but I didn't say anything because I could see that she needed to walk for a while. I tried to get her to talk to me, to tell me what was in her heart, but she was looking very forlorn, and any attempts on my part to lift her spirits were not very successful.

"So you're really down in the dumps," I said to her.

"I don't want to go into the whole thing. It's long and boring and you've heard it before."

"No, I haven't."

"Then you've surely written it before."

"Heartache hurts," I said.

"I'm not sure it's even heartache. There's just something about us. We can't stand being together and we can't stand being apart. And yet I was certain that taking this role and changing my whole life around would . . ." Her voice trailed off and her eyes began to tear. Watching women cry upsets me to no end. And having Anna next to me made me forget that I was still groggy, hung over and half-dead from balling Silvia. We walked some more and she kept her head down and looked like a lost puppy. Her hair was loose and fell to her shoulders and now she was crying softly and there was something about the way Anna cried that afternoon that really shook me up. Because her cry sounded so hopeless and so lonely. I knew she had really been hurt by that bum and I was ready to kill him.

We arrived at the restaurant and, once inside, I wasn't terribly comfortable. This wasn't exactly my kind of joint. Lots of beards and skinny broads with frizzy hair. The walls were full

111

of photographs and drawings of weird things like clothespins and bottle caps. A few sketches showed people screwing and, though I didn't exactly approve of such art hanging in public places, at least it was more interesting to look at than clothespins.

I ordered a beer and she ordered white wine and mushroom salad and I got into a vegetable casserole which was hot and strange and not altogether bad. Maybe there was something to this kind of stuff, I started thinking; maybe I could give up meat and booze and betting and start getting into shape. Maybe I'd even try jogging.

"I don't know what he wants," she said as she nibbled on her salad. She really wasn't eating. "I thought he wanted me to do this show, and he said so, he said that's what he wants, but now that I'm doing it he seems even . . . even . . ."

"Crazier?" I suggested.

"Not crazy, but just restless and unhappy with himself. I tell him that I want to help him. We've been through so much together that now it seems stupid to throw the whole thing away."

"I'd like to break his arms. I want to know what he did to you last night."

"It's not what he did, it's just what he said."

"Tell me."

"I don't want to hear the words again and besides, it's not him, I know it's not really him. It's just what happens when he hasn't been working and when the world starts caving in on him. He can't contain the frustration and he lets it fly."

"At you."

"Only because I'm the only one around."

"He's a bully."

"He's a baby. He had this play he was reading, and there was a producer involved. Everything was set to go, Al, but then it . . ."

"I know, I know. It fell apart and he went nuts."

"He couldn't help but be down."

"You're too understanding, Anna. You're crazy to be so understanding."

"I'm not understanding enough. I thought I had it all under control, I thought I knew what he wanted and I was willing to give it to him. And now . . ."

112

"For Christ's sake, just tell me what happened."

"I already told you. He left."

"You were arguing and he got up and left."

She nodded.

"Which is how he really twists the knife in your back."

She continued to nod.

"He's dirt," I told her. "He's nothing but dirt."

"Stop it, Al!" Now she was pleading through her tears. "You don't know him. I live with this man. I love this man. I'm doing your goddamn soap opera just so . . ."

"So you want to quit? Is that what you're telling me?"

"I don't know what I want. Right now I don't know a goddamn thing except that it hurts. It hurts me and it hurts John."

"He'll be back," I announced confidently.

"Why do you say that?"

"Money. He'll be back because you'll be earning. He's probably been asking people in the business about the show. He realizes that it's a bigger deal than he had first imagined. Now he knows about me, he's found out how much power I have with the network and he sees that you might really be on to something major. For a guy who's so full of himself, he's shaking in his boots. He can't stand the fact that you're going to be successful."

And then she just said, "John." Her mouth was open and her eyes were not on mine.

"What about John?" I wanted to know.

"John," she repeated, and I realized she was looking across the room at a guy and a gal who were sitting down at a table and laughing and holding hands and obviously having a ball. "That's John."

I threw back my beer and thought a second. A crisis. We had run into a crisis. "What do you want to do?" I asked her.

"I, I . . ." But she couldn't talk. I could see her head shaking and her hands shaking. I could see that she was on the verge of tears again, and I could see the anger and hurt and rage building. I didn't know what the fuck to do. And then suddenly he spotted us and he got up from his table and walked across the restaurant and stood there, inches away from me and from her.

I looked at him and I thought to myself that he was good-looking, all right, just like a hundred guys I had known from the old neighborhood. The kind that were always stuck on themselves. The movie-star types with long, black, wavy hair and big asses which they swaggered like women. He had a sneer on his face and I hated him.

"You want to introduce me to your friend?" he asked.

I guessed that he thought by taking the lead he would push the pressure off himself onto her. A miserable strategy if there ever was one. I looked at Anna who looked at him and then looked at me and I said, "I'm Al Gonfio."

He ignored me—as though I weren't there—and said to her, "Pretty bold of you showing up here with your old man."

I didn't know what he meant by "old man," but I didn't like it.

"You pig," she said, looking over at his table where his girl-friend who wasn't at all ugly was waiting for him. "You don't have the decency to . . ."

"Don't talk about decency," he shot back.

"This is Al," she said. "He writes . . ."

"Don't tell me what he writes," John snapped. He wouldn't give her a chance to talk. He was browbeating her to death.

She fought back in a voice which was just as tough as his. "You show up at my favorite restaurant with some trick . . ."

"Trick? Are you kidding? Do you know who Sally Bernstein is? Have you seen her work? She's got her own show over at . . ."

"Leave me alone, John. Get the hell out of here and leave me alone."

"Just thought I'd say hello," he quipped.

"You've said it, and I don't want to hear anything, I don't want to hear about Sally Bernstein or . . ."

"You brought it up. You called her a goddamn whore."

"Leave the lady alone," I broke in. I had heard enough.

"Listen, Pops," he turned to me.

"Stop it, John," she pleaded. "Just turn around and get out of here."

"What are you? The proprietress of this place? What right do you have giving me orders?" he barked.

"I'm not telling," she said, understanding his potential for violence, "I'm asking."

"Well, I'm *telling*," I said.

"I warned you, Pops. Stay the hell out of this. I'm talking to the bitch, not to you."

I got up and slugged him. I slugged him square in the jaw, and he collapsed over the table next to us, and the couple eating there—two broads—screamed and when he tried to get up and come at me I slugged him again. I landed a right across his mouth. I smashed a couple of his teeth and there was some blood and Anna was beside herself and Sally Bernstein came running over and I threw a twenty on the table and took Anna by the hand.

"I'm getting you the hell out of here," I said. And before she knew it I had us back in a cab. She was sobbing, angry and confused, demanding that we go back to make sure John was all right. I told her that he wasn't all right, that he was the biggest turd to hit the streets since King Kong dropped a load on his way to the World Trade Center, but that he wasn't hurt. She wanted to know where we were going and I told her that we were going to my place. We were cutting out the bullshit and going to work.

And that's what happened. At first she was still too shook up to think about anything but John being flattened in the restaurant, but I was so exhilarated by what I had done, and I was so desperately behind in my script, that I somehow bullied my way through her apprehensions into her imagination.

"Get your mind off that asshole!" I demanded, "and think about young Brian MacNiece. Help me out, will you? Can't you see that I'm dying here?"

And she did. She helped. Slowly she turned her mind toward me and my problems and my script. We sat there in my apartment and began to discuss what was going to happen to these characters. And for a while she forgot about her Mr. Wonderful and I forgot about my Mr. Costein and little by little the story started moving, the story started exciting me, exciting Anna, because we could do with these characters whatever we liked. They weren't real. They were our puppets and we were playing a game and the game was fun and Anna was great at it. She'd close her eyes and she'd be there. Right there in Troy. And I'd follow her; I saw what she saw, and I liked what she saw. The seed had been planted and the seed was growing.

Pots and pots of coffee, hours and hours of "Brian would do

this" and "Prudence would do that." And we went on and on; we couldn't stop jabbering; we didn't want to stop jabbering. Anna, now in the easy chair, her feet folded beneath her behind, me at the typewriter banging the keys like Liberace. It was late, and we were laughing and making fun of the characters, and all the women who would be slurping up this shit. We'd talk about this hot nun and this asshole pretty boy, and the sloppier the sentiment the better, because we were doing it, we were going after the bread, the big bread, and we both knew the way to get it. We both came from the same place and we were both going to the same place. We took off our shoes and socks and we were jumping around like little kids because it didn't matter, none of it mattered, and there was more talk talk talk, more plot plot plot until we finally started to wind down and Anna rested her head on a pillow and stretched out on the couch.

Looking at Anna, looking at this exquisitely delicate creature, I started to write for real. I wrote quickly and effortlessly. I wrote as the night turned a softer black, as black became heavy gray, as light turned the gray to dawn. And by morning, I was through. My scripts were there. I felt better than I had ever felt in my entire life. I felt like picking up Anna and carrying her into my bedroom and undressing her and loving her and telling her that I understood, I understood why she was always coming over to my apartment. But I didn't. Instead I walked over to the easy chair and leaned over and kissed her on her sweet forehead. She reacted with a dreamy smile, and that was enough for me—at least for now—because I realized that she was saving my life just as surely as I was saving hers.

13

The golf course set looks remarkably real, although it consists of nothing more than a few yards of plastic grass and a painted tree of papier-mâché. Baxter MacNiece is dressed country club conservatively—Lacoste golfing shirt, softly tailored trousers. Brian MacNiece's clothes are equally understated, but they are tight enough to reveal the fine, muscular condition of his body. His blond hair glistens in the sunlight. His smile lights up the screen. The two men wait their turn to tee off from the tenth hole. Another party is ahead of them.

"Hell of a lucky shot back there, son," Baxter claims. His voice is loud and self-assured.

"Thanks," Brian answers, losing his smile. He is more than slightly annoyed that his father is so stingy with praise.

"You know," the older man says, looking around, "you should try and get out here more often. You should be making more use of this club. It's important. Do you realize that more real business is transacted on the links than . . ."

"I've heard the line before, Dad."

"It's not a line, son. It's the simple truth. And I must say that I take exception to your antisocial attitude. Ever since you and Sally moved back to Troy, you've displayed, well, almost contempt for your old circle of friends."

"What circle are you talking about, Dad?"

"The Warburton boy, for example. And Tommy Stevens."

"You happened to mention two guys who are running their fathers' companies. Two guys whom I barely knew in high school."

"Not true, Brian. Not true in the least."

"Buck Warburton's interested in staying drunk and chasing women, and Tommy Stevens is really no different. That's how they were as teenagers, and that's how they are now."

"You're not turning puritan on me, are you, Brian?" Baxter turns on his devilish smile. "I won't have any son of mine turning puritan. I've always said that a man who works hard earns more than his money. He also earns his pleasure."

"It's their style I object to. They're still kids. Overgrown fraternity boys."

"The hell with their style," retorts Mr. MacNiece. "What about their business?"

"Now we've come to the point."

"I hope to God you have nothing against new business."

"Nothing in the world. As long as it interests me."

"How do you know what's going to interest you until you get to reacquaint yourselves with these boys? Their companies are growing and their problems must be immense and highly complex."

"Business problems," Brian sighs.

"Might I remind you that our bread and butter is servicing the business of this great community."

"You sound like an ad."

Baxter angrily turns and says, "Damn it, son, you're being contrary and disagreeable. I don't know what in hell you learned back there in Yale, but in my day the professors taught us that business is what makes this country go 'round. It's nothing to be ashamed of, and as long as you go around with your nose stuck up in the air you're going to be making damn little contribution to the firm. I might take that from some other new associate, but not from my own son. If you only knew how I've looked forward to this day, how I'd run around telling everyone that you were in your second year of law school, and then your third, and then you were graduating and coming home. The day I walked down the hallway to your little office and saw you sitting there, I must tell you, son, that was a very big moment in my life. Damn big. Sure, I know that Troy takes some getting used to after the East. That's understandable. But you look at Sally, you see how she's joined the Junior League. Why she's delighted to be back in the thick of things. Small communities

118

have their comforts. And I don't want you to forget that the MacNiece name means something in Troy. Means a great deal, in fact."

"I understand that, Dad. And I don't want to disappoint you. It's just that . . ."

"It's just what? Tell me, son."

"The work is different than what I had envisioned."

"Ours is a good, solid, reputable general practice. Let me remind you that it's taken me years to develop our clientele, and I'm not ashamed to say that it's one of the most enviable in this part of the state."

"I realize that," Brian says somewhat sheepishly.

"I certainly hope so. And by the way, when you get back to the office I want you to do me a favor."

"What is it?"

"Someone named Sister Prudence came by to see me. A rather aggressive nun, I must say. Something about trouble with her landlord. The convent's lease is in dispute. The landlord wants to evict them. Sounds like a charity case to me. Anyway, I told her I would be turning over the matter to our leading expert in contracts. I gave her your name this morning and said you'd call her. Use your own judgment. If you want to bother with it, fine. A little goody-goody work might soothe your conscience. Word might also leak back to the Taggart brothers. They're awfully big in the Catholic Church and I understand their new pharmaceutical plant is costing something like two and a half million. Seems like they're ready to leave old man Nutley. How can a one-man legal firm service a company of that size? Anyway, Brian, you do as you see fit. The nun's your baby, all the way." Baxter laughs heartily.

"Thanks," Brian says without a great deal of excitement.

"Let's go," Father orders. "Looks like the tee is ours."

The actors march off camera. Another station break, another commercial.

Brian's office is extremely small. His Yale law degree hangs on the wall and a color photograph of his wife Sally sits on the credenza behind his desk. He is wearing thin tortoiseshell glasses, reading a brief, when the intercom buzzes. He picks it up, listens and says, "Show her in, please." He returns to his reading, and a few seconds later Sister Prudence is escorted into his office by a secretary. He gets up, comes from behind his desk and asks the nun to be seated. Her face—the depth and the radiance of her beauty—startles him, and he finds himself struggling to stop gazing at her with such intensity.

There is only her face. The rest is covered by her black habit.

As he returns to his swivel chair, as he walks behind his desk, she sees the firmness and strength of his body under his charcoal flannel suit. He sits down, he takes off his glasses, he speaks to her.

"You mentioned a lease on the phone. I hope you have brought it with you." She is struck by the fact that he is all business. There are no pleasantries, as though a discussion of anything other than business would frighten him.

"Yes, I have brought the lease, but before you look at it, I want you to know how grateful I am for your time. I know you are busy, and there certainly must be more profitable cases than this one."

"Please don't thank me, Sister, before I have done anything."

"I feel confident that you will help. There's something about you which gives me confidence."

He looks at her quizzically. His father was right; she is a most aggressive nun. There is something about her. Something about her being in his office . . .

"The lease," he reminds her. "I hope you have brought the lease."

"Of course," she says, startled from her reverie, from her prolonged examination of the length of his blond hair, the width of his nose, the kindness in his eyes. From a small attaché case, she takes out the lease and places it on his desk. It is some six pages long. He looks it over quickly.

"It's rather unusual for a convent to have a short-term lease," he says. "I don't quite understand."

"It was a matter of necessity. Seven years ago, as I understand it, we had to relocate because of a fire. This was the only property in the vicinity that was suitable."

"You weren't here then," he presumes.

120

"No, I wasn't."

He wants to ask her where she was, where she comes from, why she became a nun. But he says not a word. He knows better. There is no reason to get personal.

"If you don't mind, Sister Prudence," he finally says, "I'll take this lease tonight and study it before giving you my opinion one way or another."

"That would be wonderful." She is enthusiastic. She is about to say something else, but she stops herself. There is a brief but very nervous lull. The lawyer and the nun look at each other. The gaze lingers on for a few seconds too long. Finally, in embarrassment, he says, "Well, then, you can expect to hear from me tomorrow."

"Would you like me to tell you about my meeting with Mr. Adams, the landlord?" she asks. "He is quite a peculiar man, quite a unique personality."

"I would rather study the lease first. Then we can talk about personalities."

"Yes," she answers, "by all means. And thank you, thank you again."

She extends her hand and he takes it. They touch. They shake hands tentatively. And the camera stays on them, the camera stays there as they both seem the slightest bit reluctant to end the meeting.

"You must be tired," Hanford Seames said to Anna Calzolari.

"I can't wait to get this habit off. Between the lights and this costume, I'm about to drop."

"If you did, I'd be there to catch you."

She smiled and said nothing.

"How about some dinner?" he asked. "There's a little Cuban place on the West Side that'll make you a believer in the Revolution."

"I wouldn't need much convincing."

"So we're on?"

"Not tonight."

"How come?"

Anna hesitated. "I'm afraid I'm all acted out."

"This is no act," Hanford argued.

"It's just that I have other plans," Anna told him, thinking of how, only last night, John had called and spoken—much to her delight—about coming back.

14

Anna was happy. She was happy because me and Dick and Howard and everyone else at the show were happy. (We hadn't heard from Costein, but that was only because he was waiting to see a few more ratings. When a new segment is introduced in a soap, its success is often a matter of word of mouth—housewife calling housewife—and it takes a while for the word to get around.) But Anna was mainly happy because Palermo had come back.

This evening she busied herself around the apartment—watering the plants, clearing away dishes. At one point she actually heard herself whistling, something Anna was not inclined to do. Still, tonight was special: Her television role was working out. She had been at it over two months, and her salary seemed enormously high. And John had come back, his moods had been even, almost serene; they had fought less in these past few days than in any other period that Anna could remember. And now in only an hour or so they would be attending a party, a happy Thanksgiving party with the promise of food and friends and the kind of fun Anna hadn't enjoyed in far too long.

John emerged from the bathroom, naked and lovely, the dark hair on his chest glistening with the wet of the shower. Anna looked at him, admiring the wonderful leanness of his body, the definition in the muscles of his stomach, the bold swell of his thighs, the broad width of his nose, his neck, his arms, his cock.

She went to him and, despite the fact that he was still dripping with water, she kissed and hugged and whispered, "Don't walk around here like that. I'll wind up attacking you and we'll miss the party."

"Can't do that," he replied, obviously in a good mood himself. "Too many people I need to see. Couple of directors and producers are going to be there. And I understand at least one is very interested in meeting me."

"That's wonderful!" she exclaimed.

"We'll see what happens, but apparently a few big films are going to be shot after the first of the year here which require dark Italian types with thick New York accents. Big productions, big money."

"I can feel it," Anna said. "All week I've felt that your world is coming together, honey."

"How did your taping go today?" he asked, demonstrating highly unusual consideration.

"Everyone was really pleased. I think I've got the character down."

"You had that nun nailed the first minute you put on the habit, didn't you?"

"It was sort of natural."

"I just don't want to see you sneaking into church when I'm not looking."

"We could make love in the confession booth," she said. "That's something I've always wanted to do."

They laughed and kissed and John started getting dressed while Anna showered. He put on the new clothes he had bought this week—with her money—and they made him look dramatic and even more handsome. The black twill pants were tight around his ass, tight around his crotch. He wore the gray wool shirt with the tiny collar and left the top three buttons undone. He put a racing-green cashmere scarf around his neck, and then went for the last item, the best item: a thin blood-red belt of genuine snakeskin which had cost him—or her—$40. He couldn't resist, and he bought it because he knew that Anna would appreciate the choice. He splashed on a great deal of cologne and went to his drug drawer where he sat down and prepared his evening entertainment. He took his time as he

123

rolled a half-dozen exceptionally fat joints and carefully stuffed a vial with a half-gram of fresh cocaine. For good measure, he treated himself to a quick snort and then walked over to the mirror for inspection. Goddammit, he thought to himself, this is going to be *my* fucking night.

Anna appeared in her robe. She looked at him and praised his clothes, praised his taste, didn't say a word about his extravagance. For a second, the thought of his indulgence crossed her mind, but she remembered to be happy because he was happy; she remembered to be happy because he was there.

She wore a billowy skirt that a friend had brought back from Turkey a year ago—it was yellow and green and pleated and made her feel free—and a simple but strikingly elegant bone-white silk blouse that she had bought the day that she cashed her first *Search for Happiness* paycheck. It had cost $80 in one of the Village's better boutiques.

John, already a little high, didn't comment on her appearance. "What do you think?" she finally had to prod him.

"I think we should smoke a joint before we go."

"I mean about the way I look."

"You always look fine," he said, still not noticing the new blouse or the fact that tonight she had chosen to wear her hair down, letting it fall to her shoulders.

No matter, she decided. The rhythm was right. The evening was going to be good.

The grass *was* good. It brought a certain serenity to her eyes. John seemed smoky and enchanting and when he said, "I just need a little kick in the head and then we can go," she didn't object. She watched him line up a thin row of snow and snort it through a straw and when she said, "I think I'll have a hit myself, the taping can really be tiring," he hesitated, just for a second—as if to say, this is mine, not yours—but he finally prepared her a small treat and handed her the straw. The cocaine picked her up and a few minutes later they were flying out the door.

They wore coats and they wore hats—his a taxi-driver-looking cap, hers a wildly-feathered floppy model. They looked terrific on the street—young artists on their way up, young artists throwing caution to the wind—and John hailed a cab which sped them out of SoHo, out of the Lower East Side, over to the old West Village.

The party was in a penthouse in an apartment building on Sixth Avenue. The host was a fashion designer, a local celebrity named Eloise, who knew both John and Anna from just being around the Village art scene. Eloise was a kook who had hit big. She was one of New York City's more flamboyant dressers. She was not pretty, but the fact that tonight she was wearing an orange tubular space suit and green glasses the size of the moon made you forget what she once might have looked like. "I call this Disco Venus," she described her outfit to Anna and John, "after my new rock group. I'm doing all their things—have you heard?—down to their jocks. I'm into painting hair, I'm into painting teeth, I may wire the group in neon, I may live in a missile, I'm the first designer of the nuclear age, I'm delivered, I'm primitive, and I welcome you two beautiful creatures to my party."

"Eloise is really fucked up," John whispered to Anna as they edged their way toward the throbbing heart of the party.

The penthouse was large and split-leveled. There were disco lights and two bars serving booze. Eloise was throwing a hell of a bash. The place was jammed, the music was pulsating. The guests ranged from punk rockers—in angry T-shirts and palm tree buttons from Fiorucci—to salt-and-pepper publishers, petite ballet dancers, avant-garde composers with wrinkly noses and dirty fingernails, high-fashion models incredibly tall and tight-faced. Everyone was impressed that he or she was actually there, impressed with the other guests, straining to see and looking to be seen, and everywhere the cloying aroma of weed or hashish, conversation hyped up by the gin and the Scotch and the wine, the extravagance of Eloise, the madness of the Village, the success of bohemia and Thanksgiving in the big city.

John and Anna went their separate ways. It was impossible to stay together at such affairs. There was a time when Anna had tried—she preferred to spend the whole evening with John —but she had learned long ago that he liked to roam and navigate from one whirling cocktail circle to another, talking here, pausing there, lingering and moving on at will. Anna had taught herself not to mind and tonight—especially tonight—she had no

125

hesitation about tackling this party on her own. She milled around for a while, she hung around the edges of conversations, she was deciding whom to look at or listen to next when someone said, "Why, if it isn't the highest paid nun in America."

"Gwen!" Anna exclaimed, ignoring her friend's sarcasm. "I'm really glad to see you. I've meant to call, I've meant to . . ."

"Intentions really don't mean crap, do they?" Gwen asked.

She was wearing satiny beige pants and a brown Danskin top which pressed and expanded her enormous breasts.

"Let's not fight," Anna pleaded. "It's a party. It's Thanksgiving."

"And you've got one shitload of stuff to be thankful for."

"I'm not unhappy, Gwen."

"Why should you be? You've got the grace of God and the glory of the networks on your side."

"How's the play coming?" Anna asked, again sidestepping her friend's sarcasm. "I hear you have a fine replacement."

"You've heard right. And it looks like we have the deal with PBS."

"That's wonderful."

"Do you really think so?" Gwen asked angrily, turning her head so her soft bouncy curls did a small dance atop her head.

"Yes, I think so. I want you to succeed. You mean a great deal to me."

"I'd like to believe that."

"There's no reason not to, Gwen. I did what I did out of necessity."

Gwen glanced over at John Palermo charming a group of women. She pointed out the scene to Anna. "Look," Gwen said, "that's your necessity. He's as necessary as scarlet fever."

"I don't want to hear it anymore, Gwen. Your snipes are boring."

"And how do you think I felt," Gwen finally exploded, "when I turned on the tube the other day and saw you playing that candy-assed nun? Do you think I was bored? Do you think I was thrilled to see someone with your talent doing some dip-shit part in a goddamn cartoon for retarded adults?"

"It's a joke," Anna argued. "I close my eyes and go through the motions like it's a joke, like it's a dream."

126

"It's no dream and it's no joke because you're good, you're real. You're so good it scares me. And it's a waste and a shame and it stinks. It really does stink, Anna." Now Gwen was shouting, and even in the din of the celebration, her voice could be heard above the music and conversation.

Suddenly John, who had heard the last remark, appeared at Anna's side. "What you need," he said to Gwen, "is a little less self-confidence and a lot more stiff cock."

Gwen shot him the finger, whirled around and lost herself in the party. Anna started to follow her, but John intervened. "Fuck that bitch!" he exclaimed. "She just wants her tits squeezed."

The rest of the party was downhill from there. John continued circulating among the festive. He found a director and discovered that there was indeed a movie but no part. He found an agent who had once refused to accept John as a client and who, contrary to the spirit of Thanksgiving, refused once again. And as John's spirits dampered, so did Anna's. She danced a few dances with an old friend of hers. She spoke to a couple of her ex-colleagues from the Living Rock Theatre, and by their aloofness she knew that they shared Gwen's attitude. Someone offered her a burning pipe stuffed with dope and she accepted it with thanks; she kept the marijuana in her lungs for a very long time and when she finally exhaled she wanted to cry. She had come to the party feeling like a star; now she felt like a traitor.

When John saw that he wasn't scoring with the directors and the agents, he turned to the women, and he made sure that Anna was watching. He approached an ex-girlfriend and kissed her on the mouth. He danced with a redheaded model, continually rubbing his crotch against hers. He smoked and he drank and when Anna said she wanted to go, he said that she'd have to wait. He tried one more hustle—a playwright whom he had known at City College—but the playwright didn't remember John and didn't feel like talking about his new play which was about to be produced. "Call me when you have a chance," he told John, and then added, "sometime after the first of the year."

By the time they left it was after two. Three whole turkeys had been devoured and only the stragglers were left. Eloise herself had deflated her space tubes and passed out in a chair. The disco tape continued to run, but the dancers had cut the rhythm in half; now they moved in slow motion. Earlier, in frustration and anger, John had actually tried to pick up a girl, but he had been spurned. That only made matters worse.

He was furious in the cab, furious and stoned, and all he spoke of was the asshole director and the asshole agent, the assholes of the world who think they're so fucking important they won't give you the time of day. Well, what difference does it make? he said, because their movies and their plays are only shit anyway, shit and nothing but shit and Eloise is a freak and the whole goddamn party was nothing but a bunch of freaks. Anna knew to remain silent, though she worried that even her silence might be too loud.

Back in the loft he finished off the vial of coke, offering none to Anna. Then he ripped off his shirt and his pants and stood in front of their mattress/bed and demanded that she come to him. She did, she gave him what he wanted, and she was not altogether displeased. Now he lay on the bed and he said to her, "I want you to get undressed and talk like Gwen. I want you to pretend that you're Gwen, and I'm going to pretend that you're Gwen, I'm going to be playing with Gwen's huge tits and sucking Gwen's fat cunt. I'm going to be fucking Gwen and you're going to be Gwen getting fucked by me."

"I don't like that, John. It's not a game that I like."

"You get pissed at me when I get up and leave, well, one of the reasons I leave is because I get tired of the same old shit. And if you're too goddamned square to do a little role-playing number, I've had it. I swear I've had it."

"We can play games, we can have fun, but not with Gwen."

"I'm telling you that I want you to be Gwen. Talk like Gwen, goddammit, or I'm getting the hell out of here!"

She knew that he'd act on his threat. She thought for a second, and she decided to do it.

She searched for her friend's speech patterns, her friend's accent. She said a few things in Gwen's voice—about the size of Gwen's breasts, about how bad Gwen wanted to be fucked by John—and it worked. She was good at it; she was superb.

He became excited and he told her to talk more, to talk in that nonstop, hustling way in which Gwen spoke. And he pictured Gwen's Danskin top and Gwen's breasts as he fondled Anna, as

128

Anna sucked him again, even as he sucked her. Even as he bit her, as she cried in protest, as he bit harder, as she tried to move away, as he turned her over, and jackhammered her from behind, too suddenly, too quickly, calling her Gwen, having her say yes, yes, she was Gwen. And by the time he had come, her small breasts were bruised and her womb cried for more. She demanded more. And this time, aroused by the scene, still aroused by the thought of fucking Gwen, he answered her cry. She lay on her back. She raised her legs straight to the ceiling. And she took him. And he slammed against her, hard, harder, she demanded, as she cried, as she felt the bone of his soul up in her heart, up in her throat. As she faded and sank into the softness of the sea.

15

The scenery boys have done a good job with the park. On camera, it looks real. There's a bench, several bushes, a bed of flowers and a narrow pathway. Brian, in suit and tie, is seated on the bench reading a book. He seems very far away. Suddenly someone calls his name—"Mr. MacNiece, Mr. MacNiece." He looks up and sees Sister Prudence standing in front of him. He puts down his book. He seems almost too startled to speak.

"How nice to see you." She speaks before he does. "Do you often come here?"

"Why, no, but today the sun was shining for the first time in a week, and I felt like walking rather than eating."

"What a lovely idea," she says, "and what a happy coincidence for both of us."

"Please sit down," he offers. She joins him on the bench. "Do you come here often?" he asks her, only now adjusting to her presence.

"Ursula is just across the street. You knew that, didn't you?" she questions him.

He hesitates. "Oh, yes, of course."

"May I ask you what you're reading?" she inquires.

"Certainly. Just a book of poetry." He fingers the book somewhat nervously.

"Who is the poet?" Sister Prudence persists.

"T. S. Eliot."

"And which of his poems?"

"The *Four Quartets*. Do you know them?"

"Yes, I love them. I always thought them to be prayers. I've always felt them as stunningly beautiful meditations."

"They allowed you to read such non-Catholic poetry in your religious schools?"

"As much as they allowed you to read poetry in law school." He smiles. "I've always read what I've wanted to read," he says. "I'm not much good when restrictions are placed on me."

"I'm afraid," she replies, "that deep down I'm the same way." She thinks about what she has just said and adds, "Besides, Eliot's poetry is rather religious, don't you agree?"

"I suppose it depends upon your point of view. I find that his poems contain more questions than answers."

"I understand. But at a certain point, there's a definite declaration of faith."

"I must say that I'm surprised that we're having this discussion," he declares.

"Why?" she asks.

"Because I intended to call you as soon as I walked back to the office and discuss not T. S. Eliot, but rather your lease with S. J. Adams."

"Let's discuss it now," she urges. "Mr. Eliot can wait."

"It's a very tight lease. I'm surprised that you people ever agreed to it."

"I explained that those were very different circumstances. And different people."

"I see very little hope, Sister Prudence, except perhaps in reasoning with this man."

"I've tried."

"And what about the mother superior?"

130

"She's entrusted this matter to me. If she could have been effective, I know she would have tried."

"Then I will call Adams," Brian announces. "I'll set up a meeting and see what I can do."

"What could you possibly do? I practically begged the man."

"I'm certain that begging is not the way. I'd like to take another approach with him. But before I do, I may give him a call, just to sound him out. I can't promise you anything, Sister Prudence."

"You've said that before."

"And I say it again because it's true. Right now you'll just have to have a little . . . a little faith in me."

She smiles broadly and says simply, "That won't be difficult."

The camera leaves them looking at each other. In a few seconds a man will tell us why Bufferin is stronger than aspirin.

"That Cuban restaurant is hotter than ever," Hanford mentioned again.

"The heat's gotten to you, huh?" Anna quipped.

"Listen, today you were pretty hot yourself."

"All the sizzle's coming from you."

"My stomach's empty. Come with me tonight. Let me buy you dinner."

"I can't."

"What's wrong? Due back in the convent?"

"If only it were that simple," Anna said, thinking of John. "Listen, you've still got a lot of taping ahead of you today. By the time you get through fighting with Sally and Papa Baxter, you won't even want to think about me."

"That's what you think," he winked.

We're in Brian's home. The den is pleasant. Lots of good furniture. Bentwood rocker. Big fireplace. Gleaming, stained hardwood floor. He's just gotten in from work. Sally brings him a drink. She's blond and cheerleader cute, well-meaning but shallow, the perfect suburban spouse.

"Remember that dinner party that I mentioned to you?" she asks him as she hands him his cocktail. They sit on the couch.

131

"No, not really," he answers, loosening his tie.

"You don't listen to me, Brian. I don't think anything I say sinks in."

"Please, Sally, let's not make a big thing out of it. I'm sorry I've forgotten. But tell me now, I'm listening."

"I've wanted to have a dinner party. A really elegant dinner party. I've been talking about it now for nearly six months. I think it's time that we did some real entertaining."

He's not happy to hear this, but he's too tired to fight. "If that will make you happy, fine. I'm willing."

"It's not simply to make *me* happy. It's to make *us* happy."

"I'll be happy to see you happy," he lies.

"How about three weeks from tomorrow?" she asks.

"Fine."

"That's *wonderful!*" she exclaims, taking a very long time to get out the word *wonderful*. Her speech is squeaky and the slightest bit pretentious. "Let me read you the list of people I want to invite."

He groans to himself. This is just what he doesn't want to hear. As Sally bounces out of the room to fetch her guest list, Brian rubs his eyes. We see the strain of his day, the strain of his life. Sally is back with her pencil and paper.

"I'll read the names," she says excitedly, "and you give me a nay or yea. Here goes. The Magilows, they're always fun. Naturally Tom and Pat Bromer—they're going to the Bahamas, but I think they'll be back by then. The Warburtons, the Stevenses, the . . ."

"Wait," Brian stops her. "Just wait a minute."

"What's wrong?"

"My father had nothing to do with this, did he?"

"I don't understand."

"I do. He's been after me to hustle Stevens's and Warburton's business. And I want to know if Dad put you up to inviting them."

"Honestly, Brian, I can't remember everything your father suggests to me. Darling, why are you being so difficult? It's fun to socialize. It's fun to give fancy parties and decorate the house with beautiful flowers and plan divine dinners and . . ."

"Please, Sally, let's talk about it another time."

"Is anything wrong? Did something go wrong at the office today?"

"No, nothing went wrong. I just have a new case that I want to look over, if you don't mind."

"Is it an interesting case?"

"It concerns a convent."

"A convent?"

"Yes, the Ursula sisters."

"The ones who have the school over on Hillside Avenue?"

"That's right."

"And they need your help?"

"I'm not sure. I'm not yet familiar with the case. I've met with one of the nuns. They're having a problem with the lease."

"You met with the mother superior?"

"No, it was Sister Prudence."

"She wasn't one of those modern nuns, was she?"

"I don't know what you mean."

"You know, the kind who wears dresses which show her knees."

"No, I'm afraid not. She wore the traditional habit. She did seem very young, though."

"And pretty?" Sally wants to know.

"How could I tell? Nuns cover themselves."

"Her face wasn't covered, was it?"

"No, Sally, her face wasn't covered."

"Well, was she pretty? Was this nun pretty?"

"I can't remember. She came to me with a legal problem. I was looking at her lease, not her face," he lies again.

"Young nuns have always worried me," Sally says in a very strange voice.

"Sally, what are you talking about?"

"I don't know. I just think the idea of a young, pretty girl hiding behind a habit . . . there's something, something spooky about that."

"There's nothing spooky about this nun, I can assure you. She's a highly intelligent, highly attractive . . ."

"*Attractive?*" Sally stops her husband.

He realizes his mistake, and in a huff he opens his attaché

case, pulls out some papers and begins to read. "Why don't you start getting dinner while I look over this brief?"

She gets up and starts to walk to the kitchen. She says nothing else, but, just before she leaves the living room, she turns and looks at her husband who is already absorbed in his work. Her face reveals a certain concern.

The camera dollys in on Brian's face. He looks tired and worried.

"Glad to see you're here so early in the morning." His father pops his head in his son's office. He sits down and puts his feet up on Brian's desk. Baxter's suit is gray and meticulously tailored. Brian looks collegiate in a blue blazer. "First time I can remember your being here at this hour. It's not even eight yet. Just hope you're not trying to show up the old man."

"Don't worry, Dad. It's just that this case is bothering me."

"What case?"

"Ursula. I can't believe these nuns got themselves in such a fix."

"Oh, so you decided to help them out."

"How can I refuse?"

"Easy. Say no," he says smugly.

"There's got to be some loophole." Brian ignores his father's last remark. "I'm tempted now just to pick up the phone and call the landlord."

"What's his name?"

"S. J. Adams."

"Good luck," Baxter smirked. "There's no way in hell you'll get any consideration out of that SOB. Old man Adams is the original Scrooge, son. I'll tell you that right now."

"I'm calling him," Brian states bluntly.

"You're acting foolishly, Brian," the senior MacNiece declares. "If you're not careful, you're going to make an even worse mess of this case."

That's all Brian needs to hear. "For God's sake, Dad, will you leave me alone! One day you ask me to work on this, and the next day you're already telling me what to do."

"Just trying to be helpful."

"I'll handle this in my own way, if you don't mind."

"I don't mind," the father asserts, "as long as you watch

your involvement. After this, no more *pro bono* cases. They wind up costing us more in time than we gain in goodwill. I don't want you to become obsessed with this thing."

Baxter MacNiece straightens his fine silk tie, picks himself up and leaves.

Brian picks up the phone and dials a number.

"Mr. Adams? . . . My name is Brian MacNiece and I'm representing the nuns at Ursula. I've taken the liberty of calling you, sir, because I do not have the name of your attorney, and before I go any further . . . Mr. Adams, you don't realize . . . I can't believe . . ." Brian tries to say. "I only want to stress, Mr. Adams, that . . ."

But by now Brian is listening to the sound of a dial tone. Adams has hung up in his face.

Sister Prudence is calling from Ursula. The other side of the split screen shows Brian at his desk.

"I'm sorry to disturb you, Mr. MacNiece, but I missed you in the park today."

"It's not that I go there every day," Brian tells her, speaking from behind his desk.

"Oh, then that's my mistake. I presumed that it was something of a ritual with you. In any event, I was hoping that you'd be there today. I was wondering about our lease."

"I've had time to make only one call."

"And was it fruitful?"

"It's too early to tell," Brian lies. "There's still work to be done."

"I'm not worried, I don't want you to think that I'm worried. I know that you'll accomplish exactly what needs to be accomplished. I want you to know that I have a great deal of confidence in you. I have been praying for you, Mr. MacNiece."

"If you have confidence, why the prayers?"

"The two are not mutually exclusive."

"Sister Prudence, I don't want to appear rude, but there are three gentlemen waiting for me in the conference room right now."

"By all means," she says, "attend to your business. I'm glad things are going so well for you."

"You're assuming too much," he begins to argue.

"I only assume what I feel," she answers before ending the conversation.

"Why can't we at least have a drink," Hanford pursued Anna as they both were leaving the studio. "A drink never hurt anyone."

"You're so wrong," she said.

"You're playing so hard to get," he smiled.

"I'm bushed, I really am. It feels like we taped at least a year's worth of shows tonight. Some other time."

"Promise?" he wanted to know.

"It's a probability," she maintained, "not a promise."

16

I was leaving the studio, getting ready to go home and talk to my bookie while relaxing in a hot tub (yes, I have a phone in the can for such purposes), when someone said there was a call for me. I picked up one of the phones in the control room. It was Silvia, and immediately I had to decide whether I wanted to get laid tonight. It was a question of her tits versus my tiredness. "I'm not sure, Silvia," I heard myself saying. "I'm feeling a little flat right now." She had forgiven me, she had been watching the show, now she loved Sister Prudence and was glad that she got to meet her. She wanted to know what was going to happen next.

"That's just it, baby," I said. "I gotta go home and figure that out." She told me what a good time she had when we were last together. "It was beautiful, wasn't it? she asked. "It was very nice," I told her. "It was really nice, Silvia, but right now my stomach is bothering me—too much lunch, I think—and I better go soak myself in the tub." She squealed and said that she wanted to come along. I considered it for a few seconds. Fucking Silvia in the bathtub could definitely be fun; but no, if I did anything tonight I'd go to the Garden, to the fights. Alone. Banging Silvia was one thing, but putting up with the bullshit of her life and times at the bank was another. I could just picture my patience petering out. So I got rid of her, listened to her giggle good-bye and promised her another time and place.

I grabbed my coat and was about to make my getaway when all of a sudden I was distracted by another woman, this time the Oriental chick, the one who belonged to Costein. She tapped me on the shoulder and said that the kid wanted to see me.

I felt my heart freeze. This was it. But after a few seconds, I realized that there was nothing to panic about. My meeting with the kid was long overdue. I hadn't called him and he hadn't called me. And we both knew why: the numbers were looking better every week. There had been enough time for the Sister Prudence segment to sink in and register and I knew goddamn well that the impact was being felt out there in America and over on Sixth Avenue.

"Is the kid in his office?" I asked his chic little helper who was wearing purple leather boots.

"No, he's waiting for you downstairs in his car."

I gave a little laugh. Waiting in his car, I thought to myself. Fucking guy operates like the mob. I half expected to see him sitting in the back seat between two beefy hit men.

We went downstairs and out the door. I spotted the limo. The long, this-is-a-big-shot's limo. I tried to peek inside but the windows were darkened so I hollered, "Hey, Costein! You're double-parked! Pull your head out of your ass before you get a ticket!" His secretary was a little scandalized, but an electric window smoothly descended and there he was, reading *Runner's World* magazine, all dressed up in nothing but his jogging outfit.

"So that's why you're hiding," I said to him.

"Get in, Gonfio," he ordered, "before you get arrested for disturbing the peace."

I started to climb inside and so did the secretary. "If you wouldn't mind, Miss Lee, I'd rather that you sit up front with Edgar. I'd like this meeting to be private," he announced.

Miss Lee did what she was told. There was a thick Plexiglas partition between us, the driver and the cute little Miss Lee.

"I didn't know you rated a car like this, Costein," I said as we pulled into traffic.

"It makes city life a little easier," he answered.

"Come to think of it," I reminded myself, "there was a story about Brewster Golden and a limo. The reason he quit the network and started beating our brains out down the street was because the boys upstairs wouldn't give him a car. Yeah, he switched networks over a car. And the way I hear it is that now the boys upstairs would give him the whole fucking building on Sixth Avenue to get him back."

Costein smiled, indicating that I heard right.

"So," I continued with my analysis, "they ain't about to make that same mistake twice. I bet you didn't even have to ask for the fucking limo. They probably threw it at you as soon as your numbers started looking good."

"I'm afraid your approach to these things is a little simple-minded, Gonfio," Costein quipped, crossing his legs and looking out the window through his small, dark-tinted glasses.

"As long as you're enjoying the ride, kid, it doesn't matter how you got the car."

"The trappings of the executive life are something which I hardly notice. At best, I find them amusing."

"I don't see you laughing."

"I thought we'd talk a little business, Al. I know you're always ready to talk business. Besides, our meeting's somewhat behind schedule, isn't it?"

"I figure you've been too busy practicing pinball."

Costein smiled against his will.

"You improved any?" I asked him.

"I'm not interested in games."

"Then how'd you get in TV?"

"I view this business scientifically. Naturally I have a sociological overview, but the components themselves are primarily . . ."

"We've had this discussion before. Right now I just want to know where we're going."

"I just told Edgar to drive. I had to get out of the office. My afternoon jog got beeped out and I'm trying to recover."

"Sorry to hear that," I said sympathetically, "but what the hell are you talking about?"

He pointed to a small, radiolike receiver attached to the waistband of his jogging suit, the sort of thing a doctor wears.

"So you can't even run away from it. The shit follows you everywhere."

"Emergencies must be handled."

"Well, I think you've been handling me beautifully."

"How's that?"

"By leaving me the hell alone."

"You're a lucky man, Gonfio. Very lucky, indeed."

I lit up a cigar and the kid said, "If you ran, your lungs would be clean and you'd realize what that smoke is doing to you."

I let down the window and said, "It's too fucking cold to run. And hasn't anyone told you that cigars are good for your digestion. Cigars and grapefruits."

"Let's get out here," he suggested as we pulled up to a small boutique over on Madison. "Pick us up in fifteen minutes," he instructed Edgar. "That'll give you enough time to run Miss Lee home."

"Snazzy dame," I commented as the car pulled away. "Surprised you're not making her a TV star."

He ignored me and walked into the store. I followed. Jogging shoes—the joint sold nothing but jogging shoes and shorts and shirts. I was a little more than slightly pissed. I remember reading about presidents and kings who liked to talk business with their underlings while they, the high and mighty, would take a dump. This was the same thing. The kid wanted me to watch him go about the menial chores of selecting shoes while he toyed with my whole fucking future. I had to string along but, believe me, I wasn't real happy about it.

It was around six-thirty and the joint was jumping. It was packed with bleached and streaked expensive East Side dolls, none of whom looked as though they needed to lose a pound.

"You know, kid, when I was in the army we looked on running as punishment."

"That was a different time," he answered. "You were operating under a radically altered state of values."

"Who the fuck knew about values? We just didn't like to hurt."

"Running is a meditative exercise," he explained.

"I'm sure. You meditate about your miserable aching feet."

A couple of guys who had come into the store reminded me of Hanford Seames—blond and preppy. Ad execs, no doubt. After looking around for a few minutes, we finally had someone come up and wait on us, a character who looked as though he had been rush captain of his fraternity at UCLA. What was happening to my hometown? A band of disgustingly healthy invaders were taking over.

"Let me try on the Etonics," Costein gave the order.

"How about your friend?" the salesboy asked.

"It's too late for me. I'm dying of lung cancer," I said, puffing on my cigar, gleaning a perverse sort of pleasure from smelling up this den of noble aims and pure intentions.

I sat down next to the kid as he tried on the first of what would be many pairs of shoes.

"You're running right on schedule, Al. I want to be straight and tell you that right away." As he spoke to me, he stood and bounced up and down. "Maybe I should stick with the round stud tread."

"I like this nonslip star design," the salesguy tried to sell him.

"I'm not running, kid," I said, maintaining my cool. "I'm just doing what I've always done, just doing what comes naturally."

"I'm not certain." My vice-president shook his head, not wanting to indicate whether he was talking to me or the shoe man. "What model Etonics are these?" he finally asked.

"They call them the Street Fighters," the jogging pro announced.

"Put a pair on my pal," Costein generously offered, pointing to me, trying to make me feel foolish.

"That's awfully sweet of you, boss," I told him. "I especially appreciate the fact that you wear shoes that don't need to be shined."

"You don't think I'd ask you to shine my shoes, do you?" the horse-faced veep wanted to know.

"Probably."

"You've got me wrong, Gonfio. I'm intrigued by you."

The clerk was back with the shoes. He slipped them on me and laced them up. They felt better than any shoes I had ever

140

worn. "Give 'em to me in a run of colors—gray, pink, green, the works," I said. "My uncle here is treating."

"They're just available in the blue and gold."

"Then blue and gold it is," I declared. "My college colors."

"Where'd you go to school?" Mark Costein inquired.

"I can't remember exactly. But there was a lot of ivy. And I caught it. I was so laid up with poison ivy that I decided to quit. That's when I scratched college and developed a scholarly interest in nags."

Costein let all this by him without a comment. He was busy trying on other pairs of shoes. I was still in my Street Fighters and ready to go.

"How many miles you do?" the salesman asked the kid.

"Fifty, sixty. Depends."

"Goddamn," I grunted.

"That's a week, Al."

"I figured it was a month."

"You ought to give it a try. Wonderful, stimulating exercise."

"I think I'll just wear the shoes. I don't want to get them too dirty."

"The show's better. I wanted you to know that the show's better."

"Do I get a new pair of jogging shoes every month?"

"Just keep the nun moving. You've got to keep her moving."

I resented the interference. Now the kid was telling me what to do with my own invention. I was about to tell him that when he suddenly took off, out of the store, wearing still another pair of shoes. "Just taking a little trial jog around the block," he said over his shoulder. "Wait for me."

Wait for him? What the hell else was I going to do? Chase him? He was back in a few minutes, proudly demonstrating the fact that he wasn't even winded.

"I'll take these, too," he told the guy. "And there are a few others I'd like to try."

"I'm getting bored," I announced.

"I'll drop you off at a pinball parlor in a few minutes."

"You'd be doing me a favor, kid."

"What's going to happen to Prudence?" he asked, trying to be nonchalant as he stepped into a pair of yellow training flats.

141

"You're hooked!" I exclaimed. "The fucking boss is hooked on the story."

He did not smile this time. He got up and did a few deep knee bends. He stretched and went into a little jogging jig. "They're fine," he said to the guy. "I'll take these, too."

"You think in terms of stories." Costein turned his tall attention to me. "I don't. My responsibilities go beyond . . ."

"I think I'll wear these shoes home," I interrupted him. "They're doing something strange to my head. I feel like I'm walking on air."

I saw the car pull up in front of the store. Edgar appeared. He had a limp. At least the boss had a heart; he hired the handicapped.

"Charge my account," the kid told the happy salesman who by this time had a healthy order. "Costein, Mark C."

"Yes, sir, and have a good run tomorrow."

At this point the clerk was saccharine enough to give me the runs.

"Where do you live, Al?" Mark asked.

"On top of a pinball parlor in Murray Hill."

"Climb in. I'll drop you off."

Back inside the limo, I gave my address to Edgar as Costein opened a long panel in front of us. I expected a bar, and I was glad; I could have used a drink. But instead there were a couple of tape machines and something which looked like a miniature computer. It had a typewriter keyboard and Costein started hitting the keys like a boogie-woogie piano player. The kid was hot.

"What are you looking for?" I had to ask him.

"Your current numbers." The computer was displaying all sorts of figures.

"I can tell you as of yesterday," I informed him.

"I'm looking at *today*. And it looks like you're all right."

"So I get to keep my new shoes."

"For another month, Gonfio. At least for another month."

"I'm just worried about you moving out in that fast lane, kid. The long-distance stuff can get rough, and I don't want to see that marathon do you in. Not before I make you a star."

"You're a generous sort of chap, Al."

"I mean well, Mark."

"I hope you realize now," he said, "that I'm interested in taking care of you. And I want to make damn sure that you take care of that nun. I'm very concerned about that character."

"How'd you think she'd look in a jogging outfit?"

"Don't lose her, Gonfio," he said to me as the limo pulled up to my building. "Whatever you do, don't lose the nun."

I tried to read his expression, but the dark tint of his glasses got in the way. A few minutes later he and Edgar dropped me off. And I actually found myself jogging down the hallway to my apartment. Nothing too speedy, but I was sure as hell feeling good. I had Costein going. If I weren't afraid of falling on my ass, I would have jumped in the air and clicked my heels. Yes, sir; baby had a new pair of shoes.

17

Anna was surprised; John said that he'd come with her to the milk plant. And the only reason he agreed, of course, was that he knew that I wouldn't be there. It was late Saturday afternoon. Anna hadn't been there on Friday, when we had taped a couple of episodes in which Prudence did not appear. But she had helped me write the scripts, and now she was anxious to see how they had turned out. She wanted to see the tapes.

He was already stoned when they arrived in the control room where Howie, one of the engineers, was getting ready to show them yesterday's action. But while Howie was rewinding the tape, John pulled out a fresh joint and lit up. Anna felt like saying something, but she didn't. Why antagonize him? Besides, Howie was happy to take a toke when Palermo passed the number his way. John started talking about the one time he did a commercial. He had been a spokesman for a Midwestern insurance firm, and he worked in a setup just like this one. "What a crock of shit that was," he remembered. Anna wanted to remind him that the money had been good, but she didn't. She stood in front of the monitor and watched the screen.

The scene is Brian MacNiece's dining room. A dinner party is under way. Sally sits at one end of the table, Brian at the other. A light-skinned black maid serves. Around the long, elegant table are four other couples—also young, prosperous members of Troy's up-and-coming society.

"Listen, I could tell you some stories. Oh, man, do I have some stories to tell!" the wide-faced, redheaded man exclaims.

"Buck Warburton, you *will* behave tonight," warns the frosted-haired woman sitting next to him, Buck's proud-bosomed wife whom everyone remembers as the school tramp.

"Let him go on. Let Buck tell those stories," Tommy Stevens suggests. "Especially the one about dumping ink in the librarian's goldfish bowl." Tommy Stevens is thin and tall. His greatest glory came during his days on the high-school basketball court.

"I don't think this is the appropriate time for such stories," one of the wives bravely asserts.

Brian is silent, but the camera picks up the look of consternation that he shoots to Sally.

"Yeah, there was one time," Buck goes on, ignoring his wife's pleas, "when we went egg bombing. You remember that, don't you, Brian?"

"No," Brian says adamantly.

"Well, you were there," Buck continues, "I can sure as hell tell you that much. You were there and you were drunk like the rest of us." His storytelling does not interrupt his eating. "Matter of fact, you were the one who got us the wine. Stole some from your old man, if I'm not mistaken. Then we took a bunch of eggs—must have had four dozen—and went down around Hillside Avenue and started heaving them at the cars. You should have seen a couple of those old ladies jump."

"I wasn't there," Brian insists, unable to eat.

"Maybe now you wish that you hadn't been there," says

144

Buck, whose voice grows louder with each sentence, "But you *were* there. I can see you there now."

Brian realizes that he is being tormented. We can practically see him gnashing his teeth, trying to restrain himself, wondering why in the name of God he agreed to let his wife arrange this ridiculous dinner party.

"Actually," says Larry Cooke, manager of the finest men's clothing store in Troy which happens to be his father's, "Hillside Avenue isn't what it used to be. It used to be black, but Ursula has changed the nature of the whole neighborhood. It's not quite as nasty now."

Brian listens quietly as the table begins discussing the Catholic school—how good a reputation it has enjoyed, what excellent teachers the nuns are supposed to be.

"All that's coming to a stop, pretty g.d. quick," Buck informs the group. "Brad Bullens tells me the school's coming down and a shopping strip's going up. And all the big franchises are going in there. Brad himself is going in with hamburgers or ice cream or some damn thing. He expects to clean up. Actually it's probably something this town has needed for a long time. Those big-time national franchises can generate a lot of business."

"But what about the school?" one of the well-behaved wives asks.

"There are so damn few Catholics in Troy, what difference does it make anyway?" someone says.

"That's right," another female dinner guest agrees. "I think it's really going to be exciting to see a group of new stores. And I've heard that there's going to be a *fabulous* woman's boutique in there."

"Fashion! Can you imagine?" bellows Mrs. Warburton. "Little Troy is going to be treated to a splash of fashion. How divine!"

"Brian knows a great deal about this, don't you, dear?" Sally announces, hoping to pull her husband into the discussion. She's proud that he has a professional connection with the matter, and she only vaguely remembers his role in the case.

"It's nothing I'd want to discuss," he says abruptly.

"Pretty touchy, aren't you, Brian boy?" big Buck taunts.

"Touchy enough not to break bread with you," Brian barks

145

as he gets up and leaves his own table. Everyone is silent. Seconds pass. Sally holds herself together and perseveres. "Let's just eat and enjoy ourselves," she manages to say, knowing that later—after the guests have left—she and her husband will have the biggest fight of their brief marriage.

"I think I'm going to throw up," Palermo said.

"Then get away from me," Anna warned him, half pissed.

"Don't tell me you're taking this horseshit seriously?" he questioned. "It's such unadulterated crap. It's enough to make me puke."

"You already said that," she reminded. "Now quiet. I want to watch the next episode."

"Come on, baby. Let's get out of here. I'm bored stiff."

"It'll only take a few minutes, John. Be patient. Go ahead and play the tape," she said, turning to Howie.

"Heard you were a little upset at your dinner party last night, son," says Baxter MacNiece.

Sally and Brian have finished Sunday brunch at Brian's parents' home. Mrs. MacNiece, a thin, nasal-voiced, blue-haired lady, has just invited Sally out to the garden to inspect the new crop of white and yellow roses. The men remain in the massive den decorated with the heads of wild animals which Baxter has hunted down.

"Did you hear what I said, son?" Baxter continues. "Sally said you were upset."

Brian sighs. He does not want to have this discussion. "It was nothing," he finally says.

"Who was there?"

"Why bother asking? You know better than I."

"Damn it, Brian. It's impossible to talk with you. You're on pins and needles. What the hell is wrong with you?"

"I've been preoccupied with the Ursula case," he answers honestly.

"Forget it! I told you to forget that silly matter."

"It's not in the least silly, and I can't forget it. I don't want to forget it."

"There's nothing to do about it. I already told you that Adams is an unmovable, unreasonable diehard."

"I'm close," Brian states. "I'm very close to a solution."

"There is no legal solution," his father insists.

"That's why I've been toying with other ideas."

"What sort of ideas?"

"Public-relations ideas."

"You better explain yourself, son."

"Adams will not respond to pressure," Brian says, sipping coffee from his mother's bone china cup, "but his prospective tenants might. Imagine their embarrassment when they discover the whole city of Troy is up in arms because they—these ice-cream and the burger franchises—are destroying a convent and a school."

"I don't like the way that sounds. Before you do a thing, Brian, I want to see a list of the tenants. I have a feeling that several of them may be friends or associates whom we certainly do *not* want to embarrass."

"We?"

"Yes, we. The firm. My firm, your firm. Our firm."

"My responsibility is to my client."

"Hogwash. Your responsibility is first to yourself and the people who are paying your salary."

"I don't like the way that sounds."

"We've been through this before, Brian. When you were in high school you were ready to integrate the entire public school system of the state of Ohio single-handedly."

"It happened, didn't it?"

"It happened because a few blacks had enough money to buy into white neighborhoods. But there really was no issue to begin with. No more so than today. With everyone yelling about busing, I still say . . ."

"Dad, I'm tired. I was up late last night. And I still have a great deal of research to do."

"What are you researching?" Baxter asks, his anger rising.

"I already told you. The Ursula case."

"I want you to drop it."

"You'll have to drop me first."

"You heard what I said, Brian!"

"Tell Sally I'm walking home," Brian announces, throwing a set of keys on the coffee table. "She can take the car."

* * *

Palermo was bent over laughing. He was hysterical. Howie didn't know what to make of him, so he got up and left.

"You're acting like an ass," Anna finally told him.

"*I'm* acting like an ass! What in God's name would you say about this Brian character. Talk about an ass!"

"He's not a bad actor, you know."

"*Bad!*" Palermo shot back. "The idiot couldn't act his way out of a paper bag. He reacts like a wet dishrag. He reads lines with all the subtlety of a seal."

"Well, this isn't exactly a subtle script."

"You can say that again, sister."

"But for what it is . . ."

"Don't start rationalizing, Anna. Shit is shit."

"Might I remind you"—now she was angry—"that only a few months ago . . ."

"I know, I know. I told you to do this. And I still think you should. I just don't want you to begin fooling yourself, that's all. Because I'll tell you something: outside of the goddamn TV studio these actors would die. If they had to play legitimate . . ."

"They *have* played legit parts. They do all the time. They're good, they're very good, and just because they're making a lot of money doesn't mean . . ."

"Shut up, Anna," he said to her with a hint of brutality in his voice. "I don't want to hear about it. Your *Search for Happiness* depresses the hell out of me."

Anna was quiet. The fight had gone far enough. "Let's go eat," she suggested, and Palermo agreed. He sulked during dinner, though when he made love to her later that night she thought she detected a gentleness in his touch that she had never felt before. And the next morning, in the Sunday *Times,* he was briefly mentioned in an article on Off-Broadway theater. He was very excited and absolutely convinced that something was about to happen, that his big chance was just around the corner.

18

"I don't want any of those extras saying a word," Dick the director commanded as he sat in front of me in the control booth. "If they cough, it'll cost us two hundred bucks. They're silent fixtures, is that clear?"

We were getting ready to tape after being on the set since seven-thirty this Monday morning. Everything was moving well. The story was building.

"Tell Hanford," Dick added, "that his hair is a little out of place in the back. Please let's do something about that now."

A few seconds later, we were ready to roll.

Brian and Baxter are seated around the law firm's huge conference table with a half-dozen other gentlemen. The senior MacNiece is speaking about a complex problem involving taxes. These are obviously important clients. In midsentence, the telephone buzzes. Baxter lifts the receiver angrily. "I thought I told you," he says, "that I don't want to be disturbed."

"It's urgent," the voice of the secretary replies. "A Sister Prudence is calling Mr. Brian MacNiece, and she claims it's urgent."

"Tell her that he's busy."

Brian is now out of his seat and, just as his father puts down the phone, he picks it up and has the secretary put through the call. His father turns red. The clients squirm.

"I know I shouldn't be interrupting," Sister Prudence apologizes on the other side of the split screen, "but there's a quite remarkable letter in this morning's *Troy Clarion* which I think you should know about."

"Of course, of course." He is smiling. In the background, his father has again begun to speak to the clients.

"It's a letter about Ursula."

"I know," Brian whispers.

"So you've seen it?"

"No, I wrote it."

"But it's signed by Guy Wynne."

"That's my new pseudonym."

"I don't understand."

"Come to the park at noon and I'll explain it all," he says softly.

The lighting has been adjusted for the park scene. Sister Prudence is already sitting on the bench when Brian arrives. He is without a jacket. His tie is loose, his shirt sleeves rolled to beyond his elbows. He is winded.

"I'm sorry I'm late. I had this incredibly boring meeting. You wouldn't believe how boring the formation of a new corporation can be. Especially when the clients are boring and the lawyers are boring and . . ."

"You aren't boring," Sister Prudence protests.

"Thank you, but I'm afraid I don't see it that way."

"No one who is truly boring would forge a letter like that."

"I liked the style, didn't you?" he asks happily.

"I was more interested in the content," she answers smartly. "I thought it was a wonderfully succinct presentation of our problem, but now I'm wondering what good it will do."

"We'll have to wait and see. But you have no idea how many people read those letters to the editor. Everyone in town."

"And you hope to rally support to our side."

"I hope to have the whole citizenry down on the necks of those new franchisers."

"So you've given up on Mr. Adams."

"Mr. Adams is beyond salvation, yes."

"No one is beyond salvation."

"Except Mr. Adams."

She smiles, her eyes sparkle, and she asks, "But how will we know if your letter is effective?"

"By reading the paper tomorrow. Care for a plum?" He reaches into his pocket and pulls out a plum.

150

"Thank you." She takes the plum.

"Not at all."

Brian is happy and playful, in marked contrast to his mood of recent days.

"Do you really think there will be other letters?" she asks.

"I know so," he says slyly.

"Don't tell me you've written others." Sister Prudence bites into the ripe plum. Her teeth are wonderfully white, and she is obviously savoring the succulence of the fruit.

"I haven't, but there are friends who will. Friends, by the way, who also promise to start calling Adams's new tenants."

"But haven't they already signed leases?"

"No, not yet. We have about ten days. I've checked."

"This is wonderful!" Sister Prudence claps her hands, like a little girl, like an excited woman. "This is a blessing."

"Let's wait before we start congratulating ourselves."

"I feel like I felt the first day I entered the order—all tingly and excited, as though I were on the brink of a new adventure."

"That sounds great. Perhaps I should have been a priest."

"No, you were right to be a lawyer. It was certainly meant to be. You were meant to be my"—and then she corrects herself and says—"*our* lawyer."

"You believe in fate?"

"I believe in divine purpose, yes. I believe that our instincts are divine, and that our instincts must be followed, just as you have followed yours in dealing with Mr. Adams."

"But what if our instincts lead to sinful deeds."

"Then they are not our instincts, but rather perversions of our instincts."

"Aren't you just playing with language?"

"I'm aware of no game, Mr. MacNiece. It is my heart that is speaking. Can't you hear?"

He is taken aback by her last statement—a little frightened, somewhat bewildered.

"My hearing is not all that good," he tries to jest.

"But your heart beats just as strongly and rapidly as mine."

"This case is fun. We've got old man Adams on the run."

"It's more than that," she says, her eyes riveted on his. "You've been imaginative and bold in your thinking. Surely, you've been inspired. You're acting as an agent, an agent for good."

"I'm afraid that my thinking runs along much more practical lines. I take a mundane approach to contractual problems."

"How can you say that?" she argues with lively spirit. "You've been anything but mundane. You've been . . ."

"Delighted to be able to help you; that's if everything turns out well."

"I know it will," she smiles.

"I keep worrying about your optimism . . ."

"As you keep justifying it."

"That's not my intention. It's only by accident . . ."

"It's no accident, Mr. MacNiece, that you have come to help us."

"Wait till you see my fees," he tells her.

"I won't look. I'll send them to Mother Superior and she'll send them to the bishop."

"And the bishop will call my father."

"Tell me more about your father," she inquires. "I've only met him that one time."

"He's the boss. My father's the boss of a law firm of which I, too, will be the boss."

"When?"

"Whenever he says."

"And when will that be?"

"This case is pushing back that date."

"He doesn't approve of what you're doing for us?"

"He worries about our standing in the business community."

"And that doesn't worry you?"

"Not in the least. We're a fat firm. We have enough business. It's about time we did something really decent for someone."

"Don't tell me you do indecent work."

"Just boring work."

"We're back to boring."

"Yes, I'm afraid I'm boring you. So it's your turn to explain yourself." He worries about this last question—is it the proper thing to be asking a nun?

"I don't like to think back," she answers. "There is not much there—not much food, not much love. Just a lot of of hungry mouths and hungry hearts."

152

"You have sisters and brothers."

"Many. Though I presume you're an only child."

"Spoiled rotten."

The nun laughs, and then she suddenly realizes that the meeting has lingered on longer than she had planned. She has a class to teach.

"I will report this good news," she says, "to the mother superior. And I trust you will call me as your extraordinary campaign builds steam. In the meantime, is there anything I can do to help?"

"The parents of your students could write letters to the paper as well," Brian suggests.

"I will see to it today. I will make the calls myself."

"And I'll call you," Brian tells her, "before the week is over."

"Thank you, Mr. MacNiece."

"It is my pleasure, Sister Prudence."

They shake hands, almost too formally, and go their separate ways.

"You were marvelous today," Hanford said to Anna as soon as they were through taping.

At first she didn't answer, as though she were still considering the feelings of Sister Prudence. He repeated the compliment and finally she acknowledged, "Oh, thanks," but for a split second she forgot the actor's name.

He didn't realize she was struggling to remember, and instead he talked about the ballet. Was she interested in going? Sometime, yes, she said, but not tonight.

"You lead a rigid life," Hanford teased her. "It's time to break loose. At least for a night."

She looked at him. She felt foolish standing there in her nun's habit. She wanted to accept his invitation; she didn't want to accept his invitation. Too many thoughts rushed through her head at once. She had to get undressed and put Sister Prudence behind her. She had to get home to John.

She walked back to her tiny dressing room, threw off her costume, scrubbed off her makeup. She worked quickly, hurriedly, as though she couldn't stand to be Sister Prudence for a second longer. When she slipped into her jeans and her bulky sweater, she felt immediate relief. She looked at her face in the mirror, she inspected her teeth, she widened her eyes, she shook her head, she messed up her hair. She was Anna Calzolari, and she was on her way downtown.

By habit, she took the subway. She wanted the ride, she wanted the old familiar scene, and yet she noticed very little— not the black boy with the huge radio pressed to his ear, not the old lady with the orange hair and the Bell Yarn Store shopping bag. She stood up in the crowded car, and held onto the strap above her, and still she thought of Sister Prudence and wondered why the mother superior had such confidence in her. And why Prudence had such confidence in Brian. Did it make sense? Did any of it make sense? And what was it about Brian that struck her so? He was witty and energetic, his father was a prick, his wife was a drag. A soap opera. A stupid, lousy, good-for-nothing soap opera. John was right. Shit was shit. She wanted to laugh, and at the Fourteenth Street Station, she did. For no reason, she burst out laughing and her fellow travelers looked at her and didn't think much of it. Another nut. Another nut riding the subway, laughing out loud.

As she got out of the train and ascended into the streets, she continued laughing, more than amused, more than tickled, almost hysterical. Hysterical that she was playing the part of this nun with a legal problem, that she was actually putting on that idiotic costume and reading those idiotic lines. But it was fine; yes, it was fine, because the money was so good and the part was so funny, and she could do it; everyone who had seen it said that she could do it. And now she was home and she could put the part behind her. Now she could fix John something to eat; she could see about his day and share these funny moments with him, with John . . .

THIS IS GOING TO SOUND CRAZY TO YOU (the note read) SO I'LL BE BRIEF AND SAVE US BOTH A LOT OF TIME. I HAVE THOUGHT ABOUT THIS A LOT AND TODAY I'VE MADE UP MY MIND TO GO OUT TO L.A. BY THE TIME YOU GET BACK, MY PLANE WILL BE OFF THE GROUND. THERE ARE AT LEAST THREE GOOD POSSIBILITIES OUT THERE. I'VE BEEN TALKING TO PEOPLE,

154

IMPORTANT PEOPLE WITH ACTUAL PARTS, FOR A LONG
TIME NOW. I DIDN'T WANT TO MENTION IT BECAUSE
I KNEW WHAT IT WOULD DO TO YOU. AND YOU'VE
GOT ENOUGH TO CONTEND WITH. YOU'VE GOT YOUR
SOAP GIG AND I DIDN'T WANT TO SCREW THAT UP.
MEANWHILE, I REALIZE THAT I OWE YOU MONEY—
I'M HAVING TO LEAVE WITH THAT LAST $900 WE HAD
AROUND HERE—AND NATURALLY YOU'LL GET IT ALL
BACK. I COULD SAY A LOT OF THINGS ABOUT HOW I
FEEL AND ABOUT HOW YOU FEEL. BUT WHAT'S THE
USE? I NEED TO BE IN CALIFORNIA RIGHT NOW, YOU
NEED TO BE IN NEW YORK, AND THAT'S ALL THAT
REALLY MATTERS. HANG IN THERE, JOHN.

19

She read over the note, five, perhaps ten times. Her first reaction was not to believe him. John could be cruel, she thought to herself, and this was just his way of having fun. But when she went to the closet and saw that his coats and jackets were missing, when she went to the bureau and saw that his drawers had been emptied, there could be no mistake.

She began stalking the loft, pacing like a caged animal. She would be reasonable. She would sit on the bed and think this thing through. There were some people she could call, and she tried, but none of them were home. She began to pace again; she sat on the bed, folded her hands, looked up at the ceiling and closed her eyes and screamed inside her head and then began calling again, and still no one was there. No one was there, no one was there, and she had to do something. She couldn't stay in the loft, she couldn't wait here. It was crazy, this note, and the empty closet and the stupid TV show that was

155

ruining her life. And why had he run? Why now? Why hadn't he waited until she came back? But it didn't matter, because she couldn't wait and she wasn't going to wait. She had already waited too long. She had to go there and find him and talk to him and explain and make it all right. She made one call and finally got Kaufman.

She had some cash and a credit card and in the cab to the airport she didn't see the city, didn't think about what she was leaving or where she was going. It was dark and there was traffic, the traffic made her squirm and curse and the cabby told her, "Better take it easy, lady, 'cause it ain't gonna get no better," and she closed her eyes and tried to still her heart, but it was no use. For a second she considered the humiliation of chasing after this man in a taxi in the traffic and then in an airplane from one end of the continent to the other. She struggled to find her reason, but it wasn't there. John. John Palermo was her lover and her friend, her companion, her soul mate, and she understood that sometimes he couldn't take it—but that happens to all of us—and she would soothe him, she would comfort him, she would be there. Everything would be all right.

At the American Airlines terminal she ran to the desk and told the freckled-face ticket man to give her the next nonstop to L.A. "If you run you might be able to make the first night flight." There was no time to check her suitcase which she carried in her arms as she flew down endless corridors, breathless, determined to make this flight—she had to make this flight —and she screamed "No!" as they were just beginning to pull away the ramp, and they stopped, and she got on, and walked to the back of the long plane, to the very last row, and sat down where—for the first hour, over the darkened coal mines and farmlands of Pennsylvania and Ohio—she broke down and wept.

Later she had two drinks, and she felt the slightest surge of optimism. She was doing the right thing. John would be glad to see her. He would realize his mistake. Maybe they would stay there. Maybe she would find work. She would act in a repertory theater or, if need be, she would find roles in commercials. Everyone was always saying how many commercials were made in L.A. As soon as the plane landed she would call Barb,

156

her friend the dancer, who had moved out there only a year ago. She had tried to call her from New York, but no one was home. Barb had been practically begging her to come out anyway. And tomorrow morning, bright and early, Anna would call the directors and the producers and the couple of friends that she and John had in L.A. and in no time flat she would trace him down and they would be together again. Everything would work out. Everything would be fine.

The jet slid onto the runway, and Anna felt the strain in her eyes as she waited to step off the plane, as she dashed for the pay phone, clutching her suitcase and a dime and a slip of paper with Barb's number in Hollywood.

It was midnight and Anna wasn't even sure what day it was. She dialed. She waited.

"Hello," a voice covered with sleep answered.

"Barb, it's me, it's Anna."

"Anna, I, I . . ."

"I'm sorry to get you up but my plane just landed."

"Your plane? You're here? You're in L.A.?"

"I'm at the airport. It's a long story. I'll tell you everything when I get there. Do you know about the limousine service out here? Wouldn't it be best just to take a limo into the city and then a cab?"

"Anna, I don't think that . . . that it would be a good idea."

Anna listened intensely. What was wrong? She heard a voice in the background. "What are you talking about?" Anna asked.

"I can't explain right now, but please, don't come over."

"He's there," Anna said. "He's staying with you."

"Please, Anna, we'll talk tomorrow. Let me just think a minute, though. Let me give you the name of a friend of mine who . . ."

The phone went dead in Barb's ear.

Anna looked around the airport. People were milling about. The bargain fares meant that the airport was busy night and day. And John was with Barb. He had come and he had gone to Barb. And she had taken him in. He was sleeping with her right now.

Anna Calzolari walked slowly through the airport. She stopped to look at the children's paintings which lined one of the long corridors. One showed a plane flying beneath a white moon; another had a jet crashing into the sun. In a third, the beautiful blue airplane had a tail like a monkey. The drawings were free, like children, and Anna thought about her brothers and nephews and nieces scattered around the city of New York. She never saw them. And now for the first time that she could remember, she missed them, and she wondered how they would paint airplanes and moons and suns. John was with Barb.

The night was mild and balmy outside the airport and she got into a bus marked Hollywood. Her wool sweater began to irritate her skin. She had flown into a new climate, a new country. It felt like spring or summer, and the huge palm trees looked like enormous stiff soldiers. The bus went down a wide boulevard and everywhere Anna looked she saw cars for rent, motels, billboards advertising flights to Canada and Hawaii, coffee shops, strip joints. Then she was on a freeway and she tried not to think, tried not to envision John with Barb—Barb who was the most graceful of dancers, Barb who had such exquisite legs, Barb with whom she had gone to the ballet, to poetry readings, to foreign films. Anna closed her eyes, still thinking about those times, and the bus carried her toward Los Angeles, passing Marina Del Rey and Venice, all shrouded in darkness. She drifted as she traveled the Santa Monica Freeway, as the bus sped through the night. She drifted and she half-dreamed, half-slept—she had been up now for so, so long—and when she finally opened her eyes the bus had stopped, the other passengers had gotten off and the driver said, "This is it, this is Hollywood."

She took her suitcase and saw that she was on Sunset Boulevard. She came to Vine Street and walked down Vine looking for a motel. By now it was after 2:00 A.M. and the streets were empty except for a jogger in brief red shorts and a T-shirt with the images of Ernie and Bert from *Sesame Street*. He was bald and skinny and looked happy to be running. Finally, just above Melrose Avenue, she came to a motel called the Royale. She went into the lobby and waited for the clerk to respond to the buzzer she had just pressed.

"How long will you be here?" the wrinkle-skinned man behind the counter wanted to know.

158

"I don't know."

"I'll put down two nights."

"Fine."

"Cash or credit card?"

"Credit card."

She handed him her card, he ran it through the machine, and then gave her a key.

John was with Barb.

"Your room's around back," he said.

And she walked there and inside was a beat-up TV and a cheap gold chenille bedspread and a sign which said that X-rated movies were available simply by calling the front desk. She sat down on the bed and it gave way; she fell back and realized that it was a water bed. She didn't quite know what to do, so she laughed; she laughed for a very long time, though at some point the laugh turned into a cry, and the cry became a sob, a hysterical sob which lasted until she fell asleep, fully dressed, holding her sweater, floating over her water bed and her dreams—the country beneath her, the black sky above, fog and moon and make-believe suns, airports and oceans, John next to her, John next to Barb, John acting in movies, John in sunglasses, smiling and relaxed, warm and happy, and then suddenly gone, John ducking into alleys and disappearing behind rocks, John eluding her, John stepping behind his own slim shadow.

20

The phone was ringing off the wall when I walked through the door of my apartment. It was sometime after 1:00 A.M.

"Al?"

"Talk to me."

"It's Brink. Brink Kaufman."

"You don't think I recognize your voice?"

"Listen, you sound like you're in a good mood, so I hate to tell you this. Sit down."

"I don't want to sit down. I've got on my Street Fighters and I feel like standing."

"Anna Calzolari's been trying to call you."

I sat down, and then I said, "I've been out."

"So she called me instead."

"And?"

"She told me to tell you. She said she was sorry."

"About what? *Sorry about what?*"

"Sorry that she was leaving for Hollywood tonight."

That's all I remember hearing. I sat and thought for a few minutes. I wasn't going to panic, I wasn't going to faint, I wasn't going to go nuts. I realized that I had to be cool. I had to figure out how to stop shaking.

The last time I was in L.A. I fucked around with a hooker named Suzie and got a nasty case of VD. I won't go into details, but walking into the goddamn Royale Motel brought on a flood of crabby memories that I had long since suppressed. Who can forget the crabs? And somehow L.A. and Suzie and the social disease are all tied together in my head. Ever since, the city of smog has been the city of scratch and itch, the city of burning piss and failing genitals. But all that was my fault, and not Anna's, and yet here I was, chasing after her, hot on her trail like goddamn Philip Marlow.

It had taken some time. Three days, to be exact. The first thing I thought after Brink broke the news was—I'm through, I'm out, I'm dead as lead. And I knew, I knew even before Kaufman told me. She had gone after her glamour boy. He had skipped out and she had gone up like a skyrocket, she had flown the coop and nothing in the world would bring her back.

So a few minutes after talking to Brink I did what any self-respecting man would do—I cried in my fucking beer, I wept a few real tears. Not just for myself and my job and my show and my life, but also for this sweet little Italian kid from the old neighborhood who was really a honey and just happened to fall

160

for the wrong greaseball. I felt sorry for the broad because she was just setting herself up for some heavier blows to the heart. If he had run to California, imagine how much he hated her—or just had to get rid of her—or felt threatened by her big part or whatever the hell it was. So it only stood to reason that once she arrived on the scene, he'd just take off again. Or spit in her eye. No matter what, I concluded, throwing down the rest of my beer, she needed me. She needed my help and I needed her help. She was a pal, wasn't she? And besides, the girl was a star, she was *my* star, and there was no way I could let her do this to me.

It took some telephone calling the next morning. Through her relatives—I couldn't tip them off so I had to be very vague—I got Gwen's last name and through Gwen—who talked to me as though I were poison—I got Barb Fischer's number which is when I got the whole picture. I called Barb and found myself talking to John Palermo. Naturally, he hung up on me. But that didn't matter; I found out all I needed to know.

That guy was as rotten as last month's leftover egg salad. I waited till that night and got Barb on the phone—apparently John was out because she spoke freely—and that's how I learned what had happened.

"I don't want to hurt her, God knows I didn't want to hurt her," Barb told me in a wispy, faraway artist's voice. "And when John called me and said he was coming of course I invited him here. It was only natural; we've been friends for a long time. He came and it was cool, but when Anna called I freaked. I tell you, I absolutely freaked. Because I had no idea and no warning and suddenly I found myself in this absolutely ridiculous position. They're both such beautiful people, and I try to walk softly through the space I occupy, and if I let my friends into my space, they are *really* my friends. It was very hostile and ugly because John started screaming at me and then Anna showed up. She actually walked into our space and, believe me, there was not enough room, and John started screaming at her and she screamed back and said that he couldn't leave her, that he could never leave her, and well, it was a very negative scene and there was nothing I could do. Finally, John ran out the back door and said he was going somewhere else and Anna looked like she would kill him. She cried instead, she cried for a very long time, and then I invited her to stay here—it seemed only reasonable to have her share my space—but she said no. So I left her alone. She said she was in a motel somewhere in Hollywood and that she'd stay there until things cooled out between her and John. But I don't see how they can, since he is determined to find a space of his own."

Fucking weirdo, but she told me all I needed to know. Anna was in a Hollywood motel.

I got a map of Hollywood and an L.A. phone book and started calling. I began at the A's and when I got to the Rs—many dozens of calls later—I hit pay dirt at the Royale. She wasn't in, but she was registered, and from then on I was gone. I called Dick and Howard and my assistants and told them that Anna would be gone for a week and to concentrate on the other segments. They were full of questions. I told them that she was knocked out with a heavy flu bug and that I had some business in California. I suppose they figured I was going on a nag binge or maybe they figured I was having an affair with her, but I didn't give a shit what they thought. I was heading out to the Coast to save my own skin, and right then that's all that mattered. I knew I had to act quickly; there was no way I could keep Sister Prudence off the air more than a week and not cause my millions of ladies to wonder and worry.

Anna hadn't answered the phone in her room when I called from the L.A. airport. But I decided to go over there anyway; I had nothing to lose. The guy in charge of the desk looked as though he had died of a stroke last year and when I told him I wanted to ring Miss Calzolari's room, he said that there wasn't a house phone. "Room three-twenty-four," he grunted, "around in the back." I walked around the pool, which was more like a puddle than a pool, and I had butterflies in my stomach when I knocked on the door. I guess deep down inside I was still living the Raymond Chandler thriller; I was scared that I'd find something that I didn't want to see.

I was not altogether wrong. When she opened the door she looked very weak and very afraid, her face had lost its color, and even though she was beautiful—beautiful because she seemed so helpless, beautiful because she had always seemed beautiful to me—she also looked hollow and so strange that at first I was afraid that she had swallowed a bunch of pills. But after a few seconds of shock, she lunged at me and buried herself in my arms and I was amazed—amazed because she felt like a little bird—her bones were so fragile, her body so thin. And for as long as it takes for the sun to set or a man to fall in love, she held me, held so tightly that I couldn't have backed away even if I had wanted to—and I didn't—and beneath her sobs I whispered, "It's okay, baby, I'm telling you it's all going to be okay."

We stood there for a long time, me holding my child, my wounded sparrow, my wondrous little Anna. And when we finally separated, when she started to catch her breath I noticed that the orange shag carpet on the floor was filthy and she said, "This has been ridiculous, Al. This whole thing has been ridiculous." And she sat on the unmade bed with her face in her hands and I came over and sat down next to her and said, "You're wrong. It's not ridiculous, honey. It's just something you had to do."

"I've made such a fool of myself. You don't know what happened."

"I have a pretty good idea," I explained.

"You talked to Barb? Is that how you found me?"

"Yeah."

"It's hard for me to look at you, Al. It's going to be hard for me to look at anyone."

"Since when have we ever given a shit what people think?"

"It's what I think of myself."

"I'm telling you, baby," I said sweetly, "this is something which you just had to get out of your system."

"He just wouldn't see me," she started narrating the story. "And when I'd find him at one friend's place, he'd go to another. He just couldn't stand the thought of being near me anymore."

"That's because you frighten him. You remind him of everything he isn't and everything he'll never be."

"We had it worked out. I thought we had the whole thing worked out."

"Anna, just think of it this way. It's like you're waking up from some lousy nightmare that just lasted too long."

"You're wrong. It wasn't a nightmare. No one knew me like

John. He understood my needs and my wants, and he had a way about him, a way that could . . .''

"Drive you nuts before you knew it. Listen to me, Anna. The guy's a fucking psycho case. I've met him. I punched him in the fucking mouth. Do you know the last time I punched someone in the mouth? I can't remember. Someone's really got to be a menace to society to get punched out by me. I ain't that brave. I promise you. But I could see in a minute that this guy got his grins by watching you suffer. And I couldn't stand it. I still can't stand to see you still suffering.''

"I'm so glad you came, Al." She smiled through her tears, and my heart lightened. "You have no idea how glad I am, really," and she took my hand, and her skin was smooth, her fingers so small. "I thought about calling you, or calling someone. But you can't imagine how foolish I've felt, how ashamed.''

"You've got nothing to be ashamed of. I keep telling you that.''

"You may have to keep telling me for another year.''

"I will, I will.''

Anna managed a small smile and said, "At this point, I don't know what to do.''

"Well, I sure as hell do.''

"What?''

"Come back to New York.''

"I'm not sure, Al.''

"You're not, but I am.''

"What am I returning for?''

"To do what you've always wanted to do.''

"And what have I always wanted to do?''

"Show that miserable prick Palermo that you're ten times the actor he'll ever be. You're a goddamn star, and you know it, and there's no way anyone can stop you—even yourself. You don't need anyone. I'm telling you, Anna. You don't need anything but the natural talent that the Lord blessed you with.''

"Please, Al, don't get religious on me now.''

"I'm being as sincere as I can be. You're going back to being Sister Prudence. You're going to have a good time playing the part. It's a goof, and you know it, but you've always known it's

164

a tough role and that you're very good at it. And besides that, Anna, you're going to start enjoying your money. You're going to get out of that lousy, two-bit loft and find yourself a decent place. The days of living in warehouses and eating off orange crates are over. You're too good for that.''

"Are you sure you never sold encyclopedias for a living?''

"Someone else asked me something like that. Only I think it concerned Fuller brushes.''

"You could sell oil to the Arabs.''

"I don't want to sell anybody anything, Anna. I just want you to come home and be happy.''

Just come home and be happy, I thought to myself as I paid her motel bill, as I looked at the emaciated, stringy-haired guys in the lobby and wondered how she could have stayed here. At least now she knew what to do. She knew to listen to Al because Al knew what the fuck he was doing; Al knew that this gal had to get herself back into shape, back to the milk plant, back in front of the cameras. Al knew that he had to work fast.

Before we skipped out of town, I took her over to Rodeo Drive—I knew she'd like that—and we got to a few of the stores just before they closed. I told her that I needed to buy her something to celebrate my luck at the track. She laughed and said that she didn't want anything, and I told her she was lying, and then she noticed my shoes and said, "Jesus Christ, you've started jogging.''

"Costein gave 'em to me. Can you believe it?''

"No.''

"It's true. We went shoe shopping the other day. I wouldn't shit you. And the kid actually popped for a pair. To tell you the truth, they're comfortable as hell.''

"They look beautiful, Al.''

"They call them the Street Fighters which is why the kid got 'em for me. That's how he sees me.''

I'm not sure she heard my explanation because she was eyeing the goodies in the Rear Guard Panting Concern which seemed to be selling only blue jeans at a hundred bucks a throw which had skinny skinny little tapered legs and were made to fit you like a surfing suit. It didn't take much to get her inside, and

165

when she tried on a pair I could tell, by watching her watching herself, that they felt as good as they looked—she had such a terrifically sweet ass; this was definitely her style—and from there we went to a joint which sold French purses and she bought one (she wouldn't let me pay this time) in creamy auburn leather which smelled like the insides of a Mercedes and after that it was a beautiful white blouse with pink pinstripes and the tiniest collar I had ever seen in my life.

"Let's take a little walk," I suggested when the stores had closed, and as the sun was setting we strolled up one of those quiet Beverly Hills streets with the royal palm trees all bending in the same direction, the houses quiet and stately, the lawns freshly seeded and emerald green even in January. There were no dogs or dirt and I said to her, "Just like the old neighborhood, ain't it?"

At the end of the street, I pointed out the hotel on Sunset—the old Beverly Hills Hotel whose towers were a magical blue—where the Silver Clouds and Silver Shadows were silently pulling up on the immense circular drive. I took her through the lobby and into the famous Polo Lounge—me in my Street Fighters—and who should I see but a couple of the boys from the network—guys who worked for Costein on the Coast—and I introduced them to Anna who was busy looking at a movie star in the corner. We drank our dinner and we were doing fine when I asked her, "Would you like to stay here tonight?" I wasn't sure what I meant by the question, but it felt good coming out.

"I like to fly at night; maybe we should fly back tonight."

"Beautiful," I said, disappointed but still pleased that she was anxious to get back.

She was strangely quiet, as Anna is often strangely quiet, in the cab to the airport and the midnight plane to Manhattan. At first I was going to ask her about a few ideas I had been playing with—all concerning Sister Prudence and Brian—but I decided not to bother her. I bought her a couple of drinks and then let her sleep. And as we sped across the country in the middle of the night, she rested her head against my shoulder. All the lights in the cabin had been dimmed, except mine, and I put my arm around Anna and snuggled her a little closer to me. Everything was going to be all right. Everything was going to be fine. Anna was coming back with me and Sister Prudence was going to fall deeply and hopelessly in love. I felt good because I was helping everybody—Anna, myself, even horse-faced Costein. I wondered what Anna was dreaming about. I thought I knew. I thought by this time I knew her well enough to see inside her confused head. It had taken her a long time, but she was finally over a puppy love which had lasted half her goddamn life. It took this crazy trip to break the spell, but it had all been worth it. I edged her closer to me. I kissed her forehead. I took a pencil and a pad and, under the single beam of the small overhead light, I began writing. And as I imagined our silver plane flying high over Troy, Ohio, I wove fabrications and dreamed fictions about the nun and her friend the lawyer.

21

His fist comes thundering down on the desk. His eyes are wide with fury. He is in his office—stern, handsome, formal—and his son is seated across from him.

"This is *exactly* what I wanted to prevent!" Baxter MacNiece fumes.

"It couldn't be prevented."

"Look at this, it's a scandal, it's an outrage!" He points to the newspaper on his desk.

"It's the only way this case will ever get resolved."

"You've embarrassed the firm. You've embarrassed the very name of . . ."

"For God's sake, stop exaggerating."

"Exaggerating! Do you realize how many calls I've received in the past hour? Ten, twenty—I can't keep track. I've had to say that I'm out of the city. Everyone wants to know when we stopped practicing law and got into the public-relations business."

"You yourself said there was no way to win this case in the courts. So I took your advice and went public."

"Brian, you're no longer a child. You're no longer a member of the Troy High School debating squad. You're a junior member of a law firm with very serious obligations to the business community which it serves."

"You sound like the Chamber of Commerce."

"I might remind you that last year I had the honor of serving as president of the Chamber of Commerce."

"I had a client with a problem, Dad, and I have tried to find a solution to that problem."

"You've provoked the entire city. There are editorials, letters to the editor, special reports on radio and TV news. It's madness. I tell you it's madness. The franchisees who were going into that shopping strip are being bombarded by mail; they're being threatened by boycotts even before the convent is torn down."

"That's exactly what I had planned," Brian says with apparent satisfaction.

"Did you bother to learn that one of the men who planned to operate a franchise was once a client of ours?"

"You're talking about Derek Bosier. We handled his divorce, and that was ten years ago."

"It's more than that. Many of these people are connected, closely connected, with important clients of ours, through business or family."

"That could be said for two-thirds of everyone living in Troy."

"Precisely! That's precisely the point!" The camera closes in on Baxter's face. We see the well-manicured shape of his white mustache.

"You're making a mountain out of a molehill, Dad, I assure you."

"You assure *me*. That's a laugh."

"Anyway, it's too late. The public is now aware of what Adams is trying to do, and the public is the only means I have to combat him."

168

"It was foolish of you, terribly foolish."

"If it was foolish of anyone, it was foolish of you to take on the case. And that was primarily your decision, not mine. Don't you remember? You thought helping Ursula would impress the Taggart brothers. Or have you forgotten that you told me they were influential Catholics, and that you wanted their business?"

"I did want their business and I still do, but not this way."

"I thought that you'd take new business any way you can get it."

"Don't you see how you've upset this law firm? You've shaken the very foundation of a tradition based on discretion and integrity."

Brian laughs contemptuously, and then says, "This firm was long overdue for a shake-up."

"That's my decision to make, not yours."

"Not any longer, I'm afraid," he adds with a distinct sense of triumph in his voice.

The organ music swells and, after a commercial break, we come back to another scene.

Brian returns home from work that same day. He walks through the front door, scans the mail, removes his jacket, loosens his tie and settles down on a couch in the den. Sally is there, waiting for him, her hair up in rollers.

"This place has been a madhouse today. Everyone's been calling you."

"I hope you told them to try me at the office."

"It didn't matter what I said. The phone kept ringing and everyone had something to say about Mr. Adams and the shopping strip and the convent and now it's past six and I'm not even dressed and you better shower because we're going to be late."

"Late for what?"

"The Gordons. Tonight is the Gordons."

"Oh, God," he grunts.

"Please don't *Oh, God* me. I don't want it and I don't deserve it. You should have heard the conversations at the Junior League meeting today. Barbara Steedley, Derek Bosier's daughter-in-law, was there and she was all aflutter about why

169

you and your law firm were out for publicity and how awful she thought it was that your name should be in the paper and that well-intentioned businessmen were being . . ."

"I can't believe it, I simply can't believe it," Brian mutters, shaking his head.

"Well, you better believe it, because you started it and now it's all over town and frankly, Brian, I wish you had never agreed to . . ."

"A convent, a school, wants to stay where it is. I drum up some public support and everyone goes bonkers. What a town! What a pitifully small-minded community!"

"It's not the town. It's our friends, it's your father's friends, it's the people we socialize with. Couldn't you have thought about that before . . ."

"You sound like my father."

"I can think of worse people to sound like."

"I can't."

"Brian! You're speaking of your father!"

"My father is a hypocritical lecher who's been buying whores and stashing mistresses for himself and his well-heeled clients ever since I can remember!"

Tears come to Sally's eyes. "Brian!" she cries again. "I don't want to hear this talk! I won't listen to another word!"

The phone rings.

"Let it ring!" she shouts. "We're late, we have to get dressed, we have to go!"

Brian answers the phone.

"You son of a bitch," the voice on the other end growls.

"Mr. Adams, I've been waiting to hear from you."

"I just want you to know that I'm taking you to court."

"Oh," Brian reacts coolly, "on what grounds?"

"I don't know what grounds. Malicious behavior, ruining a man's business, fraudulent manipulation of public opinion— something, I'll get you on something, MacNiece."

"I'm sorry you're upset."

"No, you're not. You're glad, you snot-nosed kid. You're glad that today over half my tenants backed out just when they were about to sign in. And the other half are threatening to do the same. No one's about to touch this property now. No one's about to go against the tide of opinion you've turned against me."

"Nothing personal, Mr. Adams, I assure you."

"You've rendered my land worthless."

"You already have a quality tenant. What more do you need?"

"I'm taking you to court. I'm telling you that right now."

"That's your prerogative."

"If I were twenty years younger, I'd come over there and tan your hide."

Brian smiles. "Don't get yourself upset, Mr. Adams. It's not good for your heart."

"Tell that nun I'm not through with her yet."

"Yes, sir."

"Don't sir me."

"No, sir."

"Tell her I'm reading over that lease right now. Tell her that I have every intention of raising the rent."

"I'll do that," Brian answers as the phone goes dead in his ear.

"We've won!" he exclaims, his face breaking into an irrepressible smile.

"We're late!" Sally shouts from upstairs.

"Did you hear me? We've won! Old man Adams is giving up. That was him waving the white flag."

"I don't want to hear about the case anymore, Brian. I want you to get dressed."

He ignores her, hesitates for a few seconds and then reaches for the phone. In a great hurry, he dials a number and then asks to speak with Sister Prudence.

Hanford spotted Anna in the hallway.

"Thanks for coming down and watching me today," he said to her. "How did I do?"

"I came down to look over tomorrow's script," she answered somewhat aloofly. "Now I'm about to go home and memorize it."

"Before you get too absorbed in work, just remember that you can always read the Teleprompter. I just happen to have a couple of tickets for the Met. What do you say? Will you come with me?

She opened her mouth to say "No," but instead another word came out: "Yes," she said, "yes."

The opera chilled her blood. She was stirred in a way she had never thought possible. *La Forza del Destino* it was called—the force of destiny. From the moment that the overture broke from the orchestra, soaring over strings and winds and brass, her mind was flooded. She was transported, thrilled with the anticipation of the mighty struggle of the drama to come. When Hanford asked her, when she had accepted his invitation, she was certain the she would be bored. But now as she sat on the edge of her seat in the red splendor of the Metropolitan Opera House, she was strangely afraid, strangely excited about the newness of her life.

She had only been back two days and she had been living in the loft alone. Everyone knew to leave her alone, everyone except Hanford.

"An Italian girl," he said, "and you've never been to the opera. Impossible."

"It's not my culture," she explained.

"Not your culture! Then who's culture is it?"

"I have no idea."

"Then you must find out. You must venture forth. I promise you, you'll love it, you'll adore it. The pageantry alone will take you to the stars. And if that's not enough, I have the finest herb available in Gotham, an herb so delicate and delicious that it cannot be classified as smoke."

She had gotten stoned in the cab going uptown and, even though the smell of the weed reminded her of John, the idea of being wrecked on grass with a blond Ivy Leaguer was so new that the old association soon passed. She wore an eccentric black dress and a strange pendant—a cat's eye—that she had bought some time ago. Barreling up the island of Manhattan in the back seat of an enormous Checker cab, her feet resting on the small seat in front of her, Hanford Seames next to her in three pieces of subtle olive flannel, she felt relaxed and queenly and soon so fuzzy that nothing made much difference.

172

Until the overture. When the music hit her, she felt the muscle of her heart pull. The music got to her, and through the fine filter of Hanford's high-priced, powerhouse dope, she sailed. She didn't want to think; she just wanted to feel. And she was amazed by the audacity of the drama, by the huge woman called Donna Leonora, by Don Carlo di Vargas and Don Alvaro, by the gypsy girl named Preziosilla. And these people were leaving and arriving, battling and dying, pilgrims in disguise, women dressed as men, murders and fabulous joyous voices, all in a language which Anna understood not at all, and yet understood completely; the crazed action of her heart, the wild circumstance of devotion, impossible and forbidden love, fleeing, racing, crying in the night, the arias, the words: *Ah! seguirti fino agli ultimi confini della terra! . . . Son giunta! Grazie, O Dio! . . . Madre, Madre pietosa . . . Urna fatale del mio destino* . . . It went on and on and on, through wars and caves, as Anna made up incredible stories, as she thought of her grandmother and her grandmother's language, her grandmother's warnings about the cruelty of life and the meanness of men. Anna Calzolari's eyes were open to the wonders of the costumes and the movement onstage, then her eyes closed as she remembered the flight to California as improbable as the eighteenth-century Italy which tonight had been recreated in cardboard. Like a great painting. Like a miracle. Like an opera. Like a soap opera.

"It was a little long, wasn't it?" he asked afterward in the cab going back downtown.

"No!" Now she was the one who was high, who was up, who was reeling from the change in the night, the change from the music. "I wanted more! I wanted much more!"

"Were you getting lost in the story? Could you understand the story?"

"I understood everything, and nothing. If you understand."

"Everything and nothing," he laughed, lighting an after-the-opera joint. "How could I not understand? There is nothing else."

"I used to think that melodrama muddles the mind, but now I'm not sure. These plays—these make-believe, ridiculous stories, which have never happened, which never will happen—are happening all the time. To you and me right now."

"Of course. That's why I invited you out tonight. I'm here to straighten you out. I'm here to keep you straight."

"This is wonderful, very wonderful and very important to my life. All this is very important to my life."

Hanford put a hand to her cheek. His skin was smooth. He took many baths and showers. She wanted to kiss his silk tie. But she couldn't concentrate on him. Not now. And yet she needed to. She would try.

"Your hair is the color of wheat," she said. "Middle America."

"San Francisco. Remember?"

"The son of aristocracy."

"Doctors and teachers are not aristocracy."

"They are where I come from."

"You don't seem as though you come from anywhere."

"You say that only because you don't know me."

"I admit that. But I'm trying. Look how long it's taken me to see you on a nonprofessional basis."

"But you've succeeded. You are determined and strong, brave and true. Were you a boy scout?"

"I was." He smiled broadly. He was happy to meet her expectations.

"And you tied the girls up in knots?"

"I only learned about bondage when I got into the acting scene."

"So—you're kinky."

"As kinky as a marshmallow."

"Soft in the center."

"Hard on top."

"Hardly modest."

"But patient. I am very, very patient."

"That's the aristocracy in you."

"That's your fantasy speaking."

"And how does my fantasy sound tonight?"

"Fine. I wouldn't expect less from such an accomplished actress."

"You see this as a performance."

"I'm studying you," he said. "I'm looking to solve the mystery."

174

"What mystery?" she asked.

"There are so many mysteries surrounding you," he explained. "Your disappearing act last week, for instance."

"That was nothing," she told him.

"Just a flight of fancy?"

"Just a fancy flight."

"Trouble with a man."

"A bad bout with the blues," Anna said.

"Tell me about it," he urged, looking to learn.

"Not now." She looked out the window, out at the familiar SoHo scene.

"We have all night to talk," he said, finally letting loose with an unmistakable line.

"Everything's perfect the way it is. I don't want to disappoint you, but there's been enough drama for one night."

When he took her home, she went up on the freight elevator alone. He didn't argue. He *was* patient; he understood that time was on his side.

22

On one-half of the split screen, we see only her face under the white crown of her habit. On the other half, we see Brian beaming, the phone cradled against his neck.

"I hope I'm not disturbing you," he says.

"You never disturb me," she answers, somewhat surprised at her own provocation.

"I had to tell you the news."

"The articles and letters in the papers—I've seen them all. Opinion certainly seems to be running in our favor, and I can't help but think that . . ."

175

"It's over. The fight's over."

"What do you mean?"

"Adams just called me at home."

"And?"

"He can't go on with the shopping strip. His tenants are dropping out like flies."

"Blessed be the Lord who works in wondrous ways."

"Brian!" Sally screams from upstairs. "Who are you talking to *now?* We're late."

"I just had to let you know," Brian says to Sister Prudence.

"Yes, of course, how wonderful, how wonderful of you."

"I'm taking out your favorite sport coat, Brian," Sally persists. "And don't forget, Barbara Steedley's brother just graduated from Yale so you and he can talk about New Haven."

"Mr. MacNiece," the nun continues, "if I even tried to express my gratitude . . ."

"There's no need to. Naturally the terms for a new lease will have to be negotiated, but I doubt that Adams will give us any more trouble. He'll bark, but he won't bite. He's tired of all this negative publicity and he knows that if he attempts to raise the rent to some exorbitant amount he'll face the same kind of exposure."

"You're quite brilliant, Mr. MacNiece."

"Nothing I've done has been in the least brilliant, I can assure you."

"Brian! Get off that phone *now!*" the voice of his wife demands.

"I hear someone calling you," Sister Prudence says.

"I'm afraid it's my wife."

"I see," she answers, revealing the slightest edge of disappointment in her voice.

"I'll call you from the office tomorrow. We'll talk more about the details of concluding this matter."

"Yes, by all means, please do."

"You're infuriating me!" Sally has come downstairs and is standing next to Brian.

"I'm being dragged away," he tells the nun.

"Please attend to your responsibilities," Sister Prudence advises; "I don't want to disturb you any longer."

"No bother at all."

"Who was that?" Sally asks after the phone is hung up.

"Just a client."

"I hope it's an important client to cause us to be forty minutes late."

"Very important," Brian assures her.

"Because you know how Barbara is—she gives such glorious parties and she frets so if anyone is just the least bit late. And you don't want to offend her, do you?"

"Heaven forbid," Brian remarks, so obviously happy about his last phone conversation that he barely hears or cares what his wife is saying.

Sally slams the door behind them. She and her husband are back home. She is dressed in an elegant dark brown suit. Her blond hair is soft and luxuriant and touches the tops of her shoulders. He is wearing a camel color sport coat—it appears to be cashmere—and a solid maroon tie. He is merrily drunk; she is fuming.

"It's a disgrace," she screams, "it's horrible and I don't have to put up with it any longer! I don't have to and I won't!"

Brian goes to the bar in his den and pours himself another drink. He ignores her, which excites her even more.

"I've never been so humiliated in my life," she continues. "I can't believe you'd ever do anything like this—not to me."

"I said nothing," he halfheartedly defends himself. "I told myself that I would say nothing, and that's exactly what I did."

"That's just the point. You sat there like a bump on a log, obviously bored and contemptuous of everyone and everything around you. You were despicable."

"And I thought I acted the part of the perfect gentleman."

"Everyone there knew—everyone just knew—that you were having a perfectly dreadful time. Your mind was somewhere else. You might as well have stayed home."

"I wanted to. I told you that earlier."

"You did me no favor by coming." Sally's eyes are afire with rage; she stalks the den as she speaks.

"I can do no more than silence myself, Sally. That's the best I can do."

"Well that's just not good enough!"

"If I had really expressed myself, Sally, if I had given you and those other couples any inkling of what I thought of their conversations and their concerns . . ."

"What's wrong with them? What's wrong with their conversations?"

"It's fine if you want to hear about maids and golf courses and next week's trip to Bermuda."

"I want to hear about Bermuda," she insists. "In fact, I want to *go* to Bermuda."

"Then go."

"You're hateful." She is crying now.

He comes to her, drink in his hand, now tired and tipsy at the same time. He lowers his voice. "Sally, I'm sorry. I really am. I tried, but I just couldn't mix tonight."

"You didn't try. You did it to spite me. You look down on everyone who's not as smart as you, not as educated."

"That's not the point. That's not the point at all. It's just that I'm tired of hearing about last night's TV miniseries or some ball player's ten-million-dollar contract. I've been doing that ever since we came back to Troy, and I've reached my limit."

"Are you ashamed of me?" she asks. "Aren't I pretty enough for you? Aren't I sophisticated enough?"

"No, no, no. Listen to me. I mean . . ."

"I'll join the Book-of-the-Month Club, I'll start reading a novel a week, I'll . . ."

"You're being foolish, Sally."

"Stop saying that! I can't stand to hear that anymore!"

"I've never said it before," he protests.

"You're saying it now, aren't you?"

"It's not just you. It's this whole community. It's my father and the firm and . . ."

"Why don't you become a hippie? Why don't you drop out and live in the woods? Why don't you become a priest? Why don't you just hide your head in the sand and pretend that the world really isn't here?"

"I want none of those things."

"You don't know what you want."

"Do you?"

178

"Yes!" She is shouting again. "Yes! I know! I want to go to the country club and have heads turn when we walk in, because you are handsome and my dress is beautiful and because we are well-respected. And I'd like to go to New York or San Francisco or Europe every once in a while and stay at the old pretty hotels. And I'd like to have children, two or three children, and raise them here in Troy, because this is a fine place to raise children. Isn't it? You know that it is! You can't say that it's not!"

"Go to sleep, Sally. We'll both feel better tomorrow."

"No, we won't. You're lying. You just want to be alone. Just like you've wanted to be alone ever since you got home tonight, ever since you heard about your ridiculous case with the nun and the convent. You're like a high-school rebel, Brian. You're too old for this kind of behavior and I'm warning you—there's only so much that I'll take." She whirls around and leaves the room. He sits alone and studies his drink. He sips calmly and slowly, allowing the rancor to pass over him. A few seconds later, his face breaks into a small, warm smile, and it is almost as if we can see what he is seeing, almost as if we can read his mind.

The taping was over, and before she left the studio I cornered Anna who had been watching Hanford do this last episode for the day.

"So how was your date with him?" I asked her straightaway.

"Al, that's a personal question."

"Goddamn right. But I got a right to know."

"We went to the opera."

"The *opera!*"

"Yes, the opera."

"And?"

"It was beautiful."

"Was it in Italian?"

"Yes."

"Then how the hell could he understand it?"

"He understood more than I did."

"So how did it all end up?"

"The opera?"

179

"No, your date."

"Too personal," she kidded. "You're getting too personal."

"Listen, I'm the one writing this show."

She laughed and said, "He stole away with not so much as a kiss."

I was relieved. "You're a smart cookie. There's no reason to give it away like candy."

"You think I should charge?"

"I think you should get yourself a decent apartment and clean up your act—that's what I think."

"I'm ready."

"Good, we'll start this afternoon. Just as soon as you give me all the details of your date with glamour boy."

We talked for a little while longer and then agreed to meet at my apartment in an hour. When Anna showed up there, she was wearing the pair of Rear Guard jeans we had bought in L.A. Her hair was pulled back, her face was scrubbed; she looked more determined than depressed—determined not to be depressed.

"I clipped last Sunday's *Times*," I told her, "and made up a list. There are all kinds of possibilities. Most everything is around here."

"How come?"

"Because I don't like to walk."

I put on my Street Fighters and we went down in the street. The day was suddenly overcast, but that didn't bother me. I was finally getting Anna out of that stinking loft. It felt good to be on the case. It began to drizzle, and then it started to pour, and before we reached the first apartment house I felt like a fucking duck, splashing over puddles and quacking in the rain. No one had told me jogging shoes ain't waterproof. My feet were soaked to the bone. My feet were freezing.

"Let's run in here," Anna said, pointing to a small boutique on Lexington called Your Chic Against Mine. Not exactly my kind of joint.

"I want to buy you a raincoat," she said.

"I've got an overcoat on."

"You need something to go over your overcoat."

"You're nuts."

"Here it is. Our prayers are answered."

She had found a large, plastic, hooded poncho, a slicker that looked like a cape. It cost $2.98. She bought one for me in Day-Glo orange and one for herself in puke green. We put them on and looked like a pair of monks recently escaped from the funny farm. "I like to play in the rain," she said.

So we played in the rain. We ran around Murray Hill, from apartment to apartment. Nothing was right. Either the living room window had a charming view of a brick wall or the refrigerator was the size of a medicine chest. New York.

But we didn't give up. We kept on searching, kept on meeting half-crocked landladies with stories about their dead Irish husbands or the famous poet who lived in the penthouse. Sometimes Anna was serious, and sometimes she was sarcastic, but considering the fact that she was in the throes of changing her life—and finally putting Palermo behind her—she was doing pretty good. I was the one who was getting cranky. My feet were wet.

"One more place," she urged.

"It'd be easier to live with me," I offered, not quite understanding what I meant.

"It'll be bad enough having me in the neighborhood."

"I just don't want you mooching any sugar."

The final place turned out to be the winner. A decent apartment on Thirty-fifth Street. One large bedroom, old but not without a certain class. Light, lots of windows, blond hardwood floors, decent kitchen. "We'll take it," I told the tall landlady who looked as though she could be Mark Costein's mother.

"Are you two married?" she wanted to know.

"We're not married," I shot back, "and we won't be living together."

"Are you related?" she continued to pry.

"Yeah, she's my mother," I said.

"Will my furniture work?" Anna asked later.

"Everything will work. You'll work, I'll work, your furniture will work."

"I'm not sure, Al. Don't you think it's a little posh for a struggling actress?"

"It's not posh enough and you're not struggling."

"Why are you in such a hurry?"

"My feet are wet."

"I didn't bring any checks. I can't leave a deposit."

"I can and I did."

In the taxi back to my place I returned to our earlier discussion.

"So you had a good time at the opera last night?"

"I wish you had been there. The plot was unbelievable. It was so weird I made it up as I went along."

"And Seames, Seames had a good time?"

"Seems so."

"Don't be a wiseass."

"Ask him. I don't know."

"How can a guy have a good time if he doesn't get laid?"

"You're making me feel guilty."

"I don't mean to. I just want you to be aware of his intentions."

Anna laughed, then leaned over and kissed me on the cheek.

Back at my place, I took off my crazy poncho and my overcoat, put on a pot of coffee and felt like a million bucks. Anna was sitting at the kitchen table, looking over a script I was working on. What could be better? I had finally pulled her out of the Lower East Side. I felt so good, in fact, that I excused myself for a few minutes so I could put a little money on tonight's college basketball games. I had a hunch about Notre Dame.

When I got back to the kitchen the coffee was ready and Anna was really engrossed in the script.

"This is getting interesting," she said to me.

"You're cheating. You're getting ahead of yourself."

"Your stories are irresistible."

"Just 'cause I popped for the deposit on your apartment doesn't mean you have to bullshit me."

"No bullshit. I like Brian. I like the character."

"You better."

"I just think you're rushing things a bit."

"What do you mean?"

"Give Prudence a little bit more time."

"You think so?"

182

"I know so. Let the thing simmer."

"You're feeling better, Anna. You're really feeling better."

"I'm doing what I have to do."

"Don't put it that way."

"Listen, Al, you, of all people, have to understand. I'm determined to make some money, that's all. What's behind me is behind me."

"Just like that?" I asked.

"Of course not. But at least I got the words out."

"And at least I got you the fuck out of the rathole Lower East Side."

"SoHo," she corrected.

"It's all garbage."

"SoHo's not garbage. SoHo is art."

"Artful garbage."

"It doesn't matter."

"Nothing matters except Notre Dame beating UCLA by ten points tonight."

"A nun getting fucked by a lawyer. I can't believe it."

"You better fucking believe it, because if you don't, we're all fucked."

Guess where we had a date that night? The Grotta Azzurra at Mulberry and Broome, just for old time's sake. I couldn't resist. It was really a hell of a lot of fun. I wore a tie and Anna looked like a fashion model and I had the carbonara, and then an extra order, and the veal was like heaven and the huge pitcher of wine had fresh fruit on the bottom so that when the wine was gone and we were drunk, the fruit—the sliced peaches and pears— was drunk, too. I got up at ten thirty and went to call my man and found out the Irish had won and I was a G richer. When I returned to the table I lit up one of those beautiful Rey del Mondos and announced my good fortune.

"This is your send-off from the old neighborhood," I said to Anna who was strangely quiet again. "This is good-bye to bad times." I reached over and touched her hand. She looked up at me and began to say something, but then stopped.

"What is it?" I urged.

"Oh, I was just wondering about Mom and Dad and the rest of the family."

"Yeah, sometimes I wonder the same thing."

"They really have no idea who I am or what I want. They've never known."

"But they'd like this restaurant, wouldn't they?"

"They'd love it, sure."

"So take 'em here one night. Take the whole *famiglia*. All hundred and sixty-three. And I'll invite mine, and we'll sit around and get fat and eat this drunken fruit."

"It wouldn't work that way," she said with too much sadness in her voice.

"Then don't invite them. Invite the crowd from the theater. That dame—what's her name—Gwen. Invite the whole troupe. Take 'em here or up to someplace swanky and pay for everything with a new five-hundred-dollar bill and you'll feel better in a fast minute. Believe me."

Anna tried to smile, but she couldn't. "That's not my style, dear Al."

"Not now, but it should be. You need to develop flamboyance. Hell, you're going to be a goddamn star. I keep telling you that."

"And I keep listening, and I want it to matter, I want it to make some difference."

"It does. It already has. Sitting here, just looking at you, you're a different person than the girl who first exposed herself during the audition."

"That was funny, wasn't it?"

"Funny as hell. Funny as anything I've ever seen. Fact is, that's when I realized I loved you." I said it; I didn't know I was going to, but I said it.

She left it alone. She was obviously moved, but she remained silent for a long time. Finally she sighed. "You know I'm going through some tough times, Al."

"Of course I know it. That's why I wanted you out of that hellhole. I want you to forget."

"Forgetting's impossible."

"Nothing's impossible. Not even salvation."

"Stop it, Al. You're going too far."

"I believe it. You and me, honey, we're going to be delivered. We're going to make it. We're going to be saved."

184

"By what? By whom?"

"That horny nun. That fucking horny nun is going to save us all."

23

Sister Prudence is seated on the park bench reading a book of verse. She looks up as Brian, his blond hair in beautiful contrast to his blue suit, stands above her. They both smile radiantly.

"I'd thought you'd be coming here today," she says.

"What made you think that?" he asks especially light-heartedly.

"My instincts," she answers.

"Are your instincts always right?"

"Of course not. But I'm happy that in this case they were. I wanted to thank you for all you've done, and I wanted to thank you in person."

"I didn't come for that purpose."

"Ah, so you also had assumed that I'd be here."

"Actually," he begins to lie, "I just wanted to get away from the telephones for a while and . . . oh, I suppose I was hoping that we could conclude our business in a more pastoral setting than my office."

"I see. I didn't know that we have business to conclude today."

"Yes, there is the matter of a new lease."

"Has Mr. Adams called again with further demands?"

"Not yet." Brian stalls for time, trying to figure a way out of the maze of his modest mendacity. "But, um, before we get into that, I, I . . . I see you're reading poetry. Might I be bold enough to ask whom you have blessed with your attention?"

"Yes, by all means. John Donne."

"Isn't that somewhat racy for a servant of the Lord?"

"I might remind you, Mr. MacNiece, that John Donne was a sacred poet. He was, after all, dean of St. Paul's. He, too, was a devout servant of the Lord."

"Those were his later days. If I'm not mistaken, his youth was marked by verse of remarkable and lovely sensuality."

"That's true," she concurs with dignity.

"And is it also true that you sisters are sufficiently modernized and liberated to tackle the entire corpus of his work?" he asks.

"I'm not certain it's a question of 'we sisters,' and I certainly don't believe it has much to do with 'modernization' or 'liberation.' We are devoted to God—there can be no question of that —but we are also individuals. Our minds function, as all minds must function, quite freely."

"That sounds blasphemous to me."

"I must teach you more about the Church."

" 'Stand still,' " he recites from memory, " 'and I will read to thee / A Lecture, Love, in loves philosophy.' "

"I prefer Donne's *Elegies*," she replies, " 'By our first strange and fatall interview, / By all desires which thereof did ensue . . .' "

"So you do know the dirty poetry?"

"It's not in the least dirty."

" 'Batter my heart, three person'd God; for, you / As yet but knocke, breathe, shine, and seeke to mend.' "

"You know your Donne well."

"The holy stuff, the sexy stuff," he tells her. "I love all of it."

"Then it must have occurred to you that his passion is constant. What he once felt for women, he later felt for God."

"Physically? Do you mean what he felt *physically?*"

"Yes," the sister states, the hot glare of the studio lights approximating the hot glare of the afternoon sun shining on her forehead. "Religious love is physical love. Holy love is visceral, even erotic. Have you never walked over the Bridge of Angels in Rome, that bridge leading to Castel Sant'Angelo?"

"I have, but only as a rich college kid bumming around Europe for the summer."

186

"Don't rich college kids notice sensuous angels holding the sacred articles associated with Christ's crucifixion—the nails, the crown of thorns, the robe, the cross itself? Did you happen to see the expression on the faces of these beloved angels, the terrible mixture of pleasure and pain?"

"I'm afraid I missed that."

"And Bernini's famous statue of Santa Teresa. Surely you know it. Surely you recall the wonder of her ecstasy, the mystery of her divine swoon."

"No, I never saw that work," he confesses. "But you make it sound very appetizing."

"I'll bring you a book. The pictures can't substitute for the real thing, but the pictures will help."

He looks at her, amazed at the turn that this conversation has taken. "Is this how you speak in the convent?" he asks.

"I've always had a mind of my own."

"Then why did you become a nun?"

"Am I to take that question antagonistically?"

"I'm just confused, that's all."

"Confusion is a necessary part of growth."

"I'm not complaining, Sister. Just confessing."

"There are priests for that purpose."

"I'm not Catholic."

"They'll listen to you all the same."

"Are you encouraging me to confess?"

"I am encouraging you to speak. I feel you have the need to speak."

He is taken aback. His heart is full. He is frightened. He wants to touch her. He senses that she wants to be touched. He does nothing.

"Speaking to you is a great pleasure for me," he finally says, and then adds, "and a great relief."

"I'm glad to serve such a purpose," she answers with forced formality.

There are several seconds of nervous tension.

"I better be getting back to the office," he declares.

She is disappointed, but she is also relieved. "We never discussed the business you mentioned," she remembers.

"The business . . . yes, well, I'll call you. We'll have a meeting."

"Anytime convenient for you, Mr. MacNiece. Perhaps you could come to the convent. Mother Superior is anxious to meet you and express her thanks."

"Yes, of course. Good-bye, then."

"Good-bye, Mr. MacNiece."

Afterward, Anna and Hanford were hanging around the coffee machine. I saw him talking to her, and I quickly got over there to hear what he had to say.

"Heard you moved," Hanford remarked.

"You heard right," Anna confirmed.

"Inviting any guests over?" he wanted to know.

"It's a little too soon," I answered for her. Anna smiled.

"It's never too soon," Seames persisted.

"I'm not really settled yet," she explained.

"I can help settle you," he offered.

"Gentlemen do their propositioning in private," I said with more than a little annoyance in my voice.

"Gentlemen mind their own business," he quipped. Then, ignoring me, he turned to Anna and said, "Did I ever tell you about the place my folks have in the Berkshires? It's not much. Just a small cabin with a bedroom, kitchen and bath. But the countryside is magnificent—utterly magnificent. How about you and me getting away for a couple of days?"

"I'm busy this weekend," I informed him.

"What do you say, Anna?" He kept on the pressure.

"It's supposed to snow," Anna remarked as she took off the crown and hood of her habit, shaking loose her dark hair and wiping her forehead with a tissue.

"That'll make it better," Hanford suggested.

"Give me some time to think about it," she said.

"I'll call you tonight."

"If the line's busy," I broke in, "that's because she's talking to me."

But standing there, and looking at Anna, I had the feeling she had already made up her mind. I had the feeling he had gotten to her.

24

When I got home that night I didn't feel too good. It wasn't that I was jealous. It was just that I knew Anna, and Anna was especially vulnerable these days. I had seen how she had suffered in California, I had been with her on those rides up and down the emotional elevator, and I knew that this wasn't the time for her to launch into any full-blast love affair.

At the same time, I thought to myself, if she was going to be fucking around with someone, Hanford Seames wasn't a bad bet. At least he would keep her mind on the show. Still, I worried about his intentions. He wasn't a bad actor, and he was certainly a cut above greaseball Palermo, but for my money he was too slick. Too smooth and too slick.

I was worried about her, plain worried. I was having a hard time keeping my mind off her. Which is why I decided to call Silvia. Good old Silvia. But Silvia wasn't there, and that got me a little crazy. Where was she? What the hell was she doing out? Goddamn bitch.

So I picked up the phone and called Anna, which is what I wanted to do in the first place.

"Glad you're there, honey," I said when she answered the phone.

"You caught me just in time."

"Where you going?"

"The Berkshires."

"Shit."

"Where's Seames?" I asked.

"Right here," she answered. "Want to talk to him?"

"No! Tell him to leave the room while I'm talking to you."

Now she laughed. But she did excuse herself. She went to speak to me from the phone in her bedroom. I liked that.

"All right, Al, we're alone. Now you can tell me about condoms and IUDs."

"You're going to take care of yourself, aren't you?"

"Of course I am."

"I know these actors. I've worked with them for years."

"I've known a few myself."

"Your track record is lousy."

"Listen, Al, I'm late. Hanford wants to leave."

"What made you decide to go?"

"Who knows? It'll be nice getting out of the city for the weekend."

"If he gets weird, call me. Call me immediately."

"If he gets weird, I'll kick him in the nuts."

"That's my girl. Anna, how do you feel? Really, how are you feeling?"

"I'm feeling all right, Al. I'm just trying to think about the show, and concentrate on my part."

"You were wonderful today. Everyone said so."

"Thanks for telling me."

"When you get back, I want to hear about it."

"I'll give you every last detail."

"You promise?"

"I promise."

"Okay. You've gotta go, I've gotta go, but I just want to tell you to enjoy yourself, and be careful, be very careful, and if you need anything, call me."

The snow had begun to fall as soon as they hit the highway. Hanford drove a black Porsche, and the car looked to Anna like an elegant and erotic bomb. He wore a black corduroy cap, his blond hair peeking out underneath. His coat was bulky and his pants were relaxed and too large, causing her to wonder about the shape of his body, and especially the shape of his thighs. The night was dark and the snowfall, some sixty miles outside the city, thickened and turned to storm. Anna felt her body tense. Hanford slouched in the driver's seat—his legs were long —and he lit his expensive briar pipe. He cracked his window, and the shock of cold air felt good. Anna hadn't realized that the car had gotten so stuffy. "If the smoke bothers you," he said, obviously undisturbed by the untamed elements outside, "just let me know." She didn't answer him. The flakes had turned to hail, and the car was assaulted by the sound. Ice against metal. "You needn't be nervous," he assured her. "I've made this drive so often I could do it with my eyes closed."

She was afraid, so afraid that she dare not admit her fear to him, or even to herself. She didn't know what she was afraid of —of everything. Of this drive, this storm, this weekend. Afraid of her feelings. But why should she be afraid? Hanford knew the road; he was in control.

"You know," he said to her, so calmly, so self-assuredly, "when I was a little boy we used to come here for the summers. It was very exciting for someone raised in San Francisco to be exploring the woods of Massachusetts. And then, of course, there was Tanglewood, and those marvelous symphony concerts on the lawn, with the soft breeze of summer and the music floating on the air. Jacob's Pillow, the dancers and the poets. Marvelous, it was just marvelous."

Anna thought of her own summers, sleeping on the fire escape and escaping to the roof. Listening to the screams of Italian mothers and Italian fathers, looking down at the street below and wondering whether she could take off and fly, whether she should jump.

"And by the time I went to college," Hanford coolly continued as the storm worsened, "I used the place as a *garçonnière*." His French accent was impeccable. "I liked to date older girls, and even when I was a freshman I managed to lure a few Barnard sophomores up here. Those were the days, though, when women had much more to teach me than I could possibly teach them."

Anna listened intently. The cold seemed to exaggerate the smell of the rich leather upholstery of his Porsche. She wanted to snuggle next to him, to have him put his arm around her, but the deep bucket seats wouldn't permit it. She was glad that he kept talking—about old girlfriends and wild weekends in this Berkshires cabin—glad that he wasn't in the least apprehensive

191

about the night howling about them. She thought about her own college, in the city, living at home, traveling on the subway, then living with John and more subways, the underground of the city, reading poetry by the blinding white light, by the screeches and screams of the train. Then for a moment she made believe that she had gone to Radcliffe; she thought of herself in plaid skirts and cashmere sweaters, attracted to the blond Princeton boy, swept up by his easy charms, transported to his parents' place in the mountains. A college girl. A wealthy just-returned-from-Europe-last-summer college girl.

"There's nothing to it," Hanford rambled on. "This road looks tough, but I've driven on it when it was even rougher. This is nothing. Just a couple of twists and curves and we'll be there." He took her hand and squeezed it. She felt herself grow warm. She wished he had worn leather pants, leather like the seats of his Porsche.

When the car stopped, she could barely make out the cabin. But once inside, she saw it was more a house than a cabin. He lit a lantern, then threw wood in the fireplace. "I'll have this place warm in a second." She looked up at the ceiling, at the rows of exposed beams. Etchings of English ships and thoroughbred horses hung on the walls. The furniture was cushioned and worn. She turned to him—he was standing next to her, watching her fall in love with this mountain retreat—and *she* made the move: She opened her mouth as she kissed him, pressing herself hard against him, expressing her gratitude or her joy —she didn't know which—for his having conquered the storm, for having parents with taste and money, for having pursued her just as he had pursued those lovely college sophomores.

She closed her eyes as he kissed her neck. He let his lips linger there for a very long time, and she felt the fire against her back, against her buttocks.

"Would you like a drink?" he offered. "Some brandy perhaps?"

"That," she answered, "and a smoke."

"Let me prepare the magic potions. I'll be back in a flash."

She took off her boots and sat in front of the fire. She was wearing the blue jeans from Los Angeles. Her sweater was oversized and old and the wool had been irritating her skin.

192

When Hanford returned to the room, she had taken off the sweater and her nipples had been hardened by the cold.

"You're mad!" he told her. "You'll freeze!"

"It feels wonderful," she said, all dreamy and soft even before the first puff of smoke. She moved closer to the roaring fire, now feeling the heat against her chest, the cold against her back.

The brandy burned her throat; the marijuana filled her head like sweet fog. She half-closed her eyes and kneeled before the fire. He drank slowly, he smoked cautiously, trying to assess the situation. He prided himself in his patience with women—he knew what they wanted and how they wanted it—but she was something new; she was something different.

" 'So, so, breake off this last lamenting kisse,' " she recited to him, her eyes still half-closed, 'Which sucks two soules, and vapors Both away.' Do you know that?" she asked him.

"It sounds metaphysical to me."

"You're right. It's Donne."

"I wondered where Gonfio got his culture."

"Al is a very cultured man."

"I like what you're doing to the script."

" 'Twice or thrice had I loved thee, / Before I knew thy face or name; / So in a voice, so in a shapeless flame, / *Angells* affect us oft, and worship'd bee; / Still when, to where thou wert, I came, / Some lovely glorious nothing I did see.' That poem is called 'Aire and Angels.' "

" 'Aire and Angels,' " he repeated, feeling the grass fooling with his central nervous system.

"We are nowhere. We are suspended in space."

"Do you like that sensation?" he asked.

"I'm not certain," she answered. "I need to be grounded. I need to know whether your sophomore ladies from Sarah Lawrence knew John Donne."

"Certainly not like you know him."

"Did they recite poetry before they let you love them?"

"Not that I can recall."

"Did they smell of perfume and bubble bath?"

"All smells are lost to me except yours," he said, now kissing her beneath her ears, now kissing her on the nape of her neck.

"And a nun—do you think it's crazy to love a nun?"

"I think it's crazy to talk about it now."

" 'By our first strange and fatall interview,' " she began to recite again, " 'By all desires which thereof did ensue, / By our long starving hopes, by that remorse / Which my words' masculine persuasive force / Begot in thee.' Do you remember the lines?"

"They were yours, but they should have been mine."

"I bequeath them to you. You have the 'masculine persuasive force.' "

"I accept them."

"Just think of what we can do here. Things that can never be done on television."

"Pornographic cassettes are very popular," he reminded her.

"I don't believe in pornography."

"Just poetry."

"Yes, just poetry."

And she turned toward him and gave him her mouth, and he felt the excitement of her tongue.

" 'By our first strange and fatall interview,' " she repeated, and then asked, "Do you remember? Do you remember the first meeting?"

"Of course. Gonfio called his bookie."

"What did you think of me?"

"I thought you were beautiful."

"A beautiful graduate of Radcliffe or Barnard."

"Much, much more beautiful than that," he continued, now anxious to end the preliminaries.

He licked the tips of her nipples and her body quickened. Her heart beat faster, and she said, "The idea of this meeting, the idea of this interview, the idea of this show."

He quieted her with his mouth, on her mouth, on her small breasts, on her stomach. He loosened her jeans. He removed his shirt. His chest was blond and thick with hair and, flat against hers, she felt his ribs, and the tautness of his nipples. She drew her finger down the great length of his swollen cock. He asked her if she preferred the bedroom. "I have had a long starving hope about a fireplace," she told him. He nodded his head. He brought pillows from the couch. He removed her jeans, his pants.

He kissed her thigh. He was slow. He was achingly slow. He massaged her back, caressing each vertebra. He blew on her shoulder blades as she felt his hardness against the cheeks of her buttocks. She opened her mouth to the heat of the fire, the fire on her legs, the fire against her toes and against her throat. She wanted him. She wanted him to fuck her. But she said nothing. His index finger touched her clitoris, barely touched it, and she reached for his cock, she felt the blood and the fire there. Now they were naked before the fire, in the winter in the Berkshires, now his tongue was where his finger had been, encircling her clitoris, flicking against it, now his tongue was lower, was probing, inside, deeper and deeper inside her vagina, his tongue and his finger—now two fingers—on her clit, squeezing, rubbing, stiffening, And she came against his tongue and his fingers, and she climbed up his legs and she drew his cock inside her. She took him, she absorbed him, all of him, his cock was large and surrounded by blond pubic hair—she had never seen blond pubic hair before—and she rode him. She lifted her legs towards the snowy heavens. She felt him against the wall of her soul. Her ass on the pillow, the pillow of his parents, the cabin house in the mountain, the doctor's son, fucking the doctor's son, the doctor's son lean from San Francisco, delicious boy, delicious man, big-dicked and delicious, smooth smooth and higher, now slamming, now slamming hard, all of him against her, all of him inside her, she rose and he fell, filling, filling fine and fucking, forceful fierce ferocious fucking. He fucked her until she felt his white stream, until she melted, like flakes of snow, before the dwindling fire.

They loved in the bedroom that night, under and over the huge quilts. And the next morning, and that afternoon. The snow continued, and that pleased them both. They wanted to be snowbound. They wanted to stay where they were. She recited poetry and he listened. He talked about Princeton and eating clubs. She talked about the snow and her childhood church down in the old neighborhood, the Church of the Most Precious Blood. She told him about wanting to be a nun, and he was not all that interested. For the first time he thought that she might be a little intense for him, a little too strange. But he didn't think that for long, because the sex was spectacular. She lost herself in his body and gave and took more than any woman he had known. He prided himself in the conquest, but by Saturday night—after a day of nonstop talking and screwing—he had a slight case of cabin fever and found himself anxious to get out. By early evening the snow had stopped and they were able to drive to Stockbridge for dinner. The old inn was decorated with silver plates and pots and kettles which hung from the wall. A college student—a pretty boy from Princeton, she guessed— served them lamb and mint jelly. The crowd was clean and wealthy. She recognized a famous painter in the corner.

That night, before they made love again in the bedroom, she wanted to play games. She wanted to pretend that they were different people. She thought of John who had forced her to talk like Gwen. But Hanford refused. He said that he did not find such sport amusing. He did not like the way she looked at him. She was almost too lovely, too lost in his eyes. Still, their loving was loose and free; she spoke some words which he did not understand—perhaps it was verse—but it didn't matter. She pleased him with her mouth and he rewarded her throughout the night. "We fit together," she said before he fell asleep. "I don't know where you stop and I begin."

When they drove back to the city on Sunday, the world was still white. She complimented his driving and invited him to spend the night at her apartment. He refused. They had to be at work tomorrow morning, he told her, and he had best catch up on his rest.

25

Silvia was sick. She had stayed home from the bank to care for her cold. Her throat was inflamed, her head stuffed, and she lay in bed drifting in and out of sleep. At half-past noon, the sound of organ music stirred her. She had left the television on in order not to miss the show. This was the one thing she had been looking forward to, the one consolation of being sick. Today she got to see *Search for Happiness* at home.

The titles came up. She read STORY DEVELOPMENT BY AL GONFIO and then WRITTEN BY AL GONFIO and the SCRIPT SUPERVISOR: AL GONFIO. She was excited. She sat up in bed and fixed her gaze on the tube.

The screen shows a room in a convent, small but clean, sparse but not depressing. There is a bed, a dresser, a bookcase filled with books, a writing desk. There is a crucifix on the wall and, next to it, a black-and-white photograph of Bernini's famous sculpture of Santa Teresa.

Sister Prudence is seated on her narrow bed. She holds her head in the palms of her hands. She is praying or meditating or simply thinking. She raises her head and rubs her eyes. The camera comes in for a dramatic close-up of her face. She is far away; she is troubled. She walks over to the crucifix and kneels; she looks up and stares at the photograph of Santa Teresa. Tears come to her eyes. She shakes her head, lifts herself from the floor, walks over to the window next to her dresser. She opens the window and listens to the chirpings of distant birds. She smiles, goes to her bookcase, selects a volume, sits in front of her desk and tries to read. She cannot concentrate. Someone knocks at her door. She goes to see who it is.

"I hope I'm not disturbing you, my child," the mother superior says.

"No," Sister Prudence answers, a bit dazzled. "Not at all."

The mother superior quickly and silently walks into the room.

"Won't you sit down?" Prudence offers.

"No, thank you. I've been sitting all day. And I won't keep you for long. I simply wanted to come by and say that you have been much in my thoughts."

"Thank you, Mother Superior."

"That does not require thanks. I have been thinking of you, Sister Prudence, for a number of reasons. I am most grateful for the way in which you handled the matter of our disputed lease. I had prayed for wisdom, I had sought guidance. I was not at all certain about how to solve our problem, and when I turned to you for help, dear child, it was neither through whimsy nor chance. I had listened to the Lord and all the angels of my heart who said to look around me for strength. All the wondrous signs pointed to you, and so I made my request because I knew that somehow you were suited to find a solution. Almost miraculously such a solution materialized, and I have had very powerful feelings about this incident ever since."

"I am glad."

"I, too, am glad, but I am also disturbed."

"Disturbed?"

"Disturbed by the way this assignment has so consumed you, Sister Prudence."

The young nun is taken aback. "I didn't realize . . ." she begins to say, now stuttering, searching for the right words.

"It's nothing I can pinpoint, child. Just a feeling I have that perhaps you took this most serious task almost too seriously. Perhaps by enlisting your aid, I put too much pressure on you. Perhaps it was unfair of me to worry you so."

"No, not at all."

The mother superior puts her arm around Prudence's shoulder. "Now that the crisis has passed, my child, I want you to relax. I want you to concentrate once again on your teaching duties. I want you to be yourself once again. Am I being clear?"

"Perfectly clear."

"And if there is anything that is disturbing you, then please, Sister Prudence, please feel free to open your heart to me. I have come here for that purpose."

"Nothing," she answers much too quickly, so quickly that the older woman raises an eyebrow.

"Are you certain?"

"Yes, yes, of course," Prudence nervously replies.

"Then I will leave you now, and I will thank you again, and I will trust that you will take comfort in the Lord. Shall we pray together?"

Together, the nuns kneel before the crucifix. Mother Superior speaks. Her voice is soft and sincere: "We seek direction, we seek salvation, we seek courage and solitude in which we might come to know Thee even more, O Lord. And if we are dissuaded or distracted, if our minds grow cloudy and our thoughts confused, if we are lost or frightened, we will turn to Thee, we will . . ."

The voice of the mother superior fades. The camera zooms in on Sister Prudence whose eyes are closed and wet with fresh tears.

Silvia was crying, not loudly, but crying inside. She was moved and disturbed. She felt for Sister Prudence. She didn't know whether she wanted the nun to leave the convent and abandon her vows. It wasn't wise to get mixed up with a married man. Silvia knew that. It was a policy that she herself followed. Still weakened by her virus, she was too tired to get up and turn off the TV. And so she lay there for a long while, worrying about Sister Prudence, half-dreaming, half-sleeping, as various spokesmen sold toilet bowl cleaners, girdles and paper-back novels.

"How were the Berkshires?" I asked Anna as she walked off the set in the direction of the dressing room.

"Let's talk later. I'm a little tired now," she answered, avoiding my eyes.

"What's wrong? What happened to you this weekend? What did that bum pull on you?"

"Nothing."

"I'll kill him."

"Nothing, Al. Really."

"I want to hear about it."

"Later."

"You'll tell me everything?"

"Tomorrow."

"You're stalling. You're putting me off. Next time I'm coming along."

"Give me a break, will you, Al? I really am tired."

"What's made you so tired?"

"I'm tired from acting. That last scene was murder."

She looked different. She was talking different, and I was worried. And yet, in spite of my concern, I had to admit that her performance this morning had been nothing short of amazing. She was getting deeper and deeper into the part, and if that were

199

the case, everything had to be fine, everything had to be goddamn great.

Then why was I irritable? Why was she irritable? And why
did I have this really strong urge to run home and write Hanford
Seames out of the fucking script?

26

I wasn't going to call her that night. Who cared about her weekend? Screw it. It was her own goddamn business, not mine. The
dame was entitled to some privacy, and far be it from me to be
a busybody. If she wanted to tell me, she could—in her own
sweet time.

Leave her alone. Let her work out the thing by herself. Stay
out of the way—that's what I was thinking. But the more I
thought, the more I ate. I tore apart a roasted chicken I had
picked up at the supermarket and ate the whole thing, not so
much out of hunger but nervousness. And before I pounced on
an apple pie which had defrosted and was heating up in the
oven, I decided—if for nothing but the sake of my own health
—that I had better break down and call her.

The first words I heard myself saying were, "Tell me about
your weekend."

"It was pleasant, the weekend was pleasant."

"I want more than that."

"I think we need to know more about his father."

"Whose father?"

"Brian's."

"I want to hear about Hanford. I want to hear about the
weekend."

"He has a certain touch."

"I can imagine."

"No, you can't."

"Listen," I said, "I *invented* this guy. I know everything there is to know about him."

"He's very romantic."

"All men are romantic when they want to get laid."

"He knows how to love."

"Just like that? You went down for him just like that?" I was getting mad.

"If you're going to chastise me, I'd rather not discuss it."

She was right. "I'm sorry," I said. "I just hate guys who take advantage."

"He took advantage of nothing. Actually, he's had a very interesting life. He told me a great deal about his father. There's some jealousy between the two of them."

"Are we talking about Brian again?"

"No, Hanford."

"I don't care about Hanford's father. I don't really care about Hanford. I just want to make sure that he didn't do you dirty."

"No, he did me good. He's a sweet man."

"I'd say slick, not sweet."

"It's not for you to say. He's never been your lover."

"Don't even mention such a thing."

"He's a very deep person."

"I'd say shallow."

"You're not letting me talk."

"Sorry."

"This will take a long time."

"You want me to come over?"

"I wouldn't mind."

"Give me ten minutes."

The first thing I noticed was that she had put a photograph of Santa Teresa—the same one that was in the show—above her TV set.

"Take that down from there," I said without thinking.

"What are you talking about?"

I pointed to the photograph. "That goddamn picture."

"You're being blasphemous."

"I'm sorry, but that's a little too much for me."

"I think it's funny."

"I don't. I think it's creepy."

"It may be creepy, but it helps me to get into the part. I look at it all the time, and I think about Prudence. And anyway, she's a saint, a beautiful martyred saint. Santa Teresa."

"Listen, I love the saints as much as anyone else, but . . ."

"Look at her face. Look at the way her head leans to one side, the way her mouth is half-opened, as though she's panting or breathing heavily. . . ."

"Enough!"

"Actually, in the Cornaro Chapel in the Church of Santa Maria della Vittoria in Rome, there's another figure which is part of the sculpture. Right next to Teresa, Bernini created a smiling seraph holding an arrow, though it isn't clear whether Teresa has been pierced or is about to be pierced. But in the book she wrote about her life, called *Vida,* she talks about this. That's how Bernini got the idea. She talks about a vision brought on by an angel, an angel who came and stuck her with a burning dart, which . . ."

"I've heard enough."

"What's wrong?"

"That picture has no business hanging above your television set."

"Sister Prudence is very caught up with Santa Teresa," she went on, ignoring me. "And besides, she loves poetry. She'll use all this to justify her fling. She'll pore over Santa Teresa's writing, she'll read about the union of body of spirit, she'll convince herself . . ."

"I didn't come to hear about the saint. I came to hear about you. What happened between you and Seames?"

"I told you. He fucked me." She smiled when she said that, knowing it would shock me.

"I wish to God you wouldn't talk that way. Please, Anna."

"You asked."

"I'm also asking for a little delicacy."

"I may be in love."

"That's impossible."

"Why?"

202

"You're too good for him."

Anna threw back her head and laughed loudly. She came over and kissed me on the forehead. I liked that. "I don't really know if I'm in love," she said. "I just said that because I liked being with him and because he made me forget about everything else. I like that feeling. It's the first time I've felt free, really free, since we got back from California. And he's also different from any man that I've ever known."

"Different!" I shouted. "Jesus Christ! He looks like every college kid I've seen for the last twenty years. The guy's a walking cliché."

"You don't really know him, Al."

"What are you talking about? I keep telling you that I discovered him, I hired him, I made him up for you to play with."

"Then that's all I'm doing."

"You're playing too hard."

She laughed again. "I'm having fun."

"It's getting too complicated."

"It's just begun. It's not complicated at all."

"You're mixing up professional and personal, and I don't like it."

"You started it."

"And I'll finish it if I want to."

"Are you threatening me?"

I realized that I had to slow down. I was getting too worked up. "No," I said, "I just don't want to see you get hurt."

"I'm liking the soap more and more. It's easier for me to pretend."

"You've always been able to pretend."

"I can feel what Sister Prudence is going through. I really can. But I think we've waited long enough. I think it may be time."

"Now you're telling me how to write the show."

"You've always wanted my advice."

"Well, I don't want it now," I told her as I glanced at her bookcase which was filled with volumes of poetry. It looked as though she had checked out at least a dozen books of religious verse from the library.

"Hanford could help."

"What are you talking about?"

"Why don't we call him up and invite him over now and have a meeting, a story meeting, about what's going to happen to Prudence and Brian?"

"That's crazy."

"I think it's sensible. We're at a crossroads. We really need to discuss how these two people are finally going to come together."

"I don't want to see Seames tonight."

"I do. I think it's important." She walked over to the telephone and began to dial.

"If he comes, I leave," I announced.

"You're being awfully stubborn."

"I'm being sensible. It's you and me. That's the way we've always worked and this ain't the time to change."

"I want to see him," she said with an urgency which bothered the hell out of me.

"See the bum on your own time. I'm going to the fights," I told her as I started to leave.

"Don't go," she pleaded. "Let's not talk about me anymore. Let's talk about Prudence. That'll make things a lot easier."

"Maybe you're right. Put on some coffee, let me call my bookie, and we'll do some real work tonight. The hell with everything else."

I liked a kid named Sandro Morales in a featherweight match. He had a lot of spunk and a lot of heart. I liked him enough to put $500 behind him. I made my call, placed my bet and while Anna was busy in the kitchen, I walked around her place. She hadn't had time to buy much, and the apartment still looked unlived in. What she did have—the chairs and plants and bedspreads—was definitely out of her earlier life. There was no easy chair, no rocker. She didn't even have a bed, just a mattress on the floor, and I reminded myself that I'd have to take her shopping for all kinds of shit before the week was over. I couldn't let her go on living this way.

She came back with a pot of coffee and then went to the bedroom. She said she'd be right back. When she returned, she had put a kerchief over her hair. She mumbled something about her hair being dirty. The kerchief was dark blue, and strangely enough, it had the effect of the crown of a nun's habit. I was about to say something, but then I decided not to start up.

We sat on pillows in her living room. When she began speaking, she was very excited because she remembered the name of one of her first teachers, a nun from the old neighborhood. She started telling me nun stories and then I told her a few of my own. I told her how I managed to terrorize a few of the sisters, but how most of them succeeded in terrorizing me. She cracked up at my stories, and at one point she was laughing so hard I was convinced she was crying. Then when I asked her something about Sister Prudence she answered me—just as a goof—in Sister Prudence's voice. It was like the first time we met. I thought that was funny, but when I asked her to stop, she wouldn't. I pleaded, but it did no good, so I sat there for the next two hours, listening to her describe how she was torn between commitment and passion, between purpose and pleasure, and finally she went for the poetry and started reading me all kinds of shit, and I sat there amazed and a little afraid. But I was grateful that I was getting this—and not Seames—that I was the one to whom she finally revealed everything, all her peculiar dreams, all her soaring fantasies, and I knew that the scripts were just going to come pouring out of me—no more stumbling blocks. Costein was going to be a very happy man, because I was going to make him money, make me money, make my little Anna money. This shit she was telling me was good; this shit was real. And when I called my man, he said that Morales had won in a TKO in the fifth round.

"You better give me a key to this place," I said to her before leaving at about 2:00 A.M.

"I've already got one made up."

"Thanks, baby." I kissed her, and she opened her mouth a little bit, and I felt her tongue, and I couldn't figure out whether that was a mistake or not.

27

Mark Costein leaned back and whirled his chair around to get a glimpse of the action on the Avenue of the Americas. Black and red and striped umbrellas. The yellow blur of taxicabs. A midday downpour, the gloomy midtown traffic. He thought of his dry 6:32 A.M. run this morning and silently congratulated himself for having arisen so early. He had beaten the rain. He looked to his left, at the building across the narrow street; he stared smack into the skyscraper next door which belonged to one of the other networks. He thought of next month's 26.2-mile marathon and flipped on the television set behind him. It was almost twelve thirty. He got up from his desk and walked to the pinball machine. He smiled to himself. He'd play a quick game as he watched the show—just for the fun of it.

They are on the park bench again, Brian and Sister Prudence.

"I didn't know that you'd be here," he says.

"You did, you did," she answers quickly.

"I promise I didn't."

"It doesn't matter." He is smiling. She is nervous.

"Would you like something to eat?" he asks as he opens a bag of potato chips.

"No, nothing, thank you."

"You seem uneasy," he mentions.

"I was just wondering when you will be coming to meet the mother superior."

"Do you really think that's necessary?"

"No," she snaps.

"You've changed your mind, then."

206

"No, I just . . ."

"You have a right to change your mind."

"It's not that."

"Then what is it?"

"It's so many things, I can't begin to speak of them."

"Try."

"Why do you come here every day?" she asks him, changing the subject.

"It's not every day."

"Nearly every day."

"It's a pleasant park, a pleasant bench. Isn't that clear?"

"Nothing is clear any longer," she says.

"I've never seen you like this."

"I've never been like this."

"Is it something you want to talk about?" Brian asks with concern.

"How can I talk about it with you?"

"You can try," he repeats.

"Are you interested in the *Vida* of Santa Teresa?"

"I am if you are."

"Have you read her account of her own life?"

"I haven't. Should I?'"

"Yes."

"Then I will."

"I have the book here," she says, opening it and beginning to read. " 'Though I often see representations of angels, my visions of them are of the type that I first mentioned (that is, 'imaginary'). It pleased the Lord that I should see this angel in the following way. He was not tall, but short, and very beautiful, his face so aflame that he appeared to be one of the highest types of angel who seem to be all afire. They must be those who are called seraphim. . . . In his hands I saw a long golden spear and at the end of the iron tip I seemed to see a point of fire. With this he seemed to pierce my heart several times so that it penetrated to my entrails. When he drew it out, I thought he was drawing them out with it and then he left me completely afire with a great love for God. The pain was so sharp that it made me utter several moans; and so excessive was the sweetness caused me by this intense pain that one can never wish to lose it, nor will one's soul be content with anything less than God. It is not bodily pain, but spiritual, though the body has a share in it—indeed, a great share. So sweet are the colloquies of love which pass between the soul and God that if anyone thinks I am lying I beseech God, in His goodness, to give him the same experience.' "

Brian has been looking in Sister Prudence's eyes which are now filled with tears. "That is an extraordinary experience," he finally says.

"I've had such experiences," she tells him.

"You are fortunate."

"I am not! I am not! I have those feelings, but I am certain that they have not involved God—at least not God exclusively."

"I don't understand."

"The face of Santa Teresa as Bernini sculpted her. I dream of that face. Every time I close my eyes, I see it. Her head is tilted back, her eyes shut, she is thin and exquisite and her mouth is opened—half-opened—as though she has been loved, or is being loved or about to be loved. A seraph looks on with a golden arrow, the arrow which has been the instrument of her pleasure. Do you understand, Mr. MacNiece? Do you understand what I'm talking about?" Her voice was almost shrill. "What are we doing here, on this park bench, whispering about poetry and sculpture and . . ."

"You aren't whispering, you're practically shouting."

"I'm sorry. But I'm tired of seeing you and not understanding, not understanding how you feel or what you want."

"I don't know what to say."

"You're afraid."

"Yes, I'm afraid, and so are you."

"Tell me—what are we afraid of?"

"We're afraid of coming to this park," he says.

"You are right."

"And we are also afraid of not coming."

"I'm afraid of the pain, but I also want the pain. I keep moving toward the pain."

"Nothing has to be painful."

"We should stop talking."

208

"We should meet elsewhere," he whispers as he takes her hand. She quickly, almost violently, draws back.

"No!" she exclaims.

"That's what you've been hinting at! That's what your eyes have been saying to me for weeks now!"

"We can continue coming here. We can speak to one another on this bench."

"You yourself said that the pain is too great. We have to do something else."

"Sometimes I think I'm crazy."

"Our emotions are always crazy. They provide our surprises and our joys, even our faith."

"My faith is . . ."

"Constant," he finishes for her. "Your faith will always be constant."

"Constant or crazy?"

"Both, and neither."

"You're making no sense."

"We must meet elsewhere," he implores. "We both want to."

"I'll have to think about it for a long time."

"If you think, you won't act. We have to do something crazy. I'm telling you that we have to do something crazy."

"What is crazy?"

"The country club. The Troy Country Club. At night the golf course is deserted. No one is there. We could talk. Meet me there. There's a large tree by the first hole. I'll be there by nine thirty. Go to the back of the parking lot and keep walking straight. It's easy to find. You can walk to the club from Ursula in less than a half hour."

"That *is* crazy. And that's also impossible."

"As long as I haven't insulted you."

"I'm too afraid to be insulted."

"If you're too afraid, you won't come. The same's true for me. We can do whatever we like. It'll be interesting to see who is there—you, me or no one."

Without saying good-bye, she gets up and leaves him alone on the park bench.

* * *

Costein walked from the pinball machine over to the television set. He turned off the tube, sat back down at his desk, picked up his Dictaphone and spoke softly but clearly:

"Memo to Al Gonfio," he said into the machine. "*Search* making decent progress. How about your jogging?"

He thought of adding something else, but he changed his mind. This would do just fine. He clicked off his Dictaphone and swung around in his chair, noticing that the rain was tapering off. The park would be muddy tomorrow, but he'd manage to put in a good ten miles anyway.

"That was hot today," I said to Anna before she had time to leave the set. "Very hot. Let's have dinner and talk about it more."

"Talk about what?" she asked me.

"Prudence. Prudence getting fucked."

"I'm a little drained."

"And a little booked up," Hanford said.

"Oh, I forgot," she said. "We're going to eat."

I wanted to fire that bastard right then and there. He was moving too fast. He was showing off in front of the wrong guy. Didn't he know that I knew? Didn't he know that I was closer —spiritually closer—to her than he could ever be? What was wrong with this asshole?

"I'll call you when I get home, Al. I do want to talk to you," she told me, trying to smooth my feathers. She was a nice dame and deserved something a lot better than Mr. Princeton.

"Do you know your lines for the rest of the week?" I asked Seames.

"Yes, I do, boss. And I must say that I love them. My congratulations."

Just what I didn't need—insincere flattery.

"We better get moving, Anna," he said, "our reservations are for nine."

Reservations! They shouldn't be out wining and dining, not on a school night. What was wrong with these kids? Didn't they know that we had to rehearse and block and tape all this week? Didn't they realize that this was really a critical time in the history of *Search for Happiness?* I was going to say something,

I was going to give them a piece of my mind, but at the last second I bit my tongue. I had things to do. I had to get home to write. If I had to carry this whole fucking show on my shoulders, I'd do it. Why not? Hadn't it been that way for the past ten years? Why should it be different now?

When I got outside the goddamn heavens were having a crying fit and I was soaked and unhappy and couldn't get a lousy cab, couldn't get my brain to work right, thinking about that incredibly brilliant, wonderful actress being taken for a ride by still another sleazo, thinking how happy she made me when she acted, thinking about hitting up Costein for a raise, thinking about my birthday, my forty-sixth birthday which was next Tuesday, thinking about whether Anna knew or whether old faithful Silvia would call or whether I should go to the old neighborhood to see Mom and Dad when . . .

When the pain shot through my arm. The piercing, horrible, out-of-my-mind pain, pain all over my chest, terror pain, death pain which threw me to my knees, which had me thinking that I was going to die like a dog on the fucking, filthy streets of New York City.

I was down on my knees, contemplating my last moments on earth, when some clown passed me by and said, "What are you doing down there, looking for your contacts?"

"No, you asshole. I'm dying of a fucking heart attack. Get me an ambulance."

The wise guy thought I was kidding, and he just kept on walking.

My arm, my chest, the whole top half of my body felt like a collapsed accordion. But somehow I managed to get myself up and throw myself in a cab and tell the battle-ax in the emergency room that I wasn't going to fill out any of her goddamn forms because I was too busy having a heart attack.

The doctor was scrawny and looked about nineteen years old. He instilled absolutely no confidence in me. He ran some tests and said it wasn't a heart attack at all, but maybe a "coronary event." I thought he was talking about crowning the queen of England. He said he needed to keep me under observation for a few hours, and then I could probably go home. I told the kid that he was nuts. I wasn't going anywhere. I was staying in the lousy hospital until they fixed up my heart. The pain had subsided—I admitted that—but I also admitted that I was scared shitless, because I had really been hurting before out there on the street, and this doctor-child better as hell understand the seriousness of what I had been through.

Three hours later I was in a bed in a private room and my own doctor, Felix Schiller, who had been taking care of me for twenty years, was right there next to me. Schiller was old now, maybe seventy, maybe more, but I trusted him like my own mother.

"It was nothing, Al."

"What do you mean, nothing?" I said to him.

"It wasn't even a flutter. Not even an event."

"It hurt."

"I'm sure it did."

"Well, if it hurt, then it was something."

"It was something in your head."

"It was in my chest, Felix. I'm telling you it was in my chest and up and down my arm."

"You've seen too many soap operas."

"What am I doing sitting here arguing with you when I know goddamn well something serious as hell happened to me this afternoon?"

"Sure it was serious. It was a serious warning. You've been working too hard. You've been worrying too much." He took off his little granny glasses and wiped them with a rumpled handkerchief. "I've seen this kind of thing happen all the time, Al. You *think* you should be having a heart attack so you do your best to bring one on. You did a good job, but not quite good enough. Next time, though. Next time you may be able to pull it off."

"You think I like this? You think I'm having fun lying here and thinking about the end of the fucking universe?"

"Maybe."

"Well, I'm not! And I'm telling you something, Felix. You can take your theories and shove them. Because I'm hurting, I'm hurting real bad."

"I don't doubt that. But this is just the practice hurt. If you don't do something about losing weight or getting in shape, you'll find that practice makes perfect, and your life really will be cut in half."

"I've never known you to resort to scare tactics, Felix."

"You're the one who scared yourself, Al."

"Well, what the hell am I going to do?"

"Eat less. Try a little jogging."

"I'm against that on principle. I have an exclusive commitment to spectator sports."

"Talking of spectator sports," my old friend Dr. Schiller said, "who do you like tomorrow in the fifth race?"

We wound up talking about the nags for a half hour, and then he left and said that I should check out tomorrow morning, but I told him that I wasn't about to do that, I was going to stay another night. I didn't care what it cost. I knew myself. Something had happened to me and I wasn't about to leave that goddamn hospital. I wanted to be safe and supervised until I was certain that the heartrending pain wasn't coming back. So I stayed, and I slept, though every half hour I woke up and pinched myself on the ass just to be sure that I was still alive and kicking.

28

Anna was barely aware of the unusually mild March weather. Her elegant dress was new—she had bought it only last week —and, because it was elasticized at the waist, it gave her the appearance of being even thinner than she really was. The fabric of the dress was wool, black or dark blue—it was difficult to tell which in the darkness of the Greek restaurant.

"What is the pattern on your dress?" Hanford asked her as

he let the forkful of squid fall into his mouth. "Are they ducks or swans?"

"Neither," she replied. "They're seraphim in flight. Don't you know angel wings when you see them?"

"Apparently not."

"The seraphim reminded me of the figure next to Santa Teresa, the angel holding the magic arrow."

"I see," he said, turning away and looking at an elderly couple at the next table.

"You should really read her *Vida*," she urged.

"I don't think that's necessary, Anna."

"I do, if you're really interested in understanding Sister Prudence."

"I believe I understand her well enough, thank you."

"You sound annoyed."

"Not in the least," he lied. "It's just when I go out, I want to be *out*, away from the demands of the part. Away from the whole scene."

"Do you consider it a *scene?*"

"It *is* a scene," he insisted. "It's a sweatshop."

"Then why do you do it?"

"I do it because I want to be an actor. Because I *am* an actor," he corrected himself. "But if you think that this is the kind of stuff I really want to be doing, you're sadly mistaken."

"Do you consider the role beneath you?" she asked.

"I don't think about it. I'm doing it until something better comes along."

"At one point," she said, "I felt the same way. But something has happened."

"I've noticed."

"It's serious. There's something serious about this whole business."

"You've been spending too much time with Al."

"It's not Al. Al has his own attitudes. Al has a tremendous enthusiasm about the show which I admire . . ."

"He's money-hungry."

"It's more than that. He's a gifted writer. He really is. But he's also strangely detached."

"Not strangely, wisely."

214

"At first I thought *Search* was a joke."

"It is a joke—a well-financed joke."

"But if you're honest with yourself," she asked him as, for the first time in the evening, she touched his hand, "isn't there something about Prudence and Brian which . . ."

"I don't want to hear about Prudence and Brian, Anna." He drew back his hand from hers. "I thought I made that clear."

Anna half-closed her eyes and tilted her head slightly upward. "Sister Prudence," she continued, "is on the brink of a fabulous adventure."

"It's a soap opera," he interrupted. "It's a routine soap opera."

"It could be anything," she replied. "A poem or a play, a vision, a prophecy, a comic strip. But at some point, you read it or you see it and you experience it. You live it. Hasn't that ever happened to you?"

"Of course it's happened—but doing Shakespeare, not Al Gonfio."

She left him alone for the remainder of the meal. She ate her lamb and drank her retsina. She tried to concentrate on the pale yellow of his shirt, the epaulets on his safari jacket. His eyelashes were even blonder than his eyebrows, blonder than the hair atop his head, and, she remembered, blonder than the hair on his chest. He had shaved before dinner. His skin was smooth, free of blemishes or cuts. "When you were a child," she asked him over their cups, "did you go to camp?"

He had to smile at the question. "Yes, as a matter of fact, I did."

"Tell me about it," she urged.

"It was in North Carolina," he began to tell the story. "Somewhere in the forests of North Carolina."

"Was it exclusive?" she wanted to know.

"Exclusive as exclusive can be."

"It sounds wonderful."

"We learned how to row and whittle and trace bear tracks. And sometimes, during those nights in early August when the breezes were cool and our fourteen-year-old passions ran hot, we'd sneak out and hike five miles down the road to Camp Evergreen. That's where the girls were. And I must confess,

215

that among all the campers, I had a certain reputation—maybe I was just precocious, but . . ."

She encouraged him to keep talking, she imagined herself there, in Camp Evergreen, the child of a corporate lawyer, wearing khaki walking shorts with sweet pleats in the front, wandering through the woods, picking berries and being pursued by light-haired children like Hanford Seames, well-mannered and full of fun. She thought of these things as he painted a picture of himself as a camp leader, a young Don Juan, a sterling athlete, a tireless explorer. And when he was finished, when he was obviously pleased with his memories and his descriptions, she said to him, "I want to show you where I spent my summers. I want to show you my neighborhood."

He was surprised, but not unwilling. "Why not?" he told Anna. "You can take me on the grand tour."

They went by taxi to Mulberry Street. The streets were soaked in moonlight. The sky was unusually clear and Anna felt excited and a little afraid as she took Hanford by the hand and began walking the neighborhood that she knew so well. She began pointing out certain landmarks to him. "I've been to Little Italy before," he reminded her. "Yes," she said, "but never with me." They walked past the bakeries and the fish stores, the meat markets and the vegetable stands boarded up for the night. Outside a corner candy store, rough-looking boys boasted of sexual conquests, saying the words "cunt" and "pussy" loud enough so that Anna and Hanford could hear. He was offended, she was not. She heard the boys; she knew who they were; she had been with them, or others like them, for most of her life. And she was especially happy to be walking past them in her double-breasted, fleece-lined raincoat, in her angels-in-flight woolen dress. She looked at the maze of fire escapes running up and down the sides and fronts of buildings like some sort of cruel public sculpture. It was hideous, she thought, hideous and uglier each time she returned. But this time was different; this time she was with Hanford. She pointed out the tenement where she had been raised, where her parents still lived. For a crazed moment, she considered taking him upstairs and introducing him to her mother and her father. But it was already past ten and her father would be asleep in front of the television set, and her mother would be talking to a friend on the phone about the price of eggs and cheese, and they would both be confused and disturbed by their daughter's presence. Still, the idea intrigued her, even excited her physically; she was increasingly aware of the fact that being with Hanford in the old neighborhood was arousing her in a way that she had never quite been aroused before. When they reached the Church of the Most Precious Blood, she said to him, "Let's go in. We must go in."

"No," he answered adamantly.

"I want to," she told him. "I very much want to."

He had sensed the sensuality in this trip, and he understood that she was almost desperate to enter the church. "You go in without me," he said. "I'll wait for you."

"No," she answered quickly, "that won't work."

He saw the need in her eyes, but he could not bring himself to respond. "Please," she begged, "I want you to come inside. I want you to see my church." She grabbed his arm and practically pushed him through the door. The church was dark and smelled of incense. It was cold and damp and he stood in the very back as she approached the altar. He saw that she did not kneel; she did not cross herself. He watched her walk past the burning candles, past the saints whose faces looked like waxed dolls. He wondered what was going through her mind as she continued walking through the deserted church, up and down the small aisles. "Do you see how amazing it is?" she asked as she approached him. "Do you see how amazing and vulgar it is?" she asked him again.

"There must be a lot of churches like this," he whispered.

"No," she corrected him. "There's only this one for me. Only this one has the memories."

And she turned and kissed him and he could not respond, and she kissed him again. She tried holding him but he backed away —he was afraid now, he was repulsed and afraid—but for the moment she was stronger and quicker and once more she forced her mouth on his, her mouth and her tongue.

He was relieved when they left the church. He suggested that they take a cab to her place. She agreed. She wanted him while her mind was still flushed with contradictions and memories. She kissed him again in the taxi, and again he was not receptive. He was surprised and confused by his own reaction—this had never happened before—and when they entered her apartment he suggested that they smoke marijuana and drink whiskey. He knew that he was going to need help.

They smoked and drank and she told him how much she loved being with him, how much this evening had meant to her. She had painted him on a canvas she had abandoned in her childhood, and now that he was there, she could not let go. She could not stop looking at him. He came to her—she was sitting on her newly acquired corduroy couch; the buttons to her angels-in-flight dress were open to the elasticized waist—and he kissed her. She moaned a distant moan, and he knew that she had been waiting, that she had been exciting herself all evening. On the way to the bedroom he noticed the photograph of the saint above her television set, and he was going to ask her about it, but he remained silent.

He slipped off her dress and his own shirt and their chests were naked and close in her bed, their nipples touched and she moaned again and moved toward him. She touched him, but he didn't want to be touched. *This isn't working,* he thought to himself, *this isn't working.* And she understood and she said, "Let's just smoke another joint and pretend."

"Pretend what?" he asked.

"Pretend that we're on that golf course and that you're loving her, you're laying her, loving and laying the nun. Just pretend," she urged. "Just close your eyes and pretend, because if we can act there we can act here and it doesn't make any difference. Do it. Just do what I say."

But he couldn't. "I'm tired," he told her. "I ate too much and I drank too much and we walked too much. That's it. I'm just too tired." And he kissed her politely and put on his shirt and his safari jacket and told her that tomorrow they would be working together and that they would talk and go out later in the week. When she heard the front door to her apartment close, she put on a robe and went to her kitchenette and began to write without a second's hesitation:

Dear John,
    It's been a long time in coming, but I think I'm over you. In fact, I know I am. For weeks I waited for you to call or to simply show up at our loft. But somehow

218

I got through one day, and then another. And after each day—each day of not calling you, not calling the airlines and making another reservation and planning another trip to rescue you from life without me—I congratulated myself. I didn't call John on this Monday, I said to myself, and then I didn't call John on this Tuesday. And slowly I found that there were other things to occupy my mind—my role, and Al, and Al's plans for the show and for the part—rehearsals and makeup and tapings and seeing myself in this costume, this nun's habit. And you know something, John? I only thought of calling you thirty times each day instead of a hundred times, and the number decreased and decreased, even though I was lonely and horny when I thought of you and the thousands of things we've done together. Now for the first time in my life I am heading in a different direction. Now I try to remember the way I loved you in the beginning or the middle or at the end, and I can't. And tonight, John, tonight especially, you were nowhere near my thoughts as I walked through the past that you and I shared as silly children. Because I was not alone. I was with a man whose sensitivity and understanding is so far greater than anything . . .

And she crumbled the paper in her hand and threw it on the floor and stared out the window, into the moonlit night, and considered the scene: the lay of the land, the golf course, the terrible hunger in the hearts of the two lovers.

29

"I don't want to worry you," I said to Anna when I called her the next afternoon, "but I'm in the hospital."

"My God, what's wrong?"

"Just a little something with my heart."

"Your heart! Al, tell me what happened." I could hear the concern in her voice. It was genuine. The girl really cared about me.

"I better not talk too much right now," I said. "It's a bit of a strain."

"When can I come see you?"

"I suppose you can come now if you want to."

"Of course I want to."

I gave her the hospital name and room number, and before she arrived, I managed to persuade one of the nurses to run down a *Daily Racing Form* for me. When I heard Anna knocking, though, I put the paper away.

She ran to the side of my bed and bent over and kissed me. Her eyes sparkled and she smelled of perfume. I was glad to know that she had put on perfume just for me. "I wish you had called me before," she said. "I wish to God you had called me before."

"I did, but I knew you were out. Didn't you have dinner with Seames last night?"

"Yes, but we were back early."

"How come?" I wanted to know.

"It doesn't matter. I want to hear about you, Al. I want you to tell me what happened."

"It was kind of frightening, honey, I have to admit."

"What did the doctors say?"

"They took a lot of tests. I'm not sure what the results mean right now."

"But are you all right? Was the heart attack serious?"

"Seems like I've survived the fucking thing."

"I want to stay here with you."

"You are here."

"I mean that I want to stay here tonight."

"The whole night?"

"Yes."

"No, baby, that's not necessary."

"Tell the nurse to get me a cot."

"I appreciate it, sugar, I really do, but I'll be okay."

"I'm not moving, Al. I don't want you to have to go through this night alone. Not after everything you've done for me."

I didn't argue for long. Why should I? I was really moved by her request. I didn't know that the little girl cared that much.

"What happened with you and Seames last night?"

"I told you that doesn't matter. What matters is that you get some rest. This show's been worrying you too much."

"What's been worrying you?" I asked Anna, looking into her eyes. "You look upset."

"I'm upset, you nut, because you're upset." She kissed me again on the forehead. I wanted to take her in my arms and tell her that she made me feel all right—just the way she looked and moved, all her mystery and brilliance as an actress and a lady and a little girl. I wanted to tell her that I loved her for coming here and being with me and worrying about my dying of a god-damn heart attack. That was awfully sweet of her. And now she wanted to stay the night—imagine that!—she couldn't stand the thought of me being alone in this lousy, lonely hospital room. Anna Calzolari was really something special.

"I want to talk to you," she said, "but I won't do it if it's going to upset you."

"Nothing you say upsets me, sugar. What's it about?"

"A lot of things."

I began to worry. "What things?"

"Hanford, Brian, John . . ."

"*John?*"

221

"I wrote to him last night."

"That was a stupid fucking thing to do."

"I tore up the letter before I finished it."

"That was a smart thing to do."

"He was on my mind for the first time in a while, Al."

"How did that son of a bitch sneak back into your head?"

"Brian and I walked through the old neighborhood."

"Brian?"

"Hanford. I mean Hanford."

"What were you doing down there?"

"I wanted him to see the church."

"That was a goddamn crazy idea."

"Not so crazy. I thought it would help him understand."

"He doesn't need to understand. He just needs to memorize the fucking lines or read them off the idiot cards. *I'm* the one who understands. If you need to go down to the old neighborhood with anyone, it should be with me."

"Then you understand . . ."

"Of course I understand. I've got to go down there myself from time to time."

"Into the church as well?"

"I don't go that far. No."

"Well, I did last night. I'm not sure why. It was just something I had to do, something that I wanted to experience with him."

"How did Seames feel about it?"

"He wouldn't go in."

"Fucking anti-Catholic."

"I wanted him to understand, I wanted him to see the beginnings for himself. He finally came in, but once we were inside, I couldn't get John out of my mind. I knew that I was being foolish, but I started remembering being a teenage girl, being John's girlfriend, and wanting to get married—can you believe this, Al?—actually wanting to marry him in that church."

She told me about the rest of the evening in great detail. I was in the hospital bed in a nightshirt and she was sitting in a straight-back chair next to me. As she poured out her heart to me, she held my hand. And as I listened to her, my heart started beating faster. That scared me; I almost stopped her; maybe this

wasn't the right time, maybe I was still too weak. But I didn't
—I couldn't—say a word. I listened and I listened and I listened
some more as she went over her childhood with John, and college, and dropping out, and the play, and the deal with Gwen,
and John leaving and Hanford backing off. When she was
through, she was crying and laughing—"I don't know whether
this is silly or sad," she said to me—and I saw that it was nearly
3:00 A.M. and I asked her if she wanted a cot brought in now.
"No," she told me, "I just feel like talking. I really feel like
talking more."

Then she spoke of Sister Prudence. She spoke of Sister Prudence until the sun came up. She spoke without pause, without
hesitation, without doubt. She spoke because she had to speak
—I saw that. She had come to the hospital because she was
worried about me, but once she started talking I saw that her
need was greater than mine. Poor fucking kid. She was really
wrapped up in this part, and nothing I could say would make
any difference. Not now. She analyzed that nun from fifteen
different angles. She told me how the sister felt before she got
laid, while she was getting laid, and after she got laid. She was
getting herself excited and she was getting me excited, and I
started listening to my heart again—it was pounding something
fierce—and I wanted her to stop, I wanted her to spare me the
details of the blood and joy and the guilt and the sacred spirit of
the body and the soul, but instead of quieting her down I found
myself taking a pencil and a piece of paper and jotting down
notes. Because I knew that we were back on track again, closer
than we had ever been. And it was beautiful, and it was definitely the reason—I knew goddamn well it was the reason—
that God had thrown us together.

30

Gwen Snodes turned over in bed. Her head ached with the pain and pleasure of last night's party. When was the last time she had done something like this? She couldn't remember. Up all night, slept through the morning, and now it was past noon. Past noon, she thought to herself, as she slipped quietly out of bed, careful not to disturb him, as she put on a robe and walked into her tiny living room. There—out of curiosity, almost out of a sense of perversity—she decided to turn on the TV and watch *Search for Happiness*. It was time. She wouldn't even bother to wash up, to brush her teeth or splash water on her eyes. She'd watch the show exactly as she was—groggy, hung over, haggard and yet, in a strange way, happy about last night and this morning, happy to be sitting here and seeing what Sister Prudence was up to now.

The art director has done a fine job with the set. The moonlight looks real. The painted trees on the Astroturf golf course lawn are convincing. The mood is soft and romantic.

Brian appears. He is not wearing a coat or jacket, but a small-checked, dark blue sport shirt and light beige pants. This is the first time he has been seen in the show without a suit. He looks around nervously, glances at his watch, waits.

When Sister Prudence walks on the set she is not wearing her habit, and the result is shocking: Her black hair is loose and touches her shoulders. Her white blouse and her dark skirt, her exquisitely thin figure, her animated face—Brian can scarcely believe the effect.

"I, I don't know what to say," he manages to mutter.

"You needn't say anything," she assures him.

224

"You, you . . ." He is unable to finish the sentence.

"I look like a normal woman? Is that what you want to say?"

"No, you don't look normal at all. You look absolutely . . . ethereal. Yes, you look ethereal."

"I feel very strange."

"Ashamed?"

"No, strange. And even stranger looking at you. You are without your costume."

He smiles. "You mean my suit."

"Your uniform."

"And yours," he adds.

"They are gone. Our former selves."

"You will have to call me Brian."

"I already have been."

"I haven't heard you."

"How can you hear my dreams?"

"Why are we just standing here like this?"

"Shall we walk? Shall we sit?" she asks.

"Let's sit on the grass."

They do so, they sit quite close to each other, but they do not touch. Sister Prudence gazes up at the sky and says, "I have never seen it look quite this way."

"The sky," he reflects.

"The heavens. The heavens seem so close to us. The heavens have descended . . ."

"Or we have ascended."

"Are we climbing or sinking?" she asks.

"You haven't called me by name."

"Brian. Your name is Brian."

"And I can no longer call you Sister."

"You can if you like."

"It's impossible."

"Would you rather I call you Brother?"

He laughs. "As if this weren't enough. Now you add a cheerful note of incest."

"You're thinking in terms of sin."

"I'm not sure I believe in sin. Only foolishness."

"Have I been foolish to listen to you? Have I been foolish to listen to my heart?"

"It's hard for me to think now."

"Then don't."

"I began this. This is my doing."

"It is not. The evening belongs to us both."

She takes his hand and looks into his eyes. He brings her hand to his lips.

"You don't know how long," she says, "how long I've thought and . . ."

"Don't," he assures her, kissing her hand over and over again, "please don't say anything."

"There's no reason to be afraid," she tells him, "not now."

"Before it was you," he reminds her, "it was you who were frightened. . . ."

"It's never just me or just you. It's *us*. When I'm weak, you're strong, and when you're afraid, I'm not."

"I don't understand."

" 'By our first strange and fatall interview,' " she recites, " 'By all desires which thereof did ensue . . .' "

" 'By our long starving hopes,' " he continues from memory, " 'by that remorse / Which my words' masculine persuasive force / Begot in thee . . .' "

"Our hopes need starve no longer."

"No longer," he repeats as he takes her in his arms and kisses her. They fall back on the grass. Now lying next to each other, they stare up into the sky.

"It will be different, it will be very new," she warns him.

"Everything about you is different. Everything about you is new."

"Now I am afraid."

"Now I am not."

"I have no experience in these matters, I have no . . ."

He closes her mouth with a kiss and says softly, "You have the experience of a lifetime of loving, loving beyond yourself."

"But if this love is destructive . . ." Her resistance is weak.

"If it's love, it can't be destructive."

"It's new, it's all so new," she says as she allows him to kiss her again, and again, as they draw close, as their words—their questions and their answers—become lost as they clutch and cling and finally call each other by name, as he finally says, "Prudence," as she finally says, "Brian," as the camera pans

226

up to the glowing moon, as the strains of the organ swell, as the picture fades to black.

Gwen Snodes shook her head. She laughed to herself, but she was also strangely moved. She wasn't as contemptuous as she would have liked to have been. Angry at her own attitude, she got up and flicked off the TV. She wasn't about to get hooked on this garbage.

She went to the bathroom and washed her face. She looked in the mirror and saw that her great mass of light blond curls was in a state of revolt. She'd wash her hair later.

She returned to the bedroom. She saw that he was still there, sleeping on his stomach. He still hadn't moved. Again, she thought about seeing him at the party last night; she thought about his rather insulting approach and the way he had excited her. She thought about her own foolishness. What need did she have for this man? The sex was maddeningly sensational, but was it worth it? And would it ever be worth it—even for one night—to hook up with someone as beautiful and as bad as John Palermo?

"We need to be together tonight," she had told him that afternoon they had taped the golf course scene.

"I'm not sure," he said.

"We have to. We must," she insisted.

"I thought you were going to be with Al."

"Al's already out of the hospital. He's fine."

"I'm tired, Anna," Hanford pleaded.

"I'll cook you dinner," she offered. They were still on the golf course set.

"I'll call you when I get home."

"No," she shot back suddenly. "Let's go together. Let's leave now."

He didn't want to, but he did. The scorching scene had gotten to him, left him yearning for action and retreat at the same time. He remembered the first night in the Berkshires. He let her take over.

They changed and met in the downstairs lobby of the milk plant. She could smell the beginnings of spring in the late-afternoon air—a softness, a distant scent of trees. She pictured a golf course. She kissed him with her tongue in the taxicab. He felt her breasts, just as he had wanted to on the set. This would work, he told himself; he would be able to love her as she had never been loved before.

In her apartment, by the bed, he noticed the volumes of poetry, the editions of Donne and Crashaw, the books on Bernini and the scholarly tracts on Santa Teresa. He said nothing.

"On the rug," she begged him. "Please love me on the rug."

He was startled. At first he thought that the carpet was a piece of Astroturf that she had swiped from the set. But it wasn't; it just looked that way. It was actually a short green shag which ran the length of the bed.

When he touched her, she was already extraordinarily wet. "It happened during the show," she said. "Everything happened at once."

She wanted him quickly. He knew that, and now he was not unwilling. That would be the easiest way for both of them. He joined her on the rug, feeling foolish, even a little ashamed—he remembered the word—ashamed—for participating in the charade. But what difference did it make? She was crazy for him. A little weird, but crazy for him all the same. He would have her right away.

"I want to tell you things," she said to him.

"I don't want to hear," he insisted.

"I want to call you different names. I want to do things that I've never done, that I've never dreamt of doing . . ."

"Too much talk," he protested, "there's too much talk."

She was ready—hungry and wet—and he loved her quickly. Much too quickly. He didn't kiss her long enough. He didn't fondle her. He didn't linger or languish. He plunged. He was strong now, and he wanted to stay strong for her. Be strong inside her. And he was, but for the shortest time. Long enough for him, and him alone.

Afterward she didn't release him and he resisted. He wanted to rest or to leave or to eat or to tell her stories about his undergraduate days at Princeton. He had never met anyone like her. He hid his confusion with sophistication.

"I think we could both use a drink," he said. "Let me do the honors."

228

Still, she held him. "What were you thinking about?" she asked. "What was in your head?"

He wouldn't say. He waited for his release. "We'll talk later," he begged off. "We'll go at this hot scene again."

She let him go. She lay there for a few minutes, listening to the sound of running water in the bathroom. She fixed him dinner and later when they made love again, again on the green rug, she quoted from Donne and called him Brian. Again, it didn't last. Again, she wanted more. Again, she spoke of other scenes, other fantasies and dreams. Again, she sounded like someone else.

When he left before midnight, he told himself that it was nothing. He kissed her and she held onto him. "There's nothing to worry about," she said, wearing her billowy black robe. "If it's love, it can't be destructive."

31

I didn't mind the jogging suit. Actually, the white piping down the side might have even looked a little dashing. It was one of those $75 jobs. I figured since I got the shoes for free, I might as well splurge on the suit.

I really didn't give a shit what I looked like. Let the assholes laugh. If I appeared a little funny trotting up Lexington Avenue at nine on a Saturday morning, tough. I had convinced myself that I had to do something, and do it quickly. The doc was right. I was too young to start messing around with heart conditions.

Hell, I was in the prime of my life. I was a premier head writer, maybe the best goddamn hack that this network had ever seen. And everyone knew it, including the kid. In fact, when I took an extra day to recuperate in the hospital I must have had a dozen calls. Costein wanted to know what he could send.

Money, I said. He laughed and asked me when I was getting
out. Tomorrow, I said. And I'd be jogging on the weekend.
"You're dealing with a different generation," I told him. "Not
a candy-ass crew like my Ivy League–educated assistants who
couldn't put together a decent plot on their own to save their
lives." "Well, take it easy," Costein said. "We don't want to
lose you, not now." "Fucking A straight," I said. "You lose
me and you've lost the fastest horse on the track." "Easy,
easy," he said to me, "I want you around to finish the race."
"Don't worry, kid, I'm just getting warmed up."

I did take it easy for the next few days. I outlined the remainder of the month's stories on all the segments (except Sister
Prudence's) to my assistants and told them to flesh out the rest
by themselves. As usual, I saved the nun for myself. I hung
around the apartment and talked to the boys—my bookies and
a few other cronies—and even made a crazy bet on a Dodger-
Yankee baseball game in the Grapefruit League down in Florida. The exhibition game didn't count for anyone except me. I
dropped a couple of hundred bucks, but I didn't care because
the ratings were up and the phone kept ringing with people
asking me about my by-now-famous coronary event. I only left
the apartment once, and that was to see my girl Anna act up a
storm on the golf course. I wouldn't have missed that scene for
the world.

Toward the end of the week, though, I've got to confess that
I gained five pounds from moping around and eating crackers
and doughnuts and other useless crap. So I called up the doc
and said, Felix, I'm ready to exercise so I better come over and
get one of those $250 checkups that have made you a fucking
millionaire. Don't bother, he said, I know you like a book and
you can save your money. Go out and run for a little while, he
told me. Don't push it. Stop when you're hurting. If you can go
a couple blocks you'll be doing good. Well, fuck that, I thought
to myself. I can sure as hell go more than a couple of blocks.
How old did he think I was? So I decided to go back up to that
place on Madison—the joint that Costein took me to—and get
myself some spiffy running duds. I figured that I had done
enough talking.

I bought the gear—the suit, some socks, a couple of jockstraps—and got a good night's sleep and dreamed of flying into Vegas in the network Lear jet and woke up and remembered not to eat or drink anything, zipped up and laced up and went downstairs and did a few stretching exercises that I had read about in the runners' magazine that the guy in the store gave me. I did ten deep knee bends just for good measure and headed out toward Lexington.

I started slowly, and I thought to myself that this wasn't half bad. I took it very easy. The morning was mild and a good-looking lady whose tan told me she just got back from Florida smiled at me and I thought: Well, hell, I'm out here and I'm doing it, I'm taking off weight and building up my heart and getting strong as a fucking bull. Yes, sir. I hit Lexington and the Armenian guy in the grocery store where I buy beer pointed at me and laughed and I shot the little bastard the shaft and kept going, yes, sir, I kept going because I was jogging with the rest of the healthy young Americans, and soon I'd trim down to 150 or maybe even 140 pounds and Anna would really be surprised when she saw me all new and skinny and raring to go, racing up Lexington Avenue, past the newsstand and the little bookstore, me shuffling my feet as though I had been born in a pair of goddamn sneakers, like I was still a teenager downtown in the playground, jumping for baskets and bragging about the pussy I was getting, and thinking about Anna, about that last show she taped, the show where she throws off her habit and finally gets it on with Brian. I'm thinking about that and how she knocked out everyone, how she left the crew and Dick and Howard speechless and how she disappeared afterward with Seames and, shit, I knew where she was going and I wanted to stop her, but what could I say? And what right did I have? And anyway she was just another crazy actress, they were all crazy, but this one was especially sweet, I thought, and especially talented, this Anna Calzolari from the old neighborhood was now getting to be a big-time afternoon TV actress thanks to me and my scripts, and I wondered—now huffing and puffing just a little bit —passing by my bank and cleaners, I wondered if she appreciated everything I had done for her, because if the truth be known I was making her a star and lot of guys in my position would take advantage, goddamn right they would, they'd throw her in the rack so fucking fast her head would spin, but I was different and she was different even though I had a feeling—just a sneaking suspicion—that my day would come. Right then my knees were hurting something awful and I had a sharp pain—a long, sharp pain—just below my gut, now cutting into me like a knife, and my shoulder blades were aching and my sides were aching and it even felt like my armpits were aching and suddenly my calves turned to butter and all I could think of was wheelchairs and ambulances and I stopped.

I stopped and turned around and saw that I wasn't all that far away from my place. I stopped and reconsidered what the fuck I had been doing. I had been inflicting damage upon myself. What in the name of sanity had driven me to such ends? Why should I abuse my body and waste my energy on an enterprise that did nothing but bring misery and pain? Screw Costein and Seames and the other assholes bent on blowing up their lungs with the polluted carbon-monoxided air of New York City. I was smarter than that. I was old enough to know how to control my ambitions. I was the wise old fox and I'd be goddamned if I'd get out every morning and put myself through this torture.

I walked home very slowly. I avoided the Armenian grocer. I was sweaty and steamy and very unhappy. The bottom of my feet hurt. My Street Fighters were all fought out. I had had it. I got upstairs and shook my head—no more fads for me—and licked a new cigar and stuck it in my mouth and lit up and felt the fabulous flavor of that thick, sweet tobacco rolling around my mouth. I sat down on the couch and put my feet up on the coffee table and enjoyed this stogie more than any stogie I could remember, except one or two which were smoked after some especially glorious fucks. I felt my body smoldering and I closed my eyes and thought about those times when I would play stickball in the streets long into the afternoon and the evening when the last light of the day had faded behind the fruit stands and the butcher shops and my mother would yell at me from the window of our kitchen, screaming that I was late for dinner and the old man would take the strap to me if I didn't get there in two minutes flat and the building would smell of everyone's supper, soups and stews and coffee and scallions and . . .

I stopped remembering and answered the phone.

232

"You sound calm," Anna said to me.

"I should be, I just got through jogging."

"Jogging! After what you've been through! That's crazy!"

I could tell she was really afraid. "Don't worry, baby," I assured her, "all under doctor's supervision."

"Did you run far?"

"I wasn't counting. Pretty far. Three, maybe four miles." I meant to say *blocks,* but I didn't bother correcting myself.

"That's very far, Al. I don't think you should be straining yourself. Not now."

"Don't go worrying your pretty little head about it."

"My head doesn't feel so pretty."

"Who's been messing up your head, honey?"

"The sandman. My dreams have been so real, Al, I've been waking up every ten minutes."

"Are you alone when you wake up?"

"Yes."

"That's good."

"I'm not sure."

"You don't need to be sure. I'm sure enough for both of us. What are you dreaming about?"

"John is there, and he's talking to the mother superior, he's telling her things that I don't want her to hear."

"Forget about John."

"These are dreams, Al. I can't tell myself what not to dream."

"You can try."

"It's impossible."

"Not if you take a couple of belts of Scotch before you go to bed."

She laughed. I loved the fact that I could always make her laugh.

"I'm worried what's going to happen with the mother superior," she said to me. "I'm worried about that, and I'm worried about Brian. I have the feeling that I'm scaring him off."

"Are you kidding?" I decided to play along with her. "That son of a bitch wouldn't leave for all the tea in China."

"How can you be so sure? He seems very wary."

"He does what I tell him to do. Him and all the others."

233

"And what are you going to tell him?"

"You sound like you want to come over and help me write."

"I do, I do."

"Then what are you waiting for?"

"The word."

"The word is run."

When she arrived a half hour later she was wearing a jogging outfit. I nearly fell down laughing.

"Stop it," she said, "you'll have another heart attack."

"This is a killer. This is really a fucking killer," I told her.

She looked so cute I wanted to take a picture. Her little ass and her gorgeous little figure and her hair in a bun in the back of her head and her eyes all bright and smiling. What a sweetheart.

"Are you taking up jogging?" I asked her.

"I decided to keep you company on your runs."

"I run at funny times," I said, not wild about the idea of jogging with her. Who knew how far she could go? "And when I run I like to meditate."

"I wouldn't dream of disturbing you, then. Actually I bought this suit because Hanford suggested it."

"What a womanizer! I've heard about those guys who go out and jog at the reservoir just so they can hit on women. I'm sure he's one of the leaders of the pack."

"It might have been my suggestion, Al. You have to understand, I'm really interested in getting to know him better, and . . ."

"There's nothing more to know. It's all right there, floating on the surface."

"Let's get down to work." She changed the subject. "My head's spinning with ideas, and before I forget my dreams, I want you to hear them all."

We sat there in our jogging suits and talked all day. It was as though our jogging suits made us talk faster. She washed my dishes and fixed me a salad for lunch and a steak for dinner. We talked that night, still dressed up to jog, and somehow—through the excitement of her imagination and mine—we worked out another bunch of Sister Prudence segments. I did some explaining—I would tell her when I saw a technical problem about a certain scene or set—but mainly I listened. And while I was

234

certain that everything she was saying was going to warm the insides of Costein's calculating heart, and while I loved looking at her half-closing her eyes and speaking so sweetly about the traumas in Troy, later in the evening I grew a little alarmed: There was a point when I realized that I couldn't get her to stop talking about Sister Prudence. Not for a blessed minute.

32

I was back in the saddle again, back up in the control booth watching it happen. Naturally, all morning long everyone at the milk plant was asking me how I felt. And, to tell the truth, I felt okay, even though I was a little worried about that last work session with Anna over at my place. Not worried about the plot —the plot was dynamite—but worried about Anna, who seemed the slightest bit weird. But I pushed that out of my mind and I told everyone that hell, yes, I felt terrific, good enough to be out there jogging on the fucking streets. Though actually I had some indigestion and noisy gas problems. The Saturday jog had left me hungry as a horse all weekend and Sunday especially —when it was Chinese for lunch and a couple of submarine bombs for dinner—had left my stomach a little fucked up on this Monday morning. No matter. The definition of a pro is a guy who works on good days and bad, and so I was working, watching a new episode, and all the time thinking while I was watching, planning new scripts and weighing the odds of the opening games of the baseball season.

Anna has the habit on. She is Sister Prudence and Sister Prudence is back in the convent the morning after she snuck out. Her face is radiant, but there is also a streak of anxiety that wrinkles her forehead. She's reading a book when we hear a knock on her door. She quickly puts the book in her desk drawer; we do not see the title.

The mother superior enters, looking stern. "I have a feeling, my child," she says to Anna, "that we must no longer postpone a conversation that we promised ourselves a while back."

"I am sorry," the young nun says, "but today I am feeling quite awful."

"Are you ill?"

"Yes."

"What is ailing you?"

"I'm not sure." Sister Prudence speaks so softly that she is barely audible. She does not look up at the mother superior.

"Is it pain of the body or of the soul?" the older woman asks.

"It's both. It's everywhere."

"Then you must describe it to me."

"I can't."

"Surely there are words to describe what you are feeling."

"If there are, they are beyond me."

"If you are troubled, then you must seek the help of God. I implore you to seek of the help of God, Prudence."

"I have tried, but words have failed me."

"Words are not required. We need not seek the Holy Spirit with mere words. Surely you know that."

"I am no longer certain of what I know."

"You are doubting."

"My mind is elsewhere, Mother Superior. My mind is outside of this convent, outside of my teaching."

"I have sensed that. It's something I have seen."

"And I no longer feel what I used to feel. I no longer know what I used to know."

Mother Superior puts her hand on Sister Prudence's shoulder. "You mustn't be afraid of new feelings, my child. Even though at first they may seem absurd and contrary to everything you have ever believed, they more often than not represent the will of God."

"I want to believe that."

"We change. We grow older and we change. If we fail to

236

understand the change, then we fear it. And when we fear change, we die.''

I watched the monitor as the picture faded. Technicians and actors assembled on another set and prepared for the next segment. I spotted Anna walking off the floor. She appeared to be shaken; she looked as if she were crying.

''Where have you been? Where in the name of God have you been?'' Sally is screaming. There is terror in her voice.

''I told you I had to go back to the office. I was researching a case,'' Brian answers.

''I called a million times. There was no answer.''

''I didn't want to bother with the phones. I didn't want to be disturbed.''

''You've been working late every night for a week.''

''The case is difficult, nearly impossible. You have to understand that. . . .''

''Your mother has had a stroke.'' Sally says the words plainly, deliberately.

''My God.''

''The maid found her. She was in the den.''

''Where's Father?''

''We don't know.''

''You don't know?''

''We couldn't get you, we couldn't find him. I didn't know whether to go to the hospital or to your office. I didn't know what to do.'' Sally is sobbing as Brian runs to the phone.

He calls Henry Grieson, a senior partner in the firm, a man his father's age.

''I have to know where my father is, Henry,'' Brian hurriedly explains. ''My mother has had a stroke.''

''I can't believe it. I saw her only . . .''

''Where's the old man, Henry?''

''I don't know, Brian. I can't tell you exactly . . .''

''Don't lie to me! You know! You always know! What's the name of his mistress? What's the name of his current mistress?''

Sally holds her hand over her mouth as though she is about to scream.

237

"Brian, you've put me in a very embarrassing position," says the voice on the other end of the phone.

"The hell with your position! I want to know where my father is."

"He'd know. He'd know where you found out. I just can't, Brian. I just can't. I'll go to the hospital and see your mother myself now. I'll meet you there."

"I want the name."

"I have no name."

Brian hangs up in Henry Grieson's face and runs back out of the house, leaving his wife behind.

From a telephone in the hallway of the convent, Sister Prudence dials the number. The phone rings. Sally MacNiece's "Hello" is hardly comprehensible through the sobs. Sister Prudence places the phone gently back on the hook without saying a word.

"It's the phone for you, Gonfio," someone said to me in the control booth. I was smoking a cigar, waiting for them to set up for the next scene which we were due to start taping in fifteen minutes. Once we get under way, this shit really starts to fly.

I picked up the phone next to Dick the director. "Al Gonfio here," I announced.

"What are you doing later on this week?"

"Writing," I said to Mark Costein. That's the best answer I could think of for the boss.

"Can you write in L.A.?"

"I can do anything in L.A."

"I'd like to have you out there. We have a place on the beach and . . ."

"Who's *we?*" I broke in.

"The network."

Goddamn, I thought to myself.

"There's some people out there I'd like you to meet and, besides, I figure you can use the relaxation."

"I fly first-class," I said, deciding to play hard to get.

"Upgrade yourself from coach and pay the difference."

"That ain't the most gracious invitation I've ever received."

"Consider it more an order than an invitation. Besides, you'll like jogging on the beach."

"My Street Fighters don't like sand."

"Have you been running?"

"Only to the can."

"You're such a wise guy, Gonfio. Here I thought I was contributing to your heart attack recovery effort."

Actually, I was touched. Maybe he did care. "Thanks, kid," I said. "I'd love to go to the Coast with you."

"Miss Lee will call you later with your reservations."

"Tell Miss Lee that I love her."

"And Gonfio," he concluded.

"Yeah?"

"I'm glad you're back on the track. It's a good thing you've got your little nun revved up and running for you."

"You ain't seen nothing yet, kid. You ain't seen a goddamn thing."

Baxter MacNiece arrives in the hospital lobby. He is wearing a blue blazer and charcoal gray slacks. He sees his son pacing back and forth, nervously smoking a cigarette.

"I came as soon as I heard," he says to Brian. "How is she? Where's Dr. Kramer?"

"I don't know."

"Dammit, son, tell me how your mother is!"

"Henry finally decided to call you."

"I'm not interested in Henry, I'm interested in your mother's well-being."

"*My mother's well-being!* Don't make me laugh. Don't make me sick."

His eyes blazing with contempt, Baxter turns his back on his son; he storms off toward the information desk in search of the family doctor and his ailing wife.

Anna and Hanford went to his place after the taping. He wanted to play records—soft Brazilian music—and smoke dope. She wanted to talk about drama, to talk about the script, about the effect of affairs, of guilt and fear and far-flung fantasies. "Let's just get stoned," he said, passing her the fat-packed reefer. The marijuana took her further back into the story: her own, Sister Prudence's. She continued to talk, even though at this point she was only talking to herself.

His apartment was dark blue and decorator-designed. There were glass tables and expensive Danish chairs, and he wanted her to notice. She hadn't been here before. But she said nothing, as though she had seen the apartment before, or was not seeing it now.

"There's this one idea I have about Prudence, though. It's not so much . . ."

"You haven't seen all of my apartment."

The bedroom featured an abstract painting of a naked woman in her bath. The canvas was too large, the colors too obvious. They smoked another joint and still she did not comment about his place. Later, she kissed his cock with her mouth and her tongue for a long while, but he did not grow excited. Then he mentioned something about the show—the reaction of Baxter to his wife's stroke—and engaged her in an hour-long conversation which took the pressure off him. He wanted to make love to her; he wanted to prove something to himself, but he couldn't. Instead, when she asked him if she could spend the night, he quickly said yes. He turned on the phonograph—there were two enormous speakers which directly faced the bed so that the energy of the music could flow forth—but the pumping disco beat did nothing for him, did nothing for her.

"There is something very beautiful," she said to him, "about talking and not loving. Or making the talk the love."

He was grateful to her. He kissed her and put his arm around her. He ran his fingers over her nose and circled her small nipples with his tongue. She squirmed and then she began to speak again, bringing Hanford up to date on the swift changes that would soon take place in the life of Brian and Prudence. Telling the story, she found herself excited. He yawned and fell asleep, even as she continued to explain the plot, even as she touched herself, opened herself, even as she pressed and pushed and probed and rubbed and finally squeezed herself free, dreaming all the while of a very small room in a convent, while she said the names, her eyes now shut, her eyes now staring at Hanford, her mind moving to the feel of the golf course's plastic grass.

33

Costein looked strange in blue jeans as he walked along the edge of the Pacific Ocean on Malibu Beach. I was back in the house on the phone to my man, trying to get some action at Santa Anita—I wanted to go out there, but I couldn't; that would really have been lousy manners—and I was figuring odds in my head and looking at the roller-coaster surf and wondering what the hell I was doing back out on the crazy Coast.

Not that I really didn't know. The kid was nuts about me—it was that simple. Over three weeks had passed since my coronary event, the numbers were the highest in the history of the soap—my fucking nun had hit those housewives like a ton of bricks—and Costein was so happy he didn't know what to do. That's why he had asked me to spend the weekend at the network place in Malibu, the house where only a half-dozen or so of the big boys were privileged to stay. He wanted me to meet some of the entertainment executives in Los Angeles, and there were going to be a few parties and I could relax and do some business and have some fun and I'd have a room to myself and a typewriter. How could I say no?

At first I was a little confused. But then I realized what was happening: In a strange sort of way, the kid wanted to be my friend. I think I comforted him. I was so different from the smooth-talking management brains that bounced around the padded cells they called conference rooms and offices that he was fascinated. He also liked the fact that I'd tell him to get fucked when I felt like it. But mainly he had seen that I delivered. I had given him the goods and had noodled with his Nielsens to the tune of maybe several million bucks of ad revenue.

But in spite of Costein's friendly attitude toward me, I really didn't know the guy. He was eager and earnest and playing the network game for all it was worth—which was plenty. He was studious and scientific and sensationally hardworking and had something of a sense of humor, and still he hid behind his tinted glasses and his straight suits and his fixation on numbers. And even now, even as I looked at him through the window on the beach, I noticed that in his left hand he was carrying a black, shiny object. At first I thought it was a gun, but then I saw that it was another kind of weapon; he was holding a calculator. The kid was strolling along the fucking Pacific Ocean with a calculator in his hand! I wanted to laugh, but I thought about the two thousand banana peels that I was about to lay on a steed called Sister Swan and decided that I had nothing to laugh about.

By the time my bet was placed, he came back in the house and we sat in the den which was designed with slanted beams of roughhewn wood and a huge sliding glass door which looked out on the ocean and he told me he had been figuring out a new basis of ad rates and I told him about my nag. He asked me whether I liked this territory and I told him the long story about how I got VD out here and he laughed his ass off—I could really make the kid laugh—and he wanted to know more about my women and that's when I clammed up.

"That's getting a little personal, isn't it?" I said.

"Nothing's more personal than a social disease. And you volunteered that information."

"You'll notice that I didn't give you the name of the broad."

"Good breeding, Al," he said. "I'll have to hand you that. You're a man of good breeding."

"Don't be sarcastic, kid. It doesn't sit well on you."

"You're getting upset over nothing. I want you to relax, Al. I invited you out here so you could take it easy."

"Scared my heart's going to give out before the end of the spring viewing season?"

"You've got the heart of a lion, Al."

"Sarcasm, kid. Your sarcasm really sucks."

"I'm being sincere. I'm sincerely curious about your life."

"Nosy."

"I've always imagined that you and the Calzolari girl had something going."

242

"What!"

"Easy now. I'm not the first to assume that. After all, you have taken more than a professional interest in her."

"You're way off base, kid."

He walked toward the sliding door and stood there, staring at the ocean, his back to me. "So you're telling me that you're just friends," he said.

"I'm not telling you shit. You're the one carrying on this conversation with yourself. I hope you enjoy it."

He turned around and looked at me. He was wearing an oxford-blue, button-down shirt opened at the neck which, even with the jeans, looked as though it wanted a tie. His long horse-face, usually white as a bar of soap, was now slightly tan. "When I was jogging this morning along the beach," he started telling me, "it occurred to me that your show is effective precisely because of the relationship you enjoy with Calzolari."

"You ain't wrong, kid."

"And furthermore, it occurred to me that the relationship must certainly be more than Platonic."

"You're a snoop, and it ain't becoming." I decided to keep him guessing. I was having a good time.

"The more I jogged, the more sense it made to me," he said.

"I would have been jogging with you," I stalled, "but the doc told me to lay off for at least four months. After my coronary event, I'm going to have to ease back into it. It really pisses me off. I was just getting started, and if I do say so myself, I was in a hell of lot better shape than I had ever imagined."

"Do you love her?"

"What's wrong with you, kid? I've never heard you talking this way. I told you once—mind your own fucking business. What happens between Anna and me is strictly our own affair." I liked the way that sounded.

"And then there's talk about her and the actor who plays the lawyer. Seames, isn't it?"

"Yeah, that's his name."

"Well, here's an item from *Soap Opera Digest*"—he picked up a magazine and handed it to me—"that says Anna and Seames have been seeing each other off camera."

I looked over the two-paragraph article and said, "I can't believe you read this crap. You actually read the gossip rags."

"I read everything that has to do with my product."

"Ain't nothing but dirt."

"You still haven't said whether it's true or not."

"Let me set you straight, kid. She doesn't really give two shits about Seames. Anna's a nice kid from my old neighborhood who looks up to me like an uncle or something. When she first came to audition for the part, she was all fucked up. She was acting at a theater that was so Off-Broadway it was practically floating in the East River. But I took a liking to her and decided to take her under my wing and show her how the real world works. I saw she had something that ninety-nine percent of these dames don't have—she had heart—and to me that's more important than getting a little pussy on the side."

"So it *is* Platonic between you and her."

"It's got nothing to do with the planets."

"But does it have to do with sex?"

"It's very strong, kid. I never thought I'd hear herself say this, but it's stronger than sex."

"Curious," he mused. "Very curious."

And then, like a lightning bolt, it hit me. "Why the fuck are *you* so curious?" I asked him.

"I've already explained. *Search* is one of my big shows. The ratings share has climbed to a point where . . ."

"Don't give me that ratings share shit. You're interested in Anna. You've got a hard-on for Anna."

"I've never met the girl."

"But you'd like to, wouldn't you?"

"If I wanted to meet her, I assure you that it wouldn't be in the least difficult. After all . . ." He hesitated.

"After all, *what?*" I wanted to know.

"Nothing."

"You could fire her. Is that what you were going to say? You could fire us all?"

"You're putting words in my mouth."

"You figure you can use me to get next to her. I can't believe it. I can't fucking believe it."

"Calm down, Gonfio. The thought of this girl has you carried away."

"Look who's talking."

244

"Why don't you go upstairs and take a nap."

"That's the first intelligent thing you've said today."

I went up to my room, and while I watched a bunch of kids in black wet suits riding in on the waves, I looked at my watch and saw that it was twelve thirty. I flipped on the tube.

The screen is split. Sister Prudence is phoning from the convent. Brian is speaking from his office.

"I've tried at your home several times," she explains.

"You shouldn't call me there."

"I didn't think . . ."

"You should have thought," he snaps.

"Brian, I need to talk to you, I desperately need to . . ."

"I can't now."

"Why?"

"These last few days have been very difficult."

"For me as well."

"I can't talk now."

"I *must* talk to you."

"My mother has been very sick, Prudence. She's had a stroke."

"Will she be all right?"

"The doctors seem to think so."

"When did it happen, Brian?"

"The days are all confused in my mind."

"Then you need to be left alone."

"Very much so."

"I understand. Perhaps we'll meet in the park."

"Yes, in the park. Soon."

"And I'll say a prayer for her. I'll pray for your mother."

"It's not a question of prayers."

"It's always a question of faith."

"And fate," Brian adds before they quickly bid each other good-bye.

As the credits rolled, I decided to call her. I picked up the phone and dialed her apartment.

"How are you, honey?" I asked when she picked up after only one ring.

245

"Oh, Al, I'm fine."

"You really grabbed the fucking phone. You been waiting for my call?"

"No, I mean yes."

"You mean you're waiting for someone else's call?"

"How was your trip out there?" She knew me well enough to ignore me.

"Boring. Costein went over his latest theories of prime-time viewing habits. I drank."

"I thought you were going to cut down."

"I only drank a little. Whose call are you waiting for?"

"I just happen to be by the phone."

"Are you going out tonight?"

"Yes, Mommy."

"Seames?"

"Seems so."

"Isn't that my line?"

"It's community property at this point," she said to me.

"You sound all right, sugar. Have you been sleeping over at his place or has he been staying with you?"

"Both."

"I don't think that's a good idea. In fact, I think it's a fucking rotten idea."

"You've told me that already. You don't have to pay long-distance money to tell me that again."

"The network's paying, not me."

"Tell me about Malibu."

"Bunch of rich beach bums. Too many Porsches and not enough pinball to suit me."

"Are they going to get you laid?"

"Nice girls don't ask questions like that."

"You ask me about my sex life, I ask you about yours."

"I don't need anyone to get me laid. When I want it, I can get it."

"Just like that, huh?"

"Just like that."

"Listen, Al, I better get off. I'm expecting a call."

"Liar. Fucking liar. You told me you were waiting for me."

"I didn't say that."

"Is he still having trouble getting it up?"

246

"What I've told you was in strictest confidence. I want you to understand that."

"If you had any real confidence in me, you'd stay away from the bum. I'm warning you."

"Get yourself laid, Al. You sound like you're horny. And when you get back, I want to talk about a couple of segments. I have some problems with a few of the new scenes with Hanford."

"You mean Brian."

"Whatever," she said, sounding distracted.

"I'll call you tomorrow."

"What are you doing tonight, by the way?"

"The usual Hollywood bit. Champagne and cocaine."

"Don't strain yourself."

"Yes, Mommy. Oh, by the way, I just saw you on TV. You look pretty good out here in California. A little pale, but reasonably convincing."

She laughed and, before she hung up, she said that she loved me. She had been saying that a lot lately. And I didn't mind. I drifted off to sleep with those sweet words rolling around my brain. The window was open, the air was fresh, the sound of the ocean—waves breaking over my dreams—soft and comforting. When I awoke a couple of hours later, I called my man and found out that Sister Swan hadn't done shit. So I went downstairs in search of a drink and found Costein talking to two guys named Blevin and Saunders.

They were another couple of young big shots, stationed in L.A., a little older than the kid, but much inferior in rank. Blevin looked like the kind of jock who had been rush captain of his fraternity and Saunders told me later that he was the Frisbee champion of Southern California in his age division. We bullshat for a while—Costein fed me a bunch of questions so he could show me off to the boys—and then Blevin said, "There's a party in Brentwood that sounds like fun tonight."

"Let's skip it," I suggested, still groggy and cranky from my nap and my loss.

"Your mood's turned black, Al," Costein observed.

"It's the smog," I said. "The smog out here really fucks with my brain."

I went to Brentwood with the boys anyway. I didn't want to

247

ruin the kid's evening, and, after all, he had paid for my trip out here and he was worried about my health and in the car I performed a little bit and told the guys how I really didn't give a shit about the Nielsens; the only thing they were good for, I said, were bets. Yeah, I told them, I actually found a bookie who would let me bet against the overnight and weekly ratings, and I explained how this bookie and me had worked out a whole system for figuring odds, and how I had beat the system—because I invented it—and made a quick $20,000, and it was all a big lie but I had them believing me and Costein was beaming. Costein was really proud of me, and I figured with that one cock-and-bull story I had paid him back for my trip.

The party sucked. The house was huge and everyone was hanging around the backyard, jumping into hot tubs and Jacuzzis, and a couple of the dames were naked, but I had seen naked broads before and I wasn't about to take off my clothes. Everyone looked about eighteen years old and I felt like an old fart and I wanted to talk to Anna. It was 3:00 A.M. in New York. I called her from a phone by the pool, and no one answered. She was at Seames's. I tried getting his number from information in Manhattan but it was unlisted. That asshole. Just like him. So I forgot the whole thing and Costein introduced me to a guy who sold time for the network and he had a lot to say about *Search* but I wasn't in the mood to listen. I had dropped a lot of money today and I missed Anna, I wondered what she was doing, and I moved inside and Costein was doing a little disco dancing with a very short, very stacked woman. He was a lousy dancer. Hell, if they played a fox-trot or something sane I'd show these fools how a man is supposed to move. I may be big, but more than one woman has called me graceful on the dance floor. But I hung around the food platters and put away the shrimps and the crabs and looked at the plastic cheeseburgers which sat on the coffee table and wondered why in the name of Christ would anyone go out and buy a plastic cheeseburger to put on a coffee table. "It's sculpture," the woman said to me. She was the hostess of the party and was wearing a T-shirt with a Perrier bottle pictured across her tits. "I saw you admiring my sculpture," she added.

I wanted to tell her that her sculpture was shit, but instead I

248

asked her what she did and she said she bought TV movies for the network and when I told her I wrote *Search* she seemed a little condescending—as though her nighttime junk movies were any better than my stuff—so I cut the conversation short and walked away and stood in a corner and cut a couple of vicious farts to stink up the room as much as I could.

Later, making my way to the bathroom, I ran into John Palermo.

We saw each other at the same time. I first thought that he was going to back away and pretend that he didn't see me. But he didn't. He looked at me and he smiled. A slight, sarcastic, slimy smile, but a smile nonetheless.

"Strange seeing you here," he said through his teeth. He was wearing his shirt unbuttoned to his waist. He had gone L.A. awfully goddamn fast, I thought to myself.

"A cruel quirk of fate," I said to the bum. The more I looked at him, the more stoned he seemed.

"You look like you've put on a lot of weight, Pops."

"Out of my way, Palermo. I'm on my way to take a dump. There's something about seeing you that makes me want to move my bowels."

"There's no need to carry a grudge, Pops. I'm the one with the sore jaw."

"I can't help it if garbage offends me."

"Talk about garbage," he said, "I was just back in New York. I tried calling Anna, but I couldn't get the number."

"Don't do her any favors."

"Just give her a message for me, will you? Tell her I've seen her on the tube a couple of times and I think she's dynamite."

"I wish she had lit a fuse under your ass and blown you up years ago."

"What's wrong, Pops? They push you off the show or something? You out here peddling scripts?"

"I'm out here seeing how they package puke. And I'm thinking that you must be doing goddamn great."

"Survival of the fittest."

"Survival of the slimiest," I said, blowing out my cigar smoke and walking past him to the can.

I was constipated. Palermo had messed up my digestion, and

a few minutes later I told Costein that I had decided to go to Vegas tonight. "But it's nearly midnight," he said.

"I can make the one A.M. flight," I told him. "I've taken it before."

"Your stuff is in Malibu."

"Be a sweetheart and bring it back to New York with you." I loved the idea that my boss was going to carry my bags.

"You're nuts," he said, smiling. He liked me because I was nuts. He started telling everyone how I was going to Vegas. He and Blevin and Saunders, who were coked up, even volunteered to drive me to the airport. The kid was sober. The kid didn't like drugs. The kid jogged. On the way out of the party, I avoided the Perrier-shirted hostess, but I couldn't help but see Palermo talking to some bubble-headed model type in the corner. She was leaning against the wall and he had his hands around her waist. Her tits looked as though they had been bought on Rodeo Drive. Before I walked out the door I yelled at him, *"Va a fare a mamma te e di' che ti ho mandato io,"* which roughly translated means, "Go fuck your mother and tell her that I sent you." I figured that he was probably too goddamn thick to understand.

I love Vegas. Vegas is as beautiful at four in the morning as eight at night. Vegas is always popping, and even though I arrived with no sleep, a clogged head and a plugged-up asshole, by noon the next day I had practically pushed Anna out of my mind—she still hadn't answered her phone—and I was cooking, winning at craps and crapping in the can in my room while talking to my man Maxie and requesting something really special after dinner. And when she arrived her boobs came through the door about thirty seconds before the rest of her body—I mean this broad had knockers—and an hour later, while she was sitting on my face and I was squeezing her jugs, I thought about my phony-baloney lost weekend in L.A. and how happy I was to be back in my element, back where I could pay for my pleasure, back where things were real.

34

Anna met him in the bar at the Carlyle Hotel. She wore a simple strand of gold around her neck and her dress was the ethereal color of a pale moon in May. She was late, almost an hour late, and he was angry.

"Where the hell have you been?" Hanford barked as she bent down to kiss his cheek.

"Shopping," she said excitedly. "I've been shopping."

She smelled of all the perfumes on Fifth Avenue. Her face was fresh and her skin gleamed with softness and clarity. She radiated happiness.

"If I had known you were going to be so late," he said, trying to sustain his annoyance, "I could have gotten in another game of squash."

"I'm sorry. I really am. It's just that I, well, I went slightly out of control today."

"Isn't that occurring with too much regularity?"

"I'm defying regularity these days. I feel wonderfully mysterious, rich and sultry."

"What's making you so happy tonight?" he wanted to know, not quite sure what her ebullience was all about.

"This hotel makes me happy. This bar."

She looked around at the faces, the starched white shirts and silver cuff links, the consciousness of fashion, the scents of cologne and milk bath, the Scotch a dozen years neat and the daringly thin eyebrows of the quietly blond woman who sat across from them. She could have been Hanford's sister, Anna thought to herself before ordering a dry vermouth on the rocks.

"Very late in life," she told him, "I am discovering the wonders of shopping in midtown Manhattan."

"It's a crashing bore."

"That's because you've done it for so long."

"Clothes don't interest me the way they once did," he murmured aloofly as he removed a short piece of string from his dark tweedy sport coat. His tie was a spirited English racing green, his shirt the color of Dijon mustard.

"I love the way you dress," she told him.

"Thank you, but I don't think I've changed styles since prep school."

"That's what's so fascinating about you. You're oblivious to change, a bulwark of conservatism."

"Let's not overdo it."

"Are you happy tonight? Are you happy to be here?"

"These old hotels have their charms."

"These old hotels are new to me. Very new and very romantic." She took his hand and he began to feel uncomfortable. She looked into his eyes, and, for a moment, he felt blinded by her intensity, her beauty. He excused himself and went to the men's room where he rubbed his eyes and splashed cool water on his face. When he returned to the table, she was lost in the music.

The pianist was a middle-aged Englishwoman who smiled sweetly as she threaded her way through the nighttime of a black man's blues. She was a handsome woman, a musician of profound feeling and complex taste. She played "Prelude to a Kiss," and it seemed to Anna that the tinkle of crystal in the room was part of the musical arrangement. There was a certain poignancy, a misty sense of an era and an elegance lost, an elegance that Anna had missed down on Mulberry Street.

She sat and drank her dry vermouths while Hanford, happy to have the jazz interrupt their conversation, got bombed on Tanqueray martinis. The pianist played seven or eight songs before she stopped, and when she stopped Anna found herself applauding a bit too enthusiastically. Hanford gave her a look, as if to say, Here at the Carlyle we do our best to contain ourselves.

But this was Anna's night, and Anna was not about to be contained. She had spent nearly $3000 on jewelry and clothes, and she was happy for the extravagance. She had gone to the boutiques where the air was rarefied and the merchandise—the

252

pigskin gloves, the scarves of silk, the thin suede belts—was dangerously, erotically exquisite. She had touched and smelled and paid in cash, but she had also opened several charge accounts and she had known, sitting in the back of the cab with her packages at afternoon's end, that she was just beginning to change in mind and spirit.

Now she felt giddy. Undoubtedly it was the vermouth.

"Are you hungry?" he asked her.

"No, just looped."

"What am I to do with a looped woman?"

"Take advantage of her, for Christ's sake."

"Speaketh the servant of the Lord."

"Yes, yes, yes." She was delighted that he, and not she, had begun the game this time. "Brian and Prudence meet in Manhattan for a torrid weekend of big-city sex."

"And where do you they consummate their passion?"

"In a room in the Carlyle Hotel."

"But reservations are required."

"Reservations have been attended to," she assured him.

"For tonight?"

"For right now, this very second."

"More drinking is required," he admitted, showing the first signs of apprehension.

The waiter and the pianist returned in the knick of time. More gin, more vermouth, more salty ballads; "I Can't Get Started with You," she played. Hanford touched Anna's knee under the table. She looked at him and saw that he was tipsy, that he was ready. She took his hand and brought it to her mouth. She kissed his pinky with the tip of her tongue. She opened her purse and produced a key which she placed in the palm of his hand. He looked at it: CARLYLE HOTEL, it read, ROOM 1018. He slipped the key into the patch pocket of his sport coat. He was pleased with himself for being smooth. He was pleased with Anna for having planned. Tonight he didn't mind her strangeness. The Carlyle. The Carlyle just might work.

The room was white, the carpeting, the walls. The painting over the bed was a Venetian scene, a silent gray morning, a mournful Adriatic, the Ducale in the distance. The furniture was substantial. The windows looked over Madison Avenue. But

253

then he saw the nun's habit folded neatly on the chair next to the bed, and then he saw the picture of Bernini's Santa Teresa tacked above the television set, and then he wasn't sure. He wasn't sure whether he could play around like this.

While he was deciding, though, she changed. She put on the habit, and he looked at her as he had looked at her so many times during the taping of the show—her face crowned by white —and he heard her starting to talk to him, telling him that she had thought about this moment for so long, so very long, telling him that she had escaped the convent dreaming of his love, telling him that underneath she wore nothing. *Underneath she wore nothing.*

"It's crazy," he said to her.

"I know it's crazy, Brian, but it's happened. There's no going back."

"I wish I were stoned."

"It would make no difference. Our desires wouldn't change."

"I'm not sure I want to go through with it."

"You're sure. I can feel that you're sure."

And she took off his coat, she let him relax on the bed.

"It's a game," he complained. "It's a childish game."

But she came to him and let him feel her underneath. Her moistness underneath. And the feel of the heavy garment, the black cumbersome garment against her skin—her thighs and her buttocks—drove her, now drove him, had them moving, had them playing the game. And she lay next to him, and she let him watch her as she rubbed the fabric, the fabric of the habit, against her softness.

" 'By our first strange and fatall interview,' " she recited, " 'By all desires which thereof did ensue . . .' "

" 'By our long starving hopes,' " he continued, " 'by that remorse / which my words' masculine persuasive force / Begot in thee . . .' "

He was hard watching her, and he was happy, relieved, over-joyed at being hard. He listened to her moan, saw her watching him watching her. She twisted and turned, turned toward him, letting him see everything. The habit set her free, set her wild with the movement of her own hands, legs, fingers. He opened the door to the white tile bathroom so that the floor-length mirror faced her, so that she could now see herself. The prop, the habit itself, the garment she had worn for so many weeks. And she cried, she cried over and again, "Brian!" and he wanted to object but he didn't, because he was drunk and besides, it was working, the wholy crazy thing was working. Prudence was bringing herself. Prudence was getting over, Prudence was screaming with satisfaction. He was the hot spectator, he was horny on the sidelines, and finally he came in; watching her release, he ripped off his clothes and he came in. It was as though he dived inside. She was still wearing the garment. And now he was fucking her. Fucking her hard. The holy engorgement. He was fucking the nun who was calling him by the wrong name, but it didn't matter, not now, because her performance was sincere, her performance was splendid. She moved into him, up toward his center, she dug her fingernails into his neck, she threw her legs to the crystal chandelier in the middle of the white ceiling. She said, "Fuck me, Brian, oh, God, fuck me," and for some reason—perhaps it was the frenzy of her dance, perhaps the madness of the scene—he was unable to contain himself in the Carlyle Hotel, he was unable to last for much longer than a minute.

35

I wasn't all that unhappy to get back. I had been gone for almost a week and my two days in Vegas hadn't been overwhelmingly successful—monetarily. Also I missed Anna, though when I returned I immediately noticed that she was a little more distracted, a little less willing to spend time with me. I hated to admit it, but I saw that she was really concentrating on Seames while he seemed to be backing away from her.

I couldn't waste my life, though, worrying about this shit. I had a show to turn out, and soon after my arrival I called a writers' meeting.

I had to tell my half-ass assistants where I wanted all the segments to go—especially Sister Prudence's—and naturally they oohed and ahhed like a bunch of school kids. I couldn't blame them. Most of them haven't been writing for all that long, and whenever I present them with my long-term plots they can't help but be impressed. Actually I was a little impressed myself. When I think of the agony I had been through, when I think of how I had to whip Anna into shape, whip Costein into shape and then beat a fucking heart attack, it's a wonder I was able to do what I did.

I went back to my cubicle. I kicked out a couple of bellyaching actors. (Jeff Rosloff, the guy who played mean landlord Adams, wanted to be written back into the script. I told him there was no way. I hated to disappoint the old guy, but it's a tough business.) I saw I had a pile of phone calls. They all had to do with the show, so I decided to answer none of them. I had the *Daily Racing Form* on my desk and I was about to study it in anticipation of a substantial wager when the weekly edition of *Variety,* which was lying next to it, caught my eye. I don't know why, but I started reading the article entitled DAVID DELEON ANNOUNCES NEW PIX. DeLeon is a heavyweight producer.

"David DeLeon today announced plans for a feature to be based on on original story by Harvey Binder."

I scanned the next few paragraphs which said that the film was about street gangs in New York. But then I read:

"Starring role will be the film preem of New York legit actor John Palermo."

And then I skipped to the very bottom of the piece and saw:

"Casting will be handled by Gwen Snodes, formerly of the Living Rock Theatre in Gotham."

"Your mother is feeling much better. Much, much better." The camera comes in for a tight shot of Baxter MacNiece. He is grimacing. His face is bathed in perspiration. He is chinning himself on the parallel bars. He is dressed in a sweat suit of brilliant yellow.

256

"I'm glad to hear that," says Brian who, standing next to the older man, is lifting weights.

"It's great working out here, isn't it, son?"

"Just great," Brian answers in a monotone.

"I'm glad you found the time. You certainly look like you need the exercise. Besides, I like to see you spending more time at the club."

"We've been over that before."

Baxter drops himself from the bars and begins a series of deep knee bends. "We've been over a number of things, Brian, and yet nothing seems to change. Especially your attitude."

"And what about yours?"

"Why must we argue?"

"I'm trying not to. It's just that these past few weeks have been upsetting for me."

"I understand. But your mother has come around. She's even walking without a cane, and by the end of the month we expect her to be back in the swing of things. You know your mother. She'd die before she missed the Junior League Ball. She's having her seamstress out to the house tomorrow for measurements. She's raring to get back. She's afraid she's going to miss something. Yes, sir, Brian, that mother of yours is one hell of a woman. I'm lucky to have won her heart."

"Please, Dad, save the speeches for her. I don't need to hear them."

"You're still angry. You're still disillusioned. Well, let me tell you something about the real world, son. Let me tell you something about grown men." Baxter goes to the slant board and, with his hands behind his head, speaks between sit-ups. "There's no reason, no reason under the sun, why every once in a while we can't enjoy ourselves without harming a soul. It's all a matter of good taste and discretion. Some women are for marrying and some women are strictly for other things. And it's important—it's downright mandatory—to know the difference. In fact, knowing the difference is a sign of maturity."

"Your morality makes me sick," says the son who is now doing chin-ups at a consciously faster rate than his father.

"Your own moral judgments are severe, Brian. They are so severe that I have a feeling that they are not really being directed at me, but rather against yourself. And when that happens, I'm afraid you're in deep, deep trouble."

A middle-aged man with a large stomach walks by. "Keep up the good work, Baxter," he says, "you look fit as a fiddle. What do you owe it to?"

"Winning cases and womanizing, Charlie." The two men bellow a hearty health club laugh while Brian grits his teeth and does another dozen chin-ups.

The golf course nighttime set is hauled out by the stagehands. The plastic grass, the cardboard tree—everything is in place. Brian and Prudence arrive. He is dressed in walking shorts, she in plain white cotton slacks. The director calls for action. Tape rolls.

They embrace.

"I never thought we'd meet again," she says to him.

"I never wanted to."

"You always wanted to. And you always will. Please, now is not the time for lies."

"I no longer know a lie from the truth. I no longer know what I think or even what I feel."

"Your confusion is no greater than mine."

"And yet. . . ." he begins to say.

"Yet," she finishes for him, "we're here. Our confusion led us here."

"Our bodies."

"Our hearts."

"These days and these nights, these weeks have been impossible for me."

"I've been able to think of nothing besides you. My mind's no longer my own. I've tried to erase the thought of our last meeting, I've told myself not to dwell, to concentrate on other things, other images, but nothing works. I'm no longer in control."

"I was afraid you were angry with me. I was short with you on the phone."

"I understood. I was the one who acted hastily. I simply couldn't wait. I acted like a schoolgirl. I went to the park every day and you weren't there."

258

"I'm sorry, I couldn't get myself to meet you, there were so many things happening—Sally, my mother . . ."

"Your mother is better."

"How do you know?"

"I called the hospital every day until she was released."

"That was kind of you."

"It was the only way I had of staying close to you. I knew that when I spoke to the hospital you were probably there."

"I was."

"And that you were suffering with concern . . ."

"Or guilt that I wasn't suffering with enough concern."

"I don't understand."

"I have a difficult relationship with my parents, Prudence. It's been difficult ever since I can remember. They live in a world which is governed by social niceties and small-town prestige. My mother's main motivation for recovery has been the Junior League Ball. She'd almost die before she missed it. And my father, my father is a story unto himself."

"Tell me," she urges, holding his hand as they sit on the grass together. "I want to hear what's been troubling you."

"The old man is a hypocrite. He's an infamous whoremaster, and he lives and works in a world where such behavior is envied and admired. The night my mother fell ill he was with one of his mistresses." Brian shuts his eyes and sighs. Prudence puts her arm around him. "I know it's not for me to judge him," he says.

"You're right. You mustn't," she agrees.

"And yet how can I help it? I work with him every day. I see him operate. I hear him on the phone. He's a man without any real . . ."

"Am I wrong to say that this is the life you chose for yourself?"

"It was a choice made by a boy. A college boy who thought he had an obligation to come home, marry the high-school beauty queen and take over his father's thriving law practice."

"And you had no doubts at the time?" she asks.

"Oh, I had doubts. I had nightmares about it. My stomach did somersaults for weeks before graduation. I didn't want to leave. I wanted to stay in the ivory tower forever. I suppose that I knew I wasn't strong enough to resist the tradition. But I

259

could go on and on talking about myself. We've said nothing about you.''

"Resisting tradition," she repeats. "We *are* talking about me.''

"We both have a desperate need to speak our minds . . .''

"And examine our souls.''

"Do you think it's wrong, Prudence, to do it together?''

"We can try to stay apart. We tried once and we failed, and, I suppose, after tonight, we can start trying all over again.''

"You're a brave woman.''

"Only when held by a brave man.''

They embrace and fall, out of the eye of the camera, onto the plastic grass.

Only minutes later tape is ready to roll again. Inside the convent two nuns are weeping and speaking at the same time.

"Where is Sister Prudence?" asks the first nun.

"I don't know," answers the second. "She was not in her room.''

"We must find her and tell her quickly. We must be there when she finds out.''

"She'll be crushed. Her heart will be broken.''

"You're right. We must be the ones to tell her.''

36

Silvia wanted me to bang her. She had been knocking on my door now for weeks, ringing my phone off the fucking wall—at my office, at home, everywhere. I had been avoiding her, and not because there's anything wrong with the broad. She's no genius, but she's got those big luscious tits and she'll screw your nuts off and sometimes when all you want to do is get in and out—with no questions asked—you need a dame like Silvia. The problem, of course, is that she asks questions, too many goddamn ridiculous questions, about the show and the stars and then she wants me to take her out to eat and she tells me about the bank and the Christmas Savings Plan and all I want to do is send her home in the first available cab.

But it was Wednesday night and I had a show to write for tomorrow and I still hadn't done it because I was so far behind —and I had to concentrate before I got myself into trouble. So deep down I was a little nervous about being distracted. And yet, on the other hand, I could use a quick hot fuck and maybe —I figured to myself—one of the reasons I was having trouble writing had to do with my horniness. "Stand by," I told Silvia who called me during her lunch break to say that she wanted to come into the city tonight because tomorrow was a bank holiday and she could sleep late and maybe come over with me and watch the show being taped. "Stand by," I repeated, thinking of the size of her nipples and the way they stuck out and got good and hard and pink, "Stand by, and I'll call you later," I said, already figuring out excuses for sending her home tomorrow morning—that is, if I could see my way clear to pumping her tonight.

I put a clean sheet of paper in the typewriter, lit a cigar and was ready to get down to brass tacks when the fucking phone rang again. Half pissed, half happy for the interruption, I picked it up. It was Seames. He said he had to talk to me. I told him that actors always had to talk to me. He said it was important. I told him I was busy. He asked me about tonight. I told him I had something lined up. He offered to make it early; he said it was something really urgent, something concerning Anna. I told him I'd meet him for drinks. He mentioned the Droman Club. I told him to get fucked. I wasn't a member; that was only a onetime deal. "Meet me at the Turf Bar and Grill on Sixth Avenue," I ordered. It was a real dive from the old days. If Seames wanted to talk to me, he could meet me on my own territory. He agreed, and as soon as he hung up I called Silvia at the bank and told her I'd meet her in the lobby of my building at eight. If I was a little late, I said, wait. I had a meeting and I didn't know what time it'd be over. She was thrilled, even though she added, "Don't you see how much easier it'd be if I had my own key to your apartment?" The very mention of the idea was enough to have me cancel the date, but I thought of the way she looked running around the bedroom in panties and a bra and I let the terror pass.

The Turf is a little crummy, I'll grant you that. It's certainly seen better days. But the crowd is pleasant, or at least the crowd shares a genuine interest in horse racing, and the roast beef is cut nice and thick and the gravy is even thicker and the smell of draft beer and Irish whiskey stimulates the appetite. Besides, everyone knows me there. I've been trading at the Turf for years; there's something about the joint that brings out the best in bettors.

I made sure to arrive late. By about a half hour. I wanted Seames to see the reception I'd get when I came through the door.

"Here comes the greatest writer since Ellery Queen," said Johnny Fatboy who was slicing beef and slinging hash behind the counter the same way he'd been doing it for twenty years. "Where the hell you been, Al?" cried out Nick the bartender, "home counting your money?" "I been watching your show, sweetie," said Holly the waitress. "I been watching it every day and even when it's crowded in here for lunch I tell all the boys to shut their faces 'cause I'm watching my friend Al's show. He wrote it, I tell them, he thinks up everything, and I wouldn't miss it for a five-dollar tip, Al, I really wouldn't, especially now with everything happening between Sister Prudence and Brian. By the way, is that guy over there Brian? He looks just like him." I looked and saw Hanford sitting in a booth in the back and I muttered, "Yeah, he's one of my boys." I wasn't thrilled at the idea of Seames being recognized.

I sat down across from him and said, "How do you like the place?"

"It's fine."

"Been coming here so long I can't tell you. I like the atmosphere, don't you?"

"It's fine."

"It's real. It's down to earth. My kind of people."

262

"Al, there's something I want to talk to you about."

"Let's order first. I'm hungry."

"I thought we were just going to drink."

"I can't be in this joint without having some of that beef. You want a sandwich?"

"A beer will do."

"Holly," I yelled, "draw two and have the Fatboy cut me a thick one. Thick and rare."

"You got it, Al," she screamed back.

"There's something about the Turf that . . ."

"Listen," Seames broke in, "I've got to talk to you. I really do."

"Easy, kid," I told him, "I ain't going nowhere. Take a couple of deep breaths and tell me what's on your mind."

"It's Anna. I'm worried about Anna."

"What's to worry about?" I asked with growing suspicion.

"I don't like the way she's getting carried away with the part."

"What's wrong with you?" I challenged. "She's a goddamn dedicated actress. The girl's a genius. She's no more carried away than I am. She's just pro, that's all."

"It's more than that, and I think you know it. I've known a lot of actresses, many of them as good as Anna, but . . ."

"Let me stop you right there. You haven't known *anyone* as good as Anna. I say that because I'm a little older than you and I've seen many, many more actresses than you. I've seen them all, and I'm telling you that there's never been anyone with Anna's feel for a character."

"That's what I'm talking about. That feel. It's too strong. It's making me uncomfortable, both on and off the set."

"That may be your problem, Seames."

"Or yours, Gonfio," he shot back. "The two of you get each other crazy, staying up all night and talking about Prudence as though she were actually out there in Troy."

"Anna's been talking to you, huh?"

"Anna's been sleeping with me, Gonfio."

"You ain't telling me nothing I don't already know. That dame tells me things that she'd never dream of telling another living soul."

"Did she tell you that she likes to have me make love to her

263

in the Carlyle Hotel while she's wearing Sister Prudence's habit?''

That's when I started listening. I started listening hard. Seames filled me in on their sex life. A lot of it I had heard about from Anna. But a lot of it was new. I tried not to wince when Seames spoke, but I'm not sure I was able to stop myself. I'm not sure I wanted to be hearing this shit from this guy. I'm not sure I believed him, but, on the other hand, why else would he be spilling his guts if not to relieve himself of some burden or guilt? And besides, he even mentioned some of his own problems in performing. I thought he was being honest. So I sat there and listened as he told me that he thought Anna was too intense, too intense about Prudence and too intense about Brian and much too intense about Hanford. I ate and drank as I listened.

"I like this woman," he said to me. "I think she's smart, and I think she has great creative resources. She's a fascinating personality, and the last thing in the world I'd do is hurt her. But she's coming on too strong, Al. Much too strong. I've had this problem before with women. But in the past, one little push and the message is conveyed. I've always been able to keep my ladies at arm's length. That's the way I've structured my life. I need freedom and independence. The girls are fun, but when they start wanting to move in with their blue jeans and their makeup, I start having problems.''

"She's told you that she wants to move in?" I asked.

"Not yet. But it's coming. I know it's coming. I've been there before.''

I hated Seames's playboy attitude, I wanted to tell him to fuck off, but I also heard the ring of truth in what he was saying. I had seen it in her eyes—when she acted, when she looked at him—and I realized that he was saying things I had been denying to myself for a long, long time. I began getting a little scared and I wondered whether it was pain I was feeling in my arm or just nervousness.

"She's a very sensitive, very volatile dame, Seames. It's nothing more than that.''

"You're lying to yourself, Gonfio, and I think you know it. She's unstable. She has no idea of who she is. One minute she's a nun devoted to the service of God, the next minute she's a Park Avenue fashion model married to a Wall Street lawyer. She keeps switching back and forth. And she's distracted. There will be times when you'll be speaking to her and she won't be there. The first time she came to my apartment, for instance, she hardly noticed it. She didn't bother to look at it. And there's the business with Santa Teresa, the poetry, the . . ."

"She's a very imaginative gal. She's got a hell of a mind."

"I don't feel right about it, Al. I say that to you as one gentleman to another. I like the show, I especially like my part, and I wouldn't want to endanger my professional relationship with her . . ."

"Fucking A straight," I broke in.

"On the other hand, my private life is terribly, terribly important to me . . ."

"Terribly, I'm sure," I mocked.

"And I'm not about to get into anything I can't get out of."

I finished off my beef sandwich and thought about having Holly bring me another one. "What do you expect me to do about this, Seames? I don't like to see you crying in your beer, but what can I do?"

"You're closer to her than anyone. You've said so yourself. You're the one who gets her going. Well, I'd suggest that you've got her going a little too quickly. Calm her down. Write her out of the script for a couple of weeks. Gradually end our relationship on camera."

"That's impossible. The thing's too hot. It's too fucking good to mess up now."

"You're the genius, Gonfio. You can find alternative plots. Have her go back to God. Have her jump in the sack with Baxter, or Sally. Do something, but, for Christ's sake, disengage us."

"I don't like actors telling me how to write my show."

"I wouldn't dream of telling you how to write your show." He was trying to charm me. "I wouldn't consider such a thing. You're the writer. You're the creative force behind *Search*. And I realize you've pushed the ratings through the roof. You have nothing but respect from me. But I also know that you have feelings for Anna which go beyond the show. I know that you care for her very deeply. And if that's the case, Al, you must be aware of what's happening to her. Right now you're the only one who can help her. I don't go around divulging the intimate details of my sexual encounters as a rule, believe me. I've painted this picture only so you can start seeing her for the way she is. She's in some trouble, some serious emotional trouble, and you've got to find a way to help her out. You've got to stop pushing her deeper in.''

Normally I don't let anyone talk to me this way. But for some reason, I didn't stop Seames. I let him go on, I even bought him another beer, and after he had gone, after I had eaten another beef sandwich, I sat around the Turf until nine o'clock, just thinking and worrying, when I realized that I had sweet Silvia waiting for me in the lobby of my building.

37

It was different fucking her this time. I told her that I needed her. I actually said those words to Silvia. I said it because—at least at the time—it was true. And as a result she fucked my brains out. The dame went wild.

But that's broads for you. They're sentimental to the core, even the horniest among them. You whisper something nice in their ear while you're satisfying their soul and they gobble you up like you're Tom the Turkey. Go figure. And while you're at it, go figure why in hell I was pouring out my heart to a gal who's barely smart enough to count the change in her bank teller's booth down there in Sheepshead Bay.

I don't know. Hanford Seames must have really socked it to me, because I couldn't get that fucking conversation out of my mind. I didn't want to think about what he had said, I wanted to forget the whole rotten confusing episode, and then when I saw Silvia waiting for me I wasn't even sure it was her.

She had screaming red hair.

"Surprise!" Silvia exclaimed. "I didn't want to tell you on the phone, but I'm a red-head."

"I can see." Remember Clarabelle? Well, this dame looked just like Clarabelle the fucking clown.

"What do you think?"

"Fine, very fine."

"Do you think the color is nice?"

"Nice, Real nice."

"Someone at the bank said I look like Rhonda Fleming. One of the officers. Have you ever met Rhonda Fleming?"

"No, never."

She came in and started telling me about the bank. She wasn't even pissed off about being kept waiting for so long. I was grateful; I told her how beautiful she looked, I told her she was the sexiest thing in the city and when we went upstairs and had a couple of drinks I was happy to listen to her tales of woe about being a teller in a Brooklyn bank. I tried to picture her there counting out cash and getting back complaints, I tried to hang on to every word she said, I tried to trade off my problems for hers, but it didn't work. Hanford. Hanford sitting there telling me that shit about Anna. My Anna.

Silvia kept talking and I kept listening and finally I shut her up by putting my mouth on hers, and she was glad. She was glad to give me her tongue and push her box against my dick. She was glad to have me get to her tits and pop 'em with my lips and rub her nipples with my nose and lick her navel with my tongue. She was happy to have me all over her, and I was happy to have a way to forget about the earlier part of the evening— Hanford and his sad stories, Hanford and his accusations—and I sucked her and fucked her for as long as I could hold out which, believe me, is longer than the average dozen men you'll find out on the street regardless of age or color, and I was so glad to have her, so relieved to hide my head in her hole that I said things I had never said to her before. She responded by bathing my back with her sweet kisses. She rubbed me down until I came back up, and once I was back up I was back in, and

267

we were rocking and rolling to beat the band, we were doing the bump and the bicycle, the mambo and the mamma-too-tight. We were going and flowing and joking and poking. My bed creaked and Silvia shrieked and I gave her the last of my golden load. I managed to touch the very, very back of her box. My head might have been spinning with Anna's or Santa Teresa's or someone else's impassioned face—I don't need to remember, I don't want to remember—but my spine was being dug up by Silvia's pointy, blood-red fingernails and I was forced to call a time-out and ask the little lady to lay off. At least for now.

We lay there in each other's arms for a half hour, maybe longer. I kissed her boobs and told her how grateful I was to have her as a friend and she cuddled next to me and cooed and then started telling me the story of the cashier at her bank who was caught with his hand in the petty cash. "Silvia," I begged her, "let's just lie here and think about how beautiful the world can be." But she didn't understand and she kept on talking about her banking adventures in Brooklyn and finally I just had to tell her nicely to shut the fuck up because I wanted to think.

"Think about what?" she persisted.

"The show," I admitted.

"What about the show? What about the show?" She was anxious, almost desperate, to hear the gossip, and I decided to finally let her have it. I told her roughly what was happening between Anna and Hanford and naturally she confused them with Prudence and Brian. Which was certainly understandable.

"When a woman falls for a man," she said to me, "there's hardly anything that anyone can do. It's like magic. All those soft feelings and diamond dreams."

I had never known Silvia to speak poetically before, and frankly, I was impressed. Maybe she wasn't the dumb broad I had always thought her to be.

"And even though everything is very complicated and difficult for you right now," she continued, "I'm sure that if anyone can find a solution to these problems it's you."

We talked a little while longer, and I have to say that Silvia was really sympathetic. She felt for Anna and Prudence and me, and I decided to reward her. I decided to let her spend the night.

268

I was a little uncomfortable, but I made it clear before she fell asleep that she'd have to leave early the next morning and that she couldn't come to the studio with me because I had a bunch of boring meetings. She reluctantly agreed.

That night I dreamed that the milk plant caught on fire and everyone was burning up but somehow I managed to climb in and get Anna out and she was bleeding and her bones were broken and when I carried her in my arms she felt like a little bird and then the phone was ringing and I picked it up and it really was Anna and I thought to myself—I had saved her, I had actually saved her—and then I looked over at Silvia and realized what had happened and where I was.

"Do you have to work today?" Anna asked me while Silvia snored on.

"Of course I have to work today. I've got to knock out a couple of scripts and then the rehearsals start at . . ."

"Couldn't your assistants do that? Couldn't we take the day off and make it up tomorrow?"

"You can take the day off. We're not taping Prudence today. But if I don't show up . . ."

"Al, it's important, very, very important, that we spend the day together."

That felt good, I admit. She wanted to spend time with me. But still I was hesitant. I wasn't bullshitting; I had a pile of work waiting for me. "What's on your mind, honey?" I asked her.

"It's nothing earth-shattering, Al," she said in her faraway voice. "I just want to be with you."

"You said, 'very, very important.' "

"There are days when we need friends. And for no particular reason. Those are the days when we're lonely, or a little afraid. You understand, Al. You always understand."

"I'll be by to pick you up in an hour."

"I love you," she said. Anna Calzolari said that she loved me.

I had to give sweet Silvia the old heave-ho again. She bitched and barked a little bit, but I won her over with vague promises about dinner and a show in the not-too-distant future. She showered, I showered, we dressed and left together. I felt bad about not giving her breakfast, but I explained to her that in the TV business the action was always fast and furious and she seemed to understand.

Anna looked very thin to me. I wondered why I hadn't noticed before. I kissed her on the cheek and told her that the day was hers. I suggested that we go eat breakfast at Da Andrea in the old neighborhood, which was part candy store, part coffee shop, where the coffee was strong and the pastry sweet.

"I'd rather go to Schrafft's," she said too suddenly. "I'd like to stay in this part of town."

I didn't argue, but I was a little disappointed. I thought the old neighborhood might do us both a world of good. Still, it was Anna's day.

Schrafft's was boring to me, but I had the feeling that it was definitely exciting to Anna. She looked around at the other ladies, most of whom were well-dressed richies shooting up with caffeine before they assaulted the high-priced department stores. During breakfast, Anna drank a slim glass of tomato juice and said hardly anything. I had so much stuff ringing in my head I had to get something out. I finally did:

"I read an item about Palermo. Seems like the bum got lucky. He landed a role in a David DeLeon flick. Can you believe it? Can you fucking believe it?"

She was still looking around the room. She said nothing.

"I didn't want to mention this to you," I continued, "but I also ran into the creep when I was out on the Coast. I was with Costein at the most boring goddamn party that you can imagine, and who do you think I see hitting on some dame in the corner? You guessed it. Mr. Marijuana himself. His little eyes were red as berries. Jesus, he looked like warmed-over shit."

Still, she did not react.

"Anna," I implored, "are you listening to me?"

"Sorry, my mind was wandering."

"I saw. I was telling you about Palermo."

"Palermo?"

I thought she was kidding. I looked into the dark green of her eyes to see if she was kidding. She wasn't.

"Your ex-old man," I said to her.

"Oh," she answered, giving away nothing.

270

"You don't care? You don't care that he landed a part in a movie?"

"I'd like to go shopping today. That is, if it's not too boring for you, Al."

I was on the verge of telling her about last night's conversation with Hanford. I was about to tell her how worried he was, I was about to tell her that she was getting too weird and too kinky and that I knew what the fuck was going on and that she had better straighten up and fly right. But I didn't know how to say all those things, and I wasn't sure I could, and I didn't.

I followed her up Fifth Avenue. I saw that she wanted nothing but my company or my protection or my approval. I didn't know what the fuck she wanted. I was sort of stunned by her silence and all I could do was eye her eyeing the merchandise, in and out of Lord & Taylor, in and out of B. Altman, through the lace undies and slips, the watches and perfumes and even the furs. Farther up the street, at Saks, she tried on a million dresses and after each one she asked me, "What do you think they'd say about this in Troy?" After a while the question got stale, but she kept asking it, she kept buying stuff—nice, good-taste conservative stuff—and telling them to send it and charge it. All her talk had been about the clothes and Troy, and the more she bought the happier she became. Then she started talking about Brian. She started telling me how Brian should take Prudence to New York. Yes, she said. They should sneak away for a weekend and spend a few nights in a swanky hotel. The Carlyle? I asked her. Exactly! she answered. That's exactly what she was thinking! And she was high and buzzy and talking a blue streak as we left Saks, talking about the timing for Prudence's weekend in New York. When we got to Bergdorf she looked at dresses and wondered what Prudence would wear, what Prudence would like. I went along and, to tell you the truth, it was a lot of fun. At least she wasn't stony silent like she had been at the beginning of the day. It was just a game she was playing. We both realized that, so it was just a question of not being square and going along with it. That's what was wrong with Seames, it occurred to me: Seames was too square, Seames was a fucking jerk. So we picked out Prudence's New York City outfit—it was a suit—and I was feeling much better,

271

and I told her that I'd find a way to charge it to wardrobe, and she laughed and then took me by the hand and put me in a chair and said, "Close your eyes for ten minutes and only open them when I say so." Then she kissed me on the forehead and disappeared.

I obeyed. I sat there and rewound the tape of our whole nutty relationship and this time it all seemed okay, it all seemed to make sense, and I listened to the polite department store bells and smelled the swanky perfume around me and told myself that if this were meditation, meditation wasn't half bad and when I heard her say, "Open your eyes," I did so and there she was, standing before me in a veiled, white, frilly, June wedding dress with a long train trailing behind her. Her face was glowing, her eyes were radiant, she was a beautiful young bride and my first thought was—it's a game, it's nothing but a game, and it's harmless fun. It's kids playing with a dollhouse, it's dress-up time. Why be stuffy and serious? Why not enjoy it all, just the way Anna was enjoying it? Why be a party pooper? Why not follow her over to Tiffany and look at rings? Why not string along and play the game—just for a day, just for the afternoon —forget the pressures and problems and remember when I was ten years old and told my mother I wanted to be Superman for Halloween and put on a cape and actually felt—actually believed—that I could fly.

I took her home that night wondering whether she was right. She had argued at dinner that Prudence and Brian would have to get married, that no ex-nun would just live with a man, that both of the characters were the marrying kind. Besides, she said, it's what everyone in America wants. It's the logical conclusion to their relationship. My own instinct was to stay away from too much happiness—if there were Happiness what would happen to the Search?—and I wondered if Anna understood that even if the nun and the lawyer did get married, something would have to go wrong sooner or later. Something stopped me from saying that to her, though. She had been so happy today and there would be time for those explanations later. I didn't want to do anything to break the mood.

She asked me in and made me coffee and served me cake and

gave me a yellow pad and a fat felt-tip pen and made sure I got down everything we had talked about. She helped me through a bunch of difficult scripts, and by midnight I had done at least a week's worth of work. Not bad, I thought. Not bad at all.

Before we were through, she had fallen asleep on the couch. Poor thing. She was exhausted. She had shopped her heart out. She had been taxing her brain for me. I kissed her forehead and ran my hand over her face. Her skin was like a baby's behind. I wanted to take a picture, and as I left the apartment, I noticed *The Collected Works of St. Teresa of Ávila*, volume 1, sitting on a small table in the entryway. I opened it to where a bookmark had been inserted and read these lines from "Soliloquies, XVI, The wounds of love" which Anna had underlined in red: "O true Lover, with how much compassion, with how much gentleness, with how much delight, with how much favor and with what extraordinary signs of love You cured these wounds, which with the darts of this same love You have caused! O my God and my rest from all pains, how entranced I am! How could there be human means to cure what the divine fire has made sick? Who is there who knows how deep this wound goes, or how it came about, or how so painful and delightful a torment can be mitigated?"

38

"Of course there's nothing wrong with her," I was saying to Dick and Howard a couple of days later. I was sitting up in the control room waiting for the taping to start.

"She just seems, I don't know, a little distracted," Dick told me in his Ivy League twang.

"Bullshit. We're all distracted. What the fuck does that mean?"

"The vibes have been strange," Howard chimed in.

"What in hell do vibes have to do with this?" I asked him. "This is a soap opera, not a goddamn rock concert."

"Al," Dick continued to press as he puffed on his briar, stinking up the room with his pipe tobacco, "I think you know what I mean."

"I don't know anything except that this show is making the network money out the ass," I challenged them both. Let 'em argue with that.

"Don't be so defensive," Howard tried to smooth-talk me. "We're worried about her, that's all. Her intensity is almost too extreme."

"What do you want me to do? Fire her? Tell her not to act so goddamn good? Tell her to be a little more mediocre?"

"You're missing the point, Al," Dick said. "We think she's marvelous. Everyone thinks she's marvelous. I'm just wondering whether the pressure is a bit too much for her now. Perhaps you can write her out for a week, or at least deemphasize the segment—slightly, just slightly."

"Great!" I shouted back. "Just great! Now I got everyone telling me what to do. Why don't we call up your wives and ask them how they'd like to rewrite the show? Maybe they have some ideas for new plot development. What do you say? Huh? Maybe a few of the cameramen would like to put in their fucking two cents about this story? Let's go out on the streets and do a survey. 'Cause I don't have enough critics. I don't have enough second-guessers. I'd like some more. I'd like everyone telling me what to do, 'cause I've only been doing this shit for half my goddamn life, I've only been keeping this show on top of the goddamn shitpile for ten fucking years. That's all."

They went back to their business and a few minutes later tape was ready to roll.

Sister Prudence is back in the convent after having met Brian. She is wearing her habit and is reading a book. There is a knock on her door. She opens it. Before her stand two sisters whose eyes are wet with tears.

"We looked for you before, Sister Prudence," says one of the nuns, "but you were nowhere to be found."

"I was on a mission outside the convent. But tell me, what's wrong? Why do you both look so grieved?"

The sisters glance at each other. Who will be the one to tell her? They both start speaking at once. They stop. "Please," Prudence urges, "what has happened?"

"The soul of our beloved mother superior has returned to the bosom of Christ."

"What!" Prudence cries. "It isn't possible! Just yesterday I was with her, she was fine, she was alive and smiling and . . ."

"Her heart had always been fragile. At least so said the doctor. She preferred that no one knew."

Sister Prudence falls to her knees, sobbing. "On her desk," one of the nuns says, "was a book with a note for you. She meant for you to have it."

Prudence takes the book and thanks her sisters. She rises and embraces them, assures them that she will be able to manage alone. They leave, and through her continuing sobs, she reads the note out loud to herself, "I have been rereading this inspiring work, and I want to share its wisdom with you." The book is *The Way of Perfection* by Santa Teresa. Prudence turns to the page which is marked by a purple silk ribbon and recites these words as her cries subside: " 'My daughters, let us at least imitate somewhat the great humility of the Most Blessed Virgin whose habit we wear and whose nuns we call ourselves with confusion; because, however much we may seem to humiliate ourselves, we always fall short of being daughters of such a mother, and spouses of such a spouse.' "

"Can I see you? Can I see you now?" she asks him.

"I asked you not to phone me at home. It's late, it's very late," Brian tells Prudence.

The screen is split. There are extreme tight shots revealing only their eyebrows, their eyes, their noses, their moving mouths.

"My mother is gone."

"Your mother?"

"Mother Superior."

"Dead?"

"I must speak with you."

"I'll listen, but it's impossible for me to say much."

"She left words with me, and I'm trying to understand them. I'm trying desperately. It's almost a matter of interpretation, and I'm afraid if I interpret the words wrong then my life will be wrong. Do you understand? Do you understand what I'm saying?"

"Yes, I understand," he whispers.

"It's difficult for me to hear what you're saying."

"I must speak softly. I can't raise my voice."

"She's gone and my life is changing. I've never felt such anguish and, talking to you, I've never felt such ecstasy. I'm hopelessly imprisoned or I'm suddenly set free—I don't know which. I search my heart, Brian, and still I don't know which."

"You're free," he whispers into the phone. "You're forever free."

"Only if you will lock me in your arms, only if you will chain me to your soul."

"I will," he promises, "I will."

"I'm leaving, I'm late," Hanford said to Anna as he charged off the set.

"Where are you going?" she wanted to know.

"Nowhere, everywhere," he barked.

She wanted to know more; she pressed him for further information. But he wouldn't give. She begged him to spend the night with her. He flatly refused, and the more she insisted, the more adamant he became.

39

The bank's manager had gone to Chicago for a convention. His office was deserted, and at 12:28 P.M., Silvia quietly entered, turned on his small portable TV and sat in one of the guest chairs. She was happy to be alone with her anticipation, her frantic curiosity, her heart full of wonder and apprehension for Sister Prudence.

The hotel room is pale yellow. It is large, luxurious and appointed with furnishings both distinguished and subtle. The bed is the most enormous that Prudence has ever seen. On either side of the bed are delicate end tables with lovely Queen Anne legs; atop each table is a thin, graceful vase containing a single white rose. The symmetry is touching.

Prudence walks around the room as if in a daze. She is wearing a tailored black suit—a manly looking suit, in fact—which makes her look that much softer, that much more feminine. She pulls open the drapes and listens to the city, the faint sounds of horns and traffic far below. She walks across the room to Brian who is wearing a crisp blue seersucker jacket, white shirt, white pants and moccasin-styled loafers with bright yellow stitching. He is sitting in a stately, green, overstuffed chair reading *The New York Times*. She sits on his lap. He drops the newspaper. They speak.

"Is it possible that we're here?" she asks.

"It's not only possible," he answers, "but highly probable. Those airplane pilots usually have a good sense of direction."

"And will we actually sleep together tonight?"

"Yes," he says, "in a bed. In that bed right over there."

She kisses him and asks, "And all your excuses worked? Your mother and your father and your wife and all your lawyer friends and businessmen believed you? They really let you go to see your make-believe prospective client?"

"Just as surely as the convent believed that your Aunt Augusta was dying and demanding your presence."

"Do you know how long it's been since I've been back?"

"It must seem a lifetime ago."

"It was, Brian. It was."

"Are you going to show me the sights of your childhood?"

"No! I don't want to see that part of the city. I've forgotten that it was ever there. That's another world down there which I never want to think about again."

"Then we will play tourists."

"Oh, yes, Brian. That's just what I want to do. I want to go up to the top of the Empire State Building and be dazzled by the sky and the lights and the glamour of the city. I want to shop up and down Fifth Avenue, I want to stroll as though we're in the Easter Parade. We'll promenade and brunch at the Plaza, won't we?''

"We will if you like.''

"Yes," she says excitedly, "we'll go to intimate cafés and listen to pianists, absolutely divine pianists who'll play songs from the thirties about the way the city used to be, the penthouses and the broken hearts, and we'll munch on olives and drink martinis and think to ourselves how safe we are—because Troy is as far away as my old neighborhood, and we'll know no one but ourselves.''

"We'll need no one but ourselves," he assures her.

"And we'll never go back.''

"Not until late Monday afternoon.''

"But by then we'll be changed, we'll be different, we'll never be the same after this weekend.''

"The luxury of spending the night with you is something I've dreamed of for months.''

"On the plane, Brian, I had closed my eyes and thought I was sleeping, but I wasn't. I was in some sort of strange state, a natural state of meditation or prayer. I don't know how to describe it. But for a while I thought I was reliving all the feelings and fears I had during Mother Superior's funeral, and then I suddenly realized that wasn't it at all, it was much different and I wasn't afraid, because I felt her presence, not her dying presence but her living presence. And she understood, Brian, Mother Superior understood where I was going and why I was going and I heard her speaking, I thought I heard her whispering to me in the hum of the jets, in the midst of the clouds, and the book I was reading opened—just like that—and I looked at the words and I read them over and over again.''

"What was the book?" he asks. "What were the words, Prudence?''

She gets up from the chair she is sharing with Brian and walks over to her small overnight bag. She takes out a book. "It's Santa Teresa's greatest work," she tells him. *"The Interior Castle."* She begins to recite. "In the betrothal it is as though two wax candles were brought together so closely that the whole light is only one or that the wicks and the light and the wax

278

together are one . . . it is as though rain from the skies were to fall into a river or a fountain where everything is water, so that it is impossible to divide or separate the water of the river and the water which came from the skies . . . or as though a room had two windows through which much light would enter; although it enters divided, within the room it becomes one light." She pauses.

"The metaphors are quite beautiful," he tells her.

"The metaphors are our life. We are the metaphors. We are joined together, and now nothing must separate us. Nothing."

It took Silvia a while to get up and turn off the TV. Sitting there in the branch manager's somewhat spiffy office, she was transfixed. She was happy about Prudence's happiness, but somehow she didn't trust it. She wanted to know what was going to happen. She feared for Prudence's future. She felt as though she had to do something. And she picked up the phone and began to call the milk plant, but she stopped herself. That was silly. It was just a show. She looked at her watch and saw that she only had a few minutes before she had to be behind her teller's cage. She bought a couple of packages of cracker-and-peanut-butter sandwiches from the vending machines, and as she ate, she realized that her stomach was still churning; she was worried about the nun.

Seames stormed off the set. He looked shook. Anna chased after him.

"It's heavy. It's getting too heavy," he mumbled to himself.

"It's nothing to get alarmed about. It's simply real," she insisted.

"I'm talking to Al. I'm telling you, the script is too heavy. It's downright spooky."

"I think it's beautiful, Al is writing beautifully."

"Al is writing whatever you tell him to write!"

"The show is ours now, Hanford. Why resist that?"

"I'm discussing this with Dick and Howard. I may even go to Costein."

"They all work for Al. You know that. They all listen to Al," she reminded him.

"Listen, I've got to get out of here. I'm late."

"Late for what?" Anna wanted to know.

"Late for a goddamn date—that's what!" He was angry. He wanted to hurt her.

"Don't, please, not tonight. We need to talk," she begged. "There are so many things we need to discuss."

She grabbed him. He pushed her away. She fell to the floor, right there in the hallway in front of his dressing room. And she stayed there, as though she were kneeling.

40

One of the stagehands told me that he thought Seames had slugged her. As soon as I heard that I went looking for them. They both had gone. I called her place and she was sobbing and I figured she was hurt. I asked her whether he was there, and she said no and I called his apartment and told him to wait there because I was coming right over.

When he opened the door he was buttoning up his shirt and there was still a little shaving cream on his face and I grabbed him by the collar and picked him up a foot off the ground and ripped his fucking shirt and told him I was going to kick his ass and crack his nuts and if I didn't need him on this goddamn show I'd turn his ugly puss into cream of tuna. He was scared, I could see that lame-brain Seames was really scared, and I couldn't blame him because I must have looked like the fucking wild man of Borneo. I mean I was so pissed I could only see yellow.

"You're crazy, Gonfio, you and Anna are both crazy," he kept saying. I should have slugged him then, but the way he was shaking made it too easy—these Ivy League boys have the backbone of a baby goat—and I told him if he ever raised a hand to Anna Calzolari again I would personally break both his arms. How the fuck could he call himself a gentleman? I asked him. How the fuck could he look at himself in the mirror after brutalizing a defenseless female? If he was having trouble keeping his dick hard, why take it out on her?

Then he told me that I had misunderstood, that it was all a mistake. He defended himself by saying that he barely touched her, that she fell down because she wanted to fall down, because she wanted to be hurt and he would never strike a female. I told him he was lying through his teeth. He said he had witnesses. I said I had witnesses too. He said it was all getting too heavy for him. Which is when I told him he could get his ass off the show.

Then something funny happened: At the same time, we both realized that such a move wouldn't work. It was a juicy role and he wanted it to further his career. No doubt about that. And I had Anna to protect. Imagine her reaction if I told her that Hanford was leaving. That would mean Brian would be leaving, and that would mean real trouble for me and millions of housewives and the ratings. I could hear the channels switching to the neighboring soaps. I could see Costein's tinted glasses steaming over. I could see that this whole thing was going to be a draw.

"I'm not going anywhere, Al, and neither are you. At least not yet."

"Don't be so sure," I bluffed. "I do whatever the fuck I want to do on this show."

"What you should do is calm down. I'm telling you, this show is making us all crazy," he said, examining his ripped shirt.

I left him, half disgusted at myself for not kicking in his teeth. They were the sort of straight white teeth that were obviously the product of San Francisco's finest orthodontist. They gleamed with good breeding. But I had something of a sense of breeding myself and I knew it was stupid and self-defeating to do any damage to Seames. He had probably already shit his pants.

Down on Lexington Avenue I called Anna's apartment and when I kept getting a busy signal I started sweating because I was nervous and because summer was nearly here and for some dumb reason I had worn a wool sport jacket to work. I called her again and again and I figured she had taken the phone off the hook and I thought about going over there and making sure she was all right but I decided that I had had enough shit for one day so I took a cab down to the old neighborhood to see Artie Sappone—it had been over a year since I paid a personal visit to Artie—at the U Pick 'Em Turf Analisis.

The window of the butcher shop was smudged with dirt and the downtown air seemed thick and sad. But Artie's sign was still there, the sign which had been there longer than the fucking Statue of Liberty. Someday I would tell Artie that he had misspelled *analysis* but today wasn't the day. I was just so happy to see him, back there in the room behind the meat counter, at his little table with his papers and his beat-up black telephone. "Arturo!" I shouted. "You look like a million bucks."

I was lying. He looked old and fat and tired. There were liver spots all over his forehead, but his face lit up when he saw me because in the old neighborhood I'm something of a celebrity and when I just drop in on someone—the way I was dropping in on Artie—there was always a lot of excitement and good cheer.

"Nice of you to come by, Al. We're always talking ponies on the phone but I never see you. I almost forgot what you look like."

"The same, Arturo. I never change."

"I wouldn't say that. You look good."

"I been running."

"You mean you're jogging with the rest of those nuts?"

"A lot of the executives at the networks are into running. Supposed to be very good for your heart."

"I could understand the nags running. They run 'cause some jockey is whipping their ass. But people running. I gotta confess, Al, that never made sense to me."

"It's nothing I do too regularly. Just a little hobby I picked up."

"How's your show doing, Al?"

"Been a helluva year."

"Glad to hear that. I been worried about you, what with your luck with the horses these past months."

Artie knew. Artie knew more than anyone. But that didn't bother me, because whereas he might say something to me, he'd never breathe a word to anyone else. It was like the lawyer/

client privilege—maybe tighter—no information is more sacred and secret than the business between bookie and bettor.

"Big," I reassured him. "Six-figure big. Plus bonuses for improvement in the ratings race. I gotta tell you, Artie, I been knocking them dead this season."

"I sneak a look at your show when I can, Al, and I see that you got all this trouble with a nun. She's a very pretty girl."

"Kaufman found her for me. Brink Kaufman." Brink was an old client of Artie's.

"Imagine that."

"She comes from around here. Just down the street."

"Yeah," Artie said to me, "it's a real fascinating story and everything, but I'm wondering, Al, I'm wondering whether it's so good to have all this stuff about a sister fooling around with a man."

I loved Artie because he was an old-fashioned guy. I loved him because he was so good at what he did, but as far as the modern world went, well, Artie wasn't home.

"It's just make-believe, Artie. None of it means shit. It's all about money. You can understand that, can't you?"

"When I get to watching it, though, I gotta tell you, Al—I can really see it all happening. I mean it all seems so real."

"That's because I pour my feelings into the scripts. And believe me, Artie, those things aren't easy to write."

"I don't see how you do it. And don't get me wrong, I think it's a great show. Great story, very big words and very educational, too. Got nothing against it. But I have a hunch"—when Artie Sappone says the word *hunch* you stop what you're doing and listen with both ears—"that little girl who plays the nun is very strange. There's something very strange about her. Maybe that's why everyone wants to watch her, but it almost seems wrong to watch her because she's so strange. Do you know what I mean? The other day I'm sitting home and looking at the show and I'm actually feeling bad that I'm watching that nun. Almost ashamed of myself for not turning off the set. Like she shouldn't be doing what she was doing."

"The girl's a genius," I assured Artie.

"Sometimes geniuses are a little weird," Artie assured me.

"Who looks good to you tomorrow?" I abruptly changed the

subject. What the fuck did old Artie Sappone know about soap operas?

"Don't get me wrong, Al. I think it's a good show, and you always got all those stories going. Everyone I know loves the show, but there's something about that girl. Is she religious? In real life is she a religious person?"

"I asked you who looks good tomorrow," I repeated. I was getting a little annoyed.

"Homesick looks very sweet in the sixth. Besides that, my bones ain't twitching."

I took a Rey del Mondo out of my jacket and, together with a $20 bill, stuck it in the pocket of Artie's shirt.

"I'll call you tomorrow from the office and tell you which way I'm leaning," I told the old man.

I thought about dropping by and seeing my folks, but my talk with Artie had left a rotten taste in my mouth. Anna. He was worried about Anna and he didn't even know her. I jumped into a cab and went straight to her place without calling. It was one of those cabs where the springs had been shot for the last ten years, and I felt like a fucking bowling ball that someone had bounced down the lane. Anna, I thought to myself as I saw a bunch of nuns coming out of a fabric store at Union Square. Anna, Anna, Anna. Everyone worrying about Anna. And me worrying about them worrying, because maybe—just maybe— they were right. Maybe there was something to worry about. And maybe I should be worrying more, or doing something different. But what? She was acting her ass off, wasn't she? She was growing up. She had left all that hippie shit behind her, left Palermo, left that lousy loft, left that bunch of losers at the fucking ridiculous Living Rock Theatre. Anna was doing good. Or was she?

I tried to get her out of my mind, and I couldn't, and when I knocked on her door and she answered it she was wearing the nun's habit. And inside her apartment, on top of the television set, I saw two white candles which were lit, which were burning, and she said to me, " 'In the betrothal it is as though two wax candles were brought together so closely that the whole light is only one or that the wicks and the light and the wax together are one.' "

I was dumbfounded, I didn't know what to say, but then she laughed, like it was all a big joke, and she took off the habit and underneath she was wearing shorts, regular walking shorts, and her legs were a little thin but very, very shapely and she told me how glad she was to see me. "I've been thinking about you all evening," she said. "You must have gotten my message." And she seemed all right. "I have all sorts of ideas about the show," she told me, and she brought me a pencil and paper and coffee and cream and settled down on her sofa and I felt very secure and sure of myself because I knew it was going to be a good night, a very good night, for writing and plotting and being with my friend.

41

This was Anna's day off. She slept late, stayed in bed, read the poetry of Donne, the journals of Santa Teresa. She knew that she was killing time, but there was nothing else she wanted to do. She couldn't find the energy to get up and get dressed.

She called Hanford, but the line was busy, busy for hours. He had taken the phone off the hook.

She fixed herself something to eat—a bowl of cereal, an orange, a slice of Melba toast—she tried the newspaper, but couldn't concentrate, didn't care; tried Hanford again; closed her eyes, counted her breaths, thought of tomorrow when she could return to her life.

She walked into her living room, to the videotape machine which she had rented, slipped in the cassette which she had borrowed from the studio, the cassette that she had been studying since yesterday.

* * *

Sally and Brian open the door to their house. She is in a gown. He wears a tux. They walk into their den. The tension is apparent. He mixes himself a drink. He watches the ice swim around the rim of the glass. He stares into the whiskey. She walks around the den. Her face is tight. He sits on the couch. He sighs. He half closes his eyes. She approaches him, stands in front of him. He doesn't bother to look up. She reaches down and knocks the drink from his hand. He leaps up, but his frilly white shirt and black trousers are stained with Scotch.

"What the hell!" he shouts.

"I've been wanting to do that all night," she screams back.

"Then you should have. No one was stopping you."

"You've been acting like an ass ever since you got back from New York, you haven't said a word to me, you've been brooding and distant and I can't stand it anymore, I can't stand it, Brian, especially tonight, especially at the Junior League Ball when you told me that you'd try, you promised me that you'd mix and socialize and dance. And you did nothing but sit there and mope, you talked to no one and barely acknowledged your own parents, your very own mother and father, your mother, who has been so sick and was so brave to come tonight . . ."

"So brave! Are you kidding? When she dies she's going to have the ball transferred to the First Methodist Church cemetery so she won't miss a thing."

"How can you joke about something so serious?"

"How can you be serious about something so inane?"

"Do you know how long it took to plan this ball? Do you have any idea of the painstaking work—all volunteer, by the way—of dedicated women like your mother?"

"Their dedication is to their small vision of high society and seeing their picture in the paper Sunday morning."

"I can't stand it! Your cynicism is so deep, Brian, that I can't stand it!"

"Is it cynical to be disgusted by a gang of hobnobbing hypocrites who are jealous and greedy and shallow and mostly stupid?"

"You sound like a schoolboy railing against your mommy and daddy."

"Aren't you tired of this, Sally? Aren't you tired of these

people—the tired old set and the ambitious young set—the parents of our friends and our friends themselves who were never really our friends and only care about the size of their houses and whether they're going to Europe and is it tacky to go to Bermuda or fashionable to fly to Florida anymore? I ask you— how can you stand it?''

"It's my life. Can't you understand that? You're talking about the people I love."

"There was no love tonight. Only phony smiles in a room filled with envy."

"People enjoyed themselves. They danced and drank . . ."

"And gossiped and stabbed their neighbors in the back . . ."

"You think you're above all this. You think you're too good for Troy."

"It's choking me."

"Then get out. Get out like you got out when you went to New York. Leave on your secret business trips. Take off."

"Don't push me, Sally."

"I'm not pushing, I'm pleading. I can't take it anymore. You're simply not here. You don't look at me or speak to me, you don't touch me or make love to me or ask me whether I'm happy or sad. You're either alone in your mind or with someone else. I don't understand, I don't care anymore, all I know is that you're not a husband to me. You're not even a decent date."

Brian begins to answer, but stops himself. He realizes that he has nothing to say.

Baxter MacNiece's tie is solid blue, his dress shirt is a field of soft gray squares. He runs a comb through his thick gray hair as Brian enters his office.

"Just in time," the older man announces. "I was just about to take out my putting green. I'll challenge you to a little match."

"I've come to talk to you, Dad." Brian's expression is sober and straight. He appears tired and bedraggled.

"We can talk while we shoot," Mr. MacNiece answers as he pulls the strip of artificial grass from the closet and brings out a ball and a couple of clubs.

"I'm not interested in golf right now, Dad. This is serious."

"Well, talk, for God's sake. I'm a much more receptive listener when I'm polishing up my putting. Don't mind me. Just tell me what's on your mind, son." Baxter sets up the apparatus and solidly plants his feet in the plastic grass. Brian stands next to him and begins to explain.

"It's hard for me to say all this to you. It's hard for me to admit much of it to myself, but I've really been having a difficult time, Dad, here in the office and especially at home. I thought my attitudes would begin to change, and for a while I fooled myself with the old adage that time would heal all."

Baxter taps the ball into the cup and breaks into a broad smile. Then he begins the process all over again.

"I've thought about this from a thousand angles, and I've come to a thousand conclusions," Brian goes on. "And yet nothing makes sense, at least not yet, and I thought that, even though things have been strained between us, Dad . . . I thought, well, that this might be an instance where we could sit down and talk. Or at least I thought it was worth a try."

With perfect form, Baxter hits the ball again, though this time he misses the cup. "Glad you decided to confide in me, Brian. Wise choice. Wise choice indeed. Now, why don't you tell the old man about this woman you've been seeing on the sly."

Brian is shocked. "How did you know?" he asks.

"At my age, you see these sort of things coming. I wasn't actually convinced until your mother had her stroke. There was something about your reaction to my being, shall we say, indisposed that evening which made me wonder. Why, I thought to myself, should you be so outraged if indeed you weren't more outraged at yourself than me?" He hits the golf ball. He misses the cup.

"It's not *that* kind of affair," Brian retorts.

"Who are you to presume what kind of affairs I, or anyone else for that matter, indulges in? We have a difficult time understanding our own flings without pretending to understand anyone else's."

"This *is* different, Dad, I assure you."

"The first one always seems different. It's all so secretive and sinful to you that the passion is naturally exaggerated. But you'll see, son, as time goes on, as you become more experienced in such matters, that it will be nothing more than a footnote, an

288

asterisk, a passing fancy. It will be nothing more than a fond
memory."

"You're wrong. You're dead wrong."

Baxter continues to play with his putting, gently knocking the
ball here and there, not bothering to look up at his son as he
continues to expound. "I think back to my first one," his father
says, "and believe me, I had your attitude exactly. I adored
her. I bought her flowers and candies and promised her that
sooner or later I would leave your mother and rush her to the
altar. She was a splendid woman. Simply splendid. A fine rear
and a stupendous front, and when we loved, the world stopped
and waited, and when we were through, we recited poetry to
each other—yes, your old man actually memorized Keats and
Byron—and when I went home to your mother my mind was a
million miles away."

"And what happened?"

"A friend from law school was visiting me at the time and I
discussed the matter with him. He was a bit more mature and
worldly about such things and he said—I'll never forget this—
'Baxter,' he said, 'some women are for loving and other women
are for living.' "

"That's the most hackneyed sentiment I've heard in my life,"
Brian counters.

"It may be hackneyed, but it happens to be true. Believe me,
son, it's true. From then on, I knew that whatever outside activ-
ities I might enjoy, your mother would always be there—for
what really counts, for living."

"But you've done nothing but live a lie."

"I don't believe in lying. Might I remind you that I'm an
attorney, an officer of the court." Baxter putts, and his shot is
right on the money. He smiles with enormous satisfaction.

"Your marriage is a farce," his son accuses.

"I tell your mother what I see fit to tell her. There's absolutely no reason to hurt her."

"You're rationalizing."

"I'm reasonable. I try to be reasonable in everything I do,
and I suggest, son, that you could do worse than follow my
example. This romance that you've mentioned—I'd forget it.
Or at least I'd put it on the back burner for a few months."

"It's not as easy as that."

"It's never easy to walk away from good sex."

"Damn it, it's more than good sex! This woman is something extraordinary!"

"They all seem extraordinary in bed."

"It's more than that! I'm telling you that it's more than that!"

"Take it easy, son. I'm on your side. I've been there before, I know how sweet those stolen kisses can be."

"This woman is a saint!" Brian is shouting at his father, but his father continues to focus on his putting.

"Remember that old song that Sinatra used to sing with Tommy Dorsey? What was it called? 'The Night a Sinner Kissed an Angel.' Something like that. Well, that's how we all view it the first time."

"She's a nun," Brian states flatly, not quite believing his own words.

"*A nun?*" Baxter interrupts his golf game.

"Yes."

"That nun from Ursula? That nun with the lease problem?"

"Yes."

"I don't believe it."

"We're very much in love."

Suddenly Baxter's face turns red and he flies into a rage.

"You are forbidden to see her again. *Forbidden!* Do you understand me?"

"This is the attitude I expected."

"I don't give a hang what you expected. I'm telling you, for the first and last time, that your seedy little affair must be ended, for the sake of the reputation of this law firm—not to mention the reputation of your own family."

Brian turns around and leaves his father's office, slamming the door behind him.

Anna was excited, thrilled. She wanted to . . . wanted to kiss him, hug him for being so brave, so strong, for standing up to Baxter. For needing her and loving her, for wanting her so badly.

She punched the rewind button and ran the tape back to the beginning. She sat and watched it all happen again, the drama still dancing about her head.

290

42

Costein's apartment was full of weird art, just the kind of shit that makes me sick. There were huge white canvases with a couple of red blobs; there were paintings of empty gas stations, there were pictures of soap bars and boxes of Band-Aids. I didn't even want to think how much he paid for this crap. But there was so much of it—all over the living room and dining room—that I felt I had to say something.

"What do you think about when you look at this stuff?" I finally asked. I didn't want to be entirely nasty since he had invited me over for dinner.

"What do you think about when you look at any painting?" he asked back.

"If it's a painting of the ocean, I think about the ocean. The way it feels to get wet at Coney Island. If it's a picture of a good-looking broad, naturally I think about fucking her."

"These images with which I have surrounded myself go deeper than that."

"Deeper than fucking?"

"These are the works of rather established painters."

"They may be, but I just wonder why you want to look at a painting of a gas station that doesn't even look as a good as a photograph."

"Because it's there. Because it has integrity, a certain solid stance, it is a landscape, an American landscape—real and raw —much the way, say, Turner might have . . ."

"Save the speeches. I'm impressed that you've remembered your notes from college."

"You realize, Al, that paintings can be intelligent investments."

"You might as well frame your stock certificates and hang them on the wall."

"That's an interesting suggestion."

"Are you serving food tonight or just bullshit?"

"I take it that you're hungry."

My stomach groaned a little, as if to say, "Hell, yes." My stomach, I noticed, was getting way too big. I don't know what it was—the pressure that came with my coronary event, the pressure of the show, the pressure of so much success.

"Let's have a drink and we'll eat in a few minutes," he suggested.

We stepped down into the sunken living room. All the floors were dark wood—glossy and slick—and all the walls were stark white. The furniture was tubular and metallic and uncomfortable—just like his office. The leather was stiff and there weren't any cushions and some of the chairs looked as though they were designed by orthopedic surgeons out on a sadistic tear. The coffee table was a huge, thick piece of clear Plexiglas and the magazines were all about TV ratings and the money market and the entertainment business. Nothing but cold facts. Not a trace of beaver.

"How do you like my place?" the kid asked. He was wearing a boring blue blazer and tan pants. He looked like college.

"How do I like it?" I stalled for time. "It's all right if you're preparing for life on the moon."

He laughed. These days I just couldn't do wrong by the kid. He thought everything I said was hysterically funny. He handed me a Scotch—he was drinking his high-priced seltzer—and said, "You realize that *Search* is the hottest product at the network."

"Naturally," I answered, though I hadn't realized that at all.

"But I'm wondering where you're taking Prudence next. I'm wondering because I see these next few weeks as critical."

"Every week is critical. The story can fall in on your head at any minute. You've got to keep it moving every day."

"We're moving into the summer cycle, and traditionally that means . . ."

"Save it, kid. You're lecturing the wrong boy. Remember—I'm the one who thought of this shit. I don't need to hear about no cycles. It's my story and I know just where to take it. I don't work in committees and I don't work in teams—not when it comes to Sister Prudence.''

"You work with Anna.''

"Anna works with me.''

"Wouldn't you call that a team?''

"More like a friendship.''

"That friendship interests me.''

"We've been over this before. It's none of your fucking beeswax.''

"Everything about *Search* is my beeswax. As a matter of fact, I'm calling a meeting with both of you for the day after tomorrow.''

"Good, because you can use that time to take your calculator and go into your little private can and beat yourself off. I ain't bringing Anna to any executive meetings, I can tell you that right now.''

"For one thing,'' Costein continued, ignoring my barbs, "I'm not at all certain about marriage.''

"It's a disgusting institution, you're right.''

"I'm discussing Prudence's marriage.''

"I'm bored.''

"That's what I'm worried about. I'm afraid that by marrying off Prudence to Brian you may create a happier, more blissful situation than you can handle.''

"I can handle anything.''

"You can, but the plot can't. I don't have to tell you that soaps depend on misery piled upon misery.''

"Maybe I should be taking notes. I don't know a goddamn thing about this soap opera business and I want to remember every last fucking thing you're saying to me.''

"I'm serious, Al.''

"I'm starving.''

"Once Anna has Brian, she isn't going to want to let him go. She's not going to allow you to create the kind of crisis that we must . . .''

"I'm going to buy a T-shirt which says NO ONE TELLS ME WHAT THE FUCK TO WRITE in big black letters and that way I'll avoid these asshole conversations once and for all.''

Costein stood in front of his fireplace which was surrounded by sheets of stainless steel. He didn't say anything for a long time. I looked at a painting—or whatever you call it—which was hanging in the middle of all the steel. It was nothing more than the numbers 3:05:10 printed in red.

"What does that mean?" I asked, pointing to the numbers.

"It's my best marathon time," the kid told me.

I looked down at my feet and saw with some satisfaction that I had worn my Street Fighters. Just for the occasion. And still, seeing Costein looking so lean and hungry, I wondered if he was onto something. He seemed so fucking steely and determined —he wanted to take over the network and the company that controlled the network and the corporation that controlled the company. I knew that. He wanted everything. In me he had found a gold mine. And now he was worried that I was about to blow it. He was worried that I was too personally involved in this thing. So maybe this meeting was on the level. Maybe he really did have something to say. Maybe I shouldn't be such a prick. I thought about this for a while, and then I said to him, "Listen, Mark, if you wanna get into Anna's panties, you're going to have to do it on your own time."

He laughed a little and sipped his seltzer. I had hit a raw nerve, I saw that. He was probably hurting for a broad. With all the goddamn jogging he did, he was probably too pooped to pop. He hadn't had any in a long time, and he was looking to me to pimp for my girl Anna. Well, nuts to that noise. He'd have to go chasing after his own tail.

"Dinner is served, gentlemen."

When I looked up I saw Miss Lee in a white satin pants suit, sleek and lovely and smiling like a dream of the Orient. She was carrying a tray with beautiful green salads.

"Thank you, dear," the kid said to her, and the three of us sat down and ate.

Costein was slick, I thought to myself going home in the cab that night. He had given me the right grub, the right brandy, he even had the right brand of cigar. He had fed me and filled me with his bullshit. He had shown me his swanky pad and let me know that he was fucking his high-class secretary. He thought

294

all this would impress me. But I was pleased with myself as I remembered how I wouldn't budge, wouldn't give him the meeting he wanted. I didn't tone down my language for him or his Miss Lee or anyone else. I kept the fucking faith. I ate my ass off—he was smart enough to have her make fancy versions of steak and potatoes and custard pudding for me—but I kept the faith. Until . . .

After the booze and the brandy and the cigar and the old Sinatra sides—the kid didn't miss a trick—he walked me to the door and helped me on with my coat and told me he was pleased that I had broken bread with him and, oh, yes, before he forgot, there was one more thing, one little business detail he had forgotten about. He had managed to put through a "little" salary increase for me. Of course it still wasn't what I deserved, but it was 50 percent more than I had been getting.

"Just call Miss Lee tomorrow," he said to me as I walked out the door, still a little stunned, "and tell her what time you and Anna can drop by the office later in the week."

43

Brian's mother walks with a cane. Her speech is slightly slurred, but her appearance is still meticulous; her blue-gray hair is neatly coiffured, her deep green dress is conservatively, expensively cut, her fine, emerald-cut diamond glitters under the light of the studio. She sits in the sun-room, adjacent to her and Baxter's bedroom, in an extravagantly formal antique armchair upholstered in a pattern of yellow flowers. The chair resembles a throne.

Brian enters the room and stands, leans against a huge wall-to-ceiling mirror as his mother haltingly, but quite deliberately, begins to lecture him.

295

"Your father has brought to my attention a matter of great delicacy. That's why I have asked you to come over this afternoon, Brian."

"He had no right to divulge confidences which were strictly between the two of us."

"He had every right in the world." She pauses between sentences as if to gather up the strength to force out her words, to fight the gnawing effects of her stroke. "This, you must understand, is a matter that touches not only your life, but the lives of many other people who love you and whom you must certainly love. It is indeed an unpleasant and uncomfortable subject to discuss with one's son, but I find I have no choice."

"I don't want to discuss it. I refuse to discuss it with you, Mother. I feel as though I've been . . . we've both been betrayed by my father."

"You're not telling me anything that I don't already know. Baxter MacNiece is a most difficult man."

"Difficult or deceptive?"

"He's not what he seems. To you, I'm sure, he seems two-faced, and I grant you that there were times when I considered leaving him. There is little about his professional or private life that I do not know. But I've chosen to look the other way, I've maintained the good name of our family. And I have done so, I might remind you, not solely for the sake of myself or your father. I've done so largely because of you. Our standing in the community, the untarnished reputation of your father's law firm, the financial stability we've been able to establish—these, dear Brian, are yours; these are our inheritance to you. And to see you, because of some midnight madness, destroy what took so very long to create—well, I could not idly sit by and watch that happen. That's why I must urge you, Brian . . ." she stops and searches for a stronger word, "I must demand . . ." again she pauses, "I must *forbid* you to continue your utter foolishness. You're on a collision course which will destroy you."

Brian thinks before answering. After several seconds he leans down, kisses his mother on the cheek and whispers, barely loud enough for the microphone to pick up, "You don't understand. You just don't understand."

* * *

296

"Are you going to tell me where you're going?" Sally asks her husband who is coming down the stairs carrying a large black suitcase in his hand.

"Of course I'll tell you. Why should I hide that from you?"

"You've hidden so much already."

"There's no reason to destroy each other. I'm not interested in hurting you."

She laughs sarcastically. "If that were true," she says, "why in the name of reason would you be doing what you're doing?"

"I have to be alone for a while, Sally. I need time to think, time to live with myself and find out what I really want."

"There's more to it than that. There has to be more!" She has begun to cry.

"Of course there's more than that. There's everything, there's my life—what I'm going to do and where I'm going to live."

"You're leaving Troy?"

"I didn't say that."

"You implied as much."

"You want answers, Sally, and I simply don't have any."

"I have the feeling that you're lying. I think that you've been lying to me for so long that you no longer know what the truth is."

"You may be right," he concedes, bowing his head, not wanting to continue the conversation.

"Your father is not going to put up with this!" she shouts. "He already told me that he won't let you leave me. He'll kick you out of the firm first."

"He doesn't have to do that. I've already resigned."

"How can you do that? Where are you going to work?"

"I'm going to open an office and work on my own for a while. There are all kinds of people in this area who need legal help but can't afford the kind of hourly rates I've been forced to charge."

"So you're going to be a goody-goody lawyer. You're going to bleed for all the poor people of the world."

"I'm just going to try to keep myself together, Sally. I have no plans to save the world."

"But what about me, dammit! What about me! For God's sake, Brian, you just can't leave, you just can't throw away everything we've ever shared. There's too much between us, too much time, too much love."

He looks at her but does not answer. Instead, he picks up his suitcase and, walking past her, leaves the house, quietly closing the door behind him.

The park bench is brightly lit. It is noon and Brian sits there, in brown sport shirt and beige corduroy trousers, reading the poetry of John Donne.

Prudence appears. She is wearing a white pleated skirt, a white blouse. She is the radiance of the day itself. She is smiling and she sits next to him. She kisses Brian on the cheek.

"Have you left?" she asks him.

"My home, my firm—everything."

She grasps his hand. "Now it's your turn to ask me," she urges.

"Have you left?" he inquires.

"I have."

"And was it painful?"

"The pain was a pleasure. I shall carry it with me always."

"Was it difficult explaining?"

"Yes, it was difficult, of course it was difficult. But the mother superior, the new mother superior, seems understanding. And because I just met her, it was easier than it might have been."

"She didn't try to convince you otherwise?"

"I spoke from my heart, and she didn't doubt my sincerity. I told her about my feelings for Santa Teresa. I quoted those lines, 'However much we may seem to humiliate ourselves, we always fall short of being daughters of such a mother, and spouses of such a spouse.' "

"You make it sound as though leaving were effortless."

"I'm happy because we're together now, Brian, but I've never done anything more trying. I suffered. You've seen how I've suffered."

"You look marvelous."

"I feel as though I want to run through forests, leap into clouds, soar across continents and dance over rainbows. I want to sing."

298

"You realize that this isn't going to be easy," he warns her.

"Yes, but tell me what happened with Sally and your parents."

"This isn't the time. I don't want to break your spell."

"My spell can't be broken. My spell is my new life."

"Have you heard from the nursery school?"

"They tell me I can start teaching there next week. Isn't that fabulous, Brian? Everything is falling together."

"Or falling apart."

"You're distressed." She caresses his cheek.

"I'm worried that my life is changing too quickly. I've hurt so many people."

"Before this," she assures him, "you were doing far more damage to yourself."

Brian turns to Prudence. "I have this gnawing feeling that we're being rash—far too rash."

"I've taken a small furnished room. You're living in a hotel. We're moving slowly and cautiously, just as we agreed, Brian."

"There are so many changes."

"And changes are always frightening. Changes force us to reexamine who we are and what we want."

"And you're not in the least afraid."

"I'm petrified," she confessed. "But my heart's singing as it's never sung before."

"There'll be pressures, there'll be ridicule, there'll be ugliness which we can't even imagine."

"What does it matter? Our love is our shield and our strength."

"We're going to be alone."

"And never lonely."

"Our faith will be tested."

"And we'll be forever faithful."

"You see it all, don't you? You see our life happily forever after."

"I see it and I feel it. I've dreamed it and now we will live it."

The organ music swells. The camera pulls back. The lovers are left looking into each other's eyes.

* * *

I was nervous and jumpy. I watched the action from the control room, but I couldn't sit down. I couldn't relax. I watched standing up, which is highly unusual for me, but there was something, something which had me half nuts. And when Anna got through with the last segment, when she wouldn't leave that fucking bench, even when the propmen had come to break the set, I went down there and told her what I had been wanting to tell her all week, what I had meant to tell her ever since I had had dinner with Costein.

"Let's go, Anna," I said to her, offering my hand, "we gotta go see the boss."

"What boss?" she wanted to know.

"Costein."

"I can't."

"Why?"

"Brian's taking me to the opera."

"*Hanford!* For Christ's sake, will you say Hanford and not Brian?"

"Al, I'm drained. I just finished an exhausting scene."

"I know you are, sweetie," I said, backing off. "But I promised the kid this meeting."

"You still haven't told me what it's about."

"The show. He wants to discuss the show."

"There's nothing to discuss. We already know what we're going to do."

"Let's just talk to the man. What do you say?"

"No."

"You're being unreasonable."

"I'm late, Al. I have to get dressed."

"I want you to do this favor, Anna. It's important to me."

"You're going to have to explain to me what the man wants."

"The man is in charge of our professional life. He can explain it himself."

"I've never heard you talk this way before. I didn't think anyone was in charge of your life except you."

She was nailing me and I didn't like it. "He has some ideas —that's all. He wants to share them."

"What kind of ideas?"

"If I knew, we wouldn't have to have the meeting."

"There's something you're not telling me."

"I'm telling you everything I know."

And then, before she left the set for her dressing room, she said something that haunted me for the rest of the night, for the ten days that it took me to convince her to go with me to meet Costein. And as I went down to the old neighborhood and ate alone at the Grotta Azzurra, as I downed an order and a half of gnocchi, as I put away my ossobuco and a couple of loaves of that real no-bullshit bread, as I finished the *Daily Racing Form* and a pitcher of wine (with the drunken fruit at the bottom), as I thought about coffee and cake and cream and candy and flying to Vegas and fucking some fine humping honey, I heard Anna's words over and over, screaming inside my head:

"I'm marrying Brian," she said to me, "and no one can change that—not even you."

44

"How'd you like to play a game of pinball?" I asked Anna who had dressed as though we were going to a funeral—dark and severe and withdrawn. I pointed to Costein's pinball machine and asked, "Don't you think that's one crazy goddamn idea? This kid's all right. I'm telling you that he's all right."

She said nothing. She didn't even smile as we continued to sit in Mark's office waiting for him to return from a meeting down the hall. We waited there for a few minutes before the door opened and Miss Lee came in to ask whether we'd like some refreshments. She treated me just as though I didn't know she was laying her boss, and I really respected her tact and her class, and when she left to get our coffee I was tempted to let Anna in on the little secret. I thought that she might get a few laughs out of that, but then I changed my mind: Why get her confused about Costein when she was confused enough?

Miss Lee returned and the coffee was definitely executive brew. And tasting those roasted beans I thought of the torture of convincing Anna to come to this meeting, how I had to beg and plead and finally put our goddamn fucking friendship on the line. She knew what was happening. She sensed it. She realized that the show might be moving away from everything that she —or Prudence—wanted. She was determined that would never happen, and she made me promise her that no matter what Costein said, I'd stick to my own convictions. *Of course*, I said to her, *of course*. No one could make me write what I didn't want to write. I assured her that there wasn't shit to worry about.

Costein came through the door and I was glad. At long last we'd get this meeting over with. He had been pressing me now for two weeks—ever since dinner at his place—and finally I was delivering him the goods. He looked at Anna and offered his hand. He ignored me, but that was okay. Anna was a powerful lady. Men were drawn to her. Nothing wrong with that. She took his hand and they shook like two businessmen. She barely looked at him, although he was looking pretty good today. He had obviously dressed for the occasion—formal three-piece suit with an I-make-big-decisions, little blue-dotted tie.

"I was thinking about you this morning during my jog," he said to her as he slipped behind his desk and leaned back in his sleek roll-around chair. "I don't know if Al told you, but I'm something of a runner. I can't recall—it was either while I was completing my ninth or tenth mile—but somehow the show, and everything it means to me and this network, filled my head. I must say that I felt overwhelmed and, at the same time, quite exhilarated. I must have run those last two miles in under eleven minutes which, you can well imagine, is quite fast. I thought about the amount of time that has elapsed since Al introduced the Sister Prudence segment—I'm sure you realize that it's been almost a year—and I felt very proud of all of us for having committed ourselves to the quality of the concept, the dramatic concept, which has had such satisfying results in the marketplace in which we compete."

302

Oh, shit, I thought to myself, *I hope Anna is buying this crap.* But when I looked over at her, I saw she wasn't. Still, the man behind the tinted glasses continued to turn himself on:

"I understand from Al that you have had extensive experience in the avant-garde theater, Anna, and I can see from the subtlety of your performance certain nuances which are the product of a highly attuned literary sensibility. I say that to you because I consider myself reasonably well versed in the modern theater. That is, if you consider the theater of Ibsen and Chekhov modern. I presume that you do."

He waited for her to respond, she said a very soft, "I do," and I was going to pronounce them man and wife. But I kept my mouth shut.

"Yes, of course," he rattled on, "and it's strange when you think of the influence of the nineteenth-century playwrights on the drama of our times, even the commercial fare that we find ourselves discussing today. Thematically, the central dilemma of woman—who she is, what she might become—has us continually pondering . . ."

I wanted to shut him up. I wanted to tell him to get on with it. I had never heard him this bad. But I just sat there and suffered. After all, the guy had given me one hell of a raise and I owed him a little courtesy.

"Someday someone will do a fascinating study," he said to Anna, who continued to sit there expressionless, "and perhaps it will be me—if I can ever find the time—on the relationship between serious literary drama and serious commercial drama. There is a serious link, you know."

No, we don't know, you dumb asshole, I thought to myself, *and we don't give a shit, either.*

"There is, of course, another distinction to be made, the distinction between drama and melodrama. Naturally it is melodrama with which we're all concerned. And by using the term melodrama, I don't wish to be derogatory. In fact, I remember one of my graduate school professors quoting Sainte-Beuve . . ."

And on and on and on. I drank two more cups of coffee and got the foxy Miss Lee to scrounge up a few doughnuts. Chocolate covered. My favorite. I put away half a dozen while the kid started telling the story of his success. Good grades in literature classes, then business classes, then computer science and finally his conquest of the world, his trip through the bureaucratic bowels of the network. He told her everything, just as he had told me. And finally, in the middle of his analysis of the Nielsens, she interrupted him and said, without a bit of malice, "I'm sorry, but I have to go rehearse."

I wanted to kiss her. What an honest dame! She was fed up with his horseshit.

"We had better move on to the business at hand," he said.

"Brilliant idea, kid," I couldn't resist adding.

"We've reached a turning point in the show, and specifically in the segment involving Sister Prudence. You and Al have developed the character quite fully and, again, you have my congratulations. But I'm afraid that if she achieves what she has sought—that is, a happy and stable life with Brian—we're likely to lose viewers."

"You're wrong," Anna blurted. "The viewers are searching for happiness, just as Prudence has searched for happiness. And no one can begrudge her finding it."

"I've studied these matters in great detail," the kid argued back, "from both a textural and a technical point of view. I think I know what sells."

"Al's been doing this for longer than anyone," she shot back, turning to me for support.

I wanted to say something, but I didn't know what. I thought I had better listen, though I knew that my silence was bothering the hell out of Anna.

"The last thing I want to do," Costein lied, "is to pull rank. You're right when you say that Al's a pro. And I've learned to hold him in great esteem." I couldn't help but smile as the kid went on. "But even great writers—or especially great writers —need editors. The awesome creative powers of a writer can cause him, from time to time, to lose perspective on what does or does not work dramatically."

"The show is working," Anna stated with flat assurance. "The show is working beautifully."

"Agreed. But it's working because there's been distress, misery, exquisite dramatic tension, if you'll pardon the phrase."

"He's trying to say that we got the housewives crying their asses off," I turned and explained to Anna.

"*I know what he's trying to say!*" she snapped, looking at me as though I were a deserter. I felt like warmed-over shit.

"These are suggestions, merely suggestions." The kid was trying to be diplomatic, but he was too stuck on himself to realize that Anna saw right through him. "For instance, to see Prudence and Brian marry might be too predictable a solution to the dramatic problem. Wouldn't it be more interesting, more provocative from the viewer's viewpoint, to insert some terrible dilemma—say . . ."

"Say nothing!" Anna was practically screaming. "Because nothing is going to alter those plans! They are set, because they are right."

"Right?" Costein questioned with his casual sophistication. "What does right or wrong have to do with it?"

"Ask Al. He'll tell you," she said. "He's the man who jumps when you pull the string." And with that, she got up and left. I didn't try to stop her. I figured she just had to blow off some steam.

"A little difficult, wouldn't you say?" the kid asked me.

"Na. Just touchy."

"I'd say she's crazy." The kid had been hurt.

"Listen, Costein, don't ever let me hear you use that word in connection with her. I've never heard you bullshit so fucking much in my life. It's no wonder she got up and left. You were giving the goddamn Sermon on the Mount."

"You foul up the show, Gonfio, and you're the one who's going to be crucified."

"This is nothing more than a minor hang-up. We'll get past it."

"I always thought she was an intriguing woman, but I didn't realize you were dealing with a spook."

"You don't know what you're talking about, kid. She's a genius."

"I'm only going to tell you once, Gonfio, so I want you to listen very closely." He had stopped acting, stopped trying to impress. Now he was all business. The real Costein. "If the ratings drop, so do you."

I thought I was going to be sick in the cab going back to the studio. My stomach hurt and my head hurt and I wanted to talk nags with Artie Sappone and forget about all this crap. I wanted to go to Hawaii with Silvia and gag her and fuck her for two weeks. I was sweating for my life. I felt some strange tingling up and down my arm and wondered whether this was it. I listened to my heart and couldn't hear it and for a second I figured that it had stopped beating. I looked around and saw that I was in a traffic jam in the god-awful middle of honking screaming yellow crazy cab Manhattan. This was where my life was ending. This was where I was going to drop dead. Before my $50 G raise took effect.

But God was good to me because I didn't die. God got me back to the milk plant in one piece. God took care of me long enough to make sure I made it back to my cubicle. But once I was there, God deserted me, and Dick and Howard and everyone else were yelling in my face wanting to know where Anna was. I told them that she had left Costein's office before me. They said that she hadn't shown up in the studio. "Fuck this noise!" I screamed. I picked up the phone and dialed her at home and she picked up the phone and she was sobbing her ass off and I asked her what was wrong and she said, "Everything, everything is wrong," and I told the creeps to get out of my cubicle, I told them I was having a private conversation and then she started telling me how she hated me because I had turned my back on her and sold her down the river and I told her to wait just a fucking minute because I was getting pissed off, I told her I wasn't doing anything of the kind, I was merely listening to Costein's ideas and I owed him . . . but she hung up in my ear and that's when I knew I was really in a fucking pickle.

45

Where had the summer gone to? Where had the year gone to?

I couldn't believe that so much time had passed so quickly, but this was proof, absolute goddamn proof: the lights strung across Mulberry, the excited crowds of people, the buzz of the old neighborhood. The festival of our beloved San Gennaro. And me walking down the street, with Anna on my arm, feeling as though I owned the whole fucking world.

Anna could still do that to me. Even after all this time. Or maybe *especially* after all this time.

She called me, and she called me just in time. Because I was getting pissed. I had had about enough of her screwed-up behavior. I was on the verge of chewing her out. I had made up my mind to tell her once and for all that I was running the show and that she was interfering too goddamn much. I didn't want to, I knew it would hurt her, but I was fed up and disgusted and— while I appreciated an actress so concerned and so absorbed and so brilliant—I also half longed for the old days when I just cranked out this shit without thinking about no one or nothing.

Sure, something was a little screwy about Anna. I was no fool. I saw that as plainly as anyone. But I also saw something else; I saw that the dame was happy playing this part, really happy, and because she was happy I was happy.

It killed me that she was so angry with me, because all I wanted to do was keep *everyone* happy—her, me and Costein. I was in the middle, and the memory of that first meeting with the kid was still fresh. The asshole had wanted to fire me. And despite all this buddy-buddy bullshit, he'd fire me again in a quick minute. He was the kind of guy who jogged fifteen miles and then pissed out ice cubes. The kid was cold.

So you can imagine how relieved I was when Anna called me

up and said in that voice of hers—so young and sweet and sincere, a voice of a goddamn angel—that she wanted to be with me tonight, that she wanted me to take her to the San Gennaro Festival. After all, she told me, it was our anniversary. I melted all over the phone.

Nothing had changed on Mulberry, and nothing ever will. That's the beauty of the festival. Oh, maybe the crowds get a little larger as time goes on, and maybe you see a few more weirdos now than you did when I was a kid, but that really doesn't make any difference since there's something so weird about San Gennaro anyway. Weird and holy and wonderful, because I'm still religious enough to believe that the blood turns to liquid and the floodwaters are turned back, the cancer cells dissolve, and maybe that 20-to-1 shot nag is really going to come in. I believe in God and all His Holy Saints, and even that gal that Anna is always talking about—Santa Teresa—had something to say about suffering. Sure, she was a little weird, too, but that's the best part of our religion. It's weird because we're weird, and sometimes—though I hate to say this in public—it occurs to me that even God is a little weird. How else did we get this way? After all, aren't we created in His image?

I was talking this way to Anna, and she was loving it. She always loved listening to me because she knew I gave her the straight-from-the-shoulder shit. And we were walking along and I was testing all the taste treats, eating a little pasta here and a little pastry there, picking up on the cheeses and the olives and the piping-hot breads. I was having a goddamn ball looking around at all the sights, noticing the new boss of the festival, the *Alto Patrono,* Phil Porcino, whose daughter Patty gave me my first blow job—God bless her.

"You know what I'd like to do?" I asked her.

"Tell me," she said.

"I'd like to get out of here before they start carrying San Gennaro around. I gotta tell you; that statue has always given me the heebie-jeebies. Why don't we leave all this noise and run by the Napolitana Kitchen?"

"The way we did last year?"

"Exactly. Make this a real anniversary party. Get drunk and not give a shit."

308

"Why don't we walk?" she suggested.

I was a little tired. I had let my jogging slide and I was more out of shape than I should have been, but I said yes, sure, we'd walk over to the Village just the way we did last year.

On the way she said she had to stop to make a phone call. I asked her who she was trying to reach, half-knowing the answer already. "Hanford," she told me, and I coughed up a wad of saliva and helped irrigate the late-summer sidewalks of New York. "Fuck that bum," I told her. And she smiled at me and called him anyway and had a long talk with him while I waited outside the phone booth trying my best to look nonchalant and listen in at the same time. She got real excited and at one point yelled at him, "No! No!" but I couldn't get any of the details. When she hung up she was crying and I knew my evening was shot.

"Why do you let him do that to you?" I asked her.

"It's all going to work out, Al. Don't worry," she said, regaining her composure.

"Nothing's going to work out if you don't drop him like a hot potato."

"I believe in happy endings."

"That's just the problem. There ain't any happy endings."

"There are if we believe deeply enough, if we love with real conviction."

"You sound like an Al Gonfio soap script."

"I mean it, I believe it, Al."

"That's what worries me. You're too smart, Anna, to start feeding yourself that shit. You know what it's like out here. It's cold and it's ugly and the only thing that keeps us from going off the deep end is the hope of more money."

"That's your vision, not mine."

"Rich beyond reason," I went on. "Everyone wants to be rich beyond reason, whether we admit it or not. So rich that nothing matters, which is when we go off the deep end on the other side."

" 'He sustains the garden without water and makes the virtues grow,' " she said, her eyes still wet.

"What the hell does that mean?"

"It's Santa Teresa's way of . . ."

309

"Come on, Anna, you promised you wouldn't fuck around with the saints tonight."

"Finally everything will be joined together. We'll get home, Al. I know we'll get home."

I didn't have the slightest idea what she was talking about, but I could see that her conversation with harebrained Hanford had thrown her back into the mood I thought she had left in her apartment. I kept quiet, and so did she. We didn't say anything else until we got to the restaurant.

I ate too much. I knew I shouldn't have, but I couldn't help it. I not only ate too much, but I ate too fast, because I kept thinking about the way the Rey del Mondo was going to taste with the espresso; I wanted to hurry through the meal and light up. I jumped into my plate of penne alla carbonara like a high diver into a pool while Anna ate a lonely spinach salad.

"You know something," I said to her when I had polished off my bistecca with a big fat fried egg on top, "I haven't heard you talk about anyone else except Seames. What about your mom and your dad and your brothers? And what about your friends, all those people you knew down at the theater company?"

"I've lost track of them."

"Your friends, maybe. But what about your family?"

"I speak to them from time to time."

"They must be proud of you. Don't they watch the show every day?"

"I don't know. I don't ask them."

She was retreating, goddammit, she was getting away from me. She stared into thin air, her head was filled with thoughts that had nothing to do with me, and I felt as though I were out with a ghost.

"Listen, Anna, I got to tell you something important."

She looked at me. I didn't want to hurt her, but I kept on talking. "Your life's become too one-sided. It's too much show and too much Seames. I'm telling you straight. You're fucking up your head. You need to get out more. You need to see other people, date other men, develop some other interests. Listen to Al. You gotta snap out of it."

Then she smiled, and she took my hand. Her skin was soft—I had forgotten how soft her skin was—and her smile lit up the

310

sawdusty old Napolitana Kitchen. "I love you because you love me," she said to me, "and you love me because I love you." Just that simple. And she was right, she was a thousand times right, and no lady had ever ever ever talked to me this way. And she got up from her chair, right there in the middle of the restaurant, and came over to me and hugged me and kissed me and whispered in my ear, "Thank you for caring so much, dear Al, thank you for saving my life."

And just when the music had started between us a trio of nuns walked into the joint and sat down behind us, chattering among themselves.

"I think I'd like to leave now," Anna said, even before I had a chance to light up my cigar, and naturally I understood and got the check and paid. "Could we go uptown and continue the celebration?" she asked. "Of course, sweetie, of course." And I looked at Anna looking at the nuns and I wondered what was going through her mind. I almost asked her, but I didn't. I saw how much she wanted to leave, and I wanted to keep her good mood going.

She told the cabby the Carlyle Hotel. "The bar there is marvelous," she said, and I kind of hated leaving the old neighborhood and the Village behind, but I was happy that she was happy, and I went along.

"When I first met you," she told me in the cab, "I didn't know what to think. You're a very complicated man, Al, a very deep and complicated man. You've given me so much energy, I'll never be able to repay you."

She kept talking that way, saying all kinds of nice things, all kinds of true things that most people never realize about me. But Anna did. Anna understood. Anna was my girl.

She sat close to me in the booth in the bar at the Carlyle. To me the room looked like it was filled with a bunch of boring fat cats. Besides, there was no color TV so I couldn't sneak a glimpse at the sports reports on the eleven o'clock news. I hadn't heard what happened at the track today. But if it was a fancy-smancy bar she wanted, it was a fancy-smancy bar she got. There was a piano player playing easy-to-listen-to-rich-Republican jazz, and—just to show her that joints like this didn't intimidate me—I ordered a bottle of champagne.

311

Let it be said that on that night Anna Calzolari and Al Gonfio got drunk together. Shitfaced drunk. We talked about old times, and how much fucking water had passed under the bridge in only twelve months, we remembered all the funny times we had had together, we laughed and we poked each other in the ribs and I think we were a little loud cause all the snobs were staring at us, but who gave a flying fuck? Not us. Not my buddy Anna and me.

And I was thinking how fine I felt, I was thinking how great she was doing, I was working on our second bottle of champagne, rolling a Rey del Mondo around my mouth and stinking up the room much to the displeasure of the East Side snotasses when suddenly Anna squeezed my arm and said to me, ''I have to marry him, it's really no joke. Nothing will be right if I don't marry him.''

I looked at her through my bubbly stupor. I thought she was joking. There was no reason for her to have said that. Not now. Not here. But she wasn't joking. She was straight and she was sober and she wasn't smiling. Things were changing too fast. I didn't want to contend with this, so I didn't. I drank more and so did she, but it didn't seem to make any difference. She kept saying that to me, over and over again, and I started thinking about this day a year ago when she charmed me into giving her the part after she blew the audition, and now she was crying again, and I threw the money down on the table and I swore to God in heaven above that I never had and never would understand women.

And in the cab, on the way to her place, she kept after me, telling me how the show would fold, how she would fold, if the marriage didn't come off. It had to, she said, it just had to happen. And then she started sobbing really loud and I put my arm around her and took a tissue and dried her tears and told her not to worry, because everything would work out. Al would make sure everything would work out.

When we got to her place, she invited me up. She said she needed to talk. I needed to sleep. I had been very drunk and now I was very undrunk. It had been a long night, but I went up with her because I didn't want to leave her alone. She fixed us a big pot of hot coffee and I managed to get down two or three cups and by then she was really talking a blue streak, she was like a teenager planning her wedding, and I couldn't stop her. I just couldn't. I couldn't bear to go back to where we were earlier in the evening. I had to let her talk, and when she gave me a pad and a pencil I had to take notes, just as I always had. I had to act as though I was agreeing with everything she said. Because I didn't want to fuck her up again, and I could see that she needed to talk. Oh, Jesus, did she need to talk! And the funny thing about this dame is that when she talks she can be very charming, very fucking charming indeed. She starts acting out the part and talking in her Sister Prudence voice. So I just let her talk, figuring that afterward I could write any script I saw fit. There was no reason to upset her now.

I don't know what time it was when my eyes finally closed. Four, maybe five in the morning. She was still going strong, but I told her I just couldn't hack it anymore. I had to get some sleep. She offered me her couch but I said I had to have my own bed. She ran over to me from the other side of the room and covered my face with kisses. "You've been wonderful," she said to me, "you're always wonderful to me."

I was too tired to answer her back, so I just kissed her and began to drag my ass out of the apartment. "Wait! I almost forgot, Al. I owe you fifty dollars from last week. Let me write you a check."

"Some other time," I tried to tell her, but she already had her checkbook out and was writing furiously. She was all perky and happy.

"Here," she said, "now we're even. I have enough debts to you without this one," and she kissed me again, this time on my mouth and sent me on my way.

I put the check in the pocket of my jacket and it wasn't until late the next day—after I had examined and reexamined our second evening with San Gennaro—that I noticed that the name she had signed on the bottom of her check, in a handwriting nothing like her own, was Prudence MacNiece.

313

46

I had never seen a taping like this one. It seemed as though everyone was walking around on tiptoes. There wasn't the usual commotion, the screaming and the kidding and the last-minute rush to get ready. There was an eerie calm about the studio. Dick and Howard were quiet. The crew was quiet. The wardrobe people, the makeup ladies, even my assistants, who usually never bother to watch the taping, were quiet.

Everyone realized that this wasn't just another show, another segment to be taped, edited and thrown in the can to appear on the tube a couple of days later. This was a special moment that had everyone behaving as though they were actually in church. I was nervous. I had been eating since early morning. I wished it were already over with.

I went upstairs and sat in the control room and waited for the action to start. I settled down in a chair and opened a pack of peanuts. The sound of the crackling cellophane had people turning their heads. This was ridiculous, I thought to myself. This was crazy. I couldn't stand the tension, couldn't stand all this solemn reverence. Let's just get it over with. Let's just get the goddamn thing over with.

I looked through the glass in front of the control booth, down into the studio itself. Anna and Brian had walked onto the set. The lights were dimmed. Finally, finally this fucking segment was about to be taped. Finally I'd be able to put it behind me, put it out of my life.

Prudence is wearing a white dress. Brian is wearing a dark blue suit. They are standing in a small room. It is the bedroom

314

of the apartment they have rented together. Brian's divorce came through last week. Today is the day.

Two wax candles, long and white, sit in petite glass holders atop the bureau across from the bed. Prudence walks across the room and lights them. Brian speaks to her:

"I hope you weren't too offended by the civil ceremony."

"My mind and heart were closed. I didn't . . . I couldn't look at the man who married us. It made no difference. It was a formality, a legal formality. I felt neither shame nor guilt. I felt nothing."

"I wish there had been an easier way."

"Please, Brian, there's no need to dwell on what's past. It was necessary, and now it's done."

"I felt . . . I don't know—cold, strange, distant from you."

"I know, I know," she says, taking his hand. "I wasn't there for you. I tried, but I couldn't be there. In my mind, I had to escape from that man's office."

"Perhaps if friends or family had been there . . ."

"It's behind us. It's all behind us. Now we'll do what we promised. We'll marry ourselves."

"Do you still feel the need?" he asks her.

"Now more than ever. If not . . ."

"Never mind, Prudence. I want you to be happy. We'll do exactly as you like."

They stand in front of the two candles. They hold hands. Prudence opens a book and begins to read from Santa Teresa: " 'In the betrothal it is as though two wax candles were brought together so closely that the whole light is only one or that the wicks and the light and the wax all together are one . . .' " She hands the book to him.

" 'And yet afterward one may well separate again the one candle from the other,' " he continues, " 'and there are two candles again or the wick may be separated from the wax.' "

" 'But here in the spiritual marriage,' " Prudence reads from the martyred saint, "it is as though rain from the skies were to fall into a river or a fountain where everything is water, so that it is impossible to divide or separate the water of the river and the water which came from the skies.' "

" 'It is as though a small brook would enter the sea,' " Brian now recites, " 'and there is no means to separate the two. Or as though a room had two windows through which much light would enter, although it enters divided, within the room it becomes one light.' "

" 'It becomes one light,' " she repeats, closing the book and taking her husband into her arms.

The crew was still silent. Prudence had clung to Brian and, now that the taping had stopped, Anna was clinging to Hanford Seames.

"I never took you for being stupid, Gonfio," a voice whispered into my ear, "but this is a mistake. This is one of your more serious mistakes."

I turned around and looked up into the tinted lenses.

47

He had promised her, and now he wanted to back down. He wanted to back down something fierce. He couldn't stand the prospect of being with her for two straight days. But she had cajoled him for weeks. She knew this scene was coming. She knew she would prevail, and she knew that afterward she would have to be with him. After the wedding she couldn't stand to be alone.

The day before he had invented an excuse. He had told her that his parents were unexpectedly coming in from San Francisco, and that they were going to use the cabin for the weekend. Fine, Anna had said, she'd call an inn in the area and they'd stay there. Before he could argue, she was on the phone, and the reservations were made.

For weeks now he had treated her badly. He had put her off, he had virtually ignored her everywhere but on the set. When she called him he was barely civil. And the more she sought him, the more he spurned her. He defiantly dated other women, and he would loudly and cruelly hint of these encounters to Anna. He even thought of bringing them to the tapings, just to show them off, just to spite her. He stopped short, though, only because he was afraid of what might happen. He was content to hurt her—hurt her because she drove him mad with her devotion—but he did not want to see her completely fall apart. His role depended upon hers, and as the show gained in popularity, so did his own visibility as an actor. He wanted to keep her at arm's length, but how was that possible when they worked together day after day, for hours on end, emotionally committing themselves to parts which were becoming more and more demanding? Besides, the worse he treated her, the more tenacious she became, the more dependent, the more excited by his presence.

There was also the matter of sex. When it happened between them it was usually unsuccessful, but there were those few instances when the lovemaking was so strange and ferocious that Hanford was not quite prepared to give it up. When it worked, it worked amazingly well. They were ludicrous, these games that Anna insisted upon playing—the habit of the nun, the lines from the show, the books of Santa Teresa—and yet if the mood and the setting were right, Hanford found himself almost as impassioned, almost as crazed, almost as lost in the startling pleasures as Anna.

So Hanford hung in, seeing her and sometimes screwing her, meeting her and mistreating her and promising himself that it would be the last time, promising himself that he would end all this foolishness and yet—because of the show or the strange lure of the sex—never quite keeping his promise.

Now the wedding was over and she sat next to him in his precious black Porsche—her hand on his knee, a distant smile on her face—as they sailed over the rolling landscape toward the bright morning Massachusetts sun. He was happy because she was quiet, and she was happy because she was with him, because, after all, they had been finally married.

He knew that she was considering this trip a honeymoon. He saw by her eyes that she was elsewhere. And when she asked

317

him a question—"Are you hungry?" "Would you like to listen to the radio?"—her inflections belonged to the ex-nun. When did all this start? he tried to remember, and when would it stop? He wished that he had not agreed to this trip. He wished that he had flat told her to get lost. He wanted out.

But now that he was in, he told himself as they ate cheeseburgers at a roadside truck stop, he might as well make the best of it.

"I'm anxious to see the ratings for the wedding show," he said to her as he wiped a spot of mustard from his lower lip.

"Our love will be reflected everywhere."

"Costein's been screaming bloody murder. He's been against it from the start."

"We've had so much to overcome," she told him, her eyes shining, "and yet that's only strengthened our love and tightened the bonds between us."

I'd like to tighten a noose around your neck, he thought to himself. He considered strangling her. For a moment he thought he might actually enjoy it. But he dismissed the idea as madness. Somehow he would get through this weekend—and then nothing more. This would be it. If his career would suffer as a result, it would just have to suffer. This crazy affair was coming to an end.

"I have to tell you that the wedding scene," Hanford said cruelly, "turned my stomach."

"No one wants to be married by a judge. I can understand how you feel."

"Not just that—the whole thing. It was ridiculous. But what do you expect for a soap?"

"You'll get used to the idea," she promised him. "It'll take time because it's all so new. There are so many changes and adjustments. But sooner or later we'll settle down and begin enjoying ourselves."

It was hopeless, he decided. Absolutely hopeless. There was no getting through to her. He tried talking about movies and books—Fellini and Genet and Herzog and Mailer. He knew she was literate. In the past, their cultural conversations had been stimulating. He knew she had—or at least used to have—a critical mind. But not now. Now his every attempt to discuss a film

318

or a novel was somehow taken by her as an excuse to cite the *Vida* of Santa Teresa, or the poem about the saint by Crashaw, or the study of Teresa by Sackville-West, or the Bernini sculpture—all of which he had heard her analyze time and time again. He was bored. He was fed up.

"Santa Teresa," he said, aware that he would shock her, "was a madwoman."

"You will learn to love her through me."

"She was one of these self-consumed mystics, and mystics have never attracted me."

"So you've been reading her. You've actually been reading the books."

"I've glanced at them," he confessed.

She reached over and kissed his forehead. "I love you for that," she said.

"Her books are repetitious, tedious . . ."

But she didn't hear his protests. She was gazing out the restaurant window, out into the highway. She was distracted—she was often distracted, he noticed—and he didn't bother to call her back to this world.

At least she was looking very good these days, he told himself as they got back into the car for the last leg of the trip. Her clothes were discreetly high-fashion. The woman had taste; he couldn't deny it.

She had picked the right inn in Stockbridge. He granted her that. It was the oldest and most established, the most prestigious and expensive. She would offer to pay, he knew, and this time he would let her.

It was still light when they finished unpacking and he quickly decided to put on his tennis whites and find himself a game. He needed to get away from her for a while, he needed some release. He took a can of balls and his racket and left the room without saying a word to her. He knew he was being rude, but he was unable to stop himself; she deserved it.

He played with a young prep-school student, a boy no older than sixteen, who trounced him thoroughly. Hanford couldn't concentrate on his game. There was the rest of the weekend to get through, and he couldn't stop berating himself for having fallen into this trap. He hit the ball too hard. His serves smashed into the net. His backhand shots sailed beyond the foul line. He cursed and finally slammed his racket against the cement surface. The wood split in his hand.

When he got back to the room she was lying in bed in a pale blue silk dressing gown, reading from the works of Santa Teresa.

"How was your game?" she asked him.

He responded by grabbing the book from her hands and ripping it in half.

"I'm sorry I haven't paid more attention to you," she said.

"That's not the point! That has nothing to do with it! I'm sick of the game! I'm sick of this goddamn sick game!"

"Everything's changed," she told him. "I've tried to explain. Nothing will ever be the same. There's nothing for you to worry about. Now it's our hearts that are controlling our lives and our destiny. You're upset because the changes are so profound, but you mustn't be afraid of . . ."

"Anna, Anna. Can't you understand? It has nothing to do with changes or fear. It's the simple fact that you're, you're . . ."

"Living a life I've always wanted to live. And I'm living it only because you've made it possible by opening your mind and heart, by . . ."

He let her drone on. He reached into his overnight case and felt around for the plastic bag stuffed with grass that he had packed for moments such as this. He found the stash and sat at the small desk in the corner, rolling joints as she continued to explain the depths, the permanence, the beauty of the love that they shared.

He got stoned. She did not. She said that she didn't need dope. He agreed. She was already gone. They dressed for dinner. He was feeling a little better. He had showered and shaved and splashed on cologne. Now he put on a sport coat which was rich chocolate brown.

He smoked another joint before they went downstairs into the softly lit dining room of the inn. He got blasted, he got excited, he felt good about everything. He had hooked up with a weird woman for the weekend and somehow he'd get through it and then he'd get rid of her. He'd find a way to get rid of her. He looked forward to that and he looked forward to God-knows-what-she'd-want-to-do-later-that-night. This would be her fare-well fuck, he thought to himself. One last fuck for the road.

Anna was quiet at dinner. She sat across the table from Han-ford and gazed longingly at his face, watching him eat. By the time dinner was over, he was exasperated.

Back in their room, Anna turned her attention to the candles, the long white candles in the glass holders that she placed on the dresser, that she lit. She stood for a long time in front of the flames while Hanford shook his head and cursed under his breath. It was useless, he decided. The whole thing was useless.

She recited the words of Santa Teresa. She wanted him to join her, but he refused. As she undressed, she repeated the scene that had been taped yesterday. The sight of her naked except for white panties excited him. Her back, her buttocks, her black hair resting on her shoulders. She turned to him and said, "Let's pretend that I have not left the convent. Let's pretend that you have snuck over the wall, that you have found my room, my tiny cell, and you have entered, and now—for the first time or the five hundredth time—you want me, you want to love me among the shrines and the other sisters who are sleep-ing."

"It's repulsive," he told her. "This whole business is repul-sive to me."

But his dick was hard. She saw that and she continued to talk, describing the convent scene in great detail, coming to him and feeling him through his pants, unzipping and reaching in and bringing him out and sucking him. Sucking him hard with her lips, biting him softly with her teeth, mouthing the great length of him the way she knew he liked.

He no longer protested. Once again, he told himself that this was the final fuck. He let her call him Brian. He went along with her descriptions, he said yes, it was hard getting over the con-vent walls. He watched her grow wild with the story. He watched her write the script, right there on the spot. He let her lick him as long as she liked. He let her undress him and mas-sage him and tell him, over and again, about the poetry of their love, about the suffering they were enduring but the eternal pleasure which awaited them.

There was no use getting angry; that only excited her more.

There was no use protesting, breaking down the roles. He listened to her garbage and he tried to relax as she mouthed him again. In spite or in relief, he came in her mouth. She smiled with the seed.

"Now I have you," she said to him afterward, after he had turned his back to her, after he had told her that he was tired and not interested in any more sex games. "Now I have you," she repeated, "and I shall never let you go."

48

Silvia managed to sneak away from the bank a few minutes earlier for her lunch break. She walked quickly to Mattie's place. She and Mattie had gone to grammar school together, and now Mattie was married with two small children and a garden apartment only three blocks from the bank in Sheepshead Bay. Mattie also had a brand-new, large-screen color TV that her husband, an up-and-coming drapery salesman, brought home last month.

"Turn it on!" Silvia was screaming as Mattie, in a pink-carnation-patterned housecoat, opened the door. "Turn it on before we miss something!"

"Easy, honey," Mattie assured her friend, "you're not going to miss a thing."

A baby screamed in the next room. Mattie's three-year-old girl Lucy ran in waving a wet diaper over her head as though it were a flag. But Silvia paid no attention to this. She parked herself in front of the television as the *Search* theme soared. Mattie returned with her infant son who had been pacified with a bottle. Lucy was given a full jar of peanut butter and told that it was all hers. The room was finally quiet. The show was about to begin.

* * *

"I was quite surprised when you phoned, and I must say, I considered not seeing you at all." Mrs. MacNiece's speech is still slightly slurred. She sits in the center of her nervously formal living room. She holds an ivory cane in one hand. Her daughter-in-law, fresh in a sweetly pleated skirt, is directly across from her. The women are drinking tea from white cups of bone china.

"I am most grateful to you for consenting to meet me. I have been deeply troubled by the pain that I have caused you," Prudence confesses.

"Does my son know you're here?"

"He does not."

"Would he approve?"

"I can't speak for Brian, but I do know that the estrangement has been most difficult for him."

Mrs. MacNiece examines Prudence carefully. She sees that the young woman is dressed as smartly, and as conservatively, as her ex-daughter-in-law Sally who has moved to be with her mother in Palm Beach.

"It is an estrangement which he himself brought on."

"He felt he had no choice."

"We always have choices, don't we?" she asks with muted sarcasm.

"Yes, I agree with you, Mrs. MacNiece. The moral decision is always ours to make."

"Precisely."

"And deep in our hearts, your son and I felt that we made that moral decision."

"However you rationalized your action, the result is quite clear. Brian is no longer interested in contact with his family or his father's law firm. He has chosen to isolate himself. *That* was the decision that he made. Now I can scarcely understand why he chooses to remain in Troy."

"Troy is his home."

"I rather think that he wants to be here so he can enjoy the aftermath of the scandal. He wants to feel the shock waves for himself."

"I assure you, Mrs. MacNiece, that has nothing to do with it. *I* have been the one who has insisted upon staying."

"What in heavens for? Why not take your prize and run?"

"Because I don't believe in running, and I don't believe we have any reason to run. That's why I'm adamant about staying in Troy."

"The Troy Garden Society is due here in an hour," the old lady announces. "I would appreciate it if you state your business so that we might conclude our little get-together. There are preparations I must attend to."

"I want to bring Brian back to you and Mr. MacNiece. I want him to accept you and you to accept him as he is—my husband, a devoted son, a fine attorney."

"You want him to return to practice law with his father?"

"Nothing would make me happier. I know in my heart, Mrs. MacNiece, that he will not enjoy a moment's peace of mind until he comes to terms with his family. He loves you both a great deal, and as long as he is unable to express those feelings he'll be frustrated and incomplete."

"A reconciliation, you propose a reconciliation."

"With all my heart."

"You realize, don't you, that the antagonism between Brian and his father runs very deep at this point?"

"Yes, I realize that."

"And you think there's hope to change that?"

"I intend to speak to them both myself. It was I who caused the rift, and now I must be the one to bring them back together."

"You are a strange woman, Mrs. . . ." she pauses, she reflects, "Mrs. . . ."

"Mrs. MacNiece. Ny name is Prudence MacNiece." The former nun walks over to the older woman, kisses her on the cheek and says, "And I so much want to be a good daughter-in-law to you. That, and being a good wife to your son, are my fondest goals in life."

"It's only been a month," Brian says to Prudence. They are having breakfast in the small kitchen of their apartment. She is serving him a very professional-looking omelet. They are both dressed for work—he in a sport coat and tie, she in a dress which seems too fashionable for a schoolteacher.

324

"And in that month you've been depressed. I've seen that."

"I've never been happier in my life," he protests.

"*We've* never been happier in our lives," she corrects him. "Together it's been wonderful, and it always will. But alone, at work, you've not been satisfied. I've seen it in your eyes, in your expressions, even the way you carry yourself when you come home each night."

"It's tough getting started alone in a small town. Finding clients—and especially the sort of clients which interest me, those in real need of legal assistance—is a tricky business. There really hasn't been enough for me to do."

"I suspected as much."

"But I knew this would happen. That's one of the reasons it doesn't have me down. I'd be depressed about the lack of money, but your job provides enough to easily carry us over."

"It all seems so unnecessary, Brian."

"What seems unnecessary?"

"The separation with your parents."

"If you knew them, you wouldn't say that."

"I've met them both."

"When?" he asks with sudden surprise.

"In your mother's home. In your father's office."

"They called you?"

"No, I called them."

"Why in the name of God did you do that?"

"Because I wanted to. I felt it my duty as a daughter-in-law and as your wife. And what I learned is what I had always suspected. They so love you, Brian, they so miss you. They so want you back."

"Nonsense."

"I heard it from their lips, I saw it in their eyes."

"You caught them at a sentimental moment. They'll never forgive me for leaving Sally. Never."

"You're wrong, Brian. You must remember that they're your parents, not hers."

"They weren't hostile to you?" he wants to know.

"At first your mother was distant. In his office, your father was initially angry. But those moods didn't last."

"You charmed them and they charmed you."

325

"Is that so grave a sin?" she asks.

"I doubt their sincerity."

"They are ready to forgive."

"What have we done that needs to be forgiven?"

"It isn't us, dearest. It's them. They must forgive themselves."

"You told them that?"

"I told them that a family without love is like a garden without water. I told them that sooner or later we all must be together, and love together."

"It's very important for you to have a family, isn't it?"

"It's very important to me that you are happy, Brian, and that your work and your life here in Troy are put back in order. I've been a disruptive force for long enough."

"You've been an angel who has rescued me from the boredom of the most bourgeois life imaginable. Why you want to see me return to that life is something I can't understand."

"You never had a chance," she tells him, "to become yourself in this city. You were twisted inside. Too at odds with yourself. But now all of that can be put behind you. Now you'll be able to take your proper place, you'll be able to embrace your parents and all that is decent and good about them."

"You make it sound so easy, Prudence, but you don't know my father. You can't imagine how our marriage has infuriated him."

"You may not believe it now, Brian," she tells him as she kisses him on his neck, "but our marriage will spread happiness beyond ourselves. Our marriage will give strength to everyone —to you, to me, even to your mother and father."

"You're moving too quickly for me, Prudence. I'm not sure I want to go back. I don't think that I want to have anything to do with that firm. My instincts still tell me to leave. I'm not sure we wouldn't be better off in Cleveland or Chicago, even New York or Los Angeles."

"You must trust me, Brian. You must believe me when I say that it was our fate to meet and live in Troy. To leave now would be to admit wrongdoing and defeat. Our happiness is here, my dear. I know that as well as I know my own heart."

* * *

326

"I want her to be happy," Silvia said to Mattie. "After all she's been through, the poor thing really deserves to be happy."

"It's just a story," Mattie replied.

"I'm still afraid that something awful is going to happen to that woman. I even had a dream about it last night."

"A dream about the show?"

"About Prudence. I can't remember the whole thing, but she was hurt. Something very bad happened to her."

"Your friend Al will save her. Don't worry."

"When I ask Al what's going to happen to her next, he gets real quiet and says it's out of his hands."

Lucy dropped the peanut butter jar on the floor and Silvia suddenly realized that she hadn't eaten. But now there was no time; she had to be back at the bank, and, besides, she was too wrapped up in Prudence MacNiece—too worried about her marriage to Brian—to think about food.

"I said I'm going to be busy all week, *all goddamn week!*" He was practically screaming at her as they walked off the set.

"Tomorrow night," she pleaded, "we were going to be together tomorrow night."

"I changed my mind. I just went ahead and changed my mind."

"There are so many things to discuss," Anna argued.

Hanford wouldn't look her in the eye. He kept walking toward his dressing room.

"Get off my back, Anna. For God's sake, get off my goddamn back. This script is making me puke, and now you . . ."

"I, I . . ." she tried to say, but before she could speak, he slammed the door to his dressing room in her face. She stood there weeping, and after a few seconds managed to find her voice and shout back at him. "We will be happy! You'll see that we're going to be happy!"

327

49

A fatty farm is no fucking fun—let me tell you that right from the start.

I wasn't going to go, and then I was, and then I changed my mind again. I kept going back and forth, because it seemed like such a crazy idea—I couldn't even get myself to tell anyone that I was thinking about it—but finally Felix came down pretty hard on me.

"You've gained nearly fifteen pounds since you were in the hospital," he told me as I sat naked on his examining table. "Fifteen pounds. That's ridiculous. I thought you were scared by what you keep calling your 'coronary event.' "

"I was," I said. "So scared I started eating a lot more."

"You're going to have to find the discipline outside yourself, Al," he said to me.

"I got a lot of pressure on me, Doc. You have no idea."

"All the more reason to get away." And then he started talking about diet retreats. I didn't know what the fuck he was talking about. "Health spas," he told me, "that are really combination motels, training camps and country clubs."

"You mean a goddamn fatty farm," I said.

"That's right, Al. You need to go off to a fatty farm."

I laughed, but then I listened. The idea of being stashed away with a bunch of tubbies for two weeks was repulsive at first. I wasn't *that* fat; hell, a lot of guys weigh 180 or 190. Those joints were for the 300-pound-and-over crowd. But Felix said no, that wasn't true, they were for anyone who had a weight problem, and a lot of people used them as much for relaxation as dieting. Besides, he said, his brother Carl owned one outside San Diego, and he could give me a rate.

He showed me the brochure. He said it was an old ranch that

328

had been converted. He said it was the best one in the country. I looked at the pictures of the mountains and the blue sky and the whirlpools and the people lying around in the sun. I could feel the weight falling off me. "There is one doctor for every four guests," Felix said, "and the diet is strictly supervised."

"They'll starve me to death."

"You're eating yourself to death."

"You're selling too hard. Your brother must give you a cut."

"If you don't want to go, Al, don't go. But you've got to do something. You're carrying around too much excess baggage. That's probably why you're having a hard time at work."

Hard time at work. I didn't even want to think about it. Costein was on my ass. Seames was coming apart. And even Anna, who was getting just what she wanted, was worried that I was going to change the scripts behind her back. She was calling me three times a night and making me read everything I was writing to her.

"Maybe I could take a break," I told Felix. "Maybe I could arrange it so I could be gone a week."

"I thought you were the boss of that soap opera of yours," the doctor reminded me. "I thought you're the one who calls the shots."

That's all I needed to hear. There was no way anyone was going to stop me from going. The next day I told the staff that I was heading out to the Coast for a week. I gave the writers everything they needed. I had the plots planned for the next month. All they had to do was flesh them out. I told them I'd call them every other day. And as far as Anna went, well, I had to level with her. I told her about the fatty farm. She didn't laugh. She thought it might be a good idea. She just wanted to see the scripts that she'd be doing while I was gone. I let her read them. More domestic tranquillity for Prudence. More moves for reconciliation between Brian and his mom and dad.

That's all Anna needed to know; she was relieved and happy and immediately began to recite and memorize the lines as though they comprised some sort of sacred text. Fuck it, I thought to myself. I'm getting away from the zoo. I'm going out to California.

* * *

My last meal on the plane was a big one. I decided to fly first-class and spend the money I was going to save because of my discounted rate at the fatty farm. I thought of this as my Last Supper, and I guess I was still uneasy about leaving Anna and the show behind while everything was still in such a state of craziness and flux. So I had a couple of Scotches and I felt good and ate the celery and the cheese dip and the olives and the crackers and downed another Scotch and sampled the creamy pâtés. They actually carved the prime rib before my very eyes and the sourdough bread was hot and thick and crusty. Not to mention the authentic Boston cream pie.

What the fuck was I doing to myself? Drinking apricot liqueur and flying out the little port window across the startlingly beautiful afternoon American sky—drunk drunk drunk drunk silly and smashed, loaded and bloated and on my way to lose it, shed it once and for all, the pounds and the problems of my life as Scribe of the Soaps.

The limo was waiting outside the San Diego airport. SCHILLER ESTATE—that's what was written on the side door in fancy script lettering, that was the name of the joint. No hint of blubber or fat or weight or reduction. Everything was discreet.

"Mr. Gonfio?" the driver asked as I approached the car. I wondered how he knew it was me. There were a lot of other guys walking out of the airport a hell of a lot fatter than me. Oh, well.

"I'm your man," I told him, noticing that he could stand to lose a good fifteen pounds himself. Least they could hire skinny drivers. Lousy image, right from the start.

I was the only passenger, which was fine with me. I relaxed and watched the city pass by. Nice clean town, San Diego. We drove about fifteen miles up or down the coast—I wasn't paying much attention—until we turned off the main highway, went through a patch of mountains, away from the ocean, and continued for another ten minutes. Then I saw the sign. SCHILLER ESTATE. Same fancy lettering.

The joint wasn't bad. I was afraid that it was going to look like an insane asylum, but it didn't. Felix was right; it looked like a fancy motel. It was long and rambling and modern and secluded out there in the middle of nowhere with the mountains in the background and a few expensive-looking houses way off in the distance. Not bad, not bad at all.

The fat driver took my bags and carried them into the lobby for me where there was a woman behind a desk who smiled and rang a little bell and then Carl Schiller came out—I knew it was him because he looked like a younger version of his brother—and he shook my hand and told me how glad he was to welcome me as a guest at his estate, and I told him that I brought regards from Felix. Carl seemed like a nice enough guy with a goatee and a smile except that I noticed something resembling a rubber tire bulging slightly under his strawberry-colored Southern California sport shirt. He wasn't fat, but I sure as hell wouldn't call him skinny.

A porter showed me to my room and there was a color tube and a nice king-size bed and a view of the mountains. I still hadn't seen any other guests. I was worried that they had died of malnutrition but the porter said they were out jogging. I had forgotten about jogging. It had been a long time and I was a little out of practice.

By evening time I was starved but I knew to prepare myself and expect the worst—or the least. I showed up at the communal dining room, which was actually pretty swanky, and, before I walked in, I sucked in my stomach. The gang was already there. There were a couple of big daddies and big mamas—mountainous people who had to tip the scales at 350 or maybe even 400 pounds—but most of the crew was just routinely American fat, nothing spectacular or out of the ordinary. I noticed that there were more women than men, and that made me happy.

There was a maître d' dressed up in a fancy gray-and-red jogging suit who showed me to my seat where my name was written on a card. I was sitting at a table with three women. They were wearing tennis clothes and diamonds and their hair was made up fancy and their noses were stuck in the air and they were talking to each other about how much weight they had lost when I stopped their conversation in order to introduce myself.

They nodded politely and then went back to their bullshit. But then I interrupted them again to tell them I had just gotten in from New York where I had just wrapped up the latest episode of *Search for Happiness*. That was my show, I told them. I wrote it. I knew that every one of these rich bitches probably watched the soaps and loved them, but they weren't about to admit it in public.

Except the lady on my right. Her name was Harriet Weiden, and I could see that she was excited by the news of my profession. She started asking me some questions, and I could tell she knew the story line. She was well-spoken and had a roly-poly face. Her hair was dyed black, but that was okay because the dye job was definitely first class. She was forty, maybe fifty, a little snobby, but not too bad. I had seen worse. She told me that her husband advertised on the network and I asked her what he did and she said that he ran a bank. Which one? I wanted to know. City Security, she said. I have a good friend who works there, I told her. I was thinking of Silvia who's a teller at the City Security branch in Sheepshead Bay in Brooklyn. Who? she asked. You wouldn't know her, I said, and I dropped the subject.

They brought me a short carrot stick and a forkful of cottage cheese. I ate it and a half hour later, after I had gone through a long explanation to Harriet of how a soap opera is put together —emphasizing my own role, naturally—I realized that there wasn't going to be any more food. Dinner was a carrot stick and a forkful of cottage cheese. Dessert was coffee and a glass of water. We left the dining room and I walked behind Harriet and noticed that she had nice flabby thighs under her white tennis skirt which was short and ruffly. It was tough telling anything about her ass, but I figured it was big.

I went to bed with my stomach groaning and complaining, wanting to know why the fuck I was depriving it of a decent meal. I reminded it of the big lunch on the plane and it shut up. Until the morning. In the morning I was back in the dining room where I ate a half of a grapefruit and a single, thin, pathetic piece of Melba toast. They had to be kidding, I said. No, Harriet answered me, they don't kid around here. She had sought me out and sat next to me during breakfast, although she tried to act as though it were an accident. I could tell, though. Harriet had a hankering. She told me that she had been at Schiller's nearly a week.

332

After breakfast I went to see two doctors who ran tests and asked questions and sent me to a dietician and a gymnast who looked like a ballerina and made me nervous—he was a man with a big red mouth like a woman's—and then I was out on the track, recently and specially built for Schiller's, and after a lap I had to stop and walk and reconsider this whole fucking program. I was an adult. I was an American citizen. I didn't have to be doing this.

Yes, I did, Harriet told me. She had run up behind me and was wearing a pink sweat suit and now I saw that her ass was higher than I had expected. She was plump but she was pleasing and she told me that the first days were always the toughest, but after that I'd be fine. Lunch was an egg and dinner was an apple and in between were sit-ups and push-ups and bicycling. I was so hungry I was sick. I wanted to cry, I wanted to go home, and that night I listened to Carl Schiller lecture everyone about the glories of changing our eating habits and living forever. He had a program, he had written a book and he had appeared on the talk shows and soon there'd be a Schiller Estates in Seattle and Dallas.

Fuck him. I was empty empty empty. My stomach wasn't shrinking, it was screaming. I was dizzy and I was angry. I went to bed and dreamed about raiding a chocolate factory and eating myself to fucking oblivion.

The next morning there were four slices of orange and a cracker for breakfast. I complained to the authorities. They laughed in my face. I told myself I was going to gut it out. I got on the track and looked down at my Street Fighters and told them to go get it, but they wouldn't move. They wouldn't fight. I walked and did not run around the track once, twice and on the third lap Harriet joined me. She was out of breath. "How do you feel?" she asked. "Like warmed-over shit, if you'll pardon my French," I told her. "Let's go to your room and watch your show," she suggested, and I did all I could to keep my dick from jumping through my jogging pants.

"Ain't that strictly against the house rules?" I asked her as we jogged toward the building which housed my room. I had finally found my second wind.

"Strictly," she echoed, though it was obvious she didn't give a flying fuck.

I was a little nervous in the hallway, but she wasn't. She was the wife of a bank president and she was cool as a cucumber. Once inside I went for her but she averted me. She turned on the TV. She really wanted to watch the goddamn show.

Prudence and Brian and Mr. and Mrs. MacNiece were just sitting down to brunch at the Troy Country Club. Prudence had arranged the meeting. She was finally getting together with her new in-laws.

"She looks just stunning today," Harriet Weiden said about Prudence.

"Do you always wear your diamonds when you jog?" I asked her, noticing that her emerald cut was the size of my pinky.

"The security in this establishment is very poor," she informed me as she lay back and rested her head against the backboard of my bed. "She really looks stunning today," Harriet repeated. "Who picks out her clothes?"

"I usually do. She's a friend of mine. A very close friend. A very close *personal* friend."

"I see," Harriet said, impressed with the fact that I might be involved with so young an actress.

I sat down on the bed next to Harriet. "My husband's in Zurich at this very moment," she told me.

"Thank God," I said.

"Do you find this as amusing a situation as I do?" she wanted to know.

"I'm hungry," I told her.

"Will Prudence live happily ever after?" she asked.

"She will if she has her way."

We listened to the small talk around the country club table. All of the good families of Troy were there. Everyone was staring at the MacNieces with their new daughter-in-law.

"She finally got in," Harriet said.

"She deserves it."

"She's a little manipulator."

"She's a lovely person."

"I'm talking about the character, not the actress," Harriet explained.

"So am I."

"She's extraordinary."

334

"The greatest," I said as I watched her charm her new relatives, as I watched her acting as though she were born into the upper crust of Troy society.

"When was this taped?" Harriet questioned.

"Not long ago."

"It's wonderful. Your story's wonderful. But what new catastrophe awaits the happily married couple?"

"Nothing."

"That's impossible. That's not even plausible."

"You're talking to a pro. Don't question the pro."

"I've been watching these things for twenty years. I have a certain expertise. Something has to happen. What? What's going to happen next?

"I'm going to fuck you," I said. And I did.

She was sweaty and I was sweaty. But I didn't give a shit and neither did she. She tasted salty and I pretended that her cunt was a cream puff. I ate her as though she were a casserole and she gobbled me up as though I were rare sirloin. I messed up her fancy black-dyed hair and she told me to pop her nipples with my lips, she told me that she loved to suck dick but her husband never let her, and I told her that hunger led to horniness. She said that when she saw me she knew I was a man who loved women and I told her she was right. Her tits tasted like strawberry tarts. "I wish you could have seen me last week," she said as she went down to lick my balls. "I had at least five more pounds on each breast."

I had never fucked like this before, I promise. I was fucking out of my mind. I was roaring crazy hot, and so was Harriet, who had a secret dirty mouth and a beautiful, soaking-wet box, a bush that wouldn't quit, from the front, from the back, from the side. "We came here," she cried, "just to find each other and fuck each other," and I kept humping and pumping, huffing and puffing to blow the house down. But she wouldn't come down and neither would I, and she said she had a vibrator back in her room—can you imagine the bank president's old lady with a vibrator?—but I told her that I didn't need no goddamn machine and I went back to work on her and thought about stuffed trouts and mushrooms and layer cakes and custards and massaged her with my thumb and my tongue and then my whole fucking hand, finally fucking her again straight, fucking her to the bottom of the bed, through the ground and under the earth until we got to China when she screamed and drew blood from my back and shook her fat little thighs like she was dying, like she had hit pay dirt, like I was the most wonderful goddamn man she had ever met in her life.

Harriet made me feel great. She was a lot of laughs, this broad, and when we were through screwing I suggested that we get the fuck out of Schiller's.

"Where could we go?" she questioned.

"Out to eat."

"Just like that?"

"Just like that."

An hour later we were both packed and ready to go. I tipped the porter $10 to call us a cab. He hesitated at first—he knew he was aiding and abetting a crime—but I handed him another fiver and he started moving. The getaway was a piece of cake. Everyone, including the instructors, was in the gym and on the jogging track.

The cab arrived and we hopped in the back and when I looked at Harriet I realized—maybe because she had put on some more jewelry—that she was a lot classier than I had given her credit for.

"Where are we going?" she said.

"Vegas," I told her.

We ate and screwed our way to heaven that weekend. I didn't even fuck with the tables I was so busy fucking with Harriet who told me all about her boring life on the East Side of New York and her husband who hadn't been on hard since Ike said he would go to Korea to end the war. I told her all about Anna —she still thought Anna was my girlfriend—and we became pretty good friends, though we both understood that it was nothing more than a crazy goof.

We had a goddamn ball for two days. We checked into separate rooms—she was worried about seeing someone she might know, even though most of her pals hung around Palm Beach or Palm Springs or Palma de Majorca. I knew she was slumming, but I also knew she was getting balled right for the first time in

336

years, and I was happy to accommodate her. We slept together at night and showered together in the morning. The feeling that I had been sprung from the goddamn Big House still hadn't left me; I ate like a gorilla. I bought a box of Rey del Mondos and Harriet fed me Godiva chocolates and I probably would have snorted a little coke if there had been any around. This was fucking paradise and I wanted it to last and last and last.

I would have stayed for a third day—and so would have Harriet—if there hadn't been this message. It was waiting for me in my room and it said, "Urgent. Call Mark Costein in New York."

"How'd you find me, kid?" I asked him a few minutes later.

"You skipped out of the fatty farm. Where else would you be?"

I had to give the kid some credit. He wasn't a complete idiot. At least he was getting to know me.

"What's on your mind?" I asked him.

"The ratings."

My heartbeat quickened. Maybe I should have stayed at Schiller's Estate. Maybe I should have stuck to the diet. Maybe I shouldn't have given up my jogging.

"How do the numbers look?" I forced myself to ask.

"Al," he said to me in a voice which made me think his mother had just died, "you better get back to New York tonight. You're in serious trouble."

Harriet wanted to know what was wrong. Harriet wanted to go back with me. Harriet would have given me a blow job in the bathroom in the airplane. Harriet, poor thing, was wild for me. She had had a taste of something real, something a lot better than her husband's phony-baloney banking world, and now she didn't want to let it go.

"You're getting too serious, baby," I told her. "You're forgetting that this whole thing was nothing more than a lark."

"I like to listen to you talk. You know that, don't you, Al?"

"There's always the telephone. I'm listed."

"It won't work. We'll lose track of ourselves. I'm afraid we'll go off our separate ways."

There were a couple of tears in her eyes as I left her in the hotel lobby. I looked at her and started wondering—in the cab to the airport, on the plane back to New York—what is it about me that attracts horny women? What is it about me that turns them into tigresses? Maybe it's 'cause they realize that I'm a man who wheels and deals in fantasies. Maybe they assume I can make their fantasies come true. Or maybe it's not all that complicated. Maybe it's just the scent—they pick up the scent —or, like Harriet, they like the way I talk, or even the way I look. Maybe losing weight is bullshit after all. There are women who like a little flesh on their men.

But all that shit was behind me, I thought to myself as the plane shot up through the Nevada rain clouds. I had had enough pussy to last me through the football season. I had been on a roll. I had even picked up a few hundred bucks at the crap tables before I left for the airport. Carl Schiller's concentration camp was ancient history. I was on my way back. I was a little scared —I'll grant you that—but I hadn't lost all my confidence. Not by a long shot. If I had put the kid in his place once, I could sure as hell do it again.

I was in a rotten mood the next morning when I got to his office. Anna had called me in the middle of the night. She had heard that I was coming back and she wanted to know what was happening. "I'm sleeping, that's what's happening, honey," I groaned. She got upset and started to cry. I felt like a prick for hurting her feelings, but I also wanted to kill her for calling at 3:00 A.M. I was dead. I was dreaming of chasing Harriet around the track. I was tired. "Tomorrow," I begged off, "tomorrow night I'll tell you everything." She sounded scared, and that got me scared, and I never did get back to sleep.

Miss Lee saw I wasn't up to snuff and offered me something stronger than coffee. She was a sweet gal. The brandy did my heart good. Costein was late. I didn't give a shit. I didn't give a shit if he showed up at all. A few minutes later I was reading the sports section of the paper when I looked up and saw a couple of maintenance men carting the pinball machine out of his office. That's when I really started worrying.

"Your psychological warfare is a little obvious, kid," I said to him a half hour later when I finally got admitted to the throne room.

"I'm through playing games with you, Al. I'm telling you that right now."

"Easy."

"It's not easy. It's tough. It's tough as hell telling you what I have to tell you. It's tough because I've grown to like you."

I prepared for the worst. I sucked in my gut. I reached for a cigar.

"And don't stink up my office with that cigar!"

"Yes, sir," I said, saluting him with my index finger.

"The antics aren't going to work, Al. The funny business is over."

"You make it sound like a little dip in the ratings is the end of the fucking world. When you've been in this business as long as I have . . ."

"No more of that crap, Al. I'm telling you, no more. I've been called on the carpet for indulging you. I've been blasted from one side of this building to the other."

"I can't understand," I said, shaking my head.

"The dip wasn't a dip, the dip was a plunge."

"I'll get it back up, kid. There's nothing to worry about."

"That girl's tied you around her little finger. She has you writing the script to fulfill whatever mad fantasies are running around her brain. I tried to warn you about that. I saw it . . ."

"Come clean, kid. You're just pissed off because you'd like to get next to her and you can't."

Costein took a stack of computer readout sheets from the top of his desk and threw them at me. I ducked. I figured I better shut up. The kid was really excited.

"The game's over. I'm telling you—*the game is over!* We've

gotten murdered these past three weeks. The biggest three-week ratings decline in the history of any one network program.''

"Least we've broken a record.''

"It's not funny, Al. Not funny one little bit.''

"You're too serious, kid. Eventually we're going to be laughing about this like it was . . .''

"Look at me, Al. Look at me very closely. You do not see a smile on my face. You do not hear me laughing.''

I lit my cigar defiantly. "All right, kid. I believe you. You want to talk turkey, so let's talk turkey.''

He coughed—it was a forced cough—and leaned back in his junior God swivel chair. "I'd fire you today if I thought I could get someone in to replace you in a few days,'' he announced. "But I can't. I've tried—believe me, I've tried.''

"It's a rare skill,'' I jumped in. "I've been telling you that for . . .''

"Save it, Al. Your bullshit's not working and your show's not working. There's no way for me to make a major change, at least not for another month. Which is exactly how much time you have to get yourself in gear.''

Inside, my heart, my soul, my body sighed in relief. My bookies would be paid. My life was not yet over.

"I'll get it right. It was just a slump, kid. Nothing but a slump.''

"You'll get it right, Al, because I'm making certain that you get it right. I'm laying it all out for you. I've had studies run. We've done telephoning, we've done viewer interviewing, we've analyzed and indexed the reactions, we've matched them against the numbers—the dwindling numbers—and a pattern has emerged. It won't surprise you to learn that the drop began shortly after Prudence's wedding. You may remember that is exactly what I predicted. I warned you about too much happiness. Too much happiness and not enough search.''

I thought about what Harriet Weiden had said about the show and sucked on my cigar.

"You're going to have to make that nun suffer. She's a very good character, and no one can take that away from you, Al, but she must suffer, she must cry and weep and somehow get kicked in the head.''

340

"That's incompatible with . . . ."

"Don't start, Al, because I know what you're going to say. You're going to tell me that it won't work, that it won't play. Well, I'm telling you that it *will* work. And if you don't make it work, I'm going to find someone who will. I didn't like the idea of the wedding—I told you that from the start—and you ignored me. You did exactly what you pleased. Or exactly what pleased Prudence . . . I mean Anna. I left you alone because—I don't know why—perhaps I thought you did know something about daytime television that I didn't, maybe I was intimidated by your years of experience. Now I see that my instincts were on the money. Research says I was right, Al, and research says you were wrong. The viewers have expressed themselves. They're bored. They think the story's gone flat. They're tired of Prudence and her happiness. Millions have just tuned us out. And those who are left are only there on the chance that something terrible is going to happen to Prudence. They've been patient, and I don't intend to keep them waiting a minute longer than I have to. I've seen your new scripts and they stink. It's more happiness, more bliss, more peace and comfort in the bosom of upper-class Troy."

"But the character," I tried to argue, "has naturally developed to the point where . . . ."

"She's a drip. She's nothing but another housewife. She's living happily ever after. I don't have to tell you this, Al, but on soaps there is no happily ever after."

What could I say? Of course he was right. I couldn't deny it. Anna had been fucking with my head. I was being a patsy. The kid was sitting here telling me that I was a first-class jerk. The kid was telling me how to do my job, *my* job—imagine that!— and there was nothing I could do but sit and listen to him because I knew he was right. As right as a cold-blooded computer.

"Tomorrow morning," he said to me, "I want to see you in here with a new plot outline for Prudence. Either that, or your letter of resignation."

51

Anna sat alone in the living room of her apartment. There was no rehearsal today, no taping. She was wearing a frightfully expensive peach-colored robe of pure silk. The television was playing. In a few seconds the game show would be over and *Search for Happiness* would begin. She didn't hear the telephone ringing. She paid no attention to the unopened mail which had been piled up on her coffee table for over a week. She was only interested in what was now being shown on the screen. She heard the announcer's voice, saw the credits. She watched so intensely that her eyes didn't seem to blink. She stared, she stared . . .

Prudence and Brian arrive back home in their apartment. They are both dressed to the teeth.

"It was divine," she says to him. "Wasn't it just divine?"

"It was as it always is."

"Don't be sour, dear. It was fun. It was great fun for me."

"I'm glad you enjoyed it."

"Are you really?"

"I am glad . . . for you."

"The country club has such wonderful memories for us," she reminds him.

"My association with the club goes back further than that, Prudence."

"You have to come to terms with that, Brian. Don't you think it's time to grow up?"

He begins to argue with his new wife, but he stops himself in time. "My parents make it difficult for me," is all he says.

"You parents want the best for you," she assures him.

"I'm sorry, Prudence, but I just wasn't comfortable with them tonight. I don't trust their new attitude."

"How can you question it? They've been lovely, simply lovely to me. They've been wonderfully accepting."

"After you've worked on them for weeks."

"I did nothing more than explain to them the sincerity of our love."

"I can't help it, Prudence. I can't be at ease with them."

"They want to help you, Brian. Surely you can feel that."

"Help? What sort of help do I need?"

"Your law practice isn't exactly thriving."

"It'll take time, it won't happen overnight."

"I think your father's willing to have you back."

"He told you that?"

"He intimated as much."

"And what if I don't want to go back?"

"That's your decision to make, Brian. I'll support you in whatever you choose to do." She lightly places herself on his lap.

"Are you tired of your job?" he asks her. "Are you tired of teaching?"

"I don't know, Brian. Sometimes I think that there are other ways that I can better serve the community—charities, for example."

"The community will never accept us, not after what we did."

"But did you see how many people came up and greeted us tonight? Didn't that surprise you?"

"They did that for my parents."

"But they spoke to you. They seemed so interested in you. They're your friends."

"I have no real friends in Troy."

"You're being too severe, Brian. You do have friends. I saw the love in their eyes."

"You see love in *everybody's* eyes."

"You're needed here, Brian. The community needs you, and I'm beginning to feel that the community needs me as well."

"Please, don't start talking about the Junior League."

"They organize some wonderful programs, they do genuinely good work. Why be bitter?"

"Because Sally . . ."

"Sally was a different time and a different place. Sally is a lovely memory, a high-school sweetheart who simply . . ."

"Turned into a first-class shrew."

"It pains me to hear you talking that way."

"I'm tired, Prudence. It's been a long night."

"I want you to think about these things. Promise me that you'll give everything we discussed some thought."

Brian sighs and kisses Prudence on the forehead. "I want you to be happy," he says. "And I'm glad, I really am glad that you're enthusiastic about your new life. It's just that . . ." His voice trails off as he rubs his eyes which are heavy with fatigue.

She embraces him, and her eyes are sparkling as she whispers, "You make me happy, Brian, you make me so incredibly happy."

It was another day. Anna hadn't moved from her couch. Was it Thursday? Was it Friday? She didn't remember. She only knew that she wasn't needed in the studio today. She could stay home. She could watch the show. And she stared, she stared . . .

Brian and Baxter are naked except for bathing suits. Their bodies are still glistening with water. They are in the locker room.

Brian's chest is tan. His stomach is flat, his legs muscular and large. His father is in equally superb shape. His expansive chest is covered with thick white curls.

"Terrific swim, son. Just terrific."

The men begin to dry themselves with huge, fluffy spring-green towels.

"You know," the father continues, "there's nothing like a swim to break up the monotony of the day. How many laps did you do, Brian?"

"I wasn't counting."

"I can remember a time when you actually thought you could outswim your old man. I trust you've put those childish illusions behind you." Baxter laughs, but Brian does not. He is pensive,

344

intent on drying himself and getting out with the minimum amount of conversation.

"You know, Brian," the older man continues, "I have to tell you that your new wife makes quite an impression."

Brian says nothing.

"Yes," Mr. MacNiece goes on, "she has a certain style about her, a certain—what should I say?—panache. She's absolutely nothing like I had imagined. I have no earthly idea what she was doing being a nun. Yes, sir, she's made quite a conversion."

"*Your* conversion seems even more sudden," says the son. "Six months ago you were convinced that Prudence was going to be the ruination of us all."

"There were certain things which, I admit, I didn't understand."

"Like what?"

The camera pulls up on the men's chests as they peel off their suits, dry themselves and begin to dress.

"Like the splendid character of this lady. Why, she has real class, my boy. Genuine class."

"And you're no longer ashamed or embarrassed or worried about what your clients and your clients' wives are saying?"

"By now, son, your scandal is stale. It's been replaced. Hell, it's been outdone. Didn't you hear? Bob Calvin has run off with his daughter's college roommate. The girl's not even twenty, and Bob's my age. Lucky bastard."

"I've got to get home. Prudence is making dinner and I'm late."

"Before you run off, I want to tell you why I invited you for this swim this afternoon."

"I already know."

"And have you given it any thought?"

"I have."

"And?"

"I'm not certain, Dad."

"Well I am, son. I know you can't be making any money on your own. It's impossible to do what you're trying to do here in Troy. You need us. You need *me*. This is your firm, and I intend for you to have it. Besides, your new wife is settling down, and if you don't owe it to your mother and me, you certainly owe it to her. You didn't steal her from that convent to let her starve to death. She wants the kind of life and luxury that you take for granted. What's more, Brian, she deserves it. She's a splendid gal. Just splendid.''

''I need more time to think about it.''

''While you're thinking, I'm going ahead and tell Gladys to clean out the corner office for you. It's a little grandiose, but you'll find a way to adjust.'' He chuckles. ''And I also want you to come down tomorrow and interview a gal who's looking for a secretarial position. First-class credentials and first-class body. Girl about your age.'' Baxter puts his arm about his son's shoulders. ''Welcome to the club, boy. It's great having you back.''

Anna called Hanford. A breathless woman answered the phone. ''Can I tell him who's calling?'' the woman asked. ''No!'' Anna screamed. ''I mean yes! Tell him it's his wife, his wife is calling him.''

''Would you leave me the hell alone!'' he said when he picked up the phone.

''How can you do this? Why are you doing this to me?''

''I'm not doing anything. I'm just living my life.''

''I need you. I need you right now.''

''I'm busy.''

''Brian,'' she began to say, but the phone went dead in her ear.

52

Her crying sounded different this time. It scared me. The girl was sobbing with such hurt that I thought she was dying. Actually dying right there on the goddamn telephone. ''Wait a minute, sugar,'' I said to her, ''calm down. Just tell me what's wrong." But all she said was, "Brian Brian Brian" and I said, "Oh, fuck" and she said, "Please, you've got to help me, there's no one to help me" and of course I went running over there, of course I wasn't going to leave my little baby alone.

Her apartment looked like shit. Clothes hadn't been put away. Books and newspapers and Bibles were opened and ear-marked and lying on the floor and on the kitchen table. Pictures of Santa Teresa were tacked to the wall, draped over the TV set. Pages from old *Search for Happiness* scripts were scattered everywhere.

"What the hell happened here?" I asked her.

"I've been thinking," she said. "I've been thinking about what to do."

"I'll tell you what to do. Get a goddamn maid for the day. This place is a shithole."

"It doesn't matter. I can't be concerned." She spoke in her Prudence voice. Her Anna Calzolari New York accent was gone. But when I thought about it, I realized that it had been gone for some time; I really hadn't noticed until now.

"I don't see how you can live in a joint that looks like this. You got to get yourself together, honey."

"I went to see him," she announced as tears began to fill her lovely green eyes. She looked so helpless standing there.

"Who?" I asked.

"Brian."

"Hanford," I corrected, tiring of this fucking game.

"And there was someone else."

"I don't understand."

"When I got there he was with a woman."

"Oh, Jesus," I croaked.

"I, I . . . I didn't know what to do."

"Did he know you were coming? Did you have a date?"

"Not exactly."

"Then you shouldn't have gone," I tried to explain patiently. "You got no business dropping in on a man like that."

"I had to see him. I had to see whether . . . whether . . ."

"Whether he was cheating on you? Sounds like you were looking to get kicked in the teeth. Why the hell can't you leave well enough alone and mind your own business?"

She began to sob that same pained sob and I knew I had said the wrong thing. "I'm sorry, Anna." I tried to retreat. "I didn't mean to come down so hard on you, baby. It's just that I hate to see you walking smack into your own misery when it would be so easy to sidestep it."

"He doesn't know what's he doing. The relationship is still new. Soon he'll realize . . ."

"Anna, Anna," I stopped her. I moved to sit next to her on the couch. I put my arm around her. "You're still bullshitting yourself, baby. That's the same shit you were saying about Palermo. Can't you see that?"

She acted as though she didn't hear me. She dried her eyes and stared into space and patted my hand and said, "There's something so good about him. Deep down inside he means so well."

"Horseshit!" I hollered. "Horseshit! Hanford Seames is nothing but one of these overgrown prep-school kids who never got over his good looks. He likes to fuck around. He's got to have a different hole in every part of town. It's nothing more than that, Anna. I swear on the goddamn Bible."

"We'll be happy. It's just a question of time and adjustment."

I got up from the couch and slammed my open hand against the wall. I turned to her and I said, "Look, Anna, you're not being smart. You're not even being sensible. You caught the son of a bitch with another broad. What more proof do you need? What the hell's wrong with you?"

I was furious with her for being so blind; I was furious with myself for having gotten into the bind; I was furious at Seames for hurting her so goddamn bad. And then, out of the blue, she said, "I want to see the new scripts. Where are the new scripts?"

My heart began to thump and bump against my rib cage. I hadn't told her about my meeting with Costein. I couldn't bring myself to let her know what was going to have to happen. At least not yet. Not now.

"You have anything to drink around here?" I asked.

"I want to read the new scripts." She ignored my request. I got up and in the general mess of things found a bottle of Scotch. I poured myself a long one and took a belt. I took another shot, hoping that this one would bring me to my courage. It didn't.

"I'm behind," I half lied to her. "I've had a hell of time getting to the typewriter."

"What's wrong?" she wanted to know.

"Meetings. Everyone butting in and telling me what to do."

"Who?" she asked. "Costein?"

"He always has something to say."

"What's he saying?"

"The ratings are sinking like a lead balloon."

"And what does he want to do about it?"

"I don't know. He has all kinds of crazy ideas."

"What are they?" She kept coming at me, she wouldn't leave me alone, she smelled the trouble and I couldn't get her off the trail.

"He thinks Prudence is a little too happy. He's looking for another hook."

"Is that what that secretary is about?"

"What secretary?" I pretended that I didn't understand.

"My husband's new secretary. The one that Baxter wants him to meet."

"Oh, *that* secretary," I stalled. "Yeah, she's going to be an interesting character."

"Why? What's interesting about her?"

"A new dame is always interesting."

"I don't like her, I don't trust her, I don't want her on the show."

"Listen, baby," I tried to smooth her feathers, "I kind of have my hands tied. I need something to keep the action moving along."

"She's up to no good."

"You don't know her. You haven't seen her yet. I'm not going to write in that kind of character."

"What's she doing there? Why does Brian need a private secretary."

"He's a busy man."

"Keep her out of the script."

"I can't."

"I thought you could do whatever you want."

"I can . . . sometimes."

"Make this one of those times."

"It's something you're going to have to live with, Anna. It's only make-believe and it's not the end of the goddamn world."

"You're doing this to torture me," she cried, "You're doing this to drive me mad! You want to drive me mad!"

Her eyes were wild and her voice was desperate. I didn't know what the fuck to do. "I'm doing it to survive," I said to her. "Without something hot, we're all going under."

She didn't understand. She didn't want to understand. "It's taken so long," she told me, "so very long to build this relationship. You asked me to change my life, and I did. You asked me to trust you, and I did. I followed you, Al. I believed everything you said. I gave you my heart and my soul. I believed in everything you wrote. I made it true, Al. I made it all come true for you, and you made it all come true for me. And now you're telling me that it's a lie. You're leaving me out and you're causing me pain. Yes, *you're* the one who's causing me pain."

"There's no goddamn way in the world that I could ever hurt you, Anna. Not intentionally."

"Then show me the scripts."

"I don't have them. They aren't written yet."

"Then tell me what you're going to write."

"I don't know."

"Then let's write together the way we always have."

"We can't. It won't work this time."

"Why?"

"Because there are changes that have to be made. I already explained."

"Then you do intend to do something wrong. You're about to betray me."

"You're talking crazy, Anna. I'm not going to betray you, I'm just going to make you a bigger star. When I'm through, you're going to be the biggest fucking star in the history of daytime television."

"I only want to be happy, Al. Nothing more than that. And so far you've made me happy, and now I see that you're about to take that away, you're about to take that all away."

Her crying built and built and her body began to shake and I

350

tried to hold her but she pushed me away and I tried to comfort her but she shook her head no. I stayed there a long time but she didn't stop crying and when I got up to leave I stumbled over a book on the floor in the foyer. I picked it up. Poetry. John Donne. Opened to a page with these lines underlined in red:

> By our first strange and fatall interview,
> By all desires which thereof did ensue,
> By our long starving hopes, by that remorse
> Which my words' masculine persuasive force
> Begot in thee, and by the memory
> Of hurts which spies and rivals threatened me,
> I calmly beg . . .

53

Being stuck in the bar of the Droman Club made me even angrier. I hated the joint, and I didn't want to think about the associations that it triggered in my mind. What's worse, Hanford was late. He had bullied me into meeting him here, and now he was late. Seames was a shit, and I thought to myself how I hated his guts. He was playing squash across the street, he said to me on the phone, and he had a dinner date here. This was the only place he could possibly meet me for a drink on a Saturday night. When did he become a member of the fucking Droman Club? I wanted to know. Oh, he told me casually, some time back. He liked the atmosphere and the food when we first had lunch here, and he decided to do the club the honor of joining. It was a snap, he added. They admitted practically any Ivy League graduate. That's all I needed to hear. I wanted to put the phone to my ass and fart in his ear. I knew he was getting back at me for the time I dragged him to the Turf.

So I sat there in the dark bar and threw back one Scotch and then another and tried to strike up a conversation with the bartender but he was English and said he didn't go in much for American football. A bartender who didn't like football. I couldn't fucking believe it.

I drank a third Scotch and looked at my watch and saw that Seames was a half hour late. I got angrier and angrier. He was a good-for-nothing and a little snot and I cursed myself for having ever given him such a juicy goddamn part. If I had my way, I'd throw him off the show in a swift second. I'd bounce him on his ass. But I couldn't do that—not right now—that would *really* fuck her up, and I had hurt her enough. I could still hear her words in my ear, and I could still imagine how she must have felt when she got to his place and found another broad, and just then he walked into the bar with his big, blue, I-am-an-Ivy-League-jock canvas bag and his squash racket and his freshly showered face. He looked so good I wanted to pour my drink down the back of his blue blazer.

"You look bombed already, Gonfio," he told me. He was smiling and happy, but he wouldn't be when I was through with him.

"This ain't my idea of an ideal drinking hole."

"You're wrong. It was, in fact, your idea. I must thank you for . . ."

"All right, all right, we've been over that before. What are you drinking?"

"Tanqueray. Neat." He sounded like an ad in *The New Yorker*. He looked like an ad in *The New Yorker*.

"I don't like being kept waiting," I couldn't help but tell him.

"Sorry, old man. My opponent was sure he could take me and I had to be considerate enough to give him another two games. I must say, it worked out well for me, poorly for him."

"I don't like the way you been treating her," I came right to the point.

"Her, I presume, is your precious Miss Calzolari."

"She's your leading lady."

"There are no leading ladies in soaps."

352

"Usually there aren't. But in this case there is. And I want you to start treating her with some respect."

He laughed. The golden boy laughed at me. It took all the restraint I had to keep from belting him in the mouth. "I presume," he said, "she's cried to you about finding another woman in my arms."

"She mentioned it, yeah. I thought it was a little goddamn raunchy of you."

"She came unannounced. She called before, she heard a woman's voice and she came anyway. She wanted to see what she saw. It's the sort of self-inflicted punishment she thrives on. You know that as well as I do. The girl simply loves to torture herself."

"That's some psychological theory you learned in college."

"That's something that you and I and everyone else at the show have seen with our own eyes. It's so obvious it's comical."

"I ain't laughing."

"I don't expect you to laugh. You've made too much money on her to see it as a joke."

"She's a serious actress."

"She's a serious freak. You've got a case on your hands, Gonfio, and now you're scared that you've lost control. She can't dictate the scripts to you anymore because the scripts have become as interesting as the phone book. So now Costein has you putting the screws to her. Costein wants just what I want. Costein would like to see her bleed a little bit. And if she didn't have you twisted up in knots, you'd . . ."

"I didn't come here to listen to this shit, Seames. I came here to warn your ass. I want you to stop torturing Anna. I want you to stop showing off your other dames when you know it does nothing but drive her nuts. There's no reason to add insult to injury."

"Aren't you just talking to yourself?" he asked. "Shouldn't you be the one to stop driving her to the limits of her imagination? She can handle my real love affairs far better than the imaginary ones that you're about to write into the scripts."

"Don't tell me what I'm about to write."

"I don't have to tell you. It's already there. I see it coming,

353

and so does everyone else who has anything to do with the show —including the viewers. It's obvious and, to tell you the truth, it's good. It's what should happen. Brian *has* to cheat. His new wife is too much to take. Everyone wants to see her writhe in pain, and you know just how to accomplish that. Your ship's just about to come in, Gonfio. My hat's off to you, old man.''

''You think you're so goddamn smart, Seames, well you're not. You haven't got one fucking thing right since you opened that overeducated trap of yours. You're not going to have an affair. No one's going to hurt her and no one's going to see her writhe in pain. It's just not going to happen. There are four other segments and lots of places for misery and intrigue and fooling around. But Prudence and you are going to be happy for a while. Hearing you open your big mouth and talk about it just helped me make up my mind. Yes, sir. I take my hat off to you, Seames, because you just showed me what has to be done. Your new secretary's going to be happily married, and so are you.'' I got through with my little speech and felt great. I felt great because I knew that I was doing the right thing. To hell with Costein. To hell with Seames. To hell with all of them. For a while I had forgotten, and it took Hanford's wiseass bullshit to remind me: *I* was running the show.

''There's only one small problem with what you say,'' Seames now said with a sly smile.

''What's that?'' I challenged him.

''None of it matters.''

''What do you mean none of it matters?''

He took a long sip from his neat Tanqueray and ran his fingers through his thick blond hair. ''It doesn't matter''—now he spoke very slowly, drawing out the words with great satisfaction —''because I'm leaving the show. In a month, I'll be gone.''

54

New York City is a bitch. Especially in November. Especially this November. Fall was long gone and there was nothing to be thankful for in spite of all the Thanksgiving cheer and the turkeys trotting around the city and the supermarkets and the soap operas. Turkeys like Dick and Howard and Seames. And Costein. Especially Costein. Especially the brilliant Wizard Costein.

"Why the fuck don't you just stick your dick up Nielsen's ass and marry the guy?" I thought about saying to him as I crawled through midtown in the back of a cold, springless cab. It started to rain and then it started to pour and there was an accident in front of us and an accident behind us. The city was drowning in cold blood and bruised fenders. My gut ached and my head still hurt from all the drinks last night. I barely remembered dragging myself out of the Droman and over to the Turf where I started my serious drinking. When did Costein call to tell me that he wanted this meeting? It must have been close to midnight. He was checking up on me. Like my goddamn parole officer.

Hail started to fall and slam against the roof above my head. I sighed. I banged on the Plexiglas shield and offered the cabby —a middle-aged black guy named James T. Booker—a Rey del Mondo. He smiled and took it through the change compartment. We both lit up together and sat and waited out the jam and the storm. How did this thing with Anna get so mixed up? I asked myself. How had we fucked up so bad? And who had done the fucking up? She had changed, I had changed her, she had changed herself, and now she was changing me. I was about to get bounced. Thunder boomed. Anna had gotten too caught up in her part. Hell, it had happened to other actresses. It could happen to anyone, especially someone as genuine and talented as Anna. She left one world and found herself in another. The first world was cold and harsh and the new world was warm and cozy. It was a world I created for her, that we created for each other. She was susceptible. She liked men, she usually liked the wrong men, except for me, because she knew that I loved her, and she trusted me, and she was right to trust me because I delivered for her. I made the girl a star, I'd make her see that, and somehow she'd get used to the changes in the script, the changes in her character, because the girl could act—there was no doubt about that—and I wasn't going to let her down, I could never do anything like that. Not to a pal. Not to my little Anna.

Miss Lee was typing furiously when I finally arrived. She looked up and saw that I was wet and offered a sympathetic smile. "Would you like something warm to drink?" she asked.

"Hot arsenic," I said.

She laughed and said that it wasn't as bad as all that. I said it was worse. Which is when Costein stuck his tinted lenses through the door and told me he was ready to see me.

Today he appeared before me like an undertaker. His dark suit had a terminal look about it. His desk was piled high with computer readout sheets. God only knows the shit that went through his head. He sat down behind his desk and told me that I was all wet. I told him that it was raining cats and dogs outside. He said I should carry an umbrella. Me and the kid were talking about the weather.

"I got bad news," I said, quickly getting to the business portion of the meeting.

"It's only bad if you look at it that way," he answered.

"Don't be a wiseass," I couldn't help but say. "You don't even know what I'm talking about."

"Hanford Seames is leaving the show. He's going to England to do a movie."

The kid knew. "You have good sources," I congratulated him.

"I have *impeccable* sources," he corrected me.

"I ain't sure where to take it," I told him, "I'll tell you right now."

356

"What choice do you have? He's got to run away or die."

"It's not that easy."

"It's *just* that easy."

"I think you should offer him more money."

"I think you should stick to the scripts, Al. Stop worrying about Anna. She'll recover." Costein smiled and that pissed me off something fierce. He liked what he was about to do to her.

"This Seames thing can really fuck things up," I warned him. "It ain't that easy to bump off a character."

"Are you kidding?"

"No, I'm not kidding. I wrote the book when it comes to this stuff, and . . ."

"Al Al Al," he tried to calm me down. "I'm not interested in any books. There's nothing to do except plan Brian's demise. Surely there's some hearthrobbing manner in which this matter can be dealt with cleanly and efficiently?"

"You're talking to me like I'm a hit man."

He smiled and said, "I see this as a bit of good fortune."

"It's a disaster. I'm telling you, kid, this is a real disaster."

"Only if we want it to be."

"I'm not concerned about us."

"I'm not either, Al. I'm concerned with that Nielsen viewer, that Nielsen housewife, that lonely Nielsen lady. I want her moved, I want her shaken, I want her crying for more." The kid was slamming his fist on the desk. "I want you to look at this as an opportunity, Al, a blissful, golden opportunity to turn the show around and boost the numbers back to where they belong."

"The numbers," I mumbled, looking at the floor.

"Yes, the numbers," he reasserted. "I've spent the last three nights projecting market share against . . ."

"Save it," I begged off. "Spare me the spiel. I've seen your computer cheerleading bit before."

"You know something, Al," he said in a different tone of voice, "when I was running around the reservoir this morning at seven A.M. watching the dark clouds gather over the city, I thought about you, and I thought about me, and I came to the conclusion that we're a bit weary of one another."

You figured that one out, Sherlock, I thought to myself.

357

"At this point we've watched each other perform," he continued, "and the fascination may be over. So I humbly suggest that we forget personalities and remember that we both have a job to do for this network. The job's a simple one. It's to make money. And we make money by attracting viewers, and we attract viewers by . . ."

"I told you, kid, that I wrote the book. You don't have to read it back to me."

"I want to be absolutely certain that you understand that this is our last lap together," he announced. "I don't know how much wind you have left. I can't tell whether you're going to collapse or whether you're actually going to cross the finish line. But I can tell you this much. I'm a long-distance runner. And I'm also something of a fighter. I've stuck my neck out so far for your show it pains me to think about it. This show has helped boost my own personal ratings in this corporation—just as it has yours—and now that my stock is falling, I can't say I'm too happy about it. I don't blame you entirely. I'm a big enough man to see that at least some of the responsibility is mine. I let you push me around, Al. I see that part of my trust was misplaced. But all that is passed. The game we're playing now, my dear Mr. Gonfio, is called hardball."

Sports metaphors. The kid was feeding me sports metaphors.

"I don't have time to do your work for you," Costein went on. "I can't tell you exactly how to get rid of your Brian character. But just remember—if it doesn't come off right, there will be no second chances. The ball game will be over."

"Don't lose any sleep over it, kid," I said loudly and confidently, hoping to muffle out the groans coming from my gut.

"I'm not going to lose anything, Al. Don't worry about me. Just worry about yourself, and the spell that woman has over you. If I were you, I'd get rid of her for a while, especially now that you've got to write in these radical changes. Send her on vacation for a week."

For the first time today, I decided that the kid was making some sense.

That evening I didn't sleep. I was up all night, listening to the rain against my window and watching the television set without the sound, sitting at the typewriter, my phone off the hook, going over my conversations with Seames and Costein, thinking of all the shit I should have said, getting angrier and angrier, realizing how they wanted to hurt her—Seames because he couldn't get it up; Costein because he knew that she wouldn't have anything to do with him. Yeah, it was as plain as the nose on my face that they were pissed at her and jealous of me. They couldn't care less about Anna. To them she was just a tool. Nothing but a goddamn tool.

Which is why she needed a break. She needed a vacation. And I needed time to figure out how to break the news to her about Seames leaving. I knew that I couldn't tell her now. She wouldn't be able to handle it. But maybe with a week of fun and relaxation, she'd feel better. Maybe she'd come to her senses. So somehow I found the courage to call her, to argue with her —for hours and hours—and convince her to go away for a week. I had to make promises I knew I couldn't keep; I had to give her assurances, invent small white lies. But I knew that all this was necessary. A question of survival for all concerned. I had to get her out of town for a while. And I did.

55

Her mother called to talk to her about the show.

"Are you listening to me, Anna? I have the feeling that you're not listening to me," her mother complained.

"I'm tired, Mama," Anna explained. "We've been working very hard."

"They're working you to death, those people. I'm telling you, they're working you to death."

Her mother continued to chatter, giving her opinion about the characters in *Search for Happiness* and the situation in which they found themselves. She spoke as though these people actually existed. When she was through dissecting the show, she began to complain about how infrequently she saw her daughter. "I don't even recognize your voice anymore," she said to Anna, and when there was no reply she asked again, "Are you listening to me? I don't think you heard a word I said."

Anna hadn't. She had the phone to her ear, but she was gazing into the cluttered living room of her apartment. Her eyes focused on the cover of a book which lay on the floor in front of the couch. It was called the *Art of Ecstasy,* and it featured a large black-and-white photograph of the head of Santa Teresa from the famous Bernini sculpture in Rome. "Are you listening to me?" her mother kept asking. "You haven't heard anything I've said to you in years," she continued to protest.

"I'm going away tonight," Anna finally told her mother. "I'm going to Hawaii on vacation."

"That's wonderful. I can't tell you how lucky you are. Have a good time and send us a postcard. Your father would like that."

Anna said good-bye and put down the phone. A few seconds later she did not remember whom she had been talking to. It didn't matter. She went to pick up the book she had been looking at; she stared at the cover for several seconds. There was something about the face of the saint, something about the tilt of her head.

Anna cut up an orange into eight slices and took a very long time eating the fruit. The juice was sweet against her tongue and she wondered about Hanford. She called him, as she had been calling for two days, but the line was busy. She guessed that the phone was still off the hook. She thought about going to see him, but decided against it. Soon she would be with him in the studio; soon they would be reunited. But today was Sunday, tonight she was flying to Hawaii. She wouldn't see him for a week. She had to see him today. She had to go see him right now.

The afternoon was clear and brilliantly cold. The blue of the winter sky hurt her eyes. She went into a discount drugstore which smelled of iodine and cheap perfume. There was a revolving display of sunglasses sitting atop a display case containing Polaroid cameras. She selected the largest and gaudiest pair. The frames were lime green and the lenses were reflective, like a mirror. She paid the clerk, a small lady with bleached blond hair, $11.95 plus tax. On the way out, she thought she saw a face on the cover of a magazine that she recognized from another time in her life, but she chose not to go back to look.

She walked to the building where Hanford lived. She stood across the street from the entrance. She liked the shade that her sunglasses provided. The sky was green, the world was dark yellow. She waited. She shifted her weight from one foot to another. A man came out of Hanford's building who looked like a turtle. A woman emerged holding on to two Great Danes as though the dogs were about to take off and pull her through the clouds. She watched a fashionable young couple struggle to clean their gray poodle's feces from the sidewalk.

Anna waited patiently. For an hour, for two hours. He did not come down. She wanted to go up. She wanted desperately to go up. Instead she took off her sunglasses, threw them in a public trash can and hailed a cab. "Take me to . . ." she struggled for a place, "take me to the Carlyle Hotel." There was little traffic in the city and the driving was easy and fast. They arrived at the hotel, she paid him, she forgot to take her change, he shouted after her, she came back for her money and left him a generous tip. The bar was closed. The lobby was deserted. The hotel seemed sad. She walked up Madison, past the galleries, until she came to a small coffee shop. She remembered the eight slices of oranges; that's all she had eaten today.

The day had grown slightly warmer. Inside, the place was yellow and clean. She sat at the far end of the counter and ordered a tuna fish on toast and milk. A few minutes later, a tall handsome woman in a brown tweed suit took a stool very close to Anna's. The woman was middle-aged, though her face was not lined. She, too, ordered tuna.

After drinking her coffee, Anna turned to the woman and said, "It's rather cold today, isn't it?"

"Yes, it is," the woman answered.

"I'm waiting for my husband," Anna announced. "You know how men are on Sundays, don't you?"

"I most certainly do."

"My husband is a lawyer. A rather busy lawyer."

"I understand. Mine has been practicing for nearly forty years. Is your husband with a firm or is he on his own?"

"He's been on his own, but he's recently rejoined his father."

"How nice."

"Yes, I think it should work out."

The older woman sipped on her tea and stared straight ahead. She had obviously tired of the conversation.

"It's not easy being the wife of a lawyer," Anna said.

"Not easy at all."

"I have a great deal of time on my hands."

"I can imagine."

"And it's difficult to know what to think of, and what not to think of."

The woman was growing suspicious. She was getting uncomfortable. She asked for her check, but before she had time to pay and leave, Anna turned to her and, with a strange mix of pain and cheer in her voice, said, "Santa Teresa—the martyred saint, Santa Teresa of Avila—once said that the mind of man is like an unbroken horse that would go anywhere except where we want it to go."

"Yes, yes, certainly," the woman mumbled as she quickly paid the check and left.

Anna sat there for a long time before she decided that she had to walk.

She tried concentrating on the paintings in the windows of the galleries, but nothing stuck. A line of orange. An old barn. A 1948 Chevrolet. The images evaporated before her eyes. There were no stories behind the paintings. She felt the need for a story. Perhaps she would go to a bookstore and find a story, but the bookstores were closed. She continued walking south, amusing herself with the clothes on display, the windows which featured spring fashions. She thought about the warm weather. And then she remembered that she was going away for a week. To Hawaii. Yes, tonight she was flying to Hawaii. And she struggled with her doubts—about leaving, about being pushed out—and decided that she better get home. Perhaps leaving the city would provide some relief.

She took a cab. She packed frantically, looked at her wristwatch, saw she had only an hour to make the plane. She grabbed her ticket, grabbed another cab, found herself sitting on the jumbo jet, first-class cabin, leaving one island and going to another.

When she awoke it was daytime and she was not pleased. She wondered about the show. She wanted to be back. She thought she was making a mistake. She called Hanford from the Honolulu airport, but there was no answer.

She hated the warm weather. It was muggy and depressing. Her hotel room overlooked the ocean, but she closed the ugly red drapes and studied her poetry and the sacred journals of Santa Teresa. She sat in darkness and fear. She never went outside—not once that first day. Inside she let the television play and, much to her amazement, at twelve thirty, she saw the show, one which she had taped only a few days before.

Each day was the same. She stayed inside, ordered food from room service. Once she ventured to the edge of the water; once she walked along the beach. But she felt aimless. Scenic beauty didn't interest her. Tours and single men, pineapple cocktails and luaus—she wanted no part of them. She wanted to be back.

The week went slowly, and she looked forward only to watching *Search for Happiness* each day at twelve thirty. Nothing else had meaning for her. By Thursday she had seen the last episode in which she herself had appeared, and she knew that Friday's show would bring her news.

She awaited the hour eagerly, impatiently. Her fifth day in Hawaii, her fifth *Search for Happiness*. Twelve ten, she sat on the bed, filing her nails. Twelve twenty, she walked to the window, gazed at the mindless ocean. Twelve twenty-five, she turned on the television set, a table model, color. Twelve thirty, she stared, she stared . . .

Baxter MacNiece walks into his son's large corner office.

"I see that you must have liked that girl I told you about."

"Yes," says Brian, "I hired her yesterday. She's working out fine."

"Sweet little disposition she has, doesn't she?"

"She has a great deal of energy. I like her. I like her spirit."

363

"I bet you do, son," the older man winks. "Well," he continues, "how does it feel to be back?"

"Fine, Dad. It feels just fine."

"You don't say that with a great deal of enthusiasm."

"The readjustment will take time."

"Just let me know if there's anything you need, son. I want you to be as comfortable as possible."

The new secretary walks in. She is slim, large-breasted and blond. Her hair is especially soft and her lipstick is glossy pink. Her dress is tight across her front, her rear. "I'm sorry to disturb you," she says to her boss, "I didn't see your father come in."

"I was just leaving, honey. Just on my way out." Once more, Baxter winks to Brian and leaves his son alone with the woman.

"You said that you wanted to see me," she says, "before I left today."

"Yes, Miss Duval," Brian clears his throat, "I just wanted to make sure that you didn't have any further questions about your job."

"Oh, no, Mr. MacNiece," she singsongs. "This is quite an efficient office and I think I'm going to get along here just fine. I'm just so happy to be back in Troy."

"That's right, you mentioned to me that you had been living in New York."

"For the last five years. I loved it at first, but after a while, oh, I don't know . . ."

"The fast life was a little bit too much for you, I bet."

"Actually, Mr. MacNiece, I've been sort of partial to the fast life. It can be exciting, don't you think?"

"To be truthful, I don't know much about the fast life."

"I wouldn't have guessed by looking at you."

"What do you mean?" he asks.

"You look so . . . so experienced."

"You have the wrong impression."

"Maybe. But if I might be bold enough to say so, looks can betray intentions."

He laughs. He doesn't know what to make of his new secretary. She is pretty and smart and sexy. She is also a shameless flirt.

364

"Well," he finally says to her, "it'll be interesting to see whether your first impressions of me are accurate or not."

"Yes, sir. Very interesting." And she turns and slowly leaves his office, making sure that he has enough time to note the tantalizing swing of her hips.

She started crying, calling New York City, calling everyone, but there were no answers. She had to get back now. She was being betrayed. She called the airlines. The next plane was at six. She made a reservation, but there was the rest of the day to kill.

Suddenly she couldn't stand to be in her hotel room a second longer. She had to get out, had to walk. She dressed quickly, left the hotel, found a large street with stores and people milling about, saw a movie theater and decided to lose herself—to try to lose herself—in some story.

The theater was small. The film was by a Frenchman. It was romantic comedy about a man's obsession with women's legs. She bought a ticket, she paced the lobby for thirty minutes, waiting for the feature to end, inspecting candy under glass. She went to the phone and called New York City again. No one was in.

She took a seat in the back. The theater was not crowded. The lights dimmed. The curtains, purple and stained, opened slowly. Coming attractions. Then his face on the screen.

"He was a man," the deep voice booms, "who refused to lose, who refused to love, who refused to leave . . . THE STREETS."

John Palermo appears on the screen. He wears no shirt. His chest is wet with perspiration. He turns and runs down a dark alleyway.

"THE STREETS," the voice continues to hawk, "where passions explode like time bombs." Palermo puts his mouth against the nipple of a dark-haired woman. "THE STREETS . . . the story of a man who wouldn't run, who spit in the face of society." Palermo slams his fist into the mouth of a burly black cop. "THE STREETS . . . the daring film debut of John Palermo." Palermo is in bed with a woman. They are both naked. Anna could see the muscles in his ass, could see the woman run her hand over his back.

365

Anna ran from the theater, ran all the way back to the hotel, checked out, taxied to the airport, arrived hours early, waited, waited, walked around the newsstand, glanced down at a magazine. Saw his picture. It was there, on the cover on the magazine. UP FROM THE STREETS, the headline read, HOLLYWOOD'S BRIGHT NEW STAR. Palermo was grim in the photograph, slightly unshaven to give the effect of toughness. Anna took the magazine in her hands. Her hands were shaking. She turned to the article on John. Pictures of his small apartment in West Hollywood. John grilling a steak. John sitting at his breakfast table in his robe. John with a woman, also dressed in a robe. They have just gotten up. She is described as his live-in girlfriend. She is Gwen Snodes.

The plane back. The light outside, the darkness, the change of colors. The last episode, the new secretary, the flirting, the changes. Hours and hours of plane ride and staring. No sleep, no peace. Her thoughts were the same. Her fixation.

When the cab arrived in front of her building in Murray Hill, the driver had to wake her. Anna had fallen into a deep sleep or a swoon.

"We're here," the driver announced.

Anna opened her eyes. Her head ached with the week's confusion. She saw that her driver was a woman.

"That'll be eighteen fifty," said the lady cabby.

Anna paid. She got out. She slowly walked toward the lobby. "Wait!" the driver called after her. "I knew I recognized you. I've been looking at you for months. *You're Prudence! You're Brian's Prudence, aren't you?*"

"Yes! Yes!" Anna exclaimed, turning around, going back, embracing the lady who had left her cab. "Yes," Anna whispered and wept, "I am Prudence."

56

"I've been trying to call you. Where have you been?" she asks.

"Must I report in to you?" he challenges.

"I kept calling and calling but I couldn't get through."

"What was so urgent?"

"I had to talk to you."

"It couldn't wait?"

"I've been thinking of you all day, I've been worried. I could think of nothing else."

"That's a mistake. There's no reason to concentrate on me like that."

"I couldn't help it. I had these horrible fears."

"Your imagination is running away with itself," he tells her.

"It's nothing I imagined. It's something I felt."

"I thought you were going to try to relax."

"I tried, I couldn't."

"You'll have to try harder."

"I suppose that I'm jealous," she finally confesses.

"Jealousy is a childish emotion. Jealousy is infantile."

"I want you to tell me that I have nothing to be jealous about."

"What good will my reassurances do if you yourself continue to be so foolishly obsessed?"

"Love is always an obsession."

"I no longer know what love is," he admits.

"You no longer look at me the way you used to."

"I don't know what that means."

"You do! You do!" she protests. "You say you don't, but you do!"

"You're the one who's become a different person."

"If I've changed, it's love that's changed me."

"That's an excuse. You're just using love as an excuse."

"Love is a reality. It's the only reality I know, the only one I ever want to know."

"You're a different person." He pauses, searching for the right words. "That's all I can say—you're different, and I'm not sure if I like the changes."

"Tell me what changes you see. It's important that I know."

"Your concern with clothes, with fashion, looking a certain . . ."

"I dress to please you."

"I don't believe that."

"It's true! I dress to be the kind of woman you want me to be."

"You used to be interested in so many other things—novels, poetry, ideas."

"I still am."

"But we never talk about those things."

"I haven't because I've sensed that you're not interested."

"This conversation is annoying me. It's futile to go on talking."

"I feel as though I'm losing you, and I don't know why. You seem annoyed at everything I say. You show no interest in me. Even in the bedroom you act uninterested."

"Enough! I've heard enough! I'm tired of talking and analyzing. I'm tired of . . ." He hesitates.

"Go on and say it!" she cries. "Say that you're tired of me! That's what you were going to say, wasn't it?"

He bows his head, as if to pray. He is silent. After a painful pause he tells her, "We're just hurting each other. There's no need to do that any longer."

"Sometimes I think you want to hurt me."

"That's ridiculous. That's just more of your obsession, more of . . ."

"I want you to hold me," she pleads.

"I don't want to hold you now."

"I want you to tell me that you love me."

"Why are those words so important to you?"

"You won't say them! You won't say that you love me!"

"Stop! I can't stand it anymore! JUST SHUT THE HELL UP!"

The camera pulls back. The episode is complete.

Hanford was exhausted. This was the first scene he had done with her since she had returned from Hawaii. He had hated it. He quickly turned to leave the studio. He had no interest in conversing with her.

"Wait," she begged him. "Please. This is the only chance I have to talk to you. I nearly went crazy for a week."

"I don't want to hear about it," he said.

"You've got to listen."

"Look, honey, I don't have to do anything I don't want to do."

The crew hung on every word.

"Why did you take your phone off the hook?"

"I don't think I owe you any explanations."

"When can I see you?"

"The less the better."

"You don't know what you're doing."

"I know exactly what I'm doing. Haven't they told you?"

"Told me what?"

"I'm getting out. I'M GETTING THE FUCK OUT OF HERE!"

And before she could demand an explanation, he stormed off the set.

57

What could I do? What the fuck could I do?

I had left her alone on her vacation. I hadn't called her, hadn't bothered her. I thought she could forget me and Brian and Hanford and this whole tortured story for a while. But no; she had come roaring back, and today I watched her play this first episode in a blind fury, acting with this raging anger, or not acting at all.

She had asked me and asked me about the new episode she had seen in Hawaii. Who was that Miss Duval, she wanted to know, and when had I selected her? I couldn't tell Anna about the secret auditioning sessions that I had run, about the segments that we had taped while she was on vacation. I just couldn't. And I didn't. I didn't want her to see exactly what was going to happen. I couldn't risk it. I couldn't tell her that Brian was going to have to cheat on her, and I couldn't tell her that Brian would shortly be gone. Sooner or later, though, I knew I'd have to.

I thought about writing her a letter, but I decided that'd be chickenshit of me. I thought about taking her to dinner at the Grotta Azzurra downtown, but I remembered how now she hated going back into the old neighborhood. I just didn't know how the hell to handle it. I felt as though she was the fuse and I was the match; I couldn't let myself get too close to her.

But now I wasn't able to put her off any longer. Now the fucking plot was thickening, now there was no way to fool her.

"What does he mean that he's getting out?" she asked me after her big fight with Hanford. We were in the control room. The day's taping was over, but everyone—including Dick and Howard—were sitting around listening.

"I don't know," I lied.

"You do. You're saying that to hurt me. Everything you say now is to hurt me."

"Everything I do is to keep you from being hurt, Anna. Why can't you see that?"

Tears were running down her cheeks. She was hysterical. "Why is he going? Where are you sending him?"

"Goddammit, I'm not sending him anywhere."

"And that secretary—why won't you get rid of her for me?"

"It's part of the story, baby. It's just part of the story."

"Don't you think you better tell her the whole story?" Dick leaned over and suggested.

"Don't you think you oughta mind your own fucking beeswax?" I put Dick in his place.

370

"What?" she wanted to know. "What's the whole story?"

"These guys don't know what they're talking about. I'm the only one who knows the whole story. Don't believe anybody but me."

"I want to believe you, but I can't. It's too, too . . ."

"This ain't the place to talk," I told her. "Why don't you change and I'll take you to dinner to some nice, cozy, quiet place, and we can sit there, just the two of us, and it'll be like old times and we'll talk about all this shit until we're blue in the face and I'll tell you exactly what's been going on and you'll see that there's nothing to worry your pretty little head about. How does that sound?"

She hesitated and then said, "I suppose we can do that."

"Good. Now you just run off and get rid of your makeup and powder your nose and go home and change your clothes and whatever else you have to do to put yourself in a good frame of mind because I intend to have fun tonight. You're my date, and any guy that muscles in is gonna have to deal with me. *Capisci?*"

She managed a weak smile and retreated to her dressing room.

When I picked her up later that evening at her apartment I had never seen a woman look so beautiful. It was eerie how beautiful she looked.

Her apartment was even more of a mess—suitcases, clothes, books, papers, scripts, pencils, crackers and makeup littered everywhere. But she appeared to come from another place; she seemed like an enchanted person that night we had dinner, and when I first saw her I was sure—at least for a minute or two—that everything was going to be all right.

I decided to splurge. That would put her in the right frame of mind. Besides, I needed a good meal myself, so I decided to take her to Farnese, which is only the most expensive joint on the island of Manhattan. It's the place where the white-collar criminals hang out, the bank swindlers and the network bigwigs. Who else can afford it? A lot of people don't like the decor, but I do. It's supposed to look like one of those palaces in Venice, and there are real marble columns and cocktail waitresses in mini-togas with their tits sticking out. Reminds me a little of

371

Vegas. Lot of people go in for those snotty French eating holes over on the East Side where the chairs are uncomfortable and nothing's written in English. I figure, though, if I'm going to spend, I'm going to spend on real food, not some dumpy, creamy frog food. Which is why I like Farnese. Plus the head-waiter, Ralphie Sotsas, used to shoot craps with me down in the old neighborhood and always gives me a hell of a welcome.

Anna was quiet in the cab. She hardly said anything to me and I had to keep the conversation rolling. I was talking to myself, but that was okay because I was happy to be going out with her. And I never really mind listening to myself talk since my own bullshit is as good as anyone else's. Or maybe a little better.

We got there and Ralphie bowed and scraped and made a big deal over me and eyed Anna and asked me about the show and gave us the best table in the house. The cocktail waitress had bigger jugs than Silvia and she recognized Anna and all of a sudden got real excited.

"Haven't I seen you on television? Aren't you Prudence from *Search for Happiness?*"

"Yes, I'm Prudence," Anna said.

"I can't tell you how much I love you," said the lady with the boobs. "You're wonderful, just wonderful, and I hope that you and Brian will be very happy."

"Thank you." Anna smiled, "we have every intention of being happy."

"Oh, my God!" the waitress exclaimed. "You're talking just the way you talk on TV. I can't believe I'm really seeing you here. I feel like I know you. And when you decided to leave the convent, believe me, I suffered with you. I really did. Oh, it must have been torture on you, poor thing."

"It was," Anna confessed, "but that was a long time ago."

"And what about your father-in-law? I mean, isn't he some-thing? Him, with all his fancy mistresses. Though actually I think he's a very good-looking man considering his age."

"Considering my age, honey," I said to the broad, "I'd like to get a double Scotch on the rocks before I run out of steam here."

"Are you on the show, too?" she wanted to know.

"I *am* the show," I informed her. "I write it."

"How nice. What would you like to drink, Prudence dear, or do you drink?"

"A glass of very dry white wine, please."

"Ain't that something," I said to Anna when Miss Waitress and her bouncing jug band was gone, "the way these people get caught up in the goddamn story."

She looked at me for a long time. Her eyes were frozen and frightened and she said what she had obviously been wanting to say all night. "Where are the scripts? What's going to happen next? I have to know."

"We're going to have a long, leisurely meal and we'll discuss all that later. In the meantime let's think about food. This goddamn menu is about as thick as one of my scripts. Now let's see, we'll have to start off with a little melon and pro . . ."

"I'm not interested in eating. I'm not interested in anything but the new scripts. I have to know, and I have to know right now."

She was fucking up my timing. I had planned on tiptoeing my way through dinner and leaving this bullshit for the very end of the evening, when we'd be nice and full and mellow. But what could I do? She wouldn't take no for an answer.

"All right, Anna, I'll level with you. The changes are going to be pretty heavy. I haven't wanted to tell you because . . ."

"Just tell me what the changes are. Tell me now."

"Hanford's leaving."

"What do you mean leaving?"

"Just like he told you. He's leaving. He's going to do a movie in England."

"I don't believe you."

"That's why I didn't want to tell you. I knew it would upset the hell out of you."

"It's a lie. You're lying to me."

"I'm telling you straight, honey. He's going. But it really doesn't make any difference, because your relationship with him had to get fucked up anyway. That's what Costein's been yelling about, and I got to admit, the kid's onto something. We were getting too carried away with the marriage bit. It was too perfect and no one was buying it. That's why the ratings were flopping in my face. You can understand that, can't you?"

"I can't understand why you're doing this to me."

"It ain't me, baby. It has nothing to do with me."

"But you promised me, you said that you'd never let anyone or anything . . ."

"Anna, Anna sweetheart, listen to me, listen to Al, you got to snap out of this, you got to stop treating this horseshit like it was . . ."

"He's all I have."

"He's nothing but a snotty actor."

"He's my life."

"Your life is your talent, Anna, please believe me. And your talent is so goddamn great that it's hard for you to understand. But I'm telling you, his leaving doesn't really mean shit. You'll go on. I promise you. I have every intention in the world of expanding your part, making it even bigger and more important. You'll see, Anna, and something else you'll be happy about is money. Yeah, I was talking to Brink the other day and telling him that when your contract is up for renewal we'll really be able to hold up the fucking network. Brink is going to put a gun to their head. I'm talking about a substantial goddamn increase, Anna, I'm talking big bucks."

"Keep Brian from leaving."

"I can't."

"You must."

"I wish I could. I tried."

"Try again."

"It won't make any difference. He wants out."

"Make him stay." She was crying softly, she was breaking my heart. "You have to make him stay."

I put my hand on her cheek. She backed away, got up from the table and practically knocked into the cocktail waitress.

"Will you tell me where the telephone is?" Anna asked.

"Who do you have to call? Brian? You're worried that he's cheating on you already, huh?" The waitress winked and pointed out the phone.

Anna never came back to my table. She snuck out of the restaurant without my knowing. And I was too tired, too drained from this whole fucking mess, to chase her down.

374

58

"I've been frantic. I tried calling, but I couldn't get through."

"I wish to God you'd stop calling so much. Your calling drives me crazy."

"I just had to talk to you."

"You keep saying that, but there's nothing for us to talk about. Nothing."

"I just want an evening alone with you, an evening the way it used to be, when we read poetry to one another, when we made love as though nothing else in the world mattered."

"It all seems better in retrospect."

"It *was* that way. We made it that way for each other. And it can still be that way, it *will* be that way, if only . . ."

"We never really knew each other. It all happened much too quickly. And most of it was make-believe. We were simply playing parts, escaping from reality. I'm not who you think I am. I don't even resemble that person."

"No one knows you the way I do. I'm wasting my breath, you'll never understand, I don't know what else to tell you."

"Tell me what I know is true. Tell me that you love me."

"Why are you prolonging this? Why are you asking me to hurt you?"

"It'll be the same as it used to be. I know it will."

"And what did it used to be?"

"Something precious, something beautiful . . ."

"It was a game. Can't you see that it was all a game?"

"All right," the voice of Dick the director boomed from the loudspeaker adjacent to the set. "Let's cut out the chatter. We're ready to roll tape."

The cameras moved in. The floor manager with the head-phone pointed his finger at Anna. The segment began:

"You've been working late again," she tells her husband. "This is the fourth night in a row. I tried calling, but your line was always busy. I've been frantic. I thought something was wrong."

"I had a very involved conversation with a client."

"At this time of night?"

"Yes."

"For two hours?"

"Yes, Prudence, for two hours."

"Were you alone?" she asks. "Were you working alone?"

"Of course I was alone."

"Then why was her car there."

"Whose car?"

"When I drove by the office I saw your secretary's car. It was parked next to yours."

He scowls at her. "Dammit, I resent your spying on me. You're treating me like a suspected bank robber. You have no business . . ."

"What was her car doing there? You haven't told me. You said that you were alone."

"Her . . ." he stumbles, "her battery was dead. She, uh . . . she left her car at the office and her sister came to get her."

"I don't believe you."

"Why didn't you come up? Why didn't you come in the office and check on me?"

"The door was locked and the lights were off."

"I can't believe I'm hearing all this. You, Prudence, you of all people, sweet Prudence, trusting Prudence, Prudence the most understanding woman in the world, Prudence has turned into a shrew, a spy, a social climber, Prudence has become everything I thought she wasn't . . ."

"None of that is true! None of that is the least bit true!"

"I'm tired of this bickering."

"You still haven't told me what you were doing tonight."

"I'm not going to repeat myself."

"I don't want you to repeat yourself, I don't want to hear the

376

same lie, I want to know why you're doing this to me, I have to . . ."

"I have to get out of here before I lose my sanity." He picks up his coat and heads for the door. She runs after him.

"No!" She grabs him. "Stay! You must stay and talk and explain and I'll understand, I promise I'll understand, but I have to know, I have to know everything that happened and why it happened . . ."

"All you have to know is that I'm leaving, and I may never be back!" He opens the door. She holds on to him.

"Perfect!" Dick shouted. "That's a beautiful take."

"Let go of me!" Hanford was screaming. "Get your goddamn hands off of me!"

"You won't go away! I won't let you go away!"

"Would someone explain to this woman that I've quit, that I've quit this miserable show and that in a week I won't be here anymore? Would someone please tell her that I'm being written out of the script? Al! Where's Al?" Hanford looked past the lights into the control booth. "Is Al up there? Would Al come down here and tell Anna that I am out. *O, U, T, out.* I am gone. I am through with this woman. I am through with this madwoman. Can everyone hear me?" Now he was shouting at the top of his lungs, shouting so his voice could be heard from one end of the studio to the other. "I don't ever want to see her again, not on the show, not on the street, not on the television set. She's a pest and a bore and I'm fed up, I'm sick and tired and I'm sick and tired of being sick and tired. I'm through. Is that clear? I'm through with Anna Calzolari and I'm through with Prudence the nun and Prudence MacNiece. They've made my life miserable and I have every intention of forgetting that they ever existed. As far as I'm concerned, they're all dead. Every one of them!"

And when he turned to leave the set she was falling to the floor, falling in silence, falling in grief, falling with all the grace and impact of an actress whose art was both heartfelt and effortless.

59

After what he had done, I knew that I'd have to kill him off. Yes, sir. I was really going to fuck up this bastard good. Seames wouldn't just be written out of the script; his ass was going to be blown to kingdom come. I thought about a heart attack, but that was too painless. I thought about a mugging, the kind where the guys follow you home on a dark moonless night and then flash their long knives and let you look at their sadistic smiles before they start taking little slices our of your ear, your nose, your dick. I thought about cancer, long, lingering cancer where there's lots of time to consider your decay, where you lose your hair and then your speech and then your mind. I thought about a lot of shit, but most of it wasn't practical. I only had a week to write him out of the script. I had to do it fast, but I was still going to take as much time as I could; there's no way I wasn't going to enjoy this little chore.

And why shouldn't I? If it weren't for him, things would have been going just fine now. If it weren't for him, I wouldn't have been crazy with worry over Anna. I was worried that she had cut herself off from everyone and everything; I was worried that she didn't do anything all goddamn day but call me and ask me about the scripts. And sometimes I got mad at her and screamed and sometimes she screamed at me, and it was no good, the thing between us now was no good. I'd try to laugh it off and tell her how she was always my lucky number—I'd remind her about the day at the track a million years ago when she had picked all the winners. But she wouldn't listen to me; she didn't want to hear about anything except scripts. And I couldn't cave in. I just couldn't. I had to stick to my guns and play it close to

378

the chest because I knew if she saw how I was getting rid of Brian there's no telling what she might do.

So I had to listen to her scold and abuse and threaten me. She'd come over and start throwing a fit and then she'd search around for the scripts but I'd have them hidden in the stove or on top of the closet and she'd beg me and cry and, Jesus Christ, she'd be breaking my heart and there were times when there were tears in my eyes, too. I couldn't help myself. But I also couldn't change the direction of the show, not now, not with a new set of New Year's debts that had piled up. (I needed some relief from this nutty fucking show and fortunately had found a hot poker game with some old friends downtown, but unfortunately I wasn't on what you'd call a hot streak. This was a rotten period for my luck—my poker luck and my professional luck. I kept getting the wrong cards.) The more I made, the more freedom I had to throw it away, and sometimes I seriously thought about asking for a reduction in salary so I could pay off some of my debts.

But the show had to go on. I told that to Anna, and I tried to explain to her that everything I did was for her and for me. The material had to be fresh or we'd be fucked; I told her that time and time again, but she wouldn't listen, she wouldn't leave her Prudence role—not for a goddamn second—and I was tired of it and disgusted and saddened and maybe even a little terrified. But the show had to go on, and I had to make a living, I had to keep churning out this shit and there was nothing I could do—I had tried every kind of reasoning—to help her see the fucking light.

So here I was at the typewriter, alone at last, still trying to figure out a way—the quickest way, the most believable way—to destroy Brian MacNiece. And as my fingers hit the keys, hit them harder and harder, I thought of bashing in his brains for what he had done to Anna—that slickass fraternity boy—I thought of kicking him in the nuts, I thought of ripping him open with a nice new razor blade. But I knew I had to be reasonable and I knew I had to think of my viewers and I finally settled on a nice friendly car crash where he'd be thrown through the windshield and have his head sliced into several thousand pieces. Good-bye to bad garbage.

60

She was standing in a corner of the studio, her face only inches away from a monitor. On the monitor screen was the segment which was being taped on the other side of the studio.

Her fists were clenched, and she stared, she stared . . .

Mr. and Mrs. Baxter MacNiece are fast asleep in their darkened bedroom. They are in single beds. He snores lightly. The phone rings, startling them from their dreams. He switches on the lamp which sits atop his mahogany nightstand. He rubs his eyes as he lifts the receiver of the phone and places it next to his ear.

"Baxter?"

"Yes."

"This is Howard. Howard Gates. I've got bad news for you, Baxter, and I wish I didn't have to be the one to tell you."

"Who is it?" Mrs. MacNiece is awake and wants to know what's happening.

"Howard Gates," her husband tells her.

"The police chief?" she asks.

"Yes, now for God's sake be quiet so I can hear what he has to say. Go ahead, Howard."

"I'm afraid that your boy has been in an accident."

"What kind of accident?" Baxter questions. "Is he all right?"

"It was a crack-up out on Highway Eighteen, Baxter, and . . . and . . ."

"Accident, what accident?" Mrs. MacNiece is asking.

"Your boy's dead," Gates finally gets the words out.

"Dear God, dear God in heaven," Baxter murmers.

380

"What? What has happened?" The mother is screaming.

"Have you called Brian's wife? Have you talked to Prudence?" Baxter asks Gates.

"No, I didn't, Baxter. I thought I'd call you first because you see . . . well, your son wasn't alone. He was with a woman, a young girl named Duval. She died in the crash along with him."

"Baxter!" His wife's voice is quivering with fear. *"Baxter! What has happened?"*

"NO!NO!NO!NO!NO!NO!NO!NO!NO!NO!NO!NO!!!"
Her piercing cry shot through soundproof walls. It was a cry of terror.

"What the hell was that?" Dick wanted to know. He checked to see whether his sound track was clear or whether the final portion of the segment would have to be retaped.

Meanwhile, Anna fled. She was out of the studio, out of the building, in the streets. She was gone before anyone could comfort her, before anyone could explain.

61

How the fuck could she pull that on me? What was she trying to do—ruin my career? destroy my life? give me another goddamn heart attack?

The first night I figured she was out somewhere or just not answering her phone. I knew she'd be upset. She'd have to be upset. Hell, *I* was upset. I wish there could have been an easier way for her to have found out, but I couldn't chance it. I couldn't have shown her the script beforehand. I was afraid of what might happen. I figured that she might threaten to quit or something. And I couldn't afford to have her talk me out of it.

So I stuck to my guns and played it close to my chest and now look what had happened: Anna has disappeared off the face of the earth.

By the second afternoon—that was Wednesday—I started to feel funny in the stomach. Still no answer at her place. "She really looked bad," one of the stagehands told me who had seen her run out of the studio on Monday. "Real bad, Al." I hadn't been there that day and I had figured that she wouldn't be either, and that was another mistake I was blaming myself for as I walked over to her apartment. I buzzed her from downstairs and no answer. I went up and knocked on the door and got a little crazy 'cause I thought I smelled gas. All kinds of weird shit was running through my brain. Was I responsible? What the hell had I done to this poor gal? I knocked and knocked and there was no answer and I took out the key that she had given me and opened the door, very quickly, just to get it over with.

Now I was really afraid because the place looked as though it had been hit by a hurricane. I ran to the kitchen to see whether she had stuck her head in the oven, but the oven was off and she wasn't there and the smell of gas had been in my imagination. Scripts and pictures of Santa Teresa and clothes and empty milk cartons and more scripts and scribblings everywhere. Her bedroom door was closed, and I was scared to open it. I looked under the door for traces of blood. There weren't any. I opened the door and there were so many clothes piled on the bed—beautiful dresses and blouses and slips from Bergdorf and Bendel's—that I couldn't be sure that she wasn't under the pile. She wasn't there and she wasn't anywhere in her apartment and I was relieved until I remembered that I still didn't know where she was. All I knew was that she hadn't come home to kill herself.

I sat down on the couch and thought about it. If I were Anna, where would I go? It suddenly came to me. I snapped my fingers and said to myself, Of course, you asshole, of course! I ran to the phone and called Hanford Seames's agent. He was out to lunch. He'd call me back. I left Anna's number and went back to the couch and thought about it. He was leaving for England, or he had already left—I didn't know which. But she was bound to have followed him; that was it, that had to be it. She wasn't going to let him get away. Just like she had followed Palermo to Hollywood. I'd find out where Seames was and that way I'd find Anna. I'd calm her down because I was the only one who could calm her down. I'd show her how everything was going to be fine, just as it was fine after Palermo had left. And then . . . then I'd tell her that we needed to be together and figure out a new love interest in her life. Yeah, that'd be perfect. She'd love that. We'd invent a new boyfriend for her. Anyone she wanted. We'd get her someone really good-looking, maybe an athlete, maybe the high-school football coach, maybe . . .

The phone rang. I jumped to get it. Seames's agent. "Where is Hanford?" I wanted to know.

"London, England."

"When did he get there?"

"Yesterday morning."

"Where's he staying?"

"The Windsor Arms."

"Perfect," I said.

"He's not coming back, Al," the agent said. "I can tell you that."

"I don't want him back," I blurted out, "I just want *her* back."

One o'clock in New York. Evening time in England. I placed the call to the Windsor Arms. They said they'd have to call me back. More time to kill. More time to worry, but why should I be worried since I knew that I was hot on her trail? She was in England, she had to be England. She ran out to the airport yesterday or today and she chased him to London. I'd find her. I'd go there and I'd bring her back and everything would be fine. The show would roll along as though nothing had happened.

The phone. My heart jumped to answer it. An English operator. I could barely hear her. Lousy fucking connection. Then a man's voice.

"Hanford? Hanford, is that you?" I shouted into the phone.

"It's me. What do you want? I'm not coming back."

"I don't give a fuck if you're ever coming back, I just want Anna. Where is she?"

"I . . ." And then his voice trailed off.

383

"What did you say? I can't hear a fucking word you're saying, Seames."

Still nothing. Noise. Static. The sound of the Atlantic Ocean between him and me. I clicked the phone. I stomped my feet. I wanted to cry. I got the operator back. "We've been disconnected!" I shouted. "Get me my party back!"

"I'll have to call you back, sir. What is your number there?"

Sweet Jesus. More waiting. Back on the couch. Time to calculate. When did I need Anna for rehearsal? How long could I put off having her in a segment? Three days, four days, maybe as many as five days. How the hell was I going to get to England and back in time to work out the aftermath of Brian's death? How could I cover for Anna? I'd find a way. Prudence was my baby. I'd work on the plane over to London. Yeah, that's what I'd do. I'd . . .

The phone. The English operator. Hanford. Loud and clear. Thank God I could hear him this time.

"Listen, Gonfio, I'm on my way out the door."

"Just tell me where she's staying."

"What the hell are you talking about?"

"Anna. Where's Anna?"

"How should I know?"

"She's in England."

"Oh, God."

"You didn't know that?"

"No."

"She hasn't called you?"

"No."

"Well, she will. She'll be calling you soon."

"I'll change hotels. I'll check out of here tonight."

"Don't do that, asshole," I said. "You do that and I'll never find her. When she calls you, just ask her where she's staying. Then call me collect—at home or at the office. Keep trying until you get me."

"Who told you that she's in London?"

"A little birdie called common sense."

"I hope you're wrong."

"Fuck yourself. Just call me when she calls you and for Christ's sake don't change hotels."

384

I hung up the phone and saw that my hands were shaking. My hands never shake, but now they were shaking as though I were an old man or something. What if she wasn't in England? Where was she? Where the fuck had she gone? I got up and went into her bedroom and rummaged around and tried to see if her suitcases were there. There were a couple of overnight bags and a large canvas suitcase, but I had no way of knowing whether there were more bags that she had taken with her or whether this was everything. How the fuck could I figure any of this out? I wasn't a detective, I was a goddamn writer and I had a bunch of scripts I had to write. Who would tell Dick and Howard? And who would tell the kid? And what in the name of the Merciful Lord was I going to do now?

I looked through her medicine chest to see whether she had taken her toothbrush. She hadn't. But what did that mean? She probably had two. There was makeup, there were all kinds of things floating around the bathroom, and I couldn't figure it out anyway. Her place was a disaster area. I couldn't tell whether she was coming or going.

I called my assistants. I told them what had happened and to keep their fucking mouths shut. I told them they had to find her in England. I told them to find the numbers of all the hotels in London, especially those around the Windsor Arms, and call them and ask for her. I told them to stop writing whatever the hell they were writing and do nothing but call England until they found her.

"Who should we ask for?" one of those Ivy League birdbrains wanted to know.

"What do you mean?" I barked back.

"Well," he said, and then I thought about it, and I knew he was right and I said, "Ask for them both. Ask for Anna Calzolari and ask for Prudence MacNiece."

Then I called Howard and Dick and told them what was happening. I reminded them about Hollywood and how I got her back and told them not to worry. They had the good sense not to "I told you so" me, because if they had I would have run over there and kicked them in the balls.

At least I was organizing the troops. I got up and went to the little writing desk in her bedroom and found her address book.

At least that was something. There were no more than two dozen names in the whole book. Her parents. I spotted her parents' phone number. I called them. I hated to do it, but I had to. Her mother answered the phone.

"You don't know me, Mrs. Calzolari, but my name's Al Gonfio and . . ."

"Of course. Anna's mentioned you. You're the writer."

"That's right, I'm the writer, and I'm calling because, well, it's no big deal and I don't want you to get excited but it seems as though Anna has missed a rehearsal. It must have just slipped her mind because she forgot to call us and I was wondering if, by chance, you might happen to know where we could find her."

"You must be kidding, Mr. Gonfio. I've talked with her twice in the last year. Maybe three times. The only time I get to see her is on TV. But now that her husband has been killed she's probably just very upset. She takes this acting business so seriously. You don't think there's anything wrong, do you?"

"Of course not. As I said, this has happened before. Actresses. You know. Actresses are very high-strung and you're right, she takes this whole thing very seriously. Now what about your husband—or your sons—do you think they may have heard from her?"

"Not a chance in the world," the woman said to me in a voice which sounded like my mother and every other mother who had ever lived in the old neighborhood.

"Thank you, Mrs. Calzolari. Sorry for bothering you."

"No bother at all. Just tell my daughter to call home when you find her. And, Mr. Gonfio, there's one other thing."

"What's that?"

"Thank you for everything you've done for my daughter. I know she couldn't have gotten where she is without you."

"It was nothing, Mrs. Calzolari, nothing at all."

I hung up the phone. I wanted to choke myself. I wanted to hear Anna's key rattling in the keyhole. I wanted the door to open and I wanted to see her walking through. What were the troops doing? Why hadn't they called me? Why hadn't they found her in England? What the hell was wrong with those numbskulls?

The address book. I had to go back through the address book.

Her hairdresser. I called. He was a fairy and said that he hadn't seen her in two weeks. Fuck him. The Regency Health Spa. I called and they said that she had dropped her membership six months ago. Gwen Snodes. It had to be an old number. It had to be wrong. Snodes was living with Palermo out on the Coast. A dozen different people had told me that. I tried the number anyway. Deep Drain Plumbing answered. I hung up. Brink Kaufman. Jesus Christ! Brink Kaufman. Of course! He'd know, he was her agent, wasn't he? His new secretary picked up the phone and said that he was out of town. I said I was his oldest friend and closest business associate in the world. He went down to Miami for the races. The fucker was at Hialeah. Get him for me, I told the broad. Have him call me here, and I gave her Anna's number.

Who else? There were a few other numbers—relatives, a dentist, a doctor. A doctor, I thought. I tried him. Busy. He'll call back. Everyone was busy. Everyone would call me back. Meanwhile my life and my world were coming down around my fucking head. But they were too goddamn busy to talk to me for two seconds. The phone rang. It was Costein. He had gotten word.

"Not to worry, kid." I tried to fake it, but he heard panic in my voice.

"Do you have contingency plans? Do you have a backup procedure worked out?"

"What are you talking about? What do you think this is, a nuclear accident? I always have backup plans. I'm a writer, aren't I? and writers can invent any fucking thing they want to. This is nothing. No problem, kid, I'm telling you that it's no problem."

"You understand the timing intricacies better than I do, Al. I don't have to remind you of how critical time is at this point. You've got to keep things moving. You've made a splendid recovery. Just splendid. I don't have to tell you again that your ratings have been soaring ever since Prudence and Brian began fighting. And I don't have to tell you that I'm counting on you to keep this thing on track."

"No, you don't, and I wish that you wouldn't."

"Then I'll let you get back to work. You've got no more than another twenty-four hours to figure out what to do."

"Don't give yourself any ulcers, kid," I said as I felt a pain shoot through my gut which nearly doubled me over. I hadn't eaten and I had cramps and something that felt like diarrhea and I was too nervous to go to the can because I didn't want to leave the phone. I didn't know what the fuck to do.

The doctor called. He hadn't seen her in a year. No help. I called back Brink's office and asked her whether she had located him. Not yet. I called my assistants. No progress.

It was getting dark outside. She'd be back soon, she'd be tired from having wandered around the city, she'd be anxious to get home and kick off her shoes and relax. She'd be glad to see me, she'd laugh when she walked through the door, and I'd laugh and we'd have a drink and I'd call Dick and Howard and my assistants and the kid and maybe even her mother—why not be nice to her mother?—and tell them that the mystery was solved. Anna just went for a long walk. Or Anna just decided to go to the country for a couple of days. Or Anna just decided to check into a hotel . . . a hotel, that's it! I thought to myself, a hotel, she loved those classy hotels, the Carlyle, of course, she probably went to the Carlyle. She was there right now.

"Do you have a Prudence MacNiece registered there?"

The operator went away to check. She came back and said, "The only Prudence MacNiece we have is the one who appears on television every day at twelve thirty."

"Very funny," I said. Even the goddamn telephone operator was a wiseass.

"What about Anna Calzolari?"

Not there. The Plaza, I thought I'd try the Plaza, and the Pierre, and the Sherry Netherland, and another dozen swanky hotels, and nothing. Nothing on top of nothing. Which is when I saw her journal buried under a stack of old *Search* scripts. I didn't want to read it then because I had to eat something before I passed out. But there was nothing in the refrigerator except cheese and old tomatoes and two oranges and I couldn't leave her apartment because the phone might ring and she might be coming through the door any minute. So I opened up the notebook and began to read and wanted to stop but couldn't.

Her notes were sometimes brief and sometimes long, and they were all about Brian. Nothing but Brian. I wasn't mentioned, the show wasn't mentioned, there was nothing about acting or

388

getting paid or living in an apartment in New York City. It was all him. Once in a while she'd mention Santa Teresa and once in a while there'd be a quote from one of those poets she liked to read, but those were the only exceptions. Everything else was him and how she intended to make him happy and change her life, transform herself into the woman that he wanted her to be. Never Hanford, always Brian. There were long descriptions of her dreams, and in her dreams she was fucking him or marrying him or flying in airplanes with him. In her dreams she was always in his arms. And the more I read, the more I realized that this diary was nothing more than the show, the show that she wrote for me and I wrote for her. Her secret in-her-head life was the same life that I had given her in those scripts that I churned out. And I found myself reading faster, knowing what was going to happen—his divorce from Sally, the marriage, the reconciliation with his parents—wanting to get to the end, desperately looking for a hint of where she might have gone.

"There are bad signs," she wrote, "distressingly bad signs, but I know that the obstacles which lie before us can be overcome. I know that in my heart. If Brian isn't strong enough, then I am. Nothing can stand in our way. And nothing will, because I have come to believe that what love has begun, love can complete. There will be temptations, of course. I recognize that. But I am not afraid. When I look back and see how far I have traveled to arrive at this place, the distance ahead seems insignificant. Love has given me my strength, and I have never felt more powerful than now."

That was the last entry. Nothing about the fights with me. Nothing about trying to get the scripts. Nothing about the lousy ratings. Nothing about Miss Duval. Nothing about Hanford quitting. Not one fucking clue.

Kaufman called. He didn't know shit. He hadn't talked to her in a month. I wanted to scream in his face, but I didn't. It wasn't Brink's fault. I asked him how they were running down there. He laughed and said he had won a bundle. Fucking liar. I got off the phone. Where the hell were my assistants? I called them. They were still in the office. Nothing. Over a hundred hotels in London and nothing. What about boardinghouses? Wasn't London full of those bread-and-breakfast boardinghouses? She could be in one of those joints. Impossible to track down, I was told. There were thousands of them. Well, try a couple of dozen, I ordered. Maybe we'll get lucky. Keep at it, I told them. Your job depends on it. Your job and my job and everyone else's job.

I was bushed. I was about to faint. Nothing to eat, getting late, no Anna. I wanted to cry. I wanted to go home. I had to get out of this apartment because it drove me out of my fucking mind. Her smells and her pictures of Santa Teresa. I'd leave and come back tomorrow morning. I left a note that said CALL ME, I LOVE YOU, WHERE HAVE YOU BEEN?

I went to a deli and ate myself sick. I opened the door to my place and the phone was ringing and I was sure it was good news but it was Silvia. Silvia wanting to get laid. I wanted to laugh, but I couldn't. I told her that she was a wonderful lady but my life was ending. Anna was missing and I couldn't do shit until I found her. Silvia understood. Silvia was almost as upset as I was. She started going on and on, telling me how worried she'd been, how she knew something really terrible was going to happen. When I finally got her off the phone I realized that it was the first time in my life that I had turned down tail. I never thought I would live to see the day.

I called the office and told the assistants to go home. We'd start again tomorrow. I tried to sleep but I couldn't. My cigar tasted like stale manure. I had the runs. I had to find her. I thought about her until 3:00 A.M., I kept calling her apartment, and when I fell asleep I dreamed about her. I was in Chicago in my dreams, sitting in a train car running around the Loop when I thought I saw her on Michigan Avenue going into a movie. I jumped out of the car and I didn't kill myself. I ran into the movie theater. She wasn't sitting in any of the seats. She was on the screen. I ran on the stage and screamed at the screen and they chased me out of there for being crazy and outside was the old neighborhood, outside was the Lower East Side and the beautiful Festival of San Gennaro and I was lost in the maze of people, knocking around, and she was the little girl, the *principessina* all so beautiful and in white, but it wasn't her, of course it wasn't her, but that *was* her, going into the church, the Church of the Most Precious Blood, and I followed her in and she ran behind the statue of the Madonna and I chased her, I followed her and I caught her in my arms. It was Anna! It was my Anna! But the phone woke me up and she wasn't there, my dream faded away and it was Costein saying that if she didn't turn up by noon we should call the cops.

I wanted to go to England but he talked me out of that. He said we should call Scotland Yard instead. Once again, the kid was right. And I spent all that day and the next day, walking back and forth from her place to mine, making thousands of calls, to everyone, everyone who had the slightest knowledge of her, everyone she had ever known, and nothing, dear God, nothing on top of nothing on top of nothing. And I spent an hour on the phone talking to Scotland Yard, describing her, explaining the situation, and the New York City cops came by and Costein pulled some strings and got the FBI on the case and two guys who looked like thugs came by and I had to tell the story, the same sad fucking story over and over again, until I was sick, sick to my stomach and sick at heart, because I felt that now she might not be coming back, she might never be coming back, and I didn't know whether she was alive or dead, I didn't know what had become of her, and I still had a script to write, I still had to put something on the air, because the show goes on, the goddamn fucking show goes on, and I was the genius who had to figure out what to do next.

"It's impossible. She can't simply disappear like that."

"Well, she has."

"Have you done everything? Have you called everyone there is to call?"

"Everyone."

"And the police have no clues?"

"The police can come up with nothing."

"There are other people beside the police."

"There's the FBI. I've called them. I've spoken to them. They've said that they'll try to help."

"And what about her family? Have you checked there?"

"I have, and I learned nothing."

"Why? Why would she leave now? Why would she decide to vanish from the face of the earth?"

"I can't say. I wish I knew. She's always been a strange and unpredictable person. But then again, which one of us really knew her?"

"Do you think she might have done herself harm?"

"I've thought about that."

"And . . . and what do you think? Tell me."

"My opinion is just an opinion. Yes, I think she may have done herself harm."

"What can we do? There must be *something* we can do."

"I've thought of everything, believe me. I've traced down every possible clue. I've spent literally thousands of dollars on phone calls, I've even hired a private detective agency."

"How long has it been?"

"Nearly ten days."

"If we only knew why . . ."

"If we only knew *where*."

"And yet there's nothing to do but wait . . ."

"And pray."

The camera pulls back to show Mr. and Mrs. MacNiece climbing into their separate beds. He switches off the lamp and the screen goes blank.

Costein walked into the control room. He saw me sitting there. He put his hand on my shoulder. "You've done what you've had to do," he said.

"I suppose so," I answered him.

"You haven't heard anything."

"No," I told him. "Have you?"

"Not a thing."

392

"Every day that goes by makes me think . . ."

"Don't be too hard on yourself, Al. The show's going to shape up just fine without her."

I wanted to punch him, but I didn't. I went home and slept and walked the streets and came back home and drank and slept and walked the streets again until late Sunday night when the phone call came.

63

The plane ran into a storm. I might have guessed that was going to happen. The fucking jet was doing loop-the-loops. And guess what? I didn't give a shit. Let the lightning strike. Let the thunder roar. Let the sky close in and the clouds turn black and the winds rip the fuselage in half. Let the passengers go spilling out and falling on the earth like bird shit. I was rooting for the storm to get worse. I didn't give a flying fuck what happened. I was drunk, downright deadass drunk, drunk in my head and drunk in my heart, depressed and disheartened and nearly destroyed. My soul was not in good shape. It was the worst trip of my life.

I couldn't stop going back over everything, couldn't get myself to think of anything but Anna. How it had started. How it had progressed. And now how it was ending. The plane hit another air pocket and I picked up the scent of puke. A woman down the aisle was throwing up her guts. I was envious. I wanted to throw up, throw up this last year and a half in my life. This nightmare.

Everyone told me that it wasn't my fault. Everyone knew that I'd be taking it hard. Everyone was trying to be nice. But I didn't need sympathy. I knew what had happened. I saw it. I did it. And now I was going to face it like a man. I had to. I couldn't live with myself any other way.

Costein kept telling me not to worry. He said that everything was going to be fine, just fine. The ratings had jumped through the roof. What more could he want? I had delivered. I had given him just what he needed. I was a goddamn hero. "The story is developing beautifully," he said to me before I left for the airport in New York. Those were his actual words.

The kid was happy because the kid had ice water running through his veins. The kid plugged the computer up his asshole every morning and the kid started to hum. The kid knelt in the first pew of the Church of High Ratings Share.

But at least he had some kind of religion, I thought to myself as the plane finally glided out of the soup of the storm into the clear morning light. At least he believed in something. At least he prayed to the God of the Numbers. What about me? Oh, hell, I had tried going to church during these past five days. I had even slipped into the confession booth. But what the fuck could I tell the man? I hadn't gotten laid right in months. I hadn't been to the track. I couldn't concentrate long enough to bet. What were my sins? That I loved her too much, that I cared for her as a father cared for a daughter? Did I ever touch her? *Ever?* Did I ever even *try* to seduce her? Shit, I was so pure I made myself sick.

We were close—that was the main thing. I thought I knew her. I *knew* I knew her. But now I remembered the warnings; there had been warnings from everyone—Dick and Howard and Seames and the staff, my assistants, even the stagehands. Not that I needed the warnings. I saw it coming before anyone. I just thought that I was in control. I thought I could take care of everything. And I was wrong.

But maybe it had to happen this way. Maybe I wasn't at fault after all. Hell, she made more money than she had ever dreamed of. She got herself a whole wardrobe of fine clothes, didn't she? And she loved those clothes. She had class. Natural class. She looked like a model. And her apartment. I almost forgot that I had found that apartment for her. I made sure she moved into a good neighborhood. I got her out of the crummy Lower East Side, crummy SoHo. I brought her home from Hollywood. I told her that Palermo was nothing more than a bum. If she had only listened to me about everything else, about Seames, about this show, about . . .

The plane landed in Cincinnati with a thud. I was half-pissed that we had made it. A crash might have saved me. A crash might have been more merciful than this trip.

I changed planes. The prop job was less crowded. I tried to sleep. I tried to play solitaire. I tried to read the local rag. I tried to eat the slop that the stewardess set before me. Peas. Two slices of baloney on stale white bread. A Tab. I wanted a drink. They were out of booze. They didn't carry much booze, she said, on these short flights.

Dayton was just another airport. I went to the Hertz counter. They wanted to give me a compact. I said I was too big for a crappy compact. I wanted to be comfortable. I wanted something bigger. They didn't have anything bigger.

The compact gave me cramps. I followed Highway 75 north and wondered why anyone would want to live out here in the wilds of Ohio. What was Ohio anyway? What did people do here? Were they farmers? Did they work in factories? They did what everyone else in America does: They watched TV.

TROY, OHIO. It really existed. I was actually there. I didn't know whether to laugh or cry or shout for joy. I just shook my head in disbelief. I was driving through Troy, Ohio. There was nothing special about it except a restaurant called the Helen of Troy. I thought that was kind of cute. Everything else was straight-ahead, wholesome Americana. A little dismal, a little dull, another small town in the middle of the world doing nothing but minding its own business.

Finding the the place wasn't hard. They told me how to get there on the phone and I had a map with the street marked in red. But when I got there, I couldn't go in. Something kept me from parking the car, so I drove around, I drove around and around peaceful little Troy, Ohio, thinking about it, thinking about the fact that I was driving through a dream. Except that the dream wasn't a dream. I was driving through a real city and the city was called Troy. It was in the state of Ohio, and I was there. In it.

I drove back and parked. I was scared. Dear God in heaven, I was very scared. I didn't want to face this. I wanted to run back where I came from, get into the car and race down the highway to the plane which flies to Manhattan. I wanted out, but I was going in.

The hallway was dark and smelled funny. I felt faint. I realized that my breath might stink of booze so I put a stick of gum in my mouth. I began chewing but I was afraid that I was chewing too loudly. Everything was so quiet in here. My shoes were loud against the marble floor. I wanted to tiptoe. I didn't want to draw attention to myself. I wanted to run away. I didn't want to go into the office.

But I did. I announced myself. She said welcome. She said wait. She left. She came back. She escorted me into another room. I sat down in a large leather chair. On the other side of the desk she extended her hand. The mother superior extended her hand and smiled.

"I'm so glad you came," she said.

"I didn't feel as though I had any choice."

"We always have choices, don't we?"

I didn't want lectures. I just wanted to get this over with. The mother superior was old. Her lips were wrinkled. Her skin sagged.

"As I explained to you on the phone, Mr. Gonfio, we are quite fortunate that our convent is attached to a private Catholic hospital. The great majority of our sisters are nurses and, in the case of Miss Calzolari, our medical experience has proven to be a great blessing."

"Yes, of course," I said.

She explained how the hospital worked, where the funding came from, what splendid facilities they had. I couldn't listen to her. I couldn't do anything but remember the phone call that had come last night. The one from the psychiatrist, the guy with the baritone voice who said he was calling from Troy, Ohio. I thought he was a fucking practical joker. I wanted to tell him to screw himself. I almost did, but he was already relaying the story: how someone had spotted her on the golf course at the Troy Country Club, crying, and after that how she had been seen walking down the main street of Troy talking to strangers, saying, "We have to save Brian, someone has to save Brian, please, for God's sake, please help me save him, help me find him, I must find him," and then how she went from store to store asking about Brian and Baxter and her mother-in-law and the law firm and her apartment until finally someone recognized her, a clerk in the drugstore, a woman who began to discuss the show with her. And that, and only that, calmed her down, the psychiatrist said. She sat down in the drugstore and talked a very long time, and the woman saw that Anna was not in her right mind, and the woman didn't know what else to do so she called the police. The police came and Anna got hysterical and they had to restrain her and they took her to the emergency ward of the public hospital and shot her up with sedatives and when she came around the next day she grew hysterical all over again and said that she had to go back, she had to go back, there was nothing to do but to go back. She kept screaming about Ursula, and the nurses understood, because they watched the show—everyone in Troy watched the show—and they called Mount Mary's convent and hospital and spoke to the mother superior who had agreed that if the child needed help, then help certainly would be offered.

"Would it help if I came there?" I had asked the shrink after telling him how close Anna and I had been.

"I can't say. It might, or it might not. I'm certainly willing to take a chance. Don't expect to take her home with you, though, Mr. Gonfio. She's going to be here for a while, I suspect. A long, long while."

After that I spoke to the mother superior and the next morning I was on my way to Ohio.

"She's been very calm," the elderly woman told me now. "I wouldn't want you to say anything that would upset her. I'm just hoping that seeing you will have an even greater calming effect on her."

"I'll be very gentle with her. I've always been gentle with her."

"I'm sure you have been. But I do want you to understand that she is still—how should I put this?—still in character."

"I understand."

"I will have her brought here now."

I waited. I looked at my watch. I fidgeted with my tie. I studied the crucifix behind the mother superior's desk. Outside the sky was darkening. The storm had caught up with me. I wished that the mother superior had offered me sherry. I needed something.

She entered the room escorted by a sister. She was wearing a white gown. She looked at me but she did not look at me. Her eyes were wild. My eyes were filled with tears. I got up and took her hand. I kissed her hand. "Anna," I whispered, "dear, sweet Anna." She looked at me. She looked through me. She turned to the mother superior and said, "The sisters promise that my habit will be ready by morning. They say they are working very hard to make the alterations. I trust that I haven't put you to too much trouble."

"Not at all, my dear," said the mother superior. "Not at all. Your friend has come to visit you from New York. Don't you want to greet your friend?"

I turned to her and said, "I've missed you, Anna, I've missed you very much." I tried to control my tears, but I couldn't. Her eyes wouldn't let me. Her eyes were wild. Her green eyes were wild.

"I must dress now and go to Mass," she said to the mother superior. "I am afraid that I'm going to miss Mass, and I can never miss Mass again. We are servants of the Lord, and our obedience must be absolute." Then she paused and said, "May I be excused now, Mother Superior?"

"Of course, my child."

But before she left, she finally turned to me and looked me straight in the eyes and whispered, "I couldn't bear the life you gave me. So I came back to where I belong."

I tried to answer, but I couldn't. I couldn't do anything but watch her leave the room and close the door behind her. And when she was gone, I put my head in my hands and broke down, weeping like a child.

64

"I assure you that she's in capable hands."

"I know you want to help her."

"She must help herself. And in due time, she will."

"I appreciate the way you have taken her in."

"There wasn't a moment of doubt on our part. She is a child of God, and she has come to us for aid. In her own peculiar way, she has reached out to us, and we are touched."

"What about the medical aid?"

"There will be a doctor's care, certainly. But there will also be a spiritual care. Between the two, I am hopeful about her future."

"Then you don't see this as a setback?"

"Not in the least. I am optimistic. I think that she has inner strength, and I am certain that she will be able to utilize that strength in the not-too-distant future."

"Do you think she'll be accepted by the other sisters?"

"I don't see why not. They have expressed nothing but love for her, and she, in turn, has been appreciative of their concern."

"You know, when I think about this whole strange episode, I can't help but be amazed—that after all this, she would wind up here."

"It was inevitable. I believe it happened because God wanted it to happen."

"I know you'll watch over her."

"I will care for her as though she were my own daughter."

"Thank you for your time."

"Feel free to call me whenever you want word of her."

Baxter MacNiece shakes the hand of the mother superior, turns and leaves her office.

Mark Costein got up and switched off the TV in his swanky, new, top-of-the-world office.

"I've got to hand it to you, Gonfio, you're a clever man. You're a real jewel." The kid came over and patted me on the back.

"Thanks," was all I could manage to say in reply.